The Ravanmark Saga
Book Two

I0639981

Redeemer

of the

Realm

Sandra Miller

Redeemer

of the

Realm

Redeemer of the Realm

Published by Onda Mountain Books

Cover Art

© Kriscole | Dreamstime.com

© Mega11 | Dreamstime.com

Cover Design

By Karri Klawiter, www.artbykarri.com

Copyright © 2014 by Sandra Miller.

Discover other titles by Sandra Miller at
www.sandra-miller.com

Chapter One

BOILING POINT

ireworks lit up the nighttime sky, casting colors like glittering confetti over the Great Palace. In the Outer Ward, people drank in the streets, and shouted, and celebrated like no one had seen since the Queen Mother's wedding thirty years ago.

In the Inner Ward, things were a bit more orderly. An enormous congratulatory line snaked through the ward, up the middle of the Great Hall, and on the royal dais to the throne of the new King Dorramon. People waited in this line for hours, smiling and chatting, to approach the throne and kiss the royal signet ring. It was a once-in-a-lifetime affair, happy but solemn, heavy with the weight of tradition and responsibility. The Great Hall overflowed with people, from the nobility and the courtiers in their fine, flowing garments and jewels, to the peasants from the Outer Ward in the best their shabby wardrobes had to offer. It was a spectacle like none of them had seen before, or would see again.

Alannys watched the proceedings from a place of honor on the dais, beside the throne. She knew she was hopelessly out of place there — what could a failed middle school music teacher have to offer the glittering assemblage around her? Beside her, in the royal throne, sat the very King of Ravanmark himself, under his regal purple cloak and golden crown. And on the other side of the throne stood Queen Mother Farrine, an imposing presence in her own right, her withering gaze commanding the unquestioning respect of every person in the hall.

Alannys shifted her weight to her other foot, her hand creeping to Songstrike's ornate, aged bronze handle. Just touching the sword seemed to give her courage—it hummed in the back of her mind, singing calming melodies with words she could almost hear. She knew people weren't used to seeing women wearing gowns and swords, but she couldn't care much about it, while Songstrike crooned to her. Dorramon had brought her the gown himself, and told her to wear Songstrike, and it was a good thing she had, with everything that had happened. She knew she had no place here...but Dorramon had asked her to come, had even commissioned her gown to match his coronation clothes—how could she have refused? It was, after all, an important occasion.

Alannys sighed, and shifted her weight back to the original foot. Important occasion, sure, but the display around her was ridiculous, especially with the serious issues facing Ravanmark. But it was also touching and humbling. Either way she looked at it, she could not change things, so she stood and tried to pay attention to the endless stream of subjects filing past the throne. Some of the people smiled and nodded at her, some of them scowled and looked away. Most paid her no attention at all, and that was perfectly fine with her.

Arch-Prince Raman stood next to her, looking as though he belonged there in a blue velvet doublet, with a golden circlet in his blond hair. In the shadows of the torchlight, the jagged scar down the left side of his face was less visible than usual, and Alannys realized, as if for the first time, that he was a ruggedly handsome man in his own right. "Lady Alannys," he said quietly, favoring her with a sidelong glance that felt sharp, "are you well? You seem...twitchy."

Alannys tightened her grip on Songstrike, and forced herself to hold still. "I'm fine. I think I just—have other things I need to do."

Raman wasn't looking at her sidelong now—he gaped at her in disbelief, or something that looked an awful lot like it. "Things to do? What things could be more important than this?"

"The songs," she said, aware of the tremor in her voice but helpless to control it. "I have to find the songs."

"Now? You have to find the songs of the Redeemer right now?"

Do any of you really believe this woman is the Redeemer? The person who will restore to Ravanmark its lost heritage and its Muses—this female, alien, creature? Only a few hours ago, Lord Malrec had called her out for a fraud—here, on this very dais—in front of the nobles and the people. She could still hear his voice, sharp and sneering, in her mind. She closed her eyes. How could she hope to make Raman hear what she heard, to make him feel what she felt when she heard it? How could she make him see the importance of the songs that would prove her at last—or disprove her?

"Alannys?"

Her eyes popped open. "I'm sorry, Raman. I have to find them, that's all." She broke abruptly out of the royal reception line, pushing past the startled peasants in front of her, and hopping down the red granite steps as fast as she could. Their murmurs did not bother her; she had already lingered here too long, and she expected most of them could see that.

"Alannys?" The voice was Dorramon's. It rang behind her, confused and worried.

For just a moment she froze. But she couldn't do it, she couldn't turn to face him now or she would never leave. He of all people had to see why she had to go. She shouldered aside the next person in line, not even glancing at the woman's face, and hurried toward the big double doors.

A grip of iron closed around her upper arm, jerking her backwards and spinning her around. "What in the Seven Hells do you think you are doing?" The growling voice rumbled in her ears, low and intense. She recognized it as Raman's in the same instant she looked up to see him glowering down at her. He was clearly working hard to control himself, but his face was almost purple with rage.

"I—I told you," she stammered, "I have to go."

Raman gave her arm a shake so violent it rattled her teeth. She'd never seen him so angry—what had she done to provoke this? "Not that!" He winced and lowered his voice, hissing at her in his fury, determined that none should overhear. "Dorramon spoke to you. You can't have missed it. Your *king* spoke to you." He gave her another shake. "And you didn't even acknowledge him! We've just had a disaster of a coronation. The Dark Alliance has openly declared war. The people are restless and afraid. And now every person in this room has seen you publicly snub the new king. Do you have any *idea* what you have done?"

The tension hung there, yawning and terrible, waiting to swallow her. She could feel the hundreds of eyes on her, the unnatural stillness of the room, Raman's fingers grinding painfully into her arm as he awaited her answer. But most of all she could feel the shame, the horrible, burning guilt—because everything he had said was true.

Everything.

Alannys jerked her arm free and strode back to the foot of the stairs. Her legs shook and her face was on fire, but she did her best to stand tall. People scattered before her, as though they found her fearsome—or maybe they didn't want her scandal, her shame, to rub off on them.

She knelt to the floor, dropped herself in a heap there at the base of the steps. "My Lord King, I beg your forgiveness. I meant no insult—I forgot myself. Please, your Highness, I beseech you—forgive me."

She was laying it on thick, and she knew it. Dorramon would not have needed—or wanted—such an apology from her. But Raman was right; she'd done damage here, and to fix it, she was going to have to be extreme.

"You have given no offense." Dorramon's voice surrounded everyone in the hall, soft and calm. "There are none here who have cause for complaint with our Redeemer. Rise now, and be on your way with our gratitude that you stayed with us this long."

She clambered to her feet, tears burning at the backs of her eyes. He should have punished her, made an example of her—he must have known that. But he hadn't the heart to do it—she could see the affection in the clear blue eyes looking back at her, could see that he would shield her with his position as long as he could. His expression was somber, his dark hair cutting a stark contrast to his pale face—Alannys knew he felt the gravity of the situation as well.

And as Raman grabbed hold of her arm again and hauled her out of the Great Hall, she found herself looking back at those eyes and wondering—how long could he keep that up?

How much would that affection cost him, in the end?

♫

"What *was* that?" Raman's tone was low, but it boiled over with anger. He dragged Alannys through the Inner Ward faster than she would ever have tried to cross it on her own, seemingly oblivious to the way she stumbled trying to keep up with him. "What could you *possibly* have been thinking?"

"I don't know," she admitted. She couldn't even defend herself—it really had been inexcusable. "I just—I have to find the songs."

He stopped and rounded on her. "*That's* your excuse? The *songs*? Alannys, even if you did find them, what could you do with them tonight?"

They were in the far side of the ward, in the shadows of the keep. It gleamed white and beautiful in the light of the twin moons. It saved her; no one else would witness her humiliation. But at the same time, the royal keep—that glimmering monument to the man she had just gravely insulted—shamed her all the more. Tears stung her eyes and she shook her head, not trusting herself to speak just then.

The fireworks glittered merrily overhead, crackling and casting their bright colors across the ward. They also illuminated Raman's face, hard and angry, regarding her over his crossed arms. Nothing she saw there raised her spirits.

He turned away from her, jerking open the door to the keep and holding it, gesturing curtly that she should go inside. She did, and he followed. "Look, Alannys, I don't understand. Dorramon has taken so many risks for you—even this coronation. He made it as much about you as him. He's risked his entire reign for you, you know—after everything he's done, if you fail, he's going down with you. He's done everything humanly possible for you." His voice echoed in the high vaults of the vestibule, carrying the sting of accusation.

"I know." She could hear the strain in her words. "And I'm grateful."

"Are you?" Raman fell in step beside her, walking her

down the corridor to her chambers. "Are you really? Because honestly, from where I'm standing, I can't see it. He's done so much for you, risked so much for you — and all that he asked was for you to be there tonight. But you left, and you would have done it without a word."

She flinched away from his assessment, but she couldn't deny the truth of it. "Dorramon would understand why I had to leave," she said, reaching for her door. Maybe she would have some peace inside. This felt too much like badgering, for all that everything he said was true.

"Dorramon wouldn't have raised a fuss, you mean. There's a difference." To her horror, he charged right into her sitting room behind her. "But let's say you're right. What does he know that I don't? Make me understand, too. I would love for this to make sense."

Alannys rubbed at her temples. "I don't know how to explain it to you, if you don't already know. Look around you, Raman!"

Music crammed her sitting room. Stacks of ancient papers lined the red velvet sofa, leaving barely enough room for her to sit down. Music was scattered haphazardly around the area rug, and stacked on the stone floor, tall enough that it covered the bottom of the huge tapestry on the wall. The top of the table in front of the couch could not be seen for all the music on it.

"Merciful Muses!" Raman ran a hand through his hair, his composure finally shaken. "I didn't know there was that much music in all of the Great Palace."

"There is, and more comes in every hour." She sank down onto the open spot on the couch.

Raman lifted one of the sheets gingerly, all trace of anger gone. "And you must search through these, for the Song of Raising and the Song of Joining?"

"I have to. Ravanmark has deep hurts that the

Redeemer cannot heal without them."

He glanced at her. "That's a rather neat way of sidestepping the issue of whether the Redeemer is you. Investiture ceremony aside, I'm not getting the impression you're feeling it."

"How could I? I've never felt like some legendary hero, Raman. I'm just an ordinary middle school music teacher who ran to Ravanmark when she had nowhere else to go. And Lord Malrec just announced to the world a few hours ago that I can't possibly be the Redeemer."

"Is that what this is about?" The arch-prince pursed his lips, staring over her head at the tapestry on the wall behind her. "Alannys, you can't worry about what other people say — especially people like him. This is about you. You stood in the Great Hall in front of hundreds of witnesses and swore to perform the acts of the Redeemer or die trying. Didn't you believe then?"

She looked away. "Let's face it, Raman, I could look through these stacks for the rest of my life. I may never find the songs. In that case it wouldn't matter anyway." She heaved a sigh and scrubbed at her eyes. To think that a few short months ago she had thought teaching middle school was difficult! "Lord Malrec brought me here, to this world, to be his weapon. Do you think he would have done that, if there was the slightest chance I might be the Redeemer?"

"Who can say why Malrec does anything? If he thought it would benefit him, he wouldn't hesitate. You can't avoid this forever. You are carrying Songstrike, the fabled sword of Soth. That proves to anyone who places any credence in prophecy that you are the Redeemer."

"I thought you didn't believe in prophecies?" She looked at him pointedly.

Raman pinched the bridge of his nose between his thumb and forefinger. "How did you manage to turn this into a conversation about me? Look, all I really want to say is, be careful. Be careful what you say, and even more careful what you do. Dorramon has done so much for you —he deserves your support, first and foremost, no matter what."

The sitting room door flew suddenly open, smashing into the wall with a bang that startled them both. They turned and found Tralice standing in the doorway, her dress rumpled and her curly black hair disheveled. Her face looked damp and red, and her chest heaved as she panted for breath.

"My Lord," she gasped, "I must ask you to leave."

"Am I to take orders from the servants now?" Raman grumbled, but the words had no bite.

"I am sorry, my Lord," Tralice said, with a deep curtsey, "but King Dorramon himself summoned me here and instructed me to inform you that you are to trouble the Lady Alannys no further."

"Dorramon! Of course!" He threw up his hands in frustration. "A coronation is only the most important thing that happens in Ravanmark, and he specifically asked her to be there. But of course he defends *her*." The two women stared at him, wide-eyed and unmoving, and he shook his head. "Ah, well—I know when I'm outnumbered. I suppose I'll return to the coronation myself—this is the closest I am ever likely to be to one."

That remark was probably intended to elicit a laugh, but Alannys couldn't do it. Raman's sarcasm was just a little too sharp. Of course, he never would have had a coronation, but if things had worked out differently, he would have had an investiture ceremony as Duke of the now defunct Holding of Archford. Another loss in the realm's great history of losses. So much now rode on her shoulders. The stakes were enormous.

But she didn't know how to express any of that to him

now, and so she watched in uneasy silence as he stomped across the room and let himself out.

He slammed the door behind him.

Alannys and Tralice flinched away from the sound, and turned to look at each other.

"Thank you," Alannys said, not sure what else she could say. For a maid to stand up to an arch-prince like that—it must have taken a lot of courage, and Alannys felt bad for being the reason it had been necessary.

"Ach, my Lady, think nothing of it. The king sent a page to fetch me to rescue you. The boy gave me as much of the story as he knew. But my Lady, why did you leave the coronation? It's a night to celebrate and relax."

"Not for me, Tralice," Alannys said darkly. "I have work to do. Even if all the people in Ravanmark are determined not to notice it, we are in serious trouble."

"Well—yes, my Lady. But it isn't really your fault. You did wonderful things for Ravanmark. You prepared the Great Palace for the news that their king is a musician, all by yourself."

Alannys eyed her maid doubtfully. "You think so?"

"Well..." Tralice shifted uncomfortably. "The coronation passed without bloodshed, and that's good enough for me."

"We did win that battle," Alannys said, turning to look at the stacks of music around her. "But what of the war? In the rest of the realm, opinions against the Talents run as strong as ever. And what can I do about that?"

"Please, my Lady, don't be so hard on yourself. Lord Malrec and the Dark Alliance aren't out winning the war tonight either."

"They don't have to. The public already hates Talent. The burden is on us to change that. But you're right. I can't do anything about it tonight. Except this." She sighed, and dropped herself onto the couch, reaching for the nearest stack of music. She worked her way through the papers, trying to sort it as she went. So far she hadn't found anything that looked to be the Song of Joining or the Song of Raising. So many of them didn't have titles—some didn't even have words. It was slow going.

She worked through the stack, sorting the music as well as she could. Tralice quietly put out most of the lanterns in the room—a not-so-subtle hint, Alannys imagined—but she continued to work until her eyes closed of their own volition and she slept.

♫

Lord Malrec swept into Castle Glennayre's cavernous library like the cold wind of death, his velvet cloak billowing behind him. Without a word he stopped, and dropped a parcel on the open pages of the book Princess Delline was studying. He folded his arms and waited in imperious silence, one eyebrow raised high on his steep forehead.

Princess Delline regarded the brown paper package for a moment, then raised her blue eyes to Malrec. Those eyes —that face—such a match for that of her twin brother, the king...it was all he could do to look at her, sometimes. 'Marriage of convenience' had such a rational sound to it, but he found it no treat to live one out, day after day.

Delline obviously had no such thoughts in her own head, looking up at him through eyes that were soft, and a smile that said she was honestly happy to see him. "What is this, my Lord?"

"It is the skin of the luch-ul." He spoke quickly, his words clipped. "Larric brought it back from the taxidermist this morning. The eel was skinned as you specified, with no lengthwise cut."

"Wonderful." Delline's tone was dry. She darted a glance at the package. "What do you want me to do with it?"

"Actually I was rather hoping you could answer that

question for me, my dear." Lord Malrec unfolded his arms, then crossed them again. Delline had a most annoying habit of parceling information out to him a piece at the time.

If his feelings reflected in his tone, however, Delline gave no indication of it. "I see." Her quill had gone dry, and she tapped it idly against her paper. "Ask me again in six weeks."

"What?"

She smiled sweetly at him, apparently enjoying her game. "The skin must age for six weeks before anything further is done with it. It should be rubbed inside and out with a special herb mixture, wrapped in a linen cloth, and laid out on stone." She dipped the quill and wrote, scratching swiftly across a fresh sheet of paper.

"Rubbed inside and out? How is that possible when the skin has no lengthwise cut?"

"I didn't say it would be easy. This collar is necessarily difficult to construct." She handed him the paper.

Lord Malrec glanced over the list in his hand. "Mortherwort, borage, wormwood...chamomile, hyssop—we have all of those in our gardens, so—hold, Herb of Silence?"

"Ah, yes." Delline sounded pleased that he had mentioned it—he was suddenly irritated with himself for playing into her hands. "You will only find that mentioned in the oldest texts. It doesn't grow in Ravanmark. I can give you a description of the plant and its leaves, but you will have to find a source for it."

"I *know* what it *is!*" Malrec exploded. Delline stared at him, her eyes wide with shock, and he drew a slow breath in and out, trying to gain control of his temper. "I've used it before, when I Talent-proofed the tower room. But I don't have any now, and I don't know where to find it."

"Ah. It will be hard to find, I am sure, but in the end it

will be worth the effort, don't you think? If you wish to control the voice of the music mage, it is your only option."

Malrec hoped she could not tell his smile was forced. Another dose of the Herb of Sight—another risking of his own life to find the things he needed. This damned music mage was turning out to be more trouble than he had ever dreamed, and he had yet to see any benefits from her presence in Ravanmark. "Of course, my dear. I shall have Kalyn see to the preparation of the skin at once." He scooped up the parcel and stormed back out of the library.

♫

"Lady Alannys!" The voice was low but intense, pushing her from sleep with its urgency. "Lady Alannys, you must wake up!"

Someone was shaking her. Alannys sat up in her bed, scrubbing at her eyes with the heels of her hands. The faint light outside her window said that the sun was rising. "Tralice? What is it?"

The maid grabbed hold of her arm, pulling as though she intended to haul Alannys out of the bed by force. "*Hurry,* my Lady! It is the Baroness of Orinthal!"

"The baroness?" Suddenly Alannys was on her feet. "Here?"

"*Yes,* my Lady!" Tralice helped her into a robe, then gave her a healthy shove towards the archway to the sitting room.

Alannys raked her hands through her hair, hoping to look more awake than she felt. "Good mor—"

Before she had even gotten the words out, Baroness Lae knelt at her feet, her blond hair floating around her head like gossamer, tear tracks on her pale skin. "Forgive me, my Lady, but I must beg your help. Do not forsake me!"

Alannys stared down at her in utter confusion. She had only known the baroness a short while, but she knew Lae wasn't prone to histrionics. What could have caused this?

"My Lady!" Alannys caught Lae by the arm and pulled her to her feet. "What happened?"

"Men, my Lady!" Baroness Lae's eyes were wide with fear. "Armed men in dark cloaks—they stormed the Raven's Nest early this morning!"

"The inn? What did they want there?"

"*Me,* my Lady! They sought me and my girls—to take us by force to my husband!"

Alannys's mind raced. Lae's husband was the awful Baron Prubard of Orinthal—currently in Glennayre Holding as part of Lord Malrec's Dark Alliance. He wanted to drag the Baroness and her twin babies *there?* "No," she said reflexively. "No, we can't allow that."

Baroness Lae clutched Alannys's arm, squeezing it tight. "Thank you, my Lady! But what can we do?"

That was the same question Alannys was struggling with herself. "Where are your daughters right now?"

"In the courtyard, with their nurse. It's dark under the trees—we thought they could hide from those men, if they should come here."

"They won't," Alannys said, and in that answer she saw their way out of this. "The entrance from the Outer Ward is guarded, and there are guards in the keep as well. Come with me."

Alannys hurried out of her chambers, leading Baroness Lae to the next door down the corridor. "Here." She grabbed the door and threw it open. "You can stay in here. I'll have a guard stand at the door."

Lae stepped hesitantly inside the room. These chambers were a match for Alannys's own, but instead of a tapestry, a massive bookshelf covered the wall. Papers crammed it, some in loose, tumbling stacks, some bundled together and tied, some rolled like scrolls. All of them were covered with the same precise handwriting. "What is this place?" she asked, turning in a slow circle.

"These are Delline's old chambers."

"The princess?" Lae gasped. "Are you certain I may stay here?"

"Positive. I'll clear it with the king officially after he's awake, but for now, if anyone asks, just tell them I told you to stay here."

"Oh, thank you, Lady Alannys, thank you! I know there isn't much I can do for you, separated from my house like this, but if there is ever anything you need, please come to me."

Alannys looked at her in sudden inspiration. "Actually, my Lady, I am in dire need of some help right now. I can't get anyone else to help me; the servants are all too afraid of music, and Dorramon and Raman are too busy. Do you remember the stacks of papers in my sitting room? I am searching for two songs. It's taking forever, and I can use every extra pair of hands I can get."

"I shall of course be happy to offer whatever assistance I can," Lae said, though she sounded dubious. "I do not know how to interpret the symbols of the Muses, though."

"I know. You won't need to read music for this—we're just reading the lyrics, looking for things that could possibly be the songs we need. It isn't hard, but it is time-consuming, and time is the one thing I feel I don't have."

"I shall be happy to help," Lae repeated. "It is the least I can do. I really can't thank you enough for everything you're doing, for me and for the realm. I pray to the Muses for your success."

"Me, too," Alannys told her, grimly regarding the stacks of paper crowding the bookshelf. "Me, too."

♫

The stacks of music in her room held Alannys's attention until the noon gong rang from the high tower. Her stomach clamored for food, finally overriding her sense of duty. She stood up, pressing her hands against her back and stretching to audible pops and snaps.

A quiet tapping at the door interrupted her. "Come in," she called.

The door swung open, and Tralice walked in, her hips swaying prodigiously behind the silver platter she carried. "Ho! and what a fine day it is, my Lady. I've brought your lunch."

Alannys moved a stack of music aside so Tralice could put the tray on the coffee table. "Thank you, Tralice. I'm sorry for the trouble."

"Ach, my Lady, it's no trouble at all. But how long are you planning to take your meals this way, if you don't mind my asking?"

"I don't know." Alannys thumped the music down next to the sofa, glaring at it as though her predicament was somehow its fault. "As long as it takes, I suppose."

Tralice made a clucking sound of disapproval. "His Majesty isn't going to like that. He seems a bit put out, if I may say so, about eating without you. He says the dining room feels empty."

"I know."

"I wouldn't be in a hurry to upset him, myself. The songs have been missing for hundreds of years, my Lady —a few more weeks won't matter. They aren't that urgent."

"I know. I know!" Her own shout startled her, and she stopped, forcing herself to calm down. "But it feels urgent to me."

Tralice looked at her uncertainly. "My Lady?"

"I know it doesn't make sense. But it's all I can do. They're all getting ready for war out there. I can't do that. I can't strategize, I can't train troops, I can't even fight decently. Finding these songs is about all I can contribute." Alannys threw her hands up in frustration. "And I can't even seem to do that!"

"Calm down, Lady Alannys. Nothing is as bad as it seems. Why don't you come eat in the dining room with King Dorramon? You've been pushing yourself too hard. A break would do you good."

Alannys shook her head. "I'm sorry, Tralice. But I can't afford the time away. Besides, how could I face him and report failure? He knows why I'm eating in here."

"I don't know. If I had such a man as the king interested in me, I wouldn't waste my time with dusty old papers. What if his interest should wane? My Lady—"

"Thank you, Tralice," Alannys said sharply.

Tralice took the hint. With a quick curtsey, she left the room.

Alannys stared at the closed door, washed over by a wave of regret. Tralice had done nothing to deserve that— the maid had only ever been her friend, and everything she had said was true.

She contemplated the unmoving, unfeeling door in something like fear, suddenly wondering if her drive to find the songs would cost her all her friends. Or—

Or if it already had.

♪

Alannys ate her lunch slowly, working through more of the music as she did. By the time she finished, her eyes felt permanently crossed. A sharp pain pounded behind her right eye, hammering to dust her will to continue working. She rubbed at her eyes, raked her fingers through her hair, and stood up. Tralice was right; she couldn't keep this up. And besides, she had promises to keep.

It was time to face the king.

Her steps dragged as she left her room. She knew it wouldn't be easy. She hadn't seen him since the coronation. She had failed him them, and in the intervening time she had failed to recover the songs they needed. She loved him with all of her heart, and all she could do was let him down. What could she say to him now?

Some of the courtiers in the Great Hall nodded greetings to her, others turned pointedly away, their noses held high. It wouldn't have been reasonable to expect anything else, but it was still disappointing.

Dorramon never held her to protocol, but she knew better than to let her manners slip now. After the disastrous faux pas she'd committed at the coronation, she knew she had to be extra careful. She knelt at the foot of the stairs, head bowed, until a page on the dais stepped forward.

"The Crown of Ravanmark recognizes Lady Alannys of Gale, Redeemer of the Realm. His Majesty bids you approach."

It was a ritual greeting, but the page's grave tone didn't let on. She had yet to see a page in the Great Palace who didn't take himself very seriously. "Thank you." She stood and approached the throne, keeping her eyes on her feet, unsure what sort of reception to expect.

Strong hands fell on her shoulders, and she looked up to find Dorramon standing there beaming at her, his blue eyes twinkling. "Alannys."

Her cheeks flushed, and she curtsied. "My Lord King."

He wrapped his arms around her, gathering her into a crushing hug. "I was beginning to wonder how long you were going to avoid me."

"I wasn't avoiding you," she said quickly. Too quickly, perhaps—she could see his eyebrows twitch, and she knew he'd caught the lie. She felt her face flush.

Dorramon laughed out loud. He pulled over a chair for her and sat back down in the throne, gesturing for her to sit as well. "What brings you here?"

Alannys spread her skirts and sat down. "I need to talk to you about Baroness Lae."

"Ah. Yes, I hear you've been quite busy."

"What?"

"You'll find," he said with humor, "there's very little that happens in the palace that I don't know about—especially when the Royal Guard are involved."

"Ah—yes, of course," Alannys stammered, trying to hide her surprise. "I see. You've heard, then, what I did to keep her safe for the moment."

"Indeed. It was well done." He drummed his fingers on the arm of the throne. "Give her Delline's chambers permanently. It seems my sister will have little use for them."

"Thank you, Dorramon. She'll be thrilled. Should I have someone empty the rooms?"

The king shrugged. "I don't know why. I'm hardly going to have Delline's things delivered to her in Castle Glennayre. Lord Malrec can damn well provide for her now. If there is anything in there the baroness can use, she is welcome to it. If not, she can have it all thrown into the moat. It's all one to me." His expression smoldered.

Alannys reached out and hesitantly patted his hand. The familiar electric tingle that accompanied any contact of their bare skin threatened to undo her, and she hastily withdrew her hand. Better for her not to touch him, she decided, when she was trying to maintain her already shaken composure. "I will see to it. It is kind of you to keep her here, but I think it is also wise. She seems to have very sharp insight into political matters."

"Yes. I think I shall have her appointed as some sort of official advisor to the Crown. That should keep Prubard gnashing his teeth for a while."

She frowned, wondering about his dark tone. "You are in a particularly nice mood. Has something happened?"

Dorramon glanced at her sidelong. "Nothing I shouldn't have expected. Demonstrations against the

Crown have begun in Glennayre. Lord Malrec is apparently mustering an army."

Alannys sighed. "You're right, we knew that was coming. Lord Malrec has been grooming the people of Glennayre Holding for this for many years."

"Have you had any luck finding the songs?"

She couldn't look him in the eye. "No. Baroness Lae has promised to help me, so the search will soon be faster, but so far it's no better." Her tone burned with frustration she couldn't hide.

"I see." He sat silent a moment, gazing out among the nobles and the hangers-on crowding the hall. Some of them, she could see, were waiting with thinly veiled impatience for her audience to conclude so they could approach for audiences of their own, but Dorramon didn't appear to notice. "I know these songs are important to you, Alannys, but I don't think you should put too much pressure on yourself trying to find them."

She looked away. "I know."

"You say that, but every time I look at you, I see further evidence that you have indeed been pushing yourself too hard. This is wearing you down, and it's got to stop."

She stood up abruptly, lighting hope in the hearts of the waiting courtiers. "I'm flattered by your concern, but really, there's no need. I had better be getting back."

She dropped a quick curtsey and turned to leave, but before she'd taken two steps, Dorramon darted from the throne and caught her wrist. "Don't patronize me. You're pale, Alannys, and the circles under your eyes are so dark they look like bruises."

"Dorramon, listen—"

"No. No, this time you're going to listen to me. I don't think you've really heard a word I've said. I could have the music locked away, you know."

She stared at him in shock. "No—no, please don't do

that."

"Why not?" His hand was warm but unyielding on her wrist, and even the familiar electricity racing across her skin felt harsh and demanding. "Give me one good reason why I shouldn't throw it all in the moat, if it's going to do this to you?"

"Because it's all I can do for you!" She saw his blue eyes widen and realized he hadn't been expecting that. "I can't win the war for you, Dorramon; I can't even help prepare for it. Finding the songs of the Redeemer is about the only thing I'm good for right now. I know it isn't urgent to you, but...it is to me."

He let go of her hand. "I had no idea you felt that way." Before she knew what was coming, he caught her by the shoulders and wrapped her in a warm embrace.

"Dorramon?"

"I should have known you wouldn't be happy if you weren't helping. But please, try not to worry about it. You won't be helping anyone if you drive yourself to collapse."

"But I feel so useless!" She was grateful that his velvet doublet muffled her voice; the petulant sound of it shamed her.

"No. You're never useless. No one who truly wants to help ever is. But you need to be patient. It may not be clear yet what you should be doing. But it will be. All in good time."

"I wish I had your confidence."

Dorramon pulled back and looked at her. "You do — just not in yourself. But that's all right. I have enough for both of us."

She couldn't help but smile back at him. "Thank you. Does that mean I can go now?"

"Yes." He frowned. "But go easy on the music, Alannys. I'm serious about that."

"Yes, your Majesty," she said, in a tone that was only

slightly facetious. She bowed low and left the dais, to the great relief of the waiting courtiers.

She never saw the long-faced, frowning ambassador who turned to watch her with narrowed eyes as she left the Great Hall.

♫

In truth, Alannys did not look forward to returning to her stacks; to the tired eyes, sore back, and stiff neck that characterized her time searching through them. She lingered outside far longer than was necessary, enjoying the sun's warmth on her face, the tickle of the cool breeze on her back, soothing her conscience by reminding it that Dorramon didn't want her rushing back to work anyway.

The Inner Ward seemed quieter than usual. Her gaze swept from the clean, blocky lines of the barracks of the Royal Guard, to the long, squat Great Hall. She turned to regard the keep, tall and gleaming in the afternoon sun. It glowed a vibrant white against the brilliant blue sky, like something in a watercolor painting. She sighed. Everyone around her worked to save it. What could she do, besides dig through dusty archives?

Somebody bumped into her, and she stumbled. "Excuse me," she said reflexively, turning to face her accidental accoster.

"You!" The man in front of her drew back from her with a hiss, his long face drawn into an expression of plain dislike, as if he smelled something objectionable.

"I'm sorry, do I know you?" Her tone was short; her anxiety had left her feeling raw. This man was unfamiliar; courtiers all looked about the same to her. He wore long, flowing silk robes that floated formlessly about him as he moved. His face was long and somehow horse-like to her eyes, with hard, beady eyes that regarded her with unwavering hostility.

"I should say not! I am an emissary of King Rathmar of Cadenda, and his daughter, Princess Varilyn."

Evidently this was supposed to impress her. "And?"

He eyed her with apparent dislike. "It is clear that you do not know—or do not care—about the grievous situation you have caused. King Dorramon has been betrothed since birth to Princess Varilyn, you audacious wretch!"

♪

Alannys stood there in the Inner Ward, blinking stupidly at the hateful, horse-faced man who had just sent her world careening. "B—betrothed?" He may as well have struck her.

"Betrothed, promised, engaged—I am sure you are familiar with the concept." He brushed at his robes as if touching her had dirtied them. "The princess is quite distraught. Reports are coming from Ravanmark of the ridiculous manner in which you have been cavorting with his Highness."

"Betrothed." She couldn't seem to get past it. She didn't know why she should feel so blind-sided. Hadn't this been hinted at, several times, in her presence? Hadn't Dorramon tried—over and over again—to tell her? She'd always brushed him off, always run from the conversation —knowing, deep down, that it had to be about something like this. He'd been the Crown Prince, after all. It was inevitable.

"Quite." He peered at her, perhaps questioning her mental faculties. "Now that King Dorramon has come into his reign, it is really time for him to honor his engagement, to begin fulfilling his responsibilities to both kingdoms. And I might point out that those responsibilities to do include you in any manner. A woman of decorum would recognize a prudent time to withdraw, and would not attempt to impose herself into the sanctified relationship of a man and his intended."

"I—I see." She did see. He was telling her, in the typical circumlocutious language of courtiers, to get lost.

"I shall consider what you have said."

He edged closer to her, inspiring in her the almost uncontrollable urge to run away. "I had hoped to take more substantial news to the princess than that of your contemplation." He paused. "It seems that perhaps this is the first you have heard of the betrothal. Is this true?"

She nodded.

"That is understandable." He waved a negligent hand. "With affairs as they have been in Ravanmark, it is easy to imagine that his Highness has been occupied with other things. And perhaps, knowing that you had not been aware, Princess Varilyn might find your behavior forgivable. But you must be willing to take the proper course yourself. She needs your vow on that."

Vow? This greasy man in the flowing robes was asking her to promise never to see Dorramon again? "I—I..."

He leaned forward expectantly.

"Thell!" The angry shout across the ward saved her. With a muttered curse, the man turned.

Raman stormed toward them. "Thell, what in the Seven Hells are you still doing here?" The arch-prince's face screwed into an angry knot.

Thell paled. "I, well, I simply paused to speak with the Lady Alannys, and—"

"I don't believe you were given permission to 'simply pause' and speak with anyone, Thell. *Especially* not Lady Alannys. Now will you heed the king, or shall I escort you to the dungeon?" Raman's hand fell on the handle of his sword.

Thell's nostrils flared. "I will take my leave of you now, Arch-Prince. King Rathmar and Princess Varilyn shall hear of this outrage."

"Fair enough. King Dorramon shall hear of *this* one."

Thell spun on his heel and stalked away, his robes flowing behind him.

Raman collared a page running by. "Whatever errand you are on, I need you to drop it. This is the business of the king."

The boy nodded earnestly, swallowing hard. "Yes, m'Lord. What would the king have me do?"

"Find Captain Grayble. Have him send two of his men on horses to follow that man. They are to make sure he goes directly to the harbor. I want him out of Ravanmark as soon as possible. Is that clear?"

The boy dipped his feathered cap in another nod. "Aye, m'Lord."

"Run, boy!" Raman sighed, watching the page disappear, then turned a narrow gaze on Alannys. "My Lady, you look terrible. Are you all right? What did he say to you?"

"I—I'm fine, I think. He wanted me to promise never to see Dorramon again."

"Seven Hells! Varilyn's a conniving bitch." Raman chewed on his lip. "I hope you didn't agree to any such thing."

"No. No, of course not." She glanced back at the Great Hall. "What did he come here for?"

Raman laughed. "Word of Dorramon's ascension has reached Cadenda. Our esteemed Ambassador suggested that since Dorramon is now King of Ravanmark, he is duty-bound to marry Varilyn as soon as possible."

"I see." She hoped she didn't sound as disappointed as she felt.

Raman glanced at her. "Varilyn can hardly wait to get her hands on the throne. Dorramon has postponed the wedding for years—because his parents were so young, and the kingdom at peace, no one forced him."

"But now Varilyn is going to try."

"I know," Raman sighed. "He doesn't have any choice, not really. He must honor the engagement. But Dorramon threw Thell out of court. If he had witnessed this little spectacle, he would have done worse. You must tell me everything he said to you."

"He was very rude," Alannys hedged, uncomfortable relating the contents of the conversation. "He implied that there was something improper going on. I didn't like him."

"That's Thell," Raman said. "He puts the ass in ambassador."

Alannys stared at him for a moment, then forced the laugh he obviously expected. It wouldn't do, under his watchful gaze, to give any sign of just how deeply this revelation had upset her. She was an idiot, that was all, a total idiot, and she preferred not to advertise the fact. There was nothing for it but to bury the hurt and the disappointment so deep they couldn't be seen.

But what she was supposed to do after that, she couldn't have said.

♫

Arch-Prince Raman tried his best to convince Alannys to go back to the Great Hall with him that instant, but she refused. All she wanted was to be back in her rooms, safe among the music stacks from foreign ambassadors and their searing condescension.

So he stalked off alone to brief King Dorramon on what had happened, and she scuttled off to her rooms, ostensibly to continue the search, but in reality just to hide.

She did work through more of the music, but she felt like she hadn't really seen a single piece she'd looked at. She could hide well enough from Ambassador Thell.

Hiding from the uncomfortable truths he'd exposed was not as easy.

Alannys sighed, raking her hands through her hair. She didn't have time for mooning around like this. Until she found a better way to contribute, her job was finding the songs. But she had to be honest—in this state she wouldn't recognize them even if they jumped up and bit her. She stood up, pushing her music aside, and began to practice with Songstrike. Working through the familiar routines gave her time to think, and some movement to distract her from her stacks.

The two songs she sought were of utmost importance to Ravanmark, and to her. She knew that. And yet she felt like she was wasting time fiddling with sheet music while the world mobilized for war. And as for her fate here, and the things Thell had told her—she just couldn't even go there. Practicing swordsmanship didn't address those concerns, but at least it allowed her to work off some of her frustration and nervous energy.

After an hour of working with the sword, she could sit back down and concentrate on the music again, still wearing Songstrike on her hip. She worked until she fell asleep on the couch, sheet music spread across her lap, and falling from her limp fingers to the floor.

The slight click of the door handle woke her. She couldn't recall a time—never, not once—when anyone had entered her room unannounced in Ravanmark. Perhaps that was what sent the feeling of wrongness deep into her brain, jolted her so suddenly awake and forced her off the couch, scattering paper around her feet.

She fell into Ready stance, hauling Songstrike from its scabbard, trying to ignore the way her hands trembled around the grip. Before the door was halfway open, a dark shape whirled in. It was a man, taller than her, wearing flowing black robes and cowl, with a black scarf pulled up under his eyes. He scanned the room, drawing his breath in a sudden hiss when he saw her.

"Help!" she shrieked. "Somebody help me!"

Her unannounced visitor pushed the door shut behind him with a foot. She had only one chance—she had to use the mindlink. No one else would hear her in time, shut in her rooms. *Dorramon! Dorramon, I need Royal Guard in here, quick!*

I know. They are on their way.

Her fright must have alerted him. Bless him for not asking questions! She would need all of her concentration to keep herself alive long enough for the Royal Guard to rescue.

Her opponent regarded her, swaying his blade before him in a hypnotizing motion. It was shorter than hers, and viciously curved. Grayble had used one in practice against her just a few days before—the blade, he said, was meant for evisceration. The curve made it hideously efficient for the purpose.

Great. She swallowed hard. Songstrike wobbled in her grasp.

He was fluid in motion, catlike. She couldn't name the precise instant when the Ready posture facing her became Ox; just suddenly he was rushing in at her, and she froze, terrified. She managed a clumsy sidestep at the last instant, raising her sword to slice at him as he passed.

Songstrike glowed with a fierce blue light. She had never seen anything like it. Neither, apparently, had Mr. Catlike Grace, who retreated into Ready position again. She pressed the slight advantage of his surprise, moving in with a slashing middle attack.

He whirled away, swinging his curved blade behind him to guard the move. She followed in close, bringing Songstrike up for a high attack this time, hoping to catch him off-guard.

It was no good. Her opponent was too experienced. He came out of his defensive maneuver with his blade raised to block. She fell back into Ready posture.

She held Songstrike in close and tracked him as he circled her. She had never seen anyone move as smoothly on their feet as this dark man. He feinted, trying to draw her into an attack, but she retained her defensive posture and he fell back.

Sweat beaded on her forehead, unheeded. Alannys and her attacker circled each other warily. Her heart pounded in her ears, and she wondered with a cold flash of fear how long she could keep this up. Her feet felt leaden and her arms shook—she hadn't eaten dinner and she'd had only a couple hours of sleep. She was running on adrenaline, and it was telling on her quickly.

Where were the guards? It couldn't have been more than a minute or two, but it felt like hours. She glanced at the door, but it remained steadfastly closed.

The cloaked swordsman chuckled, a low, dark sound that stood her hair on end. "Looking for help, little girl? Your foul music and your pathetic king can't save you now."

The words hit her like a slap, and her fear suddenly caught fire, morphing into burning, blistering anger. Who did this man think he was, to speak of Dorramon that way? How dare he invade her rooms, attack her—and insult the king!

With a wordless shriek of anger, Alannys closed the short distance to her attacker, slashing viciously with Songstrike. He backed up, neatly dodging her swings.

She pulled Songstrike in a wide middle arc. He sidestepped the attack. Before she could pull her blade back in front to guard her, he stepped close to her, and a burning, shooting pain knifed deep into her left shoulder.

Alannys cried out, jerking Songstrike around to retaliate, but he had already fallen back from her, and circled her warily. A numb sort of heat radiated from her shoulder, and she could feel her shirt sticking to her, soaking with blood.

But she couldn't see it, she couldn't look at herself to assess the damage. She dared not take her eyes off this opponent for a second, not even when the door behind her flew open again and three Royal Guards rushed in.

"Hold! Don't move!" Captain Grayble shouted. "Surrender to the Royal Guard!"

The guards fanned out behind her. The intruder's eyes flicked from her to the Royal Guards and back again.

She stepped quickly back toward the guards, her left arm hanging useless at her side. She didn't know who this man was or why he had attacked her, but she knew he would not surrender. "Why have you come here? What do you want from me?"

She might as well not have spoken. He didn't even acknowledge her, and she had not distracted him. He focused narrowly on her, swaying his curved blade in a sinuous motion that reminded her unpleasantly of a cobra preparing to strike. Captain Grayble frowned, and stepped closer to them.

The dark man whirled away from him, around her far side, between the two startled guards, and out the door.

Grayble swore. "After him! Stop him however you must, but do not let him escape!" Both guards went pounding out the door. The captain moved to follow, then turned back to her. "Stay here. Do not leave this room."

She couldn't imagine anything less likely, at that moment, than her leaving the room. She sank to her knees, shaky and light-headed, as though to demonstrate the point.

Captain Grayble gave her a look of hard concern, then ran out after his men.

♫

Dorramon glowered like a thundercloud. "You found nothing at all?" He paced in front of Alannys's couch, somehow regal even in an unbelted linen shirt and trousers. Alannys sprawled on the couch, allowing a royal healer to tend to her shoulder. Her hands looked pale to her, and her thoughts were fuzzy.

Captain Grayble shook his head, not quite meeting the king's eyes. "Not a trace, your Majesty. The man is gone. We lost him somewhere in the Outer Ward. The guards are conducting a door-to-door search as we speak, but I am not hopeful. He was too well concealed."

"Seven Hells, Grayble, tell me how this is even possible! You had this man trapped—you, and two of your men, against a single intruder. And yet he escaped!"

Captain Grayble's ears were red. "Forgive me, my Lord King—I have failed you. I have no explanation for this."

Dorramon raked a hand through his hair. He looked like he wanted to scream in frustration, but he sighed and turned to Alannys where she lay on the couch. He sat down next to her and took her hand. "Would you recognize him if you saw him again?"

She shook her head. "No. Captain Grayble is right. He was too well concealed. I could only see his eyes—if he changed his clothes I would never recognize him. I would know him if I had to fight him, though! I've never seen anyone spin as much as that fellow did."

"Neither have I," Grayble interjected. "You did very well to defend yourself against such an opponent, my Lady."

"I don't feel like I did so well," she said wryly, grimacing as the healer swabbed out her wound.

Grayble looked hard at her. "You are alive, aren't you?"

She sucked in her breath and bit her lip, watching the healer run a waxy black thread through a needle. It wasn't large, as needles went, but to her just then, it looked huge. "For now," she said. "But he got away without a scratch, and I'm getting stitches."

"My Lady, why didn't you sing? You are progressing well with the sword, but you are still no master. You could have incapacitated him with song."

Alannys shook her head. "There wasn't time for that. Music takes a certain amount of time to be effective, and I didn't have that time."

"And there's the cost," Dorramon interjected. She squeezed his hand—hard—as the healer began stitching. He held on and squeezed back. "The cost of singing can be unpredictable—you don't really know how much it will take from you until you've done it. What if the effort drained her, but he was still able to attack?"

"It doesn't matter anyway," Alannys forced out through gritted teeth. "What would I have sung, *The Man on the Flying Trapeze?*"

Both men stared at her.

"Never mind. The point is, it wouldn't have worked."

There was a small silent pause. Alannys closed her eyes and bit her lip, trying not to cry out.

Dorramon frowned. "So we don't know how he got in, we can't find him, and we wouldn't recognize him if we did. Do we know how he got into the keep?"

Grayble couldn't seem to look at him. "No, your Highness."

"It doesn't matter anyway," Alannys said in sudden frustration. "The trouble is that everyone knows where I am. There are plenty of people who want me dead—Lord Malrec even has a painting of this room, we've seen that before."

"What are you getting at?" Dorramon asked. She could hear the frown in his tone before she even looked at his face.

"I don't know how to explain it. Earlier I thought I was useless, but I was wrong. It's not just that I'm not helping —I'm actively causing problems! That man would never have breached the keep if I hadn't been here."

"So we move you to another room," Dorramon said quickly. "We post guards at your door—at your window if we must. I don't like the way you're talking. This can be handled."

"No." She squirmed as the healer pulled a stitch taut. "I'm not sure it can, Dorramon. He actually mentioned music, did I tell you that? If people hate me and my music enough to actually try to murder me, the I don't think hiding is the answer."

"Alannys..." His tone was a warning.

"Just hear me out. It makes sense." Her words came faster as she drove toward the inevitable conclusion forming in her mind. "As long as I am in the Great Palace, I put all of you in danger. Just by being here. There is only one solution to this. I have to leave."

"Leave?" Dorramon released her hand and stood, scandalized. "You can't do that, Alannys! The monster snaps at you in the palace, so you run right out into its jaws?"

She shook her head. "No, it isn't like that. I need to go to places that Lord Malrec has not painted, places where the Talents are still feared, like they used to be here in the palace. It all fits, don't you see? I've been worrying and wondering what I can do to help—this is it. I can go out into the kingdom, try to do for all of Ravanmark what I have done here."

Dorramon shook his head. He didn't even look at her. "I don't know. No matter where you go, Lord Malrec can find you. And then he can paint."

"Well—yes, but unless I'm in a location he has seen before, he is going to have to use the Herb of Sight to find me. He's not going to want to take that risk. And how many inns in how many towns do you think he can possibly have visited?" She ignored his doubtful expression and pressed on. "Besides, even if he uses the herb to find me, he will have to paint the place. That will take time. And if there is one thing I do not have, it is time.

I'm going to have to move fast; I can't stay in any one place too long. By the time he prepares a painting, I will no longer be there for him to use it on."

Dorramon sighed. "You are talking as if this is already decided."

Alannys gritted her teeth, biting back a yelp as the healer knotted off the seventeen stitches in her shoulder. "To me, it is. It is the only thing I can do. On top of everything else, I will be leading the attacks away from here. And that can only be a good thing."

"I still don't like it." He raked a hand through his hair. His hair looked as upset as he did by then, sticking out in random directions. "Look, you said these songs were important to you. If you leave, you can't find them. What about that?"

"Baroness Lae will be helping me with that. She can continue the search while I'm gone. If she finds them, you can let me know."

The king shook his head and turned away.

"My Lady, I shall accompany you." Captain Grayble knelt in front of her, his arm crossed over his chest. She regarded him fondly. He would not volunteer his opinion on her decision, but he would insist on helping her once she had made it.

"No, Captain. I'm sorry — I can't let you come with me. Dorramon needs you here. What I am trying to do is important, but Dorramon's safety is more important. I'm hoping to draw the attacks away from here, but there is always the chance that they will not follow me, and instead turn to another target inside the Great Palace."

"That is true enough," Grayble said grudgingly. "Don't you think that could be part of the plan? I cannot imagine an enemy who would feel comfortable attacking you and the king together. But if you can be coerced into leaving, so that the two of you may be dealt with separately...."

"Just so." Dorramon folded his arms across his chest. He looked haggard, and she felt bad for upsetting him. "I know I can't make you heed me, Alannys, and I won't even try. But I will ask you in the strongest possible terms to reconsider. I just can't see how leaving the palace can bring you anything but more trouble."

"I know. And you're probably right. It would be easier to stay here, and safer. But how often does the easiest, safest path prove to be the best path?"

An uncomfortable silence met this remark. Neither man could seem to meet her gaze.

"My decision is made," Alannys said gently. "I will leave the Great Palace tomorrow, in the middle of the day, for all to see. Captain Grayble, if you can arrange for the heralds to announce it somehow, that will be so much the better. I want everyone to know that I have left, and I want the news to spread as quickly as possible."

"It shall be as you wish, my Lady." Grayble crossed his arm over his chest in a salute, and left.

♫

The healer left shortly after Captain Grayble. Alannys sat on the sofa, exhausted, surrounded by a silence so heavy and tense she wasn't sure she had what it took to break it.

Dorramon stood with his back to her, staring at the wall. She could see the knotted muscles in his neck, and the sight pained her. She knew she wasn't making things any easier on him. Things just kept getting more and more complicated, and the answers were never easy.

"You're doing this because of Varilyn, aren't you?" His words were so soft she could almost believe she had imagined them, but there was nothing imaginary about the way it wrenched her heart to hear him say that name. "You're running away."

"No," she said, ignoring the guilty flare from her conscience that said maybe he was right. "Things have to change, Dorramon. Ravanmark can't go on like this."

"I know that." He didn't turn around, and the silence stretched painfully between them. Finally he turned to face her. "I'm sorry I didn't tell you sooner. You shouldn't have had to hear it from Ambassador Thell. But I don't think you should leave because of that."

"I'm not!" She started to push herself to her feet, but the pain that ripped through her shoulder left her collapsing against the cushions instead. "You don't have anything to apologize for. I know you tried to tell me, several times. I was the one hiding. You did say I couldn't run from it forever."

Dorramon's short laugh was dark. "I did say that. But it looks like you are going to try anyway. I shouldn't have waited so long—I should have told you long ago. I should have made you listen."

"Why didn't you? I mean, I know I didn't help at all, but...why didn't you ever tell me you were engaged?"

Dorramon sighed. He didn't sound angry, or impatient, just very, very tired. "Oh, Alannys, I don't know what to say. I should have told you right away, as soon as I could tell where things were headed. You had a right to know. You've got every right to be angry with me."

"No, I'm not angry." It was true. The pain gripping her heart was miles away from anger. "I'm just—I don't know what to think. I sometimes get the impression that I am very important to you. But then—I wonder, if that's the case, how could you not have told me something like that? Unless you meant to play me false?"

"No! No, how could you even think that? I've always been genuine with you. Maybe more genuine than was wise, for either of us."

"You're right. I'm sorry, that wasn't fair."

He didn't even seem to hear her. "Of course you're

important to me. Hugely important. I don't even have the words. But..." He sighed again. "Look, I don't know how well I can explain this. But this engagement has been hanging over my head since I was born, throwing a shadow over everything in my life. When I met you — it was incredible. Finally there was someone in my life who didn't know me first as the next king, who didn't know me as the future husband of a woman I never cared to marry. I just wanted to keep that — keep it special, untouched, for as long as I could. But it wasn't fair to you. I am sorry, Alannys."

She managed to climb out of the couch and went to stand next to him, keeping her left arm still at her side. "Don't apologize. Like I said, the fault is mine for not listening, because you tried. I understand how you felt — at least as much as someone like me can ever understand royalty. I love you, and nothing can change that. Not even this."

"But you're still leaving, aren't you?"

It took everything she had to see the pain clouding his eyes, and still answer that question honestly. "I have to. If people don't change their opinions of the Talents, the Dark Alliance is going to win, if for no other reason than massive public support. We can't have the population of Ravanmark rising to fight for them. And I'm the only one who can fight this battle."

Dorramon reached out and took her hand. The motion pulled on her injured shoulder, and she sucked in a breath against the sudden pain. "How will you travel with your arm that way? Alannys, are you sure this is wise?"

"No," she admitted. She held on tightly to his hand, savoring the feeling of having him close. "It isn't going to be easy, I know. But it is the only way. If music is to be accepted in Ravanmark, I'm going to have to take my message to the streets. So what else can I do?"

"You are right." He sighed, finally conceding defeat. She could almost see him swallowing his reservations, deliberately letting her go. "I just wish there was some other way."

"Me too. But it will all work out. I'll be fine."

She hoped it was true.

Redeemer of the Realm

Chapter Two

FALSE REDEEMER

The sun rose high in the sky above the Inner Ward, a fuzzy bright patch behind heavy clouds. The noon gong sounded from the tower of the keep. It was time for Alannys to go.

Quicksilver waited beside a stableboy, his saddlebags stuffed with provisions. He lifted his gray head to sniff the air, and danced sideways, seeming far more eager to be off than she was. Her beltpouch was filled with gold coins. She wore Songstrike in its scabbard, and her dagger in its concealed sheath tied to her leg. She wore her linen workshirt, and leather riding pants — clothes for heavy travel. Her violin was tied behind the saddle, covered in a blanket that hid the shape of the case.

Dorramon had adjourned court for the day so he could see her off. He stood with her at the Inner Ward gate, regarding her solemnly as she fastened her old leather riding cloak.

"Don't hesitate to come back," he told her suddenly. "Any time. There is always a place for you at the Great Palace."

Alannys thought of Princess Varilyn, and averted her gaze. "I know." She stepped forward and hugged him, ignoring the burning pull of the stitches in her shoulder. "I will miss you."

Dorramon caught her up, and his lips found hers for the most heart-wrenching kiss she had ever experienced. Music and electricity swirled in torrents around them, and she couldn't imagine, in that breathless moment, ever leaving him, ever *not* being close enough to do what they were doing right then. When they finally parted, he reached up and slipped a silken ribbon over her head. She lifted it in her hand, and the sunlight glinted off of a heavy golden royal medallion. "Show it when it can help you, and hide it when it will not. And always remember that my heart rides with you."

"Thank you, Dorramon." The gesture touched her. The royal medallion signified his protection, shouted to the world that he was watching over her, wherever she went. Thinking about it brought the specter of Varilyn before her again. She stepped back from him and hauled herself lamely up onto her horse, hoping to hide the tears burning in her eyes. If she stayed here much longer, she wasn't going to be able to leave.

An honor guard, led by Captain Grayble himself, followed her into the Outer Ward in solemn formation.

She glanced back over her shoulder once. Dorramon stood there still, watching her go. He brought his fingers to his lips, then waved them high in the air to her. The image tore at her heart, and everything in her cried out to go back.

People stopped, watching them parade past. Some people waved at her, some scowled. A few children skipped and danced along behind the honor guard, oblivious to its meaning. It felt more like a funeral procession than an honor guard. They were halfway around the Outer Ward when the sound of running hoofbeats startled her.

She looked up from her dismal contemplation of her own teardrops falling into Quicksilver's mane, just in time to see Raman ride past the guards and fall in next to her. "Raman? What are you doing here?" She wiped her hand across her face, hoping to hide her tears.

"Are you—are you *crying?*" He sounded shocked.

"No."

"Yes, you are!" Raman looked deflated. "Look, Alannys, the tears of women completely undo me. So could you just not do that anymore? I've got a tough reputation to protect, and it isn't going to help if I fall apart with you."

Alannys had to laugh. "Sounds like we've all got problems. Sorry to inconvenience you, tough guy. Did you come to say goodbye?"

"Goodbye? Hardly. I came to join you."

She stared at him, suddenly unconcerned about the state of her face. She'd been steeling herself to leave alone, but it was so *hard...* "Did Dorramon put you up to this?"

He shrugged and looked away. "He did. But only because he knew you were leaving before I did. I only have a few ceremonial functions at the palace, Alannys. I'm not needed here. And I hate to think of you going on a dangerous journey like this alone. So I came to offer you my company, for as long as you can stand it." He grinned at her, and it felt like a ray of sunshine through the heavy clouds that covered the sky.

"Oh, Raman, thank you. I'm not sure I could do this by myself."

"This is a fine time to reach *that* conclusion. You could stay here, you know. You don't have to go."

"I know." No one would make her go. But public opinion wouldn't change any other way. Only she could do what needed doing out there. And she couldn't stay here and watch Dorramon prepare to make Princess Varilyn his queen. She just couldn't.

So she would go. And what she would do then, she couldn't say.

♫

Alannys and Raman rode north for the rest of that day. Alannys had been too ashamed to admit she'd left with no clear destination in mind—she hadn't even looked at a map. The truth was that it hurt too much to be in the Great Palace knowing what she knew now—it felt like dying inside, and she had been desperate for an escape, any escape, and hadn't thought the whole thing through.

But she couldn't tell Raman any of that. When he asked, outside the palace gates, which direction she intended to go, north was the first thing that came to mind, so that was what she told him.

So they rode north, across the plains at the foot of the palace ridge, into the rolling foothills of the Cloudytop Mountains. As the hours slowly passed, the rolling hills turned to jagged mountains. The range stretched across the whole of Ravanmark, Raman told her, but the mountains were smaller here than any other place, making for the easiest crossing. "Just another reason why north was a good choice," he said, sounding satisfied.

"Another reason?" Alannys said.

"Well—yes. Lord Arik's Mirendasith Hall is almost a straight shot north from the Great Palace, and Lord Arik is one of your biggest supporters. But you knew that, right? That's why you headed this way, isn't it?"

"Of course," she lied, and let it go.

The terrain wasn't the only thing that had changed as they rode north. The wind picked up over the course of the day—by the time they rode into a little town halfway across the mountain range, the sun had sunk low on the horizon, and the wind whipped through their clothes and hair as though it sought to unhorse them. The sky loomed heavy with dark, threatening clouds, and thunder rumbled disconsolately off in the distance.

"We're in for a real storm tonight," Raman said, pulling his cloak tighter around him.

"Yes." Alannys glanced up warily at the sky—she could see lightning in the distance, spidering toward the ground in jagged, multi-pronged forks. The sight made her shiver. "We'll need an inn, and soon."

"Aye," Raman said. "Surely we'll find one here. This is the town of Crinn. It marks the border of Mirendasith Holding. We've made good progress today."

Good progress, Alannys thought. Certainly, if Mirendasith Hall was their goal. But she wasn't even sure what her goal was.

A tall, wooden wall surrounded Crinn. The heavy south gate with its black iron reinforcing strips served as a grim reminder that she had left the protection of the Great Palace far behind. Signs had been nailed to the gate, and she couldn't help reading them as she approached, though she really would rather not have.

"Any and all use of Talent forbidden here"

"Crinn will not submit to a musician king"

There were others, but they were farther out of sight, and she was unwilling to actually expend effort to read their filth. She wished there was somewhere else, anywhere else, close by that they might go. The town loomed unfamiliar and threatening in the fading light. More than ever, she was grateful for Raman's solid presence at her side. He frowned at the offensive signs, but said nothing.

Mirendasith Holding, she thought—but the name, put to this tiny, closed-in town, didn't seem to have any meaning. She remembered Lord Arik well—his friendly, magnanimous, always-gracious personality that could smooth over the roughest situations, and put the hardest-to-please person at ease. She could not imagine any connection between him and this place—to her, Mirendasith Holding, if she imagined it at all, would be somewhere breathtaking and otherworldly.

"Wow," Raman said suddenly, with a long whistle, pointing off to the right of the dirt road they followed. "That is one of the largest inns I've ever seen. Look at how decorated it is."

The gleaming white building stood three stories tall, with a large tower topped by a spire. Ornate decorations adorned the structure; flowers, spheres, scrolls—every icon of the Muses she knew, and some she didn't recognize.

"Wow, indeed. What is a place like that doing in a little nothing of a town like this one?"

"Damned if I know," Raman said, frowning. "I'd swear it wasn't here the last time I rode through this way. Guess we'd better try it out, eh?"

Alannys squinted at the fancy lettering on the sign over the carved front door. "Elossa's Ivy Crown," she read aloud.

No sooner had the words left her lips than she was abruptly plunged into utter darkness. Before she could even adjust to this change, the world around her exploded into flame. Fire consumed the great town wall, and the buildings around her—flames even licked the stone edifice that was Elossa's Ivy Crown. The storm that had brewed all day raged around her now, but the pelting rain could not stop the advancing fury of the flames.

And in the few spots of town left clear of the flames, she could see the dark shapes of people, huddled together in groups, muttering and pointing accusing fingers in her direction.

"This is *your* fault!"

♫

"Alannys?"

The voice was Raman's. He didn't sound angry, or upset, just confused — maybe about why she was cowering with her face buried in Quicksilver's mane and her eyes shut tight, riding down the street that was deserted but for them.

Alannys sat cautiously up, cracking an eye at the world around her. It was windy, and growing dark in advance of the coming storm, but it was decidedly *not* in flames. Even the Ivy Crown was safe.

And Raman was veering towards it.

"No!" she said suddenly, too loudly. Raman reined up and looked back at her, confusion plain on his face. "We can't stay there."

"What?" He looked at the inn, then back at her. "Why not?"

She realized she was shaking her head. "It isn't safe. I can't stay there. Anywhere but there. I'll camp before I go inside that building." Quicksilver danced away from the inn, as if he understood her hesitation.

Raman frowned at her. "I don't know," he said, with a doubtful glance at the sky. "Camping is likely to prove dangerous tonight — there's a corker of a storm coming. We really need proper shelter."

Alannys swallowed hard. She could hear the distant rumble of thunder, and in her mind it conflated with the roar of flames from her own personal vision of hell. "I can't do it, Raman — I can't stay there. I'll camp outside of town and you can catch up with me in the morning. I know my Second Sight doesn't put in an appearance very often, but when it does, I can't ignore it. That place isn't safe, not for me." The words tumbled out of her in a torrent; she sounded panicked and the rising wind whipped her hair into a tangled nightmare around her face.

"All right, all right," Raman said, holding his hands out in her direction. "Calm down. I'm not going to force you to stay there. Second Sight, eh? Hmm." He cast a glance around them, as though looking for inspiration in the small buildings huddled against the gathering darkness. "Look, even a town the size of Crinn is bound to have more than one inn. It's small, but it's a crossing point for the Cloudytops. We'll find another, and we'll stay there."

"What if there isn't another?" Alannys fretted. She couldn't bear to look at Elossa's Ivy Crown looming behind him now—the very sight of it felt like an ill omen after the vision she'd had.

"If there isn't another, then I'll camp with you." His tone was soothing, but the glance he gave the sky looked worried. "But I have to say I rather hope there is. This doesn't look good, not good at all."

"I agree," she said. Only as she started on down the road behind Raman with a fearful glance over her shoulder, she knew the basic difference between them...

She wasn't talking about the storm.

♫

The north gate was in sight before they found anywhere else to stay. Raman spent the ride wondering aloud how an inn that was so overtly religious could be upsetting to someone who was supposed to be the Redeemer, but Alannys didn't rise to the bait. She knew all about the symbolism of Thalia's ivy crown, sure—and the building had been plastered with the other icons of the Muses, as well. But she also remembered Lord Diabon and Lady Etherra, and she knew that religious did not necessarily mean safe.

She was pretty sure Raman knew that, too.

Raman spotted the inn first; a modest wooden building that showed age, but appeared well-kept. The sign swinging in the whipping wind read "The Weeping

Willow Inn."

"This is much better," Raman said. "And a good thing, too. I don't like the feel of this storm."

Alannys didn't, either. The lightning in the distance flashed so frequently, it never seemed to really stop. Thunder surrounded them, grating and intense, and the sound of it made Quicksilver fret and sidestep. His nerves made her nervous, too.

Raman dismounted, and went to tie his horse to the rail in front of the inn. Alannys sat anxiously on Quicksilver, trying in vain to held him still, watching his ears twitch. She felt the same way. She looked around, ill at ease with every single thing she saw. The whole town gave her the cold shivers. She was pretty sure she didn't belong there at all.

She swallowed hard, glancing over her shoulder and thinking about turning Quicksilver back toward the road and riding as hard as she could away from there.

"This again?" The voice was hard and cynical. She whipped her head around and found Raman watching her, his arms folded. "You can't run away, you know. I've already tied Quicksilver. Besides, the gates are bound to be closed, between the weather and the time."

Alannys nodded, unconvinced.

Raman sighed, and his voice turned soothing. "Look, Alannys, this isn't the Ivy Crown. We left that behind — there's nothing religious here at all. You have nothing to fear here. Except the storm. You don't want to sit there and wait for it, do you?"

Alannys shook her head and took Raman's hand, allowing him to help her dismount...admitting defeat. She followed him inside, trying hard not to look back.

She could learn to hate this town.

A short, white-haired lady greeted them from behind the wooden counter inside. She looked older than old, and she moved as slow as she talked — which was pretty slow. "Good morrow, travelers. I am Dalonna, innkeeper of the Weeping Willow." She rose slowly from her chair, as if everything hurt. "You'll be needing a room?"

"Please," Raman said. "Is anything available?"

"Oh, always. Best in the house if you want it; two silvers a night."

"That sounds wonderful. Thank you." Raman stepped forward and placed the silvers on the counter.

Dalonna squinted at him, then at Alannys. "Muses sing mercy! Arch-Prince Raman, I apologize. I did not recognize you. And this must be the Lady Alannys. It seems the rumors were true. Of course you'll have the best in the house, and there is no need for silvers."

Raman smiled. "I would be honored if you would accept my coin, Dalonna. Can you direct us to the room?"

Dalonna gestured through the opening on the west wall. "It's at the end of the main hall. Past the corridor, only door on the right. I can take you there if you wish, my Lord. But the coming storm pains my joints and makes me slow, so you may be faster alone."

'Thank you." Raman inclined his head, and took Alannys's arm. "We won't trouble you."

"I'll see that your horses are taken to the stable before the storm," Dalonna said. "Please let me know if there is anything you need. I hope you enjoy your stay."

"I'm sure we will," Raman said. Alannys smiled lamely and kept her mouth shut. 'Enjoy' was about the last thing she expected to do here — except maybe sleep.

As they left the little office and started down the hall, Alannys looked back and saw Dalonna, creaking towards the door to stable their horses.

She couldn't have said why, but the sight bothered her.

♫

Against her every expectation, Alannys did sleep, for a time. The room had one wooden table and two beds.

Raman stretched out on one, and as she climbed into the other she could practically feel her day weighing on her — from the emotional wringer of saying goodbye to Dorramon, to the unaccustomed work of a day spent on horseback, to the stressful experience of her vision in Crinn...it probably shouldn't have surprised her to find, under the adrenaline, that she was dead tired. The quilts were worn but clean, and under their heavy warmth she fell quickly asleep.

Sometime after midnight, the rippling boom of thunder — close thunder — woke her up. She woke up tensed, with every muscle knotted in fear. She lay quiet with her eyes closed, forcing herself to breathe slowly, trying to calm herself.

It didn't work. Something was wrong. She could feel it — the *wrongness* surrounding her in the darkness, like clawing fingers waiting to strangle her while she slept.

Alannys rolled over on her side, telling herself she was being crazy. Again. A fearsome storm raged outside, and it just had her skittish, that was all.

A flash of lightning threw sharp light across the room, cutting the darkness and illuminating the grim expression on Raman's face where he sat looking out the little window. The hard set of his jaw made her think that whatever he was looking at, he didn't like it very much.

"Raman?" She sat up in the bed, hearing the rain pounding against the window — and other sounds that didn't seem as though they came from the storm. She shivered. "What's going on?"

His glance flicked her direction. "Alannys. I'm glad you're awake. We need to go."

"Go? Now?" She tumbled out of the bed, fumbling around in the darkness for Songstrike and her cloak.

"I'm afraid so." She heard him whisper a curse under his breath. "I'm sorry, Alannys. You were right — I should have listened. Hurry!"

Alannys's fingers shook, slowing her down. They were going to leave? How? They couldn't leave town—it was the middle of the night; the gates were closed. Would leaving the inn be enough to save them from whatever was coming for them?

Anxiety gnawed at her, but she was afraid to ask any more questions—she wasn't sure she wanted to hear the answers. Moving as quickly as she could, she strapped on her sword, and threw her cloak over her shoulders. Cold and sleep made her injured shoulder stiff.

Raman already had the door open. He waited for her, and they hurried down the long hall. They could hear nothing but the storm outside—their footsteps seemed loud and out of place in the dead quiet of the inn.

The office was empty. Every step they took brought the noise outside more clearly into focus, and well before they reached the door Alannys recognized the angry shouts of people. What on earth was going on out there? She quickened her step, anxious to see.

The front door stood open, freely admitting the wind and rain. That, she thought, was probably not a good sign. Raman held an arm out in front of her before they reached it, stopping her. "Hold," he whispered, and she leaned forward to follow his gaze outside.

Dalonna stood just outside the inn, clutching a knitted shawl around her shoulders, weak protection against the driving rain.

Facing her was something right out of Alannys's worst nightmares—a mob. She could see the hard, angry faces, illuminated by lightning and the blazing torches they carried. The deep shadows cast on their faces and the red glow of the torches gave them all a sinister, other-worldly aspect that chilled her, and she didn't even know why they were there.

"My friends," Dalonna said, her voice wavering with age or fear, "Elossa, I beg of you—"

"Enough talk, old woman." A younger woman with flaming red hair—apparently Elossa—stepped out in front of the grumbling mob, pointing an accusing finger at Dalonna. She had high, striking cheekbones, and carried herself proudly, as though she'd have been more at home in a nobleman's mansion than in this tiny border town. "No words can change the will of the righteous. There can only be one end for a false Redeemer—you know this. Obstruct us any further, and you will meet the same end. Send out the Lady Alannys!"

"Elossa, no!" A man clutched at Elossa's arm. His hair clung to his face in damp curls, and his jawline was strong and pronounced.

Elossa tried to shake him off. "Caredry, my love, go back to the Ivy Crown. You are too tender for business such as this."

"No! Elossa, you must listen to me. This is madness! The woman has done no wrong!"

"No wrong?" Elossa's voice rose, keened like a wail of pain. "No *wrong?* The woman flaunts her foul Talent about the Great Palace—through Talent as black as witchcraft she has enchanted the very King of Ravanmark himself! And now she would bring her evil here, to us, that she might ensnare us as well? Oh, she has done wrong—great wrong. And that woman is no Redeemer! Stone the false Redeemer!"

The crowd behind her took up the chant, thrusting their torches up over their heads in time with their words. "Stone the false Redeemer! *Stone* the false *Redeemer!*"

Raman swore under his breath. "I'm sorry, Alannys. Even with everything we saw, I had no idea it could be this bad."

His face was pale and strained in the dim light that

made it into the darkened office. Looking at his face, at the tension in his posture, Alannys couldn't kid herself about it—this was bad, one of the worst situations she'd ever been in, and she had been in some pickles. These people were here for her, and they had but one purpose—to see her dead. She swallowed hard. "What are we going to do?"

"I don't know." He turned away, scanning their surroundings. "But you should come away from the door."

"But Dalonna's out there! Are we just going to abandon her to this?"

"Of course not. But before we can help her, we have to get ourselves out of here without getting killed. Now please, step away from the door."

She turned to follow him—then froze. As soon as she had begun to move, the crowd outside fell instantly silent. Her head whipped up and she looked at Raman in sudden terror. He ran to the window to see what had happened.

"Your cowardice is exposed—hiding behind the skirts of an old woman, false Redeemer!" Elossa crowed. *"We can see you!* Come out and face us, if you have any honor at all!"

Quick as a flash, Dalonna darted inside the office, slamming the door and barring it. Alannys stared in slack-jawed amazement at seeing the creaky old lady suddenly so spry.

"Soth's eye!" Dalonna said. "I hoped you would stay in your room. A fine mess this is. Get away from that window, my Lord!"

Raman jumped back from the window, just as a rock the size of his head crashed through it. "Seven Hells! Is there a back door to this place?"

"Aye," Dalonna said, "for all the good it'll do us. This way!"

She led them through the door behind the counter, through a couple of sparsely decorated rooms that looked like her living chambers, into a storage room piled with shovels, rakes, and animal feed in burlap sacks. The other side of the storage room opened into the stables. "Your horses are in here."

"I don't know where we can go," Raman said, "with the gates closed, but we'd better do it quickly. And you had better come with us."

His voice was tight and low, and at the sound of it, both women turned to look back.

Behind him, the Weeping Willow burned in a torrent of flames, dark billows of smoke pouring up into the stormy night sky.

♫

"Seven Hells!" Dalonna sounded stricken, her voice heavy with unshed tears. "This town has gone insane! Hurry, free the horses. We've got to get out of here!"

They didn't need to be told twice; Raman was already at his horse's side by the time Dalonna finished speaking, and the old innkeeper was opening the stall door to her own pony.

Alannys saw Quicksilver's familiar gray head — so covered in fine scars from his days as a Tibadoan warhorse that it appeared almost silver — peeking out over the door to one of the stalls. She ran to him, her leather boots slipping on the loose straw scattered on the floor.

"Merciful Muses!" Dalonna's shout caught her attention, and she looked up in time to see a flaming torch fly in through the window. The stable windows were just uncovered openings, so nothing impeded the torch's progress as it sailed into the building, toppling end over end.

Alannys sucked in an involuntary gasp. The window was in the middle of the long stablehouse — Raman and Dalonna were on one side of it, and she was on the other.

If that thing started a fire, she would be separated from her friends in a burning stable.

Quicksilver pawed the ground and shook his head, picking up on her nerves. The torch splashed into a water trough and went out.

Alannys sent up a silent thank-you and hurried to the others, leading Quicksilver.

Her luck was short-lived. A second torch followed not long behind the first, and this one landed in the dry hay. Before anyone had time to react, it ignited, filling the long room with choking smoke and the crackling of hungry flames.

They scrambled out of the stable, dragging their nervous mounts behind them. Alannys stared around them in utter shock.

Crinn was ablaze. Fire consumed the great town wall, and the buildings around her—flames even licked at the stone edifice that was Elossa's Ivy Crown. The storm that had brewed all day raged around her now, but the pelting rain could not stop the advancing fury of the flames.

And in the few spots in town left clear of the flames, she could see the dark shapes of people, some huddling together in frightened groups, some running bucket brigades from the well, some wailing at the destruction around them. Voices called for the opening of the gates, but no one could do that amid the flames.

And a single individual, tall and imposing, separate from the others, pointed an accusing finger in her direction.

"This is *your* fault!" The voice was like a flare, a beacon of hatred that shone clear over the sounds of the town dying around them. It took her a moment to place the voice as Caredry's voice, to recognize the dirty, bedraggled figure who stood before her now as the man who had tried to be a voice of reason earlier. "If you had never come here, none of this would have happened. Because of you, these people will lose everything!" The shifting wind blew the heavy black smoke in his direction, and he coughed raggedly, turning from her. "Elossa!"

Belatedly Alannys saw the redhead standing near them, staring into the fire consuming the Weeping Willow. Elossa turned at Caredry's call, and her gaze fell on the Ivy Crown, on the flames blackening the stone and consuming everything else it could find. She screamed in horror and ran — not away as Alannys would have expected, but *inside the burning inn.*

"Elossa!" Caredry cried, and ran after her, dodging all manner of debris. "Elossa, stop! Come back!"

"Fear not, my love!" Elossa's voice sailed back to them, sounding completely unhinged. "The Muses will protect me and my sacred place!"

Caredry disappeared inside the inn.

Alannys started after them, only to be jerked back by a vise-like grip on her arm. "What in the Seven Hells do you think you are doing?" Raman demanded.

"Raman, they're going to die in there!"

"Maybe so," Raman said, his voice hard, "but so are we and Quicksilver and all these townspeople if we don't find a way out of Crinn. You can't play hero for those two."

Not far from the iron-reinforced north gate, a group of villagers had turned the remains of a tree trunk into a makeshift battering ram and were hard at work opening up a passage in a part of the town wall that was still clear of flames. Raman and Alannys left their horses with Dalonna and put their backs into the effort as well, working against the wind, weather, and the encroaching flames to open an escape. In the rush to save themselves, the same people who had earlier howled for Alannys's blood now worked tirelessly beside her.

By the time they knocked down enough of the wall to

pass through, the flames were closing in on either side of their opening. People pushed through in a terrified rush, frantic to be away from the pit of fire and ruin that was Crinn.

Raman and Alannys joined Dalonna and the horses, and hurried toward the opening themselves. But the approaching fire totally unwound the horses. Quicksilver was a stout little warhorse, strictly trained almost since foaling, and Alannys could tell he was doing his best not to panic, following the owner who had saved him. Dalonna had wrapped her shawl around her pony's eyes, and the little mare walked with her, shying, clearly nervous.

Raman's horse, though—nothing in his noble upbringing had prepared him for the sheer terror that was fire. His eyes rolled wildly and he reared up, kicking and snorting.

Alannys turned back and saw Raman hanging onto the reins, dancing sideways to stay with his agitated mount, hauling on him and trying to wrestle him into submission. But Raman couldn't calm the terrified animal, and it was clear which one of them would ultimately win.

"There now," Alannys called, pitching her voice to carry, doing her best to imitate the lilting speak-sing she had heard Dorramon use so many times. The horse dropped his head, and she hooked her fingers into the straps of his bridle, putting her face close enough to speak into his ear.

"Alannys..." Raman's tone carried a warning.

"Be calm!" she said to the horse, still speak-singing in that peculiar, ringing tone. "Believe in my voice, and follow me!" She turned and led Quicksilver through the opening as fast as she could, and Raman followed. Dalonna had already gone through. "Everything is all right," Alannys called back to the horse, "the danger is passed. You are safe."

On the other side of the wall, she stopped and turned back to wait for Raman. To her horror, she could see Elossa, up on top of the conflagration that was Elossa's Ivy Crown, her arms extended to the heavens. "My Muses!" she shrieked. "Save me! Do not abandon me for the false Redeemer!"

"The danger has passed," she repeated, but she forgot to speak-sing and the words fell flat. The horses tossed their heads.

Raman clamped his hand around her arm and started for the woods, pulling her along. "You are not going back there. It would be your death."

Alannys said nothing, stumbling along with him. The words she had said to the horses still rang unnaturally in her ears.

But behind her, amidst the roar of the flames, she could hear Elossa screaming to the gods for rescue and retribution that never came. And she had to wonder— would the danger ever really be passed?

♫

It seemed like half an eternity later when their odd little group stopped at a cave. It was a small indentation in the rock face of the hill overlooking the woods, barely deep enough to get them in out of the rain, but the sight of it filled Alannys with relief. It had been a miserable couple of hours slogging through the wet forest undergrowth. Her teeth chattered, her hands shook, and her stomach rumbled. She sank onto the rock floor of the cave, staring out at the storm, wondering what madness had ever prompted her to leave the Great Palace.

Raman patted her shoulder sympathetically, and helped Dalonna to sit near her. "I'm sorry to make you two travel so far. We needed to be sure we wouldn't run into any of the other townspeople. They didn't seem to like you much."

Alannys was too bone-tired to do more than nod in response. Dalonna sat silently staring out at the pounding rain, acknowledging nothing. Alannys wasn't sure if Dalonna had come with them because she felt safe with them, or because she had nowhere else to go. Either way, she would have bet the old woman regretted it now.

The cave smelled of mildew and their wet horses. There would barely be room for all of them to stretch out. Still, it had to be better than spending the night in the rainy forest. Alannys sighed, wishing she could work up some enthusiasm for anything.

Raman and Alannys both carried camping supplies in their saddlebags. Between their cheese, jerky, dried fruit, and blankets, they managed to produce three meals and three beds. None of them felt much like eating, or talking, and so it wasn't long before they were all uncomfortably huddled in their blankets, listening to the horses and the storm outside.

Alannys should have been dead tired, she knew that. But she had too much on her mind, too many things to think about, and so she lay awake long after the others had gone to sleep, listening to their deep breaths and snoring.

It felt like she had been lying there for hours when she heard the slight sounds of something moving outside. She was wedged between Dalonna and Raman, with very little in the way of wiggle room. But she did her best to slip out without disturbing them, and went to stand out in front of the cave. Quicksilver whickered after her, unsettled at seeing her leave.

The fury of the storm had finally passed, and the light rain that fell over the forest now was more like a heavy mist. The impenetrable cloud cover had just begun to break, and in the faint moonlight that filtered through, Alannys could see a horse passing slowly by, bearing a single rider.

The horse glowed ethereal white in the pale light, and it moved so slowly Alannys wondered if she might be dreaming it. The rider was a slender woman, wearing a dress that looked as if it might once have been as white as her horse, but was now dirty, and appeared singed in places. Her long red hair hung down her back in damp tendrils. She stared straight at her horse's mane, glancing neither left nor right, though she passed not fifty feet from Alannys. A misty fog rolled around her horse's legs, adding to the dreamlike impression.

And then they were gone; woman and horse both disappeared off into the forest, leaving no trace of their passage behind. Alannys stared off into the trees, wondering if she had really seen that, or just imagined the whole thing.

A heavy hand fell on her shoulder, startling her. "What are you doing out here in the cold by yourself?"

She turned to face Raman, hoping he hadn't noticed the way she'd jumped. That rider had creeped her out more than she realized. "I'm sorry, I didn't mean to wake you."

"You didn't. It's impossible to get any real sleep in there. But why are you out here? Trying to catch cold?"

"No, of course not." She glanced over her shoulder, into the woods. "I heard something, so I came out to see what it was. Someone rode past."

"Just now? I don't know, Alannys. Maybe you were dreaming."

"No, there was a rider! The horse was—" She cut herself off, realizing that if she described what she had seen, there was no way Raman would believe her. It sounded too much like a dream even in her own mind. "There was a rider, that's all."

Now she just sounded obstinate. Raman smiled and patted her shoulder. "Now, now—there's no shame in a dream, especially as exhausted as you must be. But everyone else is holed up after that storm. I'm afraid the only one crazy enough to be out here right now is you." He turned and went back into the cave, calling back to her. "Come back inside, and try to get some sleep while it's still dark."

She followed him, thinking about the rider. It couldn't have been a dream. It was too eerie.

But if it hadn't been a dream, what on earth could it mean?

♫

Their night in the cave was, all taken, an uncomfortable one. Alannys figured they were probably all as glad as she was just to be alive to pass the uncomfortable night in the cave, but that didn't make it any easier to sleep on the rocky ground. None of them slept well, and first light found them rolling their blankets and packing their saddlebags.

"Today," Raman said, as they led the horses out of the cave, "we ride for Mirendasith Hall."

"No," Alannys said reflexively, and Raman looked at her in surprise. "I mean, not right away at least. We need to go back to Crinn, to see what can be done."

"What can be done?" Raman echoed incredulously. "Other than sweeping the entire town into the ashbin, you mean?"

Dalonna's face paled, and she looked away.

Alannys frowned. "Come on, Raman, that's uncalled for." They stood outside their little cave in the harsh light of sunrise, looking out over the trees at the burnt-out husk that used to be Crinn. Jagged, black shapes littered the place, and smoke still rose from them, reaching and curling like ghostly fingers up into the morning sky. "We have to try."

Raman glanced over at her, and shook his head. "All right. Back to Crinn it is."

The ride back to Crinn took considerably less time than their midnight slog away from it. But the closer they got, the more empty and wrong everything felt. Not even birdsong broke the oppressive silence. They left their horses outside town.

The town was an empty, ghostly shell. A few other people moved gingerly through the debris, searching for loved ones or surviving belongings, but it was plain that the town was unsalvageable, abandoned.

Crinn was no more.

Dalonna drifted over to the wreckage of her inn, picking through what remained. Alannys stood staring at the charred remnants surrounding her—leftovers that had been parts of people's possessions, of their homes, of their lives.

Raman clapped her on the shoulder. "Don't look like that. What happened here was not your fault."

This is your fault! She remembered the hate-filled voice, the dirty finger pointed right in her face. *Because of you, these people will lose everything!* "It feels like it is."

"I know. But that's just your over-developed sense of responsibility."

"I don't know." She saw Dalonna, kneeling in the scattered ash and debris that used to be her home and business, clutching something to her chest and weeping. "If I had never come here, this would never have happened."

"No, but something just as bad might have, *would* have, eventually. Any town that goes to torches and pitchforks, howling for blood, because a musician passes through...a town like that can't last. This would have happened anyway. You can't blame yourself for what other people do. You just have to pick up and carry on."

They picked their way through what used to be the main road through town, the same road they had ridden on yesterday, in what seemed like another lifetime. Among the devastation that surrounded them, one building still stood, reaching up toward the sky as if for mercy, with its blackened walls and crumbling spire.

"The Ivy Crown," Alannys muttered, and she began to run, clambering over the wreckage towards the stone building, a building that suddenly seemed like nothing so much as a monument to the destruction this place had witnessed.

"Alannys! Wait!" Raman sounded as though he was having some trouble keeping up, but she didn't slow down. She couldn't have said what was driving her, just— it seemed like, if anything still lived in Crinn, this ruined building covered in the icons of the Muses was where she would find it.

The front steps were cracked, and littered with ash and debris. Alannys made her way up them, carefully choosing the placement of each foot— it was plain that one wrong step here would have her hurting. The door was gone; black iron hinges hung at odd, sharp angles, holding jagged bits of charred wood. She remember the polished, carved door she had seen here yesterday, and shivered.

Inside, the place was gutted, so ravaged by fire that it wasn't immediately clear what she was looking at. The first floor of the inn was one long, open room, with high ceilings. What was left of the glass in the windows, hanging crookedly like broken teeth, looked as though it had been colored. Among the things not burned beyond all recognition, she could see the ends of wooden benches, and a stone altar.

"Is this— is this a *church?*" she said out loud, knowing there was on one there to answer her. It didn't seem right —she remember the chapel at the Great Palace, with its comfortable chairs and open places for quiet contemplation. This looked more like a setup for a single person to preach to followers, and that didn't fit with what she knew of Muse-worship at all.

"Yes..." The voice was faint, barely audible, followed by a painful-sounding cough.

Alannys froze. Someone was still alive in here? She pushed her way farther into the room, scanning the wreckage for any sign of a person.

She found him, in the back of the room near the staircase, just as the arch-prince skidded to a halt at the front door.

"Raman! Back here!" She waved her arm in the air, then knelt beside the man before her.

An enormous log beam had fallen from the damaged ceiling — landing across this man's torso. As soon as she saw the beam, she knew she and Raman could not lift it — but as soon as she saw the man's face, she knew it didn't matter. He was not long for this world. It took her a moment, through the ash, dirt, and blood, to recognize Caredry.

A hand squeezed her shoulder. "Alannys, you shouldn't run off like that. I — merciful Muses!"

Caredry's mouth twitched. He might have been trying to smile. "Arch-Prince Raman."

Raman braced against the beam and pushed, testing his strength against its massive weight. "Muses, man — what a damnable thing to happen. Just hold on."

"No," Caredry gasped, wincing as though the minute movement of the beam hurt worse than its unmoving bulk. "Too late...for me."

Raman abandoned the beam and knelt by him, next to Alannys. "I'm sorry."

Caredry's mouth twitched again. "Don't be. Need...to warn you."

"Warn us?" Alannys felt suddenly cold.

"You." Caredry's gaze wandered, but finally settled on

her. "Elossa...gone. Be careful."

"Gone?" Alannys echoed. Involuntarily her eyes flicked to the big staircase, remembering the last time she had seen Elossa — on the roof of the building, screaming to the skies.

"No," Caredry said, with his peculiar smile. "Gone. Blames you...careful..."

And before Alannys had reconciled herself to what was happening, his pupils dilated, staring at nothing, and his labored breathing stilled.

♫

"May the Muses bless him and keep him," Raman said solemnly, and gently closed Caredry's eyes.

Alannys abruptly stood up and turned away. It wasn't the first time she had watched a man die — not even the first time she felt personally responsible — but it wasn't the sort of thing that got easier.

"Alannys?" Raman's voice was close; he was following her. "Are you all right?"

"No." Her voice sounded strained, like a thread pulled so taut it might at any moment snap.

Oddly enough, she felt that way herself.

"I understand," Raman said. "That couldn't have been easy for you."

"No." She wrapped her arms around herself, tight, almost as though she feared she might fall apart without the support. "I think — I think I'm in over my head, Raman. Maybe I should just go back to the Great Palace."

"Hmm." Raman put his hand on her shoulder and guided her back towards the horses. "Well, you could. No one is stopping you. Dorr would love to have you back, and that's a fact."

Alannys felt her spirits lifting just hearing those words, just thinking about Dorramon's twinkling blue eyes and warm embrace waiting for her back home.

"But Alannys..." He hesitated. "You left because you

had things to do — important things — that only you could do. If you go running back to the Great Palace the first time it gets tough, where does that leave things?"

"I don't know." She stood still, silently waiting while Raman slipped over to Dalonna. He spoke to her — probably asking her to come with them, judging by his gestures. The old woman shook her head and turned away, and Raman returned alone. "I don't know," she repeated, continuing as if he'd never been gone, "but I didn't leave to do *this*. How can I hope to make things better, when I destroy every place in Ravanmark that I touch?"

"You have a positive gift for exaggeration," Raman said wryly, helping her through the wreckage of the ruined town gate. "You had one bad experience. And it was pretty awful, yes. But it wasn't your fault. It hardly means you'll destroy every place you touch."

Alannys shook her head. Quicksilver nickered at her approach and nuzzled his velvet nose into her neck, and she patted his head.

"Look, I know this isn't what you came here hoping for. And I know it's hard to see right now, but it's possible that this is even for the best."

"What?" she gasped, her hand freezing on Quicksilver's mane. Had he really just said that?

"No, I'm serious. Think about that place, Alannys, about what we saw there. It was rotten, and not just a little. We weren't even there but a few hours, and we could smell it. Whatever Elossa brought here...those kinds of attitudes, that kind of thinking...it's like a disease. Like gangrene. And there's only one way to deal with gangrene."

"But..." She heard what he was saying, and in an abstract way she even got it. But she couldn't accept it, not when presented with the gruesome corpse of Crinn, destroyed and desolate behind her. "But not everyone was like that! Dalonna, and who knows how many others like her—there were decent people in Crinn, people who didn't deserve to have this happen to them."

"And there are always decent people everywhere who don't deserve the horrible things that happen around them. You think the people of my hometown deserved to lose everything, when Lord Malrec burned it down? But the decent people of Crinn, driven out by that fire—I really do believe they will find better lives in other places, places less poisoned by the kind of bile Elossa and her ilk spew."

"And Elossa herself?" Alannys challenged. "She had to be the rider I saw last night."

Raman shook his head. "That's not what Caredry meant."

"Assume it is. Will she find a better life somewhere else?"

"Anywhere else," Raman said flatly, "as long as she doesn't meet up with more like her and start the whole thing over again. Look, Alannys, you could spend the rest of your life feeling bad about this. But that isn't going to help you, and it isn't going to help Ravanmark. I know you don't want to commit to going through with this right now, but from where we are, we have two options: go on or go back. Are you ready to give up and go back to the palace, Ambassador Thell and all?"

If he hadn't thrown that name in there, she would have agreed. In the shock and despair of the disaster at Crinn, she had forgotten the other reasons she'd left the Great Palace—reasons that came crashing back to her now. "No. No, I can't go back."

He studied her a moment, arms folded. "No, I reckon not. Then how about this—we'll go on to Mirendasith Hall, visit with Lord Arik. Then you can decide what you want to do, when you've gotten some distance from all of this."

"All right. It's not like I have any better ideas."

But as they mounted up and rode away, it wasn't Mirendasith Hall, or even Lord Arik that consumed Alannys's thoughts.

...as long as she doesn't meet up with more like her and start the whole thing over again...

She felt an unnatural chill, wondering just exactly who Elossa might meet — and just exactly what might come of it.

♬

Without their detour to Crinn, Alannys and Raman could probably have made it to Mirendasith Hall that same day. After spending the morning in the ruins, though, they only made it about halfway there. They made it out of the Cloudytops, however, which Raman assured her was the hardest part of the journey for the horses. They rode into the town of Falhill as the sun began to set.

Alannys was relieved to see that no walls surrounded Falhill. No signs proclaimed her unwelcome, no iron-reinforced gates barred her entry or denied her exit. These things seemed to her to set the tone of the whole place, and she couldn't help but feel that things would be better here.

Falhill was much larger than Crinn. They stopped at the first inn they came to, at Alannys's insistence. The sign, decorated with a comedic drawing, said "The Thumb and Hammer Inn." Alannys couldn't remember when she had laughed so hard. Any village with a sense of humor developed enough to support the Thumb and Hammer Inn *had* to be better than Crinn. Even Raman laughed, and he hadn't had much to say since their departure that morning.

The young man behind the counter watched them with interest, and greeted them with a showy, flourishing bow.

"Ah, and who should we see at the inn this fine day but the Lady Alannys. And our Arch-Prince Raman. I am Galar. Warmest welcome to the Thumb and Hammer Inn."

Alannys glanced over at Raman, a bit taken aback, but he seemed as surprised as she was. "Thank you," she said, "I think. How did you know our names?"

"Well," Galar replied, with a wink she found truly disconcerting, "of course everyone recognizes the Arch-Prince of Ravanmark. But you, Lady Alannys...we just had a red-headed lady come screaming through town this morning, warning us all that the very devil was coming to Falhill, in the form of a Talented woman calling herself the Redeemer. And who could that be, but you?"

This felt threatening, and Alannys felt her guard go up. "For me, I call myself nothing, but others have named me the Redeemer, yes."

She must have sounded defensive, because Galar laughed, waving his hands in front of himself placatingly. "Now, now, my Lady, I meant no offense. I tell you only what she told us. For myself, I didn't find her the most reliable witness, if you take my meaning."

"Is that so?" Alannys eyed his ingratiating smile, intrigued by that remark. "Why not, if I may ask?"

Galar's smile broadened. He leaned forward, propping his elbows on the counter, ignoring the dubious looks Raman directed at both of them. "My Lady may ask anything that pleases her, if I may do the same." Alannys inclined her head, and he continued. "I've been to Crinn a time or two myself. I've seen what goes on there, since the Ivy Crown came to town and changed everything. Anything that gets that particular lady that upset...well, I would choose to side with that thing, rather than against it."

"I—I see," she said, considering it. For all that Galar

obviously liked to talk, it was hard for her to get a handle on him.

"What about you?" The look in Galar's eyes was speculative, but hard. "You have said that you call yourself nothing, but what do you believe? Are you the Redeemer?"

Ah. She should have expected this, when she gave him permission to ask anything. "That's the million-dollar question, isn't it?" she said, reminded by their expressions that the phrase was lost on everyone in the room except herself. She adopted a more serious attitude. "People will always believe what suits their interests, Galar. In the end, what I say will not convince anyone. People believe, or not, as they choose. The time has not yet come for me to prove the issue either way. What do *you* believe, Galar?"

"You are the Redeemer, my Lady," he said, studying her face, "or no one is."

Alannys blinked at him—she hadn't expected that. "What makes you say that? Songstrike?"

Galar's eyes flicked to the sword at her side, and he shook his head. "There have been false Redeemers before —we have one who lives here now, as a matter of fact, if you ask me. Of course, none of them had Songstrike, but then, none of them were friends of the Great Palace, so they would not have had access to it. Perhaps they could have wielded it, perhaps not. There's no way to know. But I do know that none of them ever gave an answer like that when asked directly if they were the Redeemer. They were full of reasons, full of promises, full of commands."

"Full of horseshit," Raman observed bluntly.

Galar laughed out loud. "Just so, my Lord. Exactly."

Alannys laughed. "I see. Well, I hope when the time comes, I can prove you right, Galar."

"Oh, you will, my Lady. I have no doubt of it."

♬

"Talk to me, Raman," Alannys said, as soon as the door

to their room closed behind them. "What is all of this about another Redeemer in Falhill? Why didn't you tell me?"

"I didn't know!" He tossed his cloak onto one of the beds. "Calm down, Alannys. This can't be the first time it's occurred to you that there might be others who have been thought of as the Redeemer — or who want to be thought of as the Redeemer."

"Actually, that's exactly what it is! I never imagined anyone would *want* that — it sounds like an awful lot of danger to me, and work, and people hating you, with very little chance of success."

"But with an incredible sword," he said, watching her closely.

She remembered her investiture ceremony, and wondered how many of her motives he suspected. Her face flushed, even as her hand crept to Songstrike's grip, as if reassuring herself it was still there. "There is that. But these others — they wouldn't even have Songstrike. Who would do that? Why? What would they get out of it?"

"How would I know?" Raman said exasperatedly. "The Redeemer is reckoned to be a singer, not a painter, so I never worried about it. The only singer I knew until you came was Dorramon, and he's never held any ideas about being the Redeemer."

"I don't like it," Alannys fretted. "After everything that happened in Crinn, to find this here...multiple Redeemers. Who would have thought?"

"Not multiple," Raman said, sitting on the edge of the bed by his cloak. "False. Whatever else we may or may not know about the Redeemer, there can be only one."

"False Redeemer? It's like Crinn all over again!" She reached to unbuckle her swordbelt, trying not to panic. "What are we going to do when they turn on that person? How do we — "

"Hold on there," Raman cut her off, holding up a hand to stop her. "Don't take that off. I don't think you should go anywhere unarmed, not even to dinner."

"What?"

"Don't you see?" His brown eyes held her, steady and somber, almost pitying. "You need to be ready to fight. Because the person they're going to call false Redeemer isn't the local guy, Alannys.

"It's you."

♬

Alannys had never seen anything quite like the tavern at the Thumb and Hammer Inn. Splintered wooden tables at haphazard angles littered the enormous room, giving the space a cluttered, crowded feel. Torches burned on the walls, and on the stone pillars supporting the massive wooden beams across the ceiling, and in tall stands scattered around the room. A fire crackled in the stone hearth. Between the warm light of the fire, the drone of voices and the clanking of metal dishes, the tavern felt welcoming and comforting—just the thing for the end of a long day of riding.

At least, it would have been welcoming and comforting if she had been anybody else. She was pretty sure Raman felt warm and welcomed. For herself, though—not so much. After their conversation in the room, she felt too much like a wanted man to be walking around in public. She had, in fact, tried to beg off of dinner entirely, but Raman had dragged her along anyway, pointing out that a goal of changing public opinion was rarely accomplished by hiding in one's room. So here she was, in the tavern, feeling like she had a target on her forehead.

With so many people and so much activity, Alannys and Raman caused no particular commotion, though. They sat by themselves at the end of one of the long tables, grateful for a seat that wasn't attached to a horse.

"Evenin'!" a serving girl greeted them cheerfully,

before Alannys even knew she was there. "Welcome, travelers. Glad to see you at the Thumb and Hammer. Name's Jia. What can I get for you?"

"Berry juice, please," Alannys said.

"And ale for me," Raman said. "Stew and bread for both of us."

Jia nodded, and went back to the kitchen, threading her way through the crowded tables.

Alannys sighed and leaned forward over the table, resting her head in her hands.

"Me, too," Raman said. "Unfortunately we have another long day's ride before we reach Mirendasith Hall."

Alannys raised her head to regard him. "I don't think we should ride again tomorrow."

The arch-prince blinked. "What?"

"Mirendasith Hall isn't our goal. We don't need to change Lord Arik's mind."

A small silence fell on the table. "I see," Raman said finally. "Does this mean you're feeling better? This morning, you wouldn't have said that."

She looked away. "I don't know about that. But I thought a lot about what you said, about going forward or going back. And as long as I'm going forward, I think I must continue to work for my purpose."

"Very well. This song is yours to sing, Alannys. What shall we do?"

She sighed. "As you said, part of the reason I left the Great Palace was to take my message to the masses. It didn't work out so well in Crinn because the masses wanted to stone me to death. But I think maybe we should stay here a couple days."

Raman cast a glance around the tavern. She couldn't tell if he approved or not. "Are you sure that is safe?"

"I don't know," Alannys said, honestly enough. She

paused while Jia handed out heavy pewter mugs, and steaming bowls of stew. "To tell you the truth, I'm not sure anyplace is really safe. Not for me. But it doesn't really matter. Like you said, I won't be able to change anybody's opinion unless I talk to people. Ultimately it isn't my safety that's important—it's the safety of Dorramon, and the safety of Ravanmark."

"I think Dorramon would say all are important. And I think he would be right." Raman took a big swallow of ale, dragging the back of his hand across his mouth. "But it's a very brave sentiment."

"Is it? I suppose it must seem so. I have to tell you, though, I certainly don't *feel* very brave."

Raman reached across the table and patted her hand. "Courage is always easier to see in others than in yourself, my Lady."

A sudden shout went up behind her. "Redeemer! Look, boys, it's the Redeemer of the Realm come to eat with us tonight."

Alannys thumped her mug down on the table and twisted around in her seat. Her hands felt suddenly cold. Called out, in public, and just when she'd begun to think things were all right!

"Calm down." Raman's low voice cut through her panic. "They do not speak of you. The people of Falhill say the Redeemer lives here, remember?"

Of course, she should have remembered that. She knew there was a pretender in town. But why did he have to be right here, right *now*? All she wanted was a hot meal and a warm bed. She wasn't in the mood for confrontation. She had never asked for this title.

The fellow standing in the doorway was young, maybe seventeen or eighteen. He had blond hair that hung just below his shoulders. His build was tall and slight, with long, graceful fingers. So this young fellow wanted to be the Redeemer? Too bad she couldn't give it to him. The title and all the headaches that went with it.

The young man raised a hand in greeting to the person who had shouted. "Good morrow, Redus! I trust all is well at the Thumb and Hammer tonight?"

"Naturally, Kiarin." Redus sat at one of the long tables, a brimming mug of ale in his hand, sloshing out as the man next to him slapped him on the back with a guffaw. "The food is hot and the company is good. What more could such as we desire?"

Kiarin shook his head, raising his arms dramatically in a gesture that encompassed the entire room. "Tonight, I fear the company could be better. A false Redeemer walks among us!"

Alannys heard Raman's chair scrape as he slid back from the table. She didn't like the sound of the conversation either. But she sat, watching Kiarin scan the room, hoping to somehow escape detection.

Her heart stopped when his eyes locked on her, then beat double-time as he approached. "It is as I have heard. I confess I had begun to hope the red-haired woman led us false. But here is our Arch-Prince Raman." He dropped a quick bow. "And you," he said, nailing her to the spot with his gaze, "must be the Lady Alannys."

She stood up. This fellow was just a boy, but she didn't like him looming over her chair like that. She still had to look up to meet his eyes, but at least she didn't feel so defenseless when she was on her feet. "You are correct. I am sorry I cannot greet you by name as well. I am afraid I am at a disadvantage here; you seem to have heard my name, while yours means nothing to me."

The words carried more of a sting than she intended. Kiarin's face hardened. "You are correct, Alannys. You are at a disadvantage, but it has nothing to do with knowledge. I am Kiarin, and I am the one true Redeemer."

He watched her closely for a reaction. She looked from his brown eyes, to his stained leather vest, to his patched trousers. "I see. Are you certain of that, young fellow?"

"Quite certain."

"I'd be careful there, kid," Raman said, his hand relaxed on the grip of his sword, as though it just happened to be resting there. "She's been invested with that title. The Great Palace—the King of Ravanmark himself—backs her claim."

"Even the king can be led astray by a pretty face," Kiarin said, and turned back to her. "If you admit your deceit now, perhaps there will be leniency for you."

"I am sure I would find that a generous offer, had I any deceit to admit." She tried to sound confident, to keep her voice from shaking. "Perhaps you should tend to your own falsehoods before you presume to counsel others."

Kiarin's hands clenched into sudden fists. "Do you dare to call me a liar? Me, the gift of the Muses, maligned by this alien woman! It is too much!"

He reached one big hand toward her, and she fell back a step, drawing Songstrike. "If you put your hand to me again, Kiarin, you won't get it back." The blade flared blue in the torchlight.

The tavern was as silent as a tomb, her hands cold around the grip of her sword. This was not how she had planned to spend her evening! Kiarin obviously had strong local support, and facing him in a crowded dining hall put her at a bad disadvantage. Fortunately Raman stood nearby, guarding her from any townspeople who might care to strike a blow in favor of their local boy.

"Songstrike!" Redus hissed. He shoved the boy sitting next to him. "Go and find Gram! Hurry, lad!"

The boy ran out the door. When his footsteps were gone, the only sound Alannys heard was her heart pounding in her ears. Why had this crazy young fool come looking for her? Was she to have no peace anywhere?

"So this is how our official, palace-approved Redeemer addresses questions — pulling a weapon on an unarmed man! That blade is rightfully mine."

She had half a mind to give it to him. It would end this farce immediately if he couldn't even lift the blade of the Redeemer. On the other hand, that particular prophecy had never been tested. Perhaps anyone could wield the sword, and what would happen then? She flexed her feet, ready to move. This encounter wasn't going to end peacefully, everyone in the room could see that. "You'll have Songstrike," she said evenly, "when you pry it from my cold, dead fingers."

Kiarin inclined his head. "As you wish, my Lady. A true Redeemer does not need a sword to fight."

Her hair suddenly stood on end. This crazy kid actually intended to sing! She would be expected to retaliate — she would have to defend herself in song, and possibly attack him. How on earth was she supposed to do that? What sort of song did a person sing to do battle?

She didn't know. Unfortunately, it appeared she would soon find out. A girl at the next table covered her ears and ran from the room. Several other townspeople followed her. Alannys stood there, still holding Songstrike defensively in front of her, while Kiarin drew breath to sing. The blade glowed steady, bright blue, and she tightened her fingers around the grip, drawing courage from its solid weight in her hands, its soothing songs in her head.

"O Muses, up on high
Lend me your support.
Smite this imposter,
This unbeliever,
This abomination in your sight."

So that was how a musician sang in battle — they improvised. If she was being less charitable, she'd say he just made something up. The tune wasn't particularly structured, and the song didn't even rhyme. His voice wasn't half bad, but this kid was not the musician he imagined himself to be. And nothing had smote her to the floor.

She needed to defend herself, though; whether it felt like it to her or not, she was being attacked. A sword could not defend her from an attack of that nature. She had to fight music with music. Perhaps it was natural that when she thought of defense, her mind turned to Songstrike.

"Songstrike glows blue
In the hands of the Redeemer.
Bring me strength!
Protect me from this imposter,
And those who would do us harm."

She paused, gauging her energy. Singing for defense didn't seem too draining, and singing with Songstrike in her hands felt invigorating — like she wasn't really singing alone. She wondered if she dared risk an attack.

Kiarin didn't seem to worry about such things. He was still singing, his face hard and determined:

"Fall! You demon!
You spawn of Soth,
Collapse to the ground and die,
Your lies are unwelcome,
Your Talent is foul,
Your life is forfeit here.
Fall!"

Alannys had heard the explanation of how music worked; she knew that it was essentially a battle of wills between the musician and their target. But she was completely unprepared for the reality of what that *felt* like, to have someone else's will wash over her like a physical force, pushing her to do things she never intended. She staggered under the weight of Kiarin's commands, fighting to keep her feet. Songstrike hummed in her mind, encouraging her to resist—and somehow, she did.

"Alannys!" The voice was Raman's, and it was sharp with fear. She forced herself to stand upright again, and jerked her attention back to the room around her. Kiarin still sang, and she still stood. Maybe she would survive this encounter after all.

She had to fight back, though. She couldn't risk an all-out attack like Kiarin was singing; she couldn't be sure of the cost, or the effect. What if she killed him? She didn't think she could live with that. But she had to end this thing before it got any worse, and to do that she had to get more aggressive.

A cry went up in the back of the room, but she couldn't turn her attention to that. Redus slumped forward onto the long table, but she couldn't think about that either. Jia swooned suddenly, and Raman lunged to catch her. She had to end this thing.

More aggressive, then. She started a new song, with a rising melody and shorter, stronger notes.

"The fury of the Muses
Flies not at me
But to those who bar my way.
End this battle!
Remove this obstruction
Allow me to do your will.
Cast this imposter aside!"

She thought the song struck a nice middle ground. It was definitely more aggressive than her first song, but she wasn't using language like "smite the imposter" and "spawn of Soth." She never actually told him to drop dead, as he had done to her.

But the song wasn't having the effect she had hoped for —she could feel it as she sang. It was like hitting a brick wall; the song could not penetrate his defenses. Kiarin had the strongest will of anyone she had ever met. Would superior Talent be enough to get her through this? She wished she knew. It didn't seem hopeful—she was still having trouble standing under the force of his command to fall.

The tavern door flew open, and an old man with wild gray hair stumbled in. "No, Kiarin!" he cried. "You must stop this!"

"Gram!" She heard the shout from the back of the room, but she didn't know who said it. "Thank the Muses!"

Alannys looked at the old man uncertainly. Everyone in the room seemed as surprised as she was. What new trouble was this?

She looked back at Kiarin in time to see him crumple to the floor.

♫

Gram's blistering oath burned Alannys's ears. "We have to get him out of here!"

Alannys looked from him to Kiarin's unconscious form on the floor, and jammed Songstrike back into its sheath. Behind her, the shocked, oppressive silence of the tavern was broken as people began to stir. She could hear whispered questions—if people were all right, who that strange musician was, if someone hadn't better go get the town reeve...

Gram gave her a meaningful look, and grabbed

Kiarin's wrists. Alannys hurried to grab one of his feet, Raman picked up the other, and together they all managed an awkward hobble out the door.

Outside, they found an old, gray, frazzled-looking mule—a good match for its old, gray, frazzled-looking owner. Gram guided them in that direction, and Alannys stumbled along after him. By that time, Kiarin's slack weight was really beginning to tell on her.

"Who are you," she managed to grunt, "and where are we taking him?"

"Help me get him on the mule," Gram said, ignoring her questions.

Alannys dropped Kiarin's foot and glared at him over crossed arms.

"Please!" Gram threw a quick, nervous look around. "We aren't going far, and I swear I'll answer all your questions when we get there. But we have to get Kiarin out of here, and the sooner the better! Do you have any *idea* what just happened?"

Alannys didn't like the way the old man was talking, but she remembered too well the discontented grumbling inside the tavern. Perhaps Gram had a point. She nodded to Raman, and together they heaved Kiarin up and draped him over the back of the mule. The mule twitched his long ears in mute complaint, but stood firm.

Gram climbed up behind Kiarin, and turned to Alannys. "Straight to the end of this road," he told her, pointing, "then the little alley on your left. Slatboard house, all the way at the end, on the right."

With a clatter of hoofbeats, he disappeared into the darkness.

"Unfriendly fellow," Raman said. "Do you think we should follow him?"

"No." Alannys sighed, looking around them for options that failed to materialize. "There's not a thing about this that I like. But he's right, I don't have any idea what just happened. And it looks like if I want to find out, my only choice is to follow him. A man just tried to kill me, Raman. I'd like to know why."

"Into the darkness, then," Raman said, and started off down the road.

"Into the darkness," she echoed, and followed him, not at all fond of the creepy chill the words gave her.

♫

Gram's directions led Alannys and Raman to a ramshackle hut on the outskirts of town. Inside, they found Kiarin sprawled on a blanket on a hay mattress, unconscious and unmoving. Gram clutched the young man's hand. He sat hunched over on the floor next to the bed, his long gray hair falling into his haggard face, only partly hiding his tears.

"So you came," he said, and then fell silent. Alannys and Raman stood there for several uncomfortable moments, but he didn't speak another word, or acknowledge their presence at all—even though he had promised them answers.

"Talk to me, Gram," Alannys said in sudden frustration. "I don't understand. Everyone in Falhill seems to believe this man is the Redeemer. But you knew this would happen."

Gram sighed, patting Kiarin's limp hand with his own gnarled one. The joints in his fingers looked puffy and swollen, and he moved them stiffly, as though they hurt. "It seemed like a harmless lie. How could I know the real Redeemer would come in my time?"

Raman dragged a rickety stool out of a corner. He brushed off the dust and cobwebs, and offered it to Alannys. She shook her head; she was too tense for sitting. He sat down, propping his boots on the foot of the bed. "Kiarin did not seem to know there was any lie. He risked his life on the belief that he was the Redeemer."

"I know, I know." Gram lowered his head into his hands. "It's my fault, all of it. Kiarin was overheard singing when he was eight years old. They hauled him out into the town square. They were going to execute him. I couldn't let them do that—Tirawyn was my only child, and Kiarin was all she had. I couldn't let them take her son. So I suggested that they should spare him. Perhaps he was the Redeemer of prophecy."

"I see." Alannys regarded the form on the bed. He did not move. "So they spared him, because they believed he could be the Redeemer. And he grew up hearing that, and now he believes that he *is* the Redeemer."

"Yes." Gram reached out to push the sweaty, matted hair back from Kiarin's face. It was the first sign of real tenderness she'd seen from the old man, and it touched her. "Now he knows he is not. What's more, the town knows, too. And false Redeemers are stoned to death."

Alannys exhaled in a puff. "It is a tricky problem." She knelt by the messy bed, checking the temperature of Kiarin's forehead and his pulse. As she expected, he was burning up, and his heart raced. His face was flushed pink, and damp with sweat. "A tricky problem, indeed."

"But not necessarily yours," Raman pointed out. "He attacked you. Or did I just imagine the part where he sang 'collapse to the ground and die?'"

Her face burned. "Well, yes. But I still would not have him stoned to death. He really believed he was defending the world from a false Redeemer. If I had wanted him dead, I would have tried to kill him while we sang."

"Didn't you?" Raman glanced at Kiarin. "He hasn't moved since." Gram buried his face in his hands.

"No. I did not do this. Kiarin exhausted himself attacking me. Gram, what sort of fellow is Kiarin?"

Gram looked up at her in surprise. "His name means 'bringer of hope.' It suits him, my Lady. Kiarin is a good man. A good, good man." His voice cracked as if he was holding back more tears.

"And his Talent—does he use it wisely?"

"Oh, yes. When Kiarin sings it is always to good ends. Tonight was the first time in his life he sang to attack."

"I see. Gram, I am sincerely sorry to see him in this state. I hope he will recover soon. I believe that he will. I've had Muse's Fever a time or two myself—it's no fun, but when he awakes, he should be fine, if tired."

She clambered to her feet, and turned away. What could she do for them? Kiarin had to be protected, but how? "Raman, we should really go. Kiarin and Gram need their rest."

Raman held his silence until they were outside. "Alannys, what are you up to?"

"Up to, Raman?" Her tone was deliberately innocent. "I don't understand. Tell me something, how is the Redeemer regarded, out in Ravanmark? Would such a person have any authority out here?"

Raman frowned. "Civil authority, you mean?"

"Hmm. Perhaps. But I am thinking more of religious authority."

"Religious authority. I'm not sure, Alannys. This isn't what you'd call well-defined. I would imagine so. Why?"

"Just curious. Come on, let's go back to the Thumb and Hammer. We need to get our rest as well. This isn't over." She walked briskly ahead, relieved to hear his footsteps pick up pace to follow.

♬

"Let's go home, children."

The town square bustled with people and activity; it was mid-morning, and they were all busy doing whatever people did in the middle of the morning in Falhill. The sun was high, the sky was clear, and that particularly shrill woman's voice had pitched that cutting remark to carry. Even over the noise of the square, it reached Alannys's ears clearly.

"The odor in the square this morning is not to my liking." The woman turned and hustled her children out of the square, her nose high in the air. The two small boys craned their necks around as they walked, goggling back at Alannys.

Alannys froze, staring after them in shocked silence. She hadn't been prepared for that, and she had to admit it stung.

Raman placed a hand on her back and guided her forward. "If I was a betting man, I would put money on you thinking of going back to the Great Palace right about now."

"I have to admit, it's looking better all the time." Alannys looked around the town square. A woman in a blue bonnet leaned close to another woman, both glancing her way and whispering. A shopkeep swept the wooden walk in front of his shop. He saw Alannys and glared at her, turning pointedly away. "Unfortunately you were right; I can't do what needs doing from there."

"We could go back to the inn, then. You don't have to tolerate this sort of behavior."

"Don't I? Things will never get better if I hide every time the going gets rough."

"True enough." Raman clapped her on the shoulder. "Lead on, then."

A panhandler sat by the walk, huddled in tattered clothes against the cold. His hat lay upturned on the ground in front of him. Alannys pulled a gold coin from her pouch, and bent to drop it in the hat.

The panhandler kicked the hat over. "Don't need coin from the likes of you."

Alannys pulled the coin back in reflexive shock. "What?"

He scooped up his hat and stuck it over his face.

Alannys straightened. "I'll be damned. I've never seen anything like these people."

They walked on. In the cobblestone road running through the center of the square, a small girl played an elaborate game with pebbles. The child looked about five, and she had short, curly black hair. She had built a little house of twigs, and various pebbles represented the people who lived in the house. Alannys stopped to watch her, fascinated.

Carriage wheels rumbled on the road, a low and ominous sound.

Alannys frowned, looking around for the girl's mother. No one was near, and the child seemed oblivious to the approaching carriage. The driver saw the child at the same instant Alannys spotted him, and she knew he would not be able to slow the carriage in time.

She ran out into the road, her perceptions a blur. She heard the driver screaming at the horses to stop. She heard Raman shouting at her. She saw the girl's brown eyes, wide with sudden fear as she realized her danger.

Alannys bent down, scooped the child into her arms, and rolled with her to the other side of the road. The carriage clattered by them. Her heart slammed in her chest, and she was a dirty, rumpled mess, but she was alive.

They were both alive.

Alannys sat up in the grass, and pushed her hair out of her face with shaky hands. "Are you all right?"

The little girl nodded. Her lower lip trembled.

"Oh dear, don't cry. It's all right. Everything is fine. What's your name?"

"Cira." Her voice trembled as much as her lip.

"Cira!" A woman in a long dress ran towards them. She clutched the girl to her chest, tears spilling down her cheeks. "Oh, Cira, thank the Muses!" She turned to

Alannys. "Thank you so much, Lady Alannys. You saved my daughter's life!"

Alannys pushed herself to her feet. "You don't need to thank me."

Cira regarded Alannys, her brown eyes solemn. "You are Lady Alannys?"

Alannys inclined her head. "I am."

"Did you really kill that man?"

"Cira!" the woman scolded.

Alannys felt the blood drain from her face. "What?"

The woman eyed her strangely, pushing a stray curl back under her bonnet. "Surely this isn't the first you've heard of it."

Raman's hand fell on Alannys's shoulder, and squeezed. "Heard of what? Alannys did not kill anyone."

The woman's frightened eyes flicked from Raman to Alannys. "I admit it's hard to believe after meeting her. She risked her life to save my daughter. But they say she battled Kiarin at the Thumb and Hammer last night. During that battle, Redus died."

Raman's hand tightened on her shoulder. She could see in her mind Redus slumping against the table at the tavern.

"I killed no one." Her voice seemed to come from a great distance away. "Those who were there should know that."

"I don't understand." The woman fidgeted, nervous, but she still stood there, waiting to hear the other side of the story. Alannys had to admire that.

"It was a song, but it was not mine. Music can't be focused, not completely. Anything you sing will affect everyone in earshot, to varying degrees. It depends on the power of the song, your determination, and the strength of their will. But I did not sing to kill anyone. Remember, Raman, how Kiarin sang things like 'collapse to the ground and die'?" Of course he meant me, but anyone in the room would have felt that. And anyone without the strength to resist it would have....would have...."

"Muses sing mercy!" the woman gasped. "If what you say is true...then Kiarin has killed his own great uncle."

♪

Alannys stood numbly in the town square, staring at Cira's mother and trying to make sense of what she'd just heard.

"I...see that you did not know this." The woman's eyes flicked between them, then darted around the square. "Cira, we must go. Lady Alannys, Arch-Prince Raman— good day." She disappeared down the cobblestone road without looking back, hurrying Cira along in front of her.

"Redus was Kiarin's great-uncle," Alannys said into the sudden, uncomfortable silence. "Then Redus was Gram's brother."

"Gram certainly didn't tell us everything," Raman said sourly. "I didn't know anyone died last night."

"Neither did I," Alannys said, shaken. Nothing had changed, but everything had changed. "Redus died. Redus died, because of our fight. I wonder how many others were injured last night?"

"I don't know, but it does explain the warm reception we've had this morning." Raman's hand moved to the grip of his sword. "Don't look now, but I think they've sent out the welcoming committee."

Alannys turned to look, pretty sure she didn't really want to see. Three men strode toward them, their faces hard and determined. They carried plain swords, and two of them wore the distinctive bronze medallions of town reeves.

Raman stepped out in front of her. "Good morrow, gentlemen. What business have you with the music mage this day?"

"What ballocks." The man looked to be about forty,

haggard and pale. His jaw worked in silent agitation. "To stand here and ask the son of Redus what business he has with his father's murderer!" He gripped his sword, tendons standing white against the leathery flesh of his hand.

"No!" Alannys blurted. "I killed no one!" The man's cold, hate-filled gaze chilled her.

"Lady Alannys speaks the truth," Raman said calmly.

"And how do you propose to prove that?" the man demanded. "Jia collapsed last night, too. That woman sings, Redus dies, Jia falls ill. Who killed Redus, if not her? What poisoned Jia, if not her song?"

"You don't understand!" Alannys cried. "I sang only in defense. My song couldn't have hurt anyone."

"No." A man wearing a reeve medallion shook his head. "A man might wield a sword in defense, but it still wounds. I am Reeve Nor. This is Reeve-second Breba. We come to serve charges."

"Charges?" Raman said sharply.

"Indeed," Reeve Nor replied. "Lady Alannys, you are charged with the murder of Redus, the poisoning of Jia, and the poisoning of Kiarin, Redeemer of the Realm. How do you answer these charges?"

Alannys swallowed hard, the sides of her suddenly dry throat grating painfully together. "This is insanity! I killed no one. I poisoned no one. And Kiarin is not the Redeemer of the Realm."

Redus's son drew his sword. "Now you can add blasphemy to her list of charges."

Before Alannys quite knew what was happening, the reeve and reeve-second had each laid hold of one of her arms. "What? What are you doing? Let go of me!" She tried to jerk loose, but strong hands gripped her arms like vises, and iron manacles clamped hard around her wrists. Pain shot like white fire through her injured shoulder. She couldn't lay a hand on Songstrike. She couldn't even reach her dagger.

"Release her!" Raman drew his sword, stepping menacingly toward them.

"Arch-Prince Raman, this is a matter of law," Reeve Nor said. "I urge you not to intervene. I believe you will find Breba and Siran quite capable opponents."

Redus's son—Siran, apparently—and the reeve-second moved to stand in front of Raman, both holding their swords at the ready.

"Seven Hells!" Raman sword. "Alannys, don't let them treat you like this. Sing!"

Siran gestured at her with his sword. "If she sings a note, I will cut her voice from her throat."

Alannys paled. When had things gotten so completely out of control? "You people are barbarians!"

Reeve Nor jerked her backwards. "Strong words for one with the blood of the Redeemer on her hands. You are coming with me."

She struggled against him, aggravating the wound in her shoulder even further, to no avail. He had already dragged her several steps away from Raman, and although she was slowing him down, she could not stop him. "Where are you taking me?"

"To a holding cell," Reeve Nor said, as though that should have been obvious. "You are to be executed for your crimes."

"Executed!" She would have collapsed if her jailer had not been holding her up.

"That's not legal!" Raman shouted. "King Dorramon will have your head!"

"Did I say executed?" Reeve Nor sounded too innocent to be genuine. "My mistake. No, of course she'll be held for a grievance hearing for the charges, as the law demands. No, what we'll have in the morning in the stoning of a false Redeemer. No grievance hearing needed for that. Of course," he said with a guffaw and a broad wink at Siran, "could be one of the relatives will pay her a little visit tonight and save us the trouble!"

"Monsters!" Raman shoved into Breba and Siran, trying to push past them, but they held him back. Oh, she should never have left the Great Palace. How could she hope to get out of this? Breba and Siran had swords, but Nor's was still sheathed. Perhaps when they were farther away she could sing? If he would just release her long enough to let her get a hand on Songstrike....

"Stop this madness!" The voice rang across the town square, strong and compelling, ringing with musical command.

The reeve stopped pulling on Alannys, and she stopped resisting. Raman froze where he stood, Breba and Siran lowered their blades. As if they had no wills of their own, they all turned as one and watched a staggering figure drag himself across the square to them.

"Kiarin!" Alannys breathed.

"My Lady, I...." Kiarin swayed, dragging the back of his hand across his sweaty brow. His matted hair hung in clumps. He took hold of her right arm and jerked her away from the Reeve. "Let go of her! My Lady, I am sorry."

Alannys eyed his feverish complexion dubiously. "Kiarin, are you sure you should be out? You look ill."

"I know, I know. Muse's Fever has taken me." He threw his head back and shouted at the sky. "I deserve it!" He wobbled, and she steadied him. "Gram has told me the truth. I risked both of our lives recklessly. I have slain Redus, injured others. And for what?"

"Kiarin?" Reeve Nor stepped forward. "I don't understand."

"The woman has bewitched him!" Siran said.

"Stay back!" Kiarin snapped. "Don't you see? Lady Alannys is the Redeemer."

"What?" Siran gasped. "Then you are a...false Redeemer?"

"No!" Alannys grabbed Kiarin's arm as he stumbled. "Kiarin is my first official Redeemer's Steward."

"Redeemer's Steward?" Reeve Nor looked doubtful. "I don't believe there is any such thing."

Alannys puffed herself up. *If you can't dazzle them with brilliance...* "There is now. I can't be everywhere, Reeve. Would you be expected to do your job with no seconds? Could you oversee the security of all of Falhill by yourself?"

"Of course not." Reeve Nor clearly did not like where this was going, but he could not argue the point.

"Well, there you have it. The Redeemer's role stretches across the whole of Ravanmark. Surely you can't expect one person to minister to the whole country unassisted? Kiarin already knows how to use his Talent to help people. He is now the Redeemer's Steward for Mirendasith Holding."

Kiarin stared at her unsteadily. "I—I thank you, my Lady." As if the words cost him the last of his tenuous control, his eyes rolled back and he collapsed into her arms.

Reeve Nor cleared his throat awkwardly. "I must apologize, my Lady. It seems we have accused you falsely. Falhill is yours. How may we serve you?"

"For starters, someone could take the Redeemer's Steward and put him back to bed," Alannys said, struggling to support Kiarin.

They laughed, but quickly complied.

♫

Alannys and Raman took their jangled nerves and retired to the tavern at the Thumb and Hammer for their noon meal. After their harrowing experience in the square, they craved the comfort of familiar surroundings.

But as soon as they stepped inside, they could tell they would find no familiar comfort here. The room cut a sad contrast to the first time they'd seen it—then it had seemed happy and alive, bustling with people and activity. Today, though, the place was a ghost town, with a bartender giving them surly looks and a serving girl who brought their food without speaking a word, or even making eye contact. She clattered their plates down in front of them and left. All the place needed, Alannys reflected, was a few tumbleweeds, and a sheriff to tell them their kind weren't welcome here.

They ate quickly in the oppressive silence. Everything about the tavern encouraged them to move along, and it was a relief to emerge back out into the sunny afternoon. Alannys heaved a pent-up sigh.

"I know," Raman said. "Try not to get too discouraged. I'm afraid it'll just take time."

"No." Alannys shook her head, heading down the same road they had walked the night before. "If there's one thing we don't have, it's time. We're going to have to do something about this."

"Do something?" Raman echoed. "Like what?"

"Just follow me," Alannys said. She didn't like dodging the question that way, but she wasn't going to give him a chance to talk her down, either. Something had to change here, and fast. She couldn't stomach the thought of another Crinn.

Raman hurried to keep up with her, and before long they stood in front of a familiar slatboard hovel. He arched an eyebrow at her, but said nothing.

Alannys raised a fist and pounded on the thin door. She could see it shaking in its loose frame.

The door opened a tiny crack, just enough for Alannys to see a single, wide eye peering out at her, partly obscured by a veil of gray, tangled hair. "What do you want?" His voice was reedy and unpleasant, but his tone was low.

Alannys did her best not to be put off by his tone—she suspected that was precisely his intent. "Good afternoon to you too, Gram. We'd like to see Kiarin."

"No!" The gnarled fingers tightened around the edge of the door, the knuckles straining suddenly white. "No—he's got Muse's Fever, you know that. Go away."

"Gram." Alannys crossed her arms. "He did have Muse's Fever, that's true. But by now he's fine—I saw him earlier. If he was up and around then, he's even better now. I told you I've had it myself. Now will you let us in?"

The eye darted in random directions—it looked quite mad, really, seen like that. "No. You can't see him. He's—he's not here."

"Not here?" Alannys knew Gram was blocking her, trying to get rid of her, but she couldn't see why. Hadn't she protected Kiarin in the square, just as much as he protected her? Hadn't Gram heard about that? "You just said he was sick. Now he's not here?"

"Just leave! You can't see him!" Gram tried to slam the door shut. He looked alarmed to find that Raman's foot, jammed between the door and the frame, made it impossible.

"It would be a shame," Raman said conversationally, "if we had to enlist the town reeves to help us, just so that we could speak to your grandson."

"The town reeves? Now you're just talking crazy. The town reeves are looking to arrest you! Get out of here before they find you!"

Alannys blinked at what she could see of the old man in surprise. Had he been holed up in here all night? Had no one explained anything when they brought Kiarin home? "No. No, Gram, we cleared that up this morning.

No one is trying to arrest us."

"Then they'll be after Kiarin!" Gram's voice was shrill and harsh, and Alannys finally understood he was beyond reason. "You're not coming in here — no one's coming in! You already took my brother from me, you aren't taking my boy!"

"Gram. Open the door." The voice was calm and confident, cutting smoothly through the old man's hysteria — and it didn't come from her, or from Raman.

The door swung slowly inward, and Alannys saw Kiarin, standing behind Gram with his arms folded. He looked pale, but his brown eyes twinkled with humor. "Ah, Lady Alannys. And Arch-Prince Raman. I wondered what could have got my grandfather so upset. You have to excuse him; he's not quite himself. He's been up all night."

"I understand," Alannys said, and she did. She remembered too well how quickly things had gone to hell in Crinn — it was easy to imagine what sorts of thoughts might have kept Gram up all night worrying.

"Then get out!" Gram exploded, waving his hands in her face. "Don't want your sympathy, woman — I want you *gone!*"

"Gram," Raman said, looking distastefully at the old man, "please, try to control yourself."

"Don't give me that! How do you like that — acting like I'm the unreasonable one here. Do you have any idea what's going to happen to him, because of you? Nobody asked you to come here, either of you! Why, I—"

"Gram." Kiarin's voice, still calm, had a hint of an edge on it, and the ringing of musical command. "Go lie down for awhile, have a nap. I'll come see you later."

Gram didn't say another word. He stomped to the hay mattress in the back of the room and threw himself down on it as if he wanted to bury himself in it.

Kiarin shook his head, and turned back to his visitors.

"I'm sorry. What was it that you wanted to talk about?"

Alannys frowned at him. "Kiarin, what was he talking about? What's going to happen to you?"

Kiarin sighed. "It's nothing you have to worry about. I should have used my head before I started singing."

"What?"

Raman put a hand on her shoulder. "Alannys, the false Redeemer charge may have been settled, but Redus still died last night. Someone will have to be held accountable for that."

Kiarin managed to smile for her, but it was a shaky, sickly smile. "That's right. The reeves told me they wouldn't arrest me until tomorrow, because of my illness. I think they're secretly hoping I'll make a run for it. But I'll be here—I can't deny what happened, and it isn't right to run from it. I'll be held for a grievance hearing at Mirendasith Hall."

"But—"

"Alannys." Raman's voice was right in her ear, hardly more than a whisper. "Lord Arik is sympathetic to the Talents, you know that. He'll know an accident when he sees it. Besides, our next stop is Mirendasith Hall. You can talk to him yourself, before the hearing."

"Please don't concern yourself," Kiarin said, and she couldn't tell if he had overheard them or not. "What did you come to talk to me about?"

Alannys hesitated, thinking about pushing harder. But Kiarin seemed resolute, and Raman was right—she would have the opportunity to intervene on her steward's behalf, soon enough. "Singing," she said finally. "It sounds like there are a few people who were injured last night. I wanted to ask you to help me sing to heal them."

"Are you serious?" Raman said. "Alannys, he just woke up from Muse's Fever, I'm not sure he's up to—"

Kiarin held out a single hand, palm out, in Raman's

direction, cutting him off. Alannys was impressed — not many people could interrupt the arch-prince without even looking at him. Kiarin, it seemed, had quite a commanding presence, when he wasn't trying to kill her. "I won't deny my part in causing this mess, so it would seem cowardly to try to get out of doing my part to clean it up. But I am curious — you are the Redeemer, I can't imagine you actually need my help to do this. Why are you asking?"

"You're right," Alannys said. She felt like fidgeting under his steady gaze; it took a conscious act of willpower to keep her hands still. "I could do this myself. But I think it would be better if you helped me — if you're up to it. Me singing to heal the injured would raise people's opinion of the Redeemer. But I won't be staying here. If you help, you'll raise their opinions of you, and legitimize your role as Redeemer's Steward. For what it's worth, helping people is far less draining than hurting them."

"I see." Kiarin nodded, considering it. "That does make sense. I have to admit I worried about what would happen after you left. If this will help stop any backlash, I think I should do it."

"Aren't you at all concerned about the risk to yourself?" Raman said.

"A little," Kiarin said, pulling his cloak off of the hook on the back of the door and sweeping it over his shoulders. "But I'm getting the feeling there are things going on here a lot bigger than me."

"Funny," Raman said dryly, "I've had that feeling ever since Alannys showed up in Ravanmark."

♫

Kiarin took the lead as soon as they left the little hut, leading them a few streets over to a house that looked much more solid than his own, with mortared rock walls and a wooden shingle roof.

"This is Colith's house," he said, by way of explanation, knocking on the door. "Colith runs a shop on the town square. Last night his son was at the Thumb and Hammer—I hear he's taken ill since."

"That would certainly explain the reception we had in the square this morning," Raman muttered.

The door swung open, revealing a cheerful-looking brunette whose expression hardened as soon as she saw them standing there. Whatever friendly greeting she had been about to say died unspoken. "Yes?"

Kiarin somehow mustered a smile in the face of her displeasure. "Kara. Good afternoon."

"Not much good about it from where I'm standing. What do you want, Kiarin?" She wiped her damp hands on a dishtowel, seeming to favor looking at it to looking at Kiarin.

His forced smile finally faded. "I'd like to see Rolin."

"No." Kara's hand clenched convulsively on the dishtowel, and her eyes darted from Kiarin to Alannys and back. "No, I won't allow it. I don't know who to blame for what happened to Rolin—some say it was you, others say it was her," she jerked her chin sharply in Alannys's direction, "but now you expect me to let *both* of you into his sickroom and I can't think of a single reason why that would be a good idea! How do I know you aren't here to finish what you started?"

"Kara." Kiarin's smile was gone as completely as if it had never been, but his voice was soft and kind. "Kara, you've known me since I was in swaddling clothes. Do you really think I would do something like that—or bring in someone else who would? Alannys and I are here to help Rolin, if there is anything we can do."

Kara bit her lower lip, looking back and forth between them, twisting the dishtowel in her hands as if she could wring from it a solution to her current dilemma. "All right," she said finally, stepping back just enough to let them pass. "But on my life, Kiarin, if anything happens to him you will not escape me."

Kiarin gave her shoulder a reassuring pat as he walked by, but said nothing. He led Alannys and Raman confidently through the house to a room in the back where a teenaged boy lay sprawled on a bed that looked too short for his lanky frame. Alannys stepped up to the bed — the boy was unresponsive, but his breathing was deep and even. He burned with fever, and yet he didn't thrash or twitch, or even sweat. She had never seen such an ominous-looking illness, and it gave her a cold chill to see him lying there like that.

"He's like my little brother," Kiarin said mournfully. "Do you think we can help him?"

"I hope so." She knelt down by the bedside. "I don't have much experience with this — I've been told it's very dangerous. But having two of us here can only help."

"Alannys." Raman's tone was warning; she looked at him in surprise and found him gripping his sword as if he thought he might have to do battle. "I do not think King Dorramon would approve of this."

She darted a glance at the pale, unmoving form on the bed. "I think you're right. But this isn't his mission, Raman, it's mine, and I have to do what I think is right."

He clearly didn't like it, but he said nothing. He set his mouth into a grim line and folded his arms, watching them as though he expected trouble.

That was probably a reasonable expectation. She knew that, but what could she do? She turned back to look at Kiarin on the other side of the bed. "I'm going to keep this simple — straightforward tune, three lines, repeating over and over. Join in when you can, stop if you get tired."

Kiarin nodded, his eyes wide.

Nothing for it now — she took a deep breath and began to sing.

"Hear us, oh Muses on high,
Help us heal our fallen friend,
And restore him to us."

She knew Kiarin probably didn't realize she was putting up a front—in actual truth she didn't have much experience singing in Ravanmark. She knew that singing to put a couple dozen hostile assassins to sleep was a big drain, but singing to raise people's spirits hardly affected her at all. Singing to change the weather made her seriously wonder if she would survive. She had only these few experiences, but they were good ones, and she felt like she had a solid understanding of what singing felt like.

Even so, she was completely unprepared for singing to heal another person. It was visceral, intense—her song opened a channel between herself and Rolin, and she had no control over how much of her own energy, her own life, flowed through that channel. If singing to neutralize the attacking assassins had felt like being tied to a running horse, doing her best to stumble along without getting hurt, singing to save a life felt like being tied to a freight train. She remembered Dorramon's warnings, and she felt the cold fist of fear grip her guts, as she realized for the first time that she could actually die here. This could kill her—*singing* could kill her. The realization terrified her, and she continued the song mindlessly, wondering frantically what she had gotten herself into—what she had gotten them all into.

And then Kiarin started to sing with her, from the other side of the bed. Two people singing the same song created a sensation unlike any she'd experienced before—suddenly, instead of dragging her along behind, the song carried her forward, rushing headlong to whatever end awaited them. Two singers created a power stronger than any she had known. It was possible she might survive this after all.

Together they sang a few more repeats of the simple song. The channel felt wider now, more intense—almost alive. And it was working; their song was having an effect, she could feel it. The soul at the far end of that channel felt nearer now, more vigorous.

The door to the little bedroom slammed suddenly open, narrowly missing Raman as he jumped out of its path. Startled, Alannys and Kiarin both dropped the song, swinging around to face the door to find Kara, glaring at them through eyes that seemed to burn in her pale face. "Kiarin! I thought you said you were here to help him!"

Alannys and Kiarin just stared at her, dazed and disoriented at their sudden disconnection from the song, and from Rolin. It was Raman who stepped in front of the bed, frowning, to address the irate woman in the doorway.

"They *were* helping," he said, "at least until you barged in shouting like that. Does everyone in this country think that music can only be used for ill?"

"What else has it ever been used for?" she shot back. "Look, all of you, I've had enough. I want you to—"

"Mom?" The voice was tired and rough—little more than a croak—but it cut instantly through their squabble, and they all turned as one to see Rolin, pushing himself up against his pillow. His pale, damp face might have been made of candle wax, but he gave them a shaky smile. "Mom, is that you?"

Kara's mouth fell open in a frank picture of shock, and she pushed past Raman to the bed. "Rolin! You're awake!"

He smiled, but he looked confused, his gaze touching each of them in turn before settling again on his mother. "What happened?"

Kara looked at her son for a long moment, biting her lip, and drew a deep breath. "I'll explain it all later," she said, and turned back to Alannys and her friends. "I'm sorry. You were right—I should not have suspected you. I've just...I've never seen music used for anything like this before. Thank you."

"You don't need to thank us." Alannys pushed herself to her feet, leaning heavily on the bed. "Your son's injury was an accident. I hope we have helped to rectify it, and that you will remember it next time music is an issue."

"Of course. Thank you," Kara said again, and then she sat down next to her son and the rest of them ceased to exist for her.

"Come, my Lady." Raman's voice was even and his expression was controlled, giving away nothing, but she had a suspicion he still didn't exactly approve of what she had done. "Let us away."

"Yes." She turned from the bed, walking toward his outstretched hand, and found herself listing hard to the left, swaying and staggering as though the floor moved under her.

"Careful!" Raman caught her arm and held her up, eyeing her critically. "You sure you're all right? You look like you've had too much ale."

"I'm fine," she said, as they walked back through the house. But she stumbled again, and Kiarin hurried to catch her other arm. "Although...perhaps I should not have started alone."

"I should say not." Raman's voice rang with indignation, catching the attention of a couple of passers-by as they stepped back out into the street. "The whole idea was ill-conceived, if you ask me. This was a risk you should never have taken. You don't owe these people anything."

Alannys felt like snapping back at him, saying something searing about the importance of her mission, and how apathy wouldn't serve any of them well, in the end. But she couldn't find the energy for it, not while she stumbled along propped between Raman and Kiarin, not really feeling her feet.

"Don't mind him, my Lady," Kiarin whispered, leaning in close to her ear. "His concern for you blinds him, I think. You did a great thing here. It makes me proud to be a Redeemer's Steward."

Alannys could feel her heart become more buoyant— even her dead feet felt lighter. She could almost have walked on her own.

Raman eyed her suspiciously. "What are you grinning for? You've just done something incredibly reckless! That isn't a compliment, you know."

"Oh, I know." She refused to say anything more, no matter how much he goaded her. She knew there would always be naysayers, and she knew nothing she could do would ever convince some people.

But for today, she had saved a villager, a boy who might not have made it otherwise. Her very first Redeemer's Steward was happy to be associated with her.

And for today, that was enough.

♫

"I swear by the Sacred Song I will never understand you," Raman grumbled, stomping along beside Alannys down a narrow dirt lane lined with small cottages that all looked very close to the same. "Anyone else would have learned their lesson after the first time. But you're going to do it again."

"Our work isn't done yet," Kiarin said calmly from her other side. Alannys thanked him, silently but fervently, for sparing her from going head-to-head with Raman just then. Truth be told, she *was* feeling the effects of Rolin's rescue, and she had her share of worries about their next stop. But they couldn't quit, because Kiarin was right— they weren't done. Aside from Redus, who was quite beyond any help they could offer, one other person had been injured that night.

Kiarin guided them to the front door of one of the cottages, virtually indistinguishable from those around it. He gestured that she should approach, and she did, feeling that her heart was suddenly in her throat.

She took a moment to collect herself, and a deep breath for courage, and knocked on the door.

The face that greeted her when the door swung open did nothing to help her nerves. An unusually tall man stood there, glaring down at her through narrowed eyes as though he had waited all day for her to show up so he could destroy her. His skin looked sickly pale in the bright sunlight, and his hair was mussed and ruffled—she guessed that a sleepless night tending to his wife had not improved his temper.

"Good morrow," she said hesitantly, unsure how to answer that hostile stare. "I am seeking the house of Jia."

"Well, you've found it," the man said shortly. "Now clear out. You've no business here."

"Jedred!" The shocked gasp came from behind the furious man in the doorway. She could see another face—a man perhaps a bit older than the first—peeking out over his shoulder. "Jedred, I know you are upset, but Jia would not want—"

"Silence, brother!" Jedred snapped. "If you truly wish to help, go back to her bedside and alert me of any change. I'll handle this. The lady was just leaving."

"Wait!" Alannys cried, catching the door before he could slam it in her face. "You don't understand. I am—"

"I know who you are." Jedred's eyes were cold, his voice flat, and she took a reflexive step backwards. "And it is all the more reason you do not belong here. Go."

"Please! Please—I only want to help!"

"*Help?*" There was nothing cold about his eyes now; they burned with a fire that was fearsome to behold. "You are mad, woman—there is no help you could possibly offer here! I don't thank you for causing this mess, and I don't thank you for sticking you nose into it now, but I will thank you very kindly for *going the hell away!*"

The door slammed with a shuddering force she could feel in her bones.

♫

"Alannys." The single word was full of compassion, as was the hand that fell on her shoulder. It surprised her, when she turned around, to see anger boiling in Raman's eyes, and to realize it was not directed at her. "Don't let it bother you. That man is a fool. He should have been begging for your help."

Alannys shook her head, and continued walking back down the street, away from the person she had come to save. Raman's outrage was flattering, but she couldn't seem to muster any of her own. She could understand only too well what drove Jedred to turn her away.

"I'm serious," Raman insisted. "You'll never be loved by everyone—even Dorramon isn't. You've done well here. You've got to hold on to that—this doesn't change it."

"Thank you," she said, and let the matter drop. She did appreciate what Raman was trying to do—especially considering his vocal opposition to her ill-fated attempt only minutes before. How could she tell him it was wasted effort—that in the face of that cold, bleak door, closed against her forever, all of his reassurances felt hollow?

Raman shook his head and looked away. She heard Kiarin's sigh from her other side and wondered what she could say to him, how she could raise his spirits when her own were so abominably low.

"Lady Alannys!" The shout rang down the quiet street behind them. "Please wait, I beg you!"

Completely against her better judgment, Alannys stopped and turned around. Running after them was the same face she had seen over Jedred's shoulder, looking only slightly less panicked now than he had then. He skidded to a halt before them, leaning over in exhaustion, bracing his hands against his knees, gasping for breath.

Alannys watched him warily, unsure what to make of this. "I'm sorry, is there—is there something I can do for you?"

"Yes," he panted. "Come back to Jedred and Jia's house."

Raman caught hold of her upper arm before she could answer, squeezing tightly in a gesture plainly meant to silence her. "I am sorry," he said coolly, "but we've already been told very clearly that we are not welcome there." He pulled Alannys's arm, guiding her away from the winded man and back to their path on the street. A crowd was beginning to form, as gossiping neighbors and passers-by stopped to watch the exchange.

The man suddenly darted out in front of them. "No, wait! Please!" He held out his hands, as if to physically bar their way. "Please. Jedred is my brother. I've been staying with him, helping him, since Jia fell ill. It was a long night for all of us, but..." He paused, shaking his head. "The way he treated you just now wasn't right. He isn't in his right mind, Lady Alannys; he's half crazy from grief and anger. And now he's fainted—no sooner did he close the door on you than he collapsed. Please, my Lady, help him—help Jia. I am sure you can save her."

Alannys could feel Raman's fingers digging into her arm, and she knew that he would have her walk away. "I feel for you and your brother," she said slowly, "I really do. But regardless of whether I *can* help Jia or not, if I do it against his expressed wishes, your brother is going to hate me."

Jedred's brother swallowed hard, not quite meeting her eyes. "Forgive me, my Lady, but I would rather he hate you for defying him than he hate himself for allowing his wife to die."

Alannys sighed. Raman's hand clenched convulsively on her arm, and she knew he'd be furious with her, but she couldn't refuse. They seriously expected Jia to die. "All right. I'll do it. You're right—I wouldn't willingly see a man put in that position either. Let's go."

So they hurried back to Jedred's house in a silence that felt oppressive and judgmental to Alannys. They crept silently through the messy living room, where Jedred sprawled with his arms and legs hanging off the couch, and tiptoed into the bedroom.

The bed they found there was extra long to accommodate Jedred's height, and in its vast expanse Jia looked even smaller and more helpless than her illness would have led Alannys to expect.

Still, Jia did not seem as far gone as Rolin had been. Music would shorten her recovery, but she would have recovered on her own, and this made Alannys inexplicably glad.

"Let me start this time," Kiarin said, and he began to sing the same song she'd made up for Rolin. Alannys joined in on the second line, when she recognized the song.

They didn't make it through three repetitions before Jia began to stir under the blankets. They stopped singing and watched, hardly daring to breathe.

The door burst open and Jedred charged into the room, roaring. Alannys's first instinct was to dive under the bed, and she might have done so, if she hadn't been so scared she couldn't move. She'd known that Jedred would eventually wake up and find out what they'd done, of course—but why couldn't he have woken after they'd left?

"You!" He leveled one big, accusing finger at her.

She saw Raman reaching for his sword and stood quickly, anxious to forestall any kind of fight. "Yes?"

He closed the distance between them in two long steps, and gathered her into a crushing hug. "Thank you." Before she'd really processed what had just happened, he released her, and turned to Kiarin, pounding him on the back. "And you, too. I'm sorry, both of you. I listened to the wrong people—everything I'd ever heard about music was wrong."

What wrong people? Alannys wondered. *Everything you heard from who?* But she kept her mouth shut. She could imagine the answers—she'd seen Elossa, and others like her. But still, this level of resistance was so widespread, so *ingrained,* it made her wonder something else...

What if Elossa was really just the tip of the iceberg, and something far bigger moved against her now—something she hadn't even begun to recognize?

Sandra Miller

Chapter Three

SAVING LIVES AND SAVING FACE

"*I* don't understand." Raman sounded annoyed, but whether it was because of his self-professed confusion, or because of the shifting, blustery wind ruffling their clothes and tugging at their cloaks, Alannys couldn't say. He pulled at his cloak, trying in vain to secure it, before giving up with an exasperated huff, settling back into the saddle as if it displeased him immensely to be there. The sun dipped low in the sky, and the angled evening light cast his features in high relief, making his sharp jaw and strong nose even sharper and stronger than usual. "You were just starting to succeed in Falhill. After you sang to heal the poisoned, you won over just about everyone in town. Why did we leave?"

Alannys glanced warily at the sky, stalling for time. The wind and the clouds reminded her unpleasantly of the storm that had chased them into Crinn, and it jangled her nerves. The horses seemed agitated, too, and she wondered what associations they had made of their own. It had been a long, slow day of riding towards

Mirendasith Hall, and she looked forward to a comfortable sleep and a little peace.

She thought the horses would agree with that, too.

"That's just it," she finally said. "I have to keep moving. As soon as I have more friends than enemies in a place, it's time to move on."

Raman shook his head. "I just don't see how you are going to succeed that way."

"It's the only way I *can* succeed." She sighed. "I can't visit every single town in Ravanmark, Raman. I couldn't do it in a year, or in ten. I have to go where I can, fight until I am winning, and let word of mouth do the rest."

"Word of mouth." Raman said the words as if they were dirty. "Gossip, you mean. Wagging tongues that would do better to remain silent."

Alannys laughed. "It's the most effective advertising, don't you know." She looked back up at the sky, where the orange light of the setting sun turned the wispy clouds to tendrils of flame, and abruptly grew serious again. "I left the Great Palace knowing that I needed to keep moving. But honestly, Raman, after everything that's happened — it's worse now. I feel...more than just motivated, I feel like I'm running from something."

"We are," Raman said darkly, "and in more ways than one. Someone has been following us all afternoon."

"Wh — what?"

He threw an irritated glance in her direction. "Please don't shout. It's much better if he thinks we are unaware."

Alannys swallowed hard and nodded. "I'm sorry." It took all the self-control she had not to turn around and look. "Why are they following us?"

"You think I know?" Raman craned his head around, peering at the massive forest coming into view ahead as though he had no greater concern than appreciating the scenery. "Whatever he's up to, he is good at what he's doing. He's stayed well back, and out of sight. But now he has started closing the distance, and frankly it's making me nervous. It's a good thing we're close to Mirendasith Hall. Stay close, in case we have to make a run for it."

"Make a run for it," Alannys echoed doubtfully. She followed his gaze to the wall of tall, twisting trees a few thousand yards away, dark and foreboding. "We're going to have to flee, through that forest—in the dark? How far is Mirendasith Hall on the other side?"

Raman's face looked tense and strained, but his mouth quirked in a smile. "We won't be out after dark, my Lady." He swept his arm in a gesture that encompassed the huge forest before them. "What you see before you *is* Mirendasith Hall."

Alannys regarded the forest again, her breath stuck in her throat. How was such a thing possible? Huge, gnarled trunks and thick, twisted branches wound and intertwined to create a dense, living curtain wall that nothing could hope to breach. The wall extended for miles, and stretched up high enough she couldn't clearly see the tops of the massive trees. "This is Mirendasith Hall? But Raman—"

"Ware the hoofbeats!" he cut her off. "He's making a run at us—*ride!*"

Raman's horse shot off ahead of her, straight toward the enormous forest, and Quicksilver followed after at a speed that felt certain to get one of them killed. Alannys held on for dear life and focused on Raman's back, comforting herself with the knowledge that he was still here—she was not alone in this nightmare.

Then he took a sudden, sharp turn toward the trees— and disappeared. Alannys couldn't see any sign of him at all, nothing that could possibly reconcile the fact that he was there a moment ago with the equally obvious fact that now he was not. Her only option seemed to be to panic, and she was really making a good go of it when Quicksilver swerved and she abruptly found herself in a narrow passage into the forest, with Raman a few paces ahead.

Was she shaking from fear, or from relief? She didn't even know, but she was certain that if Quicksilver had not been following Raman's horse so closely, she would have been lost, abandoned to whoever pursued and whatever they intended. She managed to pry loose the fingers of her right hand from their death grip on the reins, and patted her horse's strained neck. "I adore you, have I ever told you that?"

It was unlikely, she reasoned, that their pursuer could have followed as well. She hadn't even seen the entrance to the tunnel before she entered it. How could anyone—

She heard the blunt thumps of a running horse's hooves on packed dirt behind her, the crashing, tearing sounds of vegetation being destroyed, and she knew that whatever her reason said, it was wrong.

He had followed them into the forest, and all of her hope had been in vain.

♫

Alannys knew the jig was up. The narrow passage didn't even give the horses room to turn around—Raman rode in front of her and she was on her own, with a hostile pursuer behind.

It would have been an ideal time for last-minute prayers, but she was too scared to think of anything to say.

Leaves rustled above her, and she heard the sudden sound of footsteps behind her, and when she dared to look, she saw something she never would have imagined.

Three men had dropped from the trees, in matching green tunics and tights, to block the passage behind her. Whirling and kicking, spinning their staffs, they closed in on the intruder's horse and drove him back. They fought skillfully, with a nimbleness she had never seen before.

"Alannys," Raman snapped, pulling her attention from the fearsome display. "Keep your eyes forward and get moving! Leave the fighting to the castle guards."

Castle guards? She flicked Quicksilver's reins and wondered what exactly she had gotten herself into, as the horse picked up his pace through the claustrophobia-inducing passage through the forest.

'Forest' seemed a poor word to describe what loomed around them. Enormous trees, bigger around than she and Raman put together, stretched up and out of sight, their thick gnarled branches creating an impenetrable canopy that even the sharp, dying sunlight could not seem to pierce. Vines and small trees wound between the ancient behemoths, weaving a living curtain impossible to part.

This forest was old, older than any now living and possibly older than Ravanmark itself. Its density completely muffled the sounds of the battle they had left behind. The hoary trees groaned in the slight breeze, and a few browning leaves fell around them. But for this, the immense forest was silent — no sounds of birds or animals reached Alannys's ears. This silence gave her an uneasy feeling, more than anything else about the place. No birdsong, no animal sounds — there had to be other people then, people up in the trees, scaring the wildlife into silence. But *where?* She stared up into the massive canopy overhead, towering up out of her sight, but nowhere in that vast expanse of twisting, knotted branches could she see a single person, or a place where a person might stand.

Nothing moved, and yet the sensation of unseen, watching eyes prickled the hair on the back of her neck. She stared up into the dizzying immensity of the trees. Something skittered across the edge of her vision — perhaps only her imagination. "R—Raman...up there...in the trees..."

Raman did not turn around. "Yes. The entrance to

Mirendasith Hall is carefully guarded—you saw that yourself. I would expect no less, especially in days as dark as these."

Alannys clamped her mouth shut and turned her eyes to Quicksilver's mane, trusting him to get her through this and blocking as much as she could of her surroundings. The tunnel they traveled was close, with bushes brushing against her legs, and spidery, low-hanging branches forcing her to duck her head. Darkness hung over them, much heavier than she would have expected in a forest. No patches of light angled through these trees to dapple the ground.

The passage turned sharply, and wound this way and that through the ancient trees. It did not branch or split, or even widen. She had no choice but to follow Raman through to the end of the passage, assuming it even had an end.

A low whispering reached her ears. Was it the wind? Or the voices of those who watched? Her skin prickled and crawled. The sooner they were out of this creepy forest, the better she would like it.

Only, Raman had told her that this creepy forest *was* Mirendasith Hall. What if the whole thing was like this? She didn't think she could take it. She had never been particularly claustrophobic, but this cramped, narrow, *living* passage made her acutely uncomfortable. The trees pressed in around her, uncaring.

It felt like hours had passed when she finally followed Raman out into the open on the other side of the passage. Alannys gasped, her hands tightening reflexively on the reins. Nothing in her experiences in Ravanmark had prepared her for Mirendasith Hall.

The tall, twisting trees still grew here, peppered throughout the open spaces. Their huge tops canopied the place, the pale moonlight glinting through the patches between them. She could see a deep, clear, still pond reflecting that weak light.

Lanterns floated through the space, high up in the trees and through the meandering clearing before them. Some of the lanterns were carried by tall, graceful people in fitted tunics and tights, and others hung from gnarled wood posts. By their light Alannys could make out houses; tall, beautiful buildings with rounded edges and domed roofs. The doorways were arches. The curious lack of corners blended well with the ethereal forest surrounding them.

Quicksilver followed Raman automatically down a wandering dirt path. Alannys stared around her, immediately in love with this tranquil place. She had never been anywhere that felt so safe and so peaceful.

Raman dismounted in front of a long, low building that flowed artfully into and around the big trees. Alannys followed his lead without question, but she had her feet on the ground before she realized with surprise that the building was a stable. The stalls had the same arched openings she had seen on the houses, and the thatched roof had a slight dome to it.

Alannys handed Quicksilver's reins to a waiting stableboy. The stable workers wore long belted brown tunics over rust colored tights, and they blended well with the horses they tended. The horses followed the stableboys without a whinny or a backward glance, as though they would both be glad to rest.

Alannys probably should have been too tired to care about her surroundings too, but she couldn't stop staring. Now on foot, they followed a wide path lined with lanterns that led deeper into the forest. Their shoes made scuffling and crunching noises on the dirt and fallen leaves. The people of Mirendasith, she noticed, did not make such noise when they walked. They wore soft slippers and moved with a quiet economy of motion that made them entirely unobtrusive. It all felt so far removed from the noise and the bustle of the Great Palace, it might have been another world. Lord Arik's serenity seemed to infuse the entire place.

The path led them to a large...*building* seemed an inadequate word, but she didn't know what else to call it. It was bigger than the stables they had passed, bigger than Castle Glennayre, and it was formed entirely of living vegetation. Tall, gnarled trees spread wide and twisted to form the structure, which seemed to wind up out of the ground and into the forest canopy of its own accord. Alannys goggled at it, but could not credit the evidence of her eyes. "How did they *do* that?" she said, unaware that her voice was hushed in awe.

Raman flashed a quick smile in her direction. "Music. Mirendasith Hall was shaped hundreds of years ago, through song."

Alannys swallowed hard, confronted with this awe-inspiring monument to the power of music. What, she wondered, kept the hall in shape now, after so many years? Could a song maintain its power still, when its singers had long been dead?

The wide, arched opening to the building had no doors or gate, and it did not appear to be guarded. But before they were within a dozen paces of the place, a boy clothed in forest green robes approached them.

"Welcome, Arch-Prince Raman, Lady Alannys," he said, bowing to each of them in turn. "Mirendasith Hall welcomes you."

Alannys spent an uncomfortable moment wondering how he had known of their coming, and how many others knew as well. Nobody here had paid her any particular mind before now, and after all she had been through, she found she rather preferred it that way.

"Thank you." Raman sounded entirely composed. "We are grateful for your hospitality. The road has been long."

"Indeed, my Lord. Lord Arik and Lady Marin await you in the Grand Hall." He stepped to the side, gesturing them toward the open arch behind him.

"Thank you," Raman said again, and taking Alannys's arm, he escorted her into Mirendasith Hall.

The vestibule they entered spanned the height of the hall, probably three or four stories tall. It opened to the sky, and the floor was strewn with fallen leaves. Flowers grew along the path that led to the next room, and flowering bushes grew against the walls. A climbing vine had almost completely covered the bark of one trunk-wall. A pond graced one side of the room, filling in the gap between two enormous roots, and there was a small waterfall of river rock. The vestibule felt more like a courtyard than an entrance. A few people in long, flowing robes loitered around the garden, nodding amiably to Alannys and Raman.

They passed into the hallway. The long corridor was formed between the trunks of massive trees, which had grown together to form a ceiling overhead. Wherever one trunk ended and another began, a small indentation was formed, like a little alcove. Each alcove housed a different flowering plant or bush, and a few had smaller trees.

At the end of the hallway was another arched opening. Two robed men stood here, one at each side of the door. They wore their hair in long braids, and their robes matched those of the boy who had greeted them at the entrance. They inclined their heads as the pair approached.

"Lord Arik and Lady Marin are expecting you," one of the men greeted them. "Welcome to the Grand Hall." Both men stepped aside to let them pass.

The atmosphere in the Grand Hall was nothing like

Alannys expected. In stark contrast to the Great Hall at the palace, the mood here was quiet and respectful. Courtiers littered the Grand Hall, but they stood in graceful groups, and they conversed quietly if at all.

The hall itself took Alannys's breath away. It was not open to the sky, but it spanned the full height of the building. The gentle light of the lanterns suspended around the enormous room did not reach to the ceiling. The walls were lined with alcoves like those in the hallway they had just traveled, and every plant, bush, and tree in the alcoves flowered. Their fragrance was refreshing and not too heavy. The speckled granite floor was smooth and cool, with an inlaid onyx path that led to a dais on the far end of the room. On the dais were two beautiful polished wood thrones, and in the thrones Alannys saw the familiar figures of Lord Arik and Lady Marin.

The ruling couple of Mirendasith looked just as the last time she had seen them. Arik and Marin wore matching charcoal gray robes, flowing to the floor and belted at the waist with twisted silk cords. Their matching gray slippers were soft, and they each wore a simple golden circlet. Marin's chestnut hair was braided and hung in heavy loops that framed her face. The braids were thick and long —unbound her hair must have hung almost to the floor. Arik's hair fell to his waist, and small sections on either side of his face were braided, while the rest hung loose.

Lord Arik and Lady Marin did not appear surprised at their arrival. Arik stood and spread his arms wide, and the courtiers fell silent, as Alannys and Raman knelt at the foot of the dais.

"My friends!" The Lord of Mirendasith's voice rumbled like thunder in the huge hall. He descended from the dais in large, unhurried strides. "You have arrived!" Lady Marin inclined her head, and they rose to their feet.

Arik clasped Raman's hand and clapped him on the

shoulder. "I can't tell you how glad I was to hear that you had accompanied Lady Alannys on this journey. It's been far too long since we've had the pleasure of your presence in the Grand Hall, my friend, far too long." He turned to Alannys, beaming. "And my dear Alannys!" He took her hand and raised it graciously to his lips. "It is wonderful to see you again, my dear, simply wonderful. Marin and I have worried about you since we left the Great Palace—it is such a relief to see you here safely!" He scooped her into a bear hug.

Alannys couldn't suppress a painful gasp. The pressure aggravated the still-tender stitches in her shoulder, and she stiffened involuntarily in Lord Arik's embrace.

Arik stood back at arm's length, inspecting her face closely, frowning. "What's this? You are injured?"

She nodded. "I'm sorry, my Lord. It is nothing."

"Nothing? Nonsense! Raman, what has happened here?"

Raman glanced at her anxiously. "There was a cloaked swordsman, at the Great Palace. He attacked Alannys in her chambers. The Royal Guard came quickly, but Alannys was wounded. A royal healer tended to her before we left."

"Royal healer?" Arik didn't sound particularly impressed. "May I see this wound, Lady Alannys?"

What could she do? Alannys pulled back the collar of her shirt, revealing a jagged line of puckered black stitches in her shoulder. The skin burned an angry red, crusted over in places with drainage.

Arik sucked his breath in, and his eyes darted to her face. "This is nothing? I assume this swordsman was captured?"

Alannys looked away.

Raman shook his head. "No, my Lord. He escaped."

Lord Arik's face clouded. "I am not pleased to hear it.

What is the Great Palace coming to, when an attack like this can happen inside the very keep?" He shook his head. "I will have my healer tend to you here, Lady Alannys. I am sure we can speed the healing of this wound."

She smiled weakly, pulling her collar back up. "Thank you, my Lord."

Arik clapped his hands together. "But this is grim talk, not good for such a glorious occasion. The Redeemer has come to Mirendasith Hall! Tonight, we feast!"

♫

Long, narrow tables stretched back and forth across the Grand Hall, filled with food and lined with people. Beeswax candles at regular intervals gave a flickering, cheerful atmosphere to the place, and lanterns hung around the edge of the room.

The thrones had been removed from the dais, and a polished wood table now sat there. The table was large, and it comfortably sat Lord Arik and Lady Marin, Arch-Prince Raman, and Alannys. It was spread with fragrant vegetable soups, tender cuts of meat, roasted poultry, and baked breads, still warm from the brick ovens. Alannys could feel her stomach rumble, and her cheeks reddened. She had not seen a meal like this since they left the Great Palace.

"My friends," Lord Arik said, "I have heard some news of your journey. The road, it seems, has not always been smooth."

"Indeed not," Raman said, "and I fear we brought some of the roughness here with us. I apologize, Lord Arik."

Arik brushed this concern away with a magnanimous wave of his well-manicured hand. "Please, you must not give that another thought. Such things are hardly of your doing, or even your choice."

He seemed content to let the matter go at that, reaching for his goblet of wine, but Raman cleared his throat. "My

Lord, how went the fight at the passage?"

Alannys held her breath, anxious to hear the answer to that question herself. But Lord Arik didn't answer right away. Instead he frowned, and she fought the urge to groan out loud.

"Not as well as I might have hoped," Arik said solemnly, his deep voice seeming to resonate in her bones.

"Oh, no!" Alannys cried. "Did your men—did they fall?" She wrung her hands in her lap. How could she stand any more deaths on her head?

Lord Arik looked surprised. "No, no, my dear— nothing like that. You were pursued by a man swathed completely in black. My guards did as they should have done, and stood to protect you."

"And?" she prompted, almost afraid to hear the rest.

"And I am afraid there isn't much more I can tell you. He spoke no word, offered no resistance. As soon as my men appeared, he fell back. He surveyed them but for a moment, then turned and rode away."

"Well—that's great!" Alannys said, heartened by this description. "Apparently he isn't as confident taking on your men as he was the Royal Guard."

For a moment, no one at the table spoke. Arik's grim frown deepened, and even Lady Marin seemed unable to meet her gaze.

Raman finally broke the silence, shaking his head. "I don't think so, Alannys. I don't think he's given up. He knows where we are now, and he knows how to get in— he can come back later, when we aren't expecting it. And he knows that, too."

"You think he will return?" Alannys felt cold, considering it. This had to be the cloaked swordsman from the Great Palace. Her plan to lead him away was working too well—how far was he prepared to follow her? Imagining him in Mirendasith Hall made her feel suddenly sick.

Arik spoke before Raman could answer. "It would be foolish to assume otherwise. Such an attack could only have one purpose, and a man dispatched to such a purpose will not cease until he succeeds."

Alannys shivered, thinking about spending the rest of her life running, with the man in black nipping at her heels.

"But do not worry about that now," Arik said quickly. "I did not tell you this to upset you. You are safe in Mirendasith Hall, Lady Alannys. Our defenses do not relax. No harm will come to you here."

♬

After the feast Alannys and Raman were shown to their rooms. Alannys's room was right next to Raman's, and it was beautiful. The outer wall had three alcoves in it, two with flowering plants inside, and one with a little river rock waterfall that made peaceful water noises. In one corner of the room a gnarled wood branch grew up out of the floor, and an olive oil lantern had been hung on it.

The room had a large bed, big enough for at least three people. The headboard dominated the wall behind the bed —a large concoction of twisted branches that had been peeled and polished and intertwined. It was pretty, but Alannys couldn't help thinking it was also a little creepy. White lace bedcurtains surrounded the bed, and there were potted plants on either side.

A knock at the door spared her any further contemplation of her surroundings, and she hurried to answer it. Now that she was alone, being inside this oddly formed nest of living trees and branches was unsettling, and she jumped at the chance for some company.

"A thousand apologies for disturbing you, my Lady, especially so soon after your arrival in this room," Lord Arik said, "but I wonder if I might intrude?"

"Of course—come right in." Alannys stepped back to let him pass, and only then did she see that he wasn't alone.

Her misgivings must have shown on her face, because Lord Arik smiled and gave her shoulder a reassuring pat as he passed. "I believe I said I would bring someone to look at your shoulder. This is Brynth, my personal healer. If he cannot help you, there is no one who can."

Alannys froze, suddenly wishing she had not been quite so quick to welcome him. Lord Arik was one of her favorite people, but her shoulder was tender and very sore, burning like fire after its aggravation in the Grand Hall. About the last thing she wanted was someone poking at it, no matter their skill.

Brynth floated past her, an ageless man with long, silver hair, his form hidden under a voluminous brown cloak. Alannys stared after him, impressed despite herself, then shook herself out of her stupor and followed him into the room.

"I'm sorry to waste your time," she said, "but I really don't need a healer. I've already had stitches—I'm fine."

Lord Arik turned to face her, his eyebrows raised. "Fine? I would not call the wound you showed me earlier fine, Lady Alannys."

"Well, no," she said, feeling her cheeks burn, "but it is healing. These things just take time, my Lord."

"Time," Arik murmured, turning away to inspect the room as though he had never seen it before. "I do not feel that time is your friend right now. And I fear that this injury may require something more. I have brought my healer here to tend to a friend of mine whom I value quite highly. Won't you accept this poor gesture? Or does the hospitality of an old man displease you?"

"No!" She blurted the single word, startled by the implications in his words. She knew he was laying it on thick — by no stretch of the imagination was Lord Arik old — but she couldn't refuse his aid when he equated it to refusing him personally. "I—I value our friendship as well, Lord Arik. I am grateful for your hospitality, and all the care you have shown me. I would never knowingly offend you, you must know that."

"Wonderful!" Lord Arik clapped his hands together with a beaming smile. "That's all sorted, then. Have a seat, Alannys, and let's see if Brynth can do anything for you."

Alannys sighed in resignation, and dragged herself over to the sofa.

"May I see the wound, my Lady?" Brynth asked, when she seemed disinclined to do more than just sit there.

Alannys undid the top button of her linen workshirt, and pulled the collar down over her upper arm.

Brynth knelt in front of her, so close she could hear the sharp intake of his breath as he got his first good look at her shoulder.

She couldn't blame him. She didn't really want to see it herself. Back when the royal healer had stitched her up — what felt like forever ago — the cut had been clean, and the straight, even line of stitches had pulled it into a neat seam. Now, though, the entire surface seemed to bulge, embedding the stitches into the mess that was her shoulder. The wound had puckered in some places, and stretched in others, oozing matter in unhealthy shades of yellow and green.

"Tell me," Brynth said mildly, looking at her with something like accusation in his clear gray eyes, "why do you say that you don't need a healer when it is so painfully obvious that you do?"

Alannys looked away. "I'm sorry. It's a habit, I suppose — I don't like people making a fuss over me."

"Making a fuss over you?" Brynth echoed, his precise diction making the words sound foreign and strange.

"Would you rather they make a fuss over your lost arm? Would you rather they make a fuss over your remains? This is not an injury that can safely be ignored, my Lady."

"I know. I'm sorry."

Brynth made a disapproving clucking sound, and started digging through his leather bag. She sat dejected on the sofa, her shirt hanging off of her shoulder, unable to find the words to defend herself. It sounded pretty juvenile to say she didn't want anybody to mess with it because it hurt.

"Try not to feel too badly," Lord Arik said, and she looked up to find him smiling gently at her. "I have heard something of your travels, Lady Alannys, and something of what befell you before you left the Great Palace. Surely the Muses themselves must have been singing for you. The real miracle is that you were not hurt much worse. From what I have been told, you have faced some very formidable opponents."

She smiled weakly, remembering some of those opponents now, struggling to maintain her composure as Brynth began working with a small, curved pair of scissors to snip and remove her old stitches.

"That reminds me." She could hear the strain in her own voice, but thought conversation might distract her from her discomfort. "I need to ask you about something. Raman mentioned that you are well-versed in the Talents, and in artifacts of the Muses and Soth. What makes Songstrike glow blue? What does it mean?"

Arik steepled his fingers and turned away. "Ah, yes. Songstrike, the blade of the Redeemer. It is no ordinary blade. According to prophecy, only the Redeemer may wield the blade. Songstrike was a gift to Soth from the Muses, and it has many enchantments, which are related to the Talents. Unfortunately, much of that information has been lost."

For a moment, silence reigned in the guest room. Brynth finished dispensing with her stitches, and began swabbing the wound with a cloth soaked in stinging liquid. It might have been some form of alcohol—it made her shoulder feel strangely numb and blistering, burning hot, all at the same time. She bit her lip until she tasted blood, trying her best to stay quiet.

"But I do know a little," Lord Arik continued, "and I am always happy to share what I know. Songstrike will glow blue when you feel threatened. The blue indicates that it is ready to protect you, and that its enchantments are active."

Alannys closed her eyes and drew a shuddering breath, struggling to think past the pain. "What are these enchantments? What do they do?"

"I know of three. There may be others, lost to the passage of time—but I know that when Songstrike glows blue, it will boost the effect of any song you sing. It will also help shield you from the songs of others. And it will lessen any resulting Muse's Fever."

Brynth finally finishing cleaning her shoulder, and Alannys slumped back against the cushions of the couch. "These are powerful gifts. I've been incapacitated by Muse's Fever more than once."

Arik nodded. "But naturally the Muses would not wish to punish their chosen one for actions taken in defense. That is why the protection is only active when the blade glows blue."

"Wow." Alannys watched warily as Brynth uncorked a glass jar of thick, white, strong-smelling salve. She knew that had to mean more pain for her. "And to think Songstrike might be capable of other things as well, things we don't even know about. It's amazing." She shook her head. "If only I had enough skill with a sword to deserve it."

Lord Arik smiled at her. "It isn't skill with the sword that determines who wields Songstrike, Lady Alannys. Songstrike is a blade that knows its master and will suffer no other."

A heavy, awkward silence fell over the room after that remark. Brynth started to smear a thick layer of salve on her shoulder. She couldn't tell what was in it, but it burned her eyes and she had to turn her face away, still trying to think of some way to change the subject. "Songstrike is a huge help. But I've had lots of help from my friends, too."

"Yes," Lord Arik said thoughtfully. "I heard that you appointed a young man in Falhill as something called a Redeemer's Steward."

"Yes. It was something I—made up, I guess. I didn't want to see Kiarin hurt, even after I left. I still don't, even at the grievance hearing—everything that happened there was an accident. So I just made it up. It makes sense, after all. One person can't be everywhere. It seemed like a good idea to appoint other Talented people to help me."

Lord Arik held up a hand to silence her. "My apologies, Alannys—I was not asking you to defend yourself. I understand your intent. But it seems to me that this is sensible only inasmuch as you can trust other people's motives. In Kiarin's specific case, I can certainly understand the decision. You need not worry about the hearing; I will have him released, of course. There are those, however, whom it would not be wise to place in positions of such responsibility, to give blanket permission to use their Talents on others."

Alannys tried to imagine Lord Malrec as a Redeemer's Steward, and saw Arik's point. She nodded. "There won't be many stewards. Only those who have proven themselves, like Kiarin has."

"That is well," Arik replied. "We must remember that

the Dark Alliance also has no compunctions against using the Talents to aid them. They could send a Talented person to become a steward and spy for them."

"I have to admit I had not thought of that. I'll do my best to make sure that all of my Redeemer's Stewards are trustworthy."

"That is all I can ask of you," Lord Arik said, smiling once again. "I hope you do not think I needlessly challenged you. I needed to know your intentions for this new position you have created, because I am about to do something which could be seen as officially approving of it."

Alannys had no idea what to say. She could not fathom where he was going with this. Brynth was carefully sprinkling fine powder over the salve on her shoulder, but she couldn't pay attention to him, staring wordlessly at Lord Arik as he clapped his hands loudly together and called for a servant.

Immediately a servant entered, handed him a cloth bag, bowed, and left again. Lord Arik placed the bag in her lap—she was surprised by its weight.

"These are for you," he said solemnly. "I suppose I need not tell you that a rider will depart at first light, carrying one to Falhill."

Utterly confused, she reached into the bag.

What she pulled out exceeded her wildest expectations. She held a twisted silken cord, and dangling from it was a silver medallion. Engraved around the edge were the words 'Official Steward of the Redeemer of the Realm,' and in the center was a likeness of Songstrike. Alannys watched the gleaming medallion spin slowly on its cord, speechless.

"I hope you will find these useful," Arik said. "Our silversmiths worked double-time to finish them all—I do hope they are acceptable."

"*Acceptable?* Lord Arik, these are beautiful! I never expected anything like this—I don't know what to say. Thank you."

Lord Arik inclined his head and turned for the door. "I am pleased that you are pleased. I won't keep you any longer; I know you must be exhausted. Good night, Lady Alannys."

"Good night, Lord Arik."

After Arik left, Brynth produced a heavy, roughly woven square of cloth from his bag, and used it to cover the wound on her shoulder. The salve and the powder combined to form a sort of paste, holding the cloth firmly in place.

"This should speed the healing," Brynth said, pushing himself to his feet. "It will also protect the wound. When the cloth falls off, you may leave it uncovered. But for tonight, I'm afraid it won't feel very nice."

"It already didn't feel very nice." Alannys sighed. "You were right, Brynth—I knew it wasn't right, I just...I guess I'm a bit of a coward."

"I have heard some stories myself, my Lady," Brynth said, floating smoothly toward the door. "A surprising number of stories, really, for no longer than you have been here. I am not sure if the stories are entirely accurate, but regardless, one thing is very clear." He stopped in the doorway and turned to face her. He was smiling, but it was more disconcerting than his usual deadpan expression.

"You are no coward, Lady Alannys. In fact, you may be too brave for your own good."

Brynth left the room, while she stared after him, stunned, without a single word to say in her own defense.

♫

Alannys sat sprawled on the sofa for a long time after Lord Arik and the healer left, trying to convince herself to get up. She hadn't practiced with Songstrike nearly as much as she should have since she'd left the Great Palace. Here was the perfect opportunity to remedy that, and she couldn't seem to get her butt off the couch.

She finally conceded that it just wasn't happening. She had spent all day on horseback, and she was tired and sore. And now her shoulder felt as if it had been gored open again. There was no way she was practicing swordplay tonight.

In fact, she pretty much decided to stay right there on that couch until morning. Her head tipped back against the couch, her arms went limp at her sides, and her eyes drooped finally shut.

A loud knock at her door startled her out of her skin. She jumped, and her shoulder screamed at the sudden motion. She leaned over, pressing against the wound with her hand, gasping for breath and trying her best not to swear.

"Alannys? Are you awake?" Raman's voice sounded worried.

"Yes." She dragged herself to the door, and pulled it open for him. "I'm sorry, Raman. Come on in."

He stepped inside, and froze. "Muses, Alannys, you look terrible. Are you all right?"

"I'm fine. Lord Arik's healer was just here. He did a lot for my shoulder, but he also aggravated it pretty badly." She tried to wave it off, but since she was holding the door with her right hand, she gestured with her left. The pain flared up again, white-hot and eye-watering, and she winced.

"I see." He kept a close eye on her as she walked back to the couch, holding her arm stiffly by her side. "I'm sorry to hear it. Mirendasith healers are supposed to be the best there is—I'm sure it will end up healing faster."

"That's what I keep telling myself." She settled herself carefully on the couch.

He frowned, watching how gingerly she moved. "You don't have to keep doing this, you know. We can go back home. You don't have to push yourself."

"Don't I? You were right, Raman—nothing has changed at the Great Palace."

"Does this mean you want to go on?"

"It means I don't want to go back." She sighed, hating the defeated way she sounded. "Ambassador Thell hates me. And maybe he should. It seems like I've done nothing but cause trouble—for you, for Dorramon, for a foreign royal family I've never even *met*..."

"Now that's not a good attitude," Raman said. "I don't agree with that assessment. I have never seen Dorramon as happy as he has been since you came to Ravanmark. He smiles, he jokes, he laughs like a little kid. He's never had anybody he could really relate to. With you he can talk about anything—even the music that's been forbidden all his life. With you, Alannys, he becomes just a normal man."

She couldn't hide her smile. Everything Raman said was true, a reminder of exactly why her time in Ravanmark had been the happiest in her life.

"And actually, that's basically the problem," he finished glumly, squashing her triumphant smile and her fairy tale happiness under the cold, uncaring weight of reality. "Because he *isn't* just a normal man, Alannys, and he *can't* do the things a normal man would do. He can't marry you any more than—than I could have married Kalyn, no matter what my prophecy said. Even I was too important to choose my own bride, Alannys, and Dorramon is about a thousand times more important than I ever was. The future of the royal family—the future of the entire *country*—depends on him marrying well and producing a proper heir."

"I know."

"And that's not even to mention Cadenda's side of things. Cadenda's gotten big enough and developed enough they rival Ravanmark as the chief power in the world. We had to either conquer them or ally with them — they're too important to ignore any longer. So Dorramon's parents arranged his marriage to forge an alliance between two countries who traditionally don't get along very well. He can't just refuse to go through with it — we'd be knee-deep in the war Caleb hoped to avoid."

"King Caleb," she echoed, frowning. "Wasn't he from Cadenda, too? Why, if these two countries are old enemies, did the queen choose a husband from Cadenda?"

"For the same reason she arranged her son's betrothal to a Cadendan princess! Do you think no one advised her on her own marriage? Mark my words, Queen Farrine married King Caleb hoping for exactly the sort of peaceful alliance Dorramon is set to get through marrying Varilyn."

Alannys frowned, watching Raman pace the room. His expression was fierce and she was sure she had to be missing something — there was too much here that didn't make sense. "But — why is Dorramon marrying to secure the same alliance? Didn't it work?"

"No," he said heavily. "I don't think it really did. Mind you, I wasn't there at the time. But from what has happened in the years since...if any alliance exists right now, Alannys, it exists on paper only. Cadenda is not friendly to Ravanmark. They act almost like we *stole* Caleb from them somehow."

"That's strange, don't you think? We have to assume they got what they wanted out of the marriage too — one of their princes on the throne of Ravanmark. Why would they still be acting that way?"

"It doesn't really matter, does it?" Raman sounded frustrated — she hoped it was with Cadenda, not her, but she had a sinking suspicion she already knew the answer to that. "What it all comes down to is that Dorramon cannot marry you!"

"I *know* that! Why do you think I'm *here*, days away from the palace, visiting probably the one person in Ravanmark whose mind does not need changing? If I thought there was a single chance we could be together, do you think I would be doing this? The one thing I *do* understand about all of this is that it could lead to war, and I am not willing to send other people to war for my happiness!" She didn't remember getting up, but there she was, standing in front of the sofa with her hands balled into angry fists, shouting at Raman as though a single thing that had happened was his fault. She panted raggedly, feeling her control return.

"All right," Raman said, holding his hands out to her in a placating gesture, "I'm sorry. You're right, and I should have known all that." He took her arm—her right arm, carefully avoiding her injury—and helped her sit back down. "I wasn't kidding when I talked about your over-developed sense of responsibility, Alannys. You weren't even born here—you don't owe anything to this place or these people. But you always treat Ravanmark's concerns as your own." He shook his head, turning for the door. "It's just like Dorramon, really, although he's had his responsibility trained into him. Just one of the many things that make you two so perfect for each other."

He stopped in the doorway and looked back at her, and the sadness etched into the lines of his face reminded her that this was not only one of her best friends—Raman was also Dorramon's best friend and adopted brother.

"Just another reason," he said somberly, as though his words hurt him personally, "why it's a tragedy that you two can never be together."

♫

Alannys sat there on the couch after Raman left, listening to the quiet sounds of the water and telling herself she wasn't upset, really. Raman hadn't told her anything she didn't already know—she'd been through the same things in her own mind a thousand times since she'd left the Great Palace. But she certainly hadn't been expecting him to come talk about it tonight. And the conclusion was unfortunately just as inevitable when she argued with Raman as when she argued with herself.

...just another reason why it's a tragedy that you two can never be together...

Something splashed against her hand, and she stared at it, surprised. When had she started crying?

She pushed herself irritably to her feet. What did it matter when she had started? Crying was useless. It wouldn't change anything. She was tired, and sore, and the last thing she needed to be doing was sitting around bawling.

Lord Arik had assured her she would be safe here. She believed him. And yet, the talk of the cloaked swordsman at dinner had worried her. She pushed the table up against the door, and she went to bed with the dagger Raman had given her in its sheath, still strapped to her leg under her borrowed nightgown.

She couldn't sleep. She tossed and turned, paced her room, then tossed and turned some more for what felt like hours. She had the most comfortable bed she had been in since leaving the palace, and the room felt peaceful and relaxing. But her mind would not rest, replaying her conversation with Raman over and over again, until she thought she might go mad. Her wakefulness frustrated her, and her frustration pushed her farther from sleep.

It was long past midnight when she heard a small scraping sound, completely out of place in the quiet room with its water noises. She sat up in bed. What on earth was that?

A dark line marked the crevice of her slightly open

door. The door pushed inward, scooting the little table across the floor with a scrape.

Alannys screamed.

As if realizing that all hope of stealth was gone, whoever was pushing her door shoved it all the way open, toppling the little table. A dark shape spun in, wielding a curved blade.

Alannys swallowed hard, clutching at the blankets as if they could protect her. What could she do now? Songstrike was across the room on the couch, with her riding cloak and boots. Her little dagger wouldn't be of much use to her—by the time he came close enough for her to use it, she would already be reduced to ribbons by the longer reach of his sword. Desperate, she started to sing.

"Fall asleep,
Collapse to the ground,
Unhand your weapon..."

The dark swordsman bounded across the room in three long strides and jumped up on the bed, raising his blade. She rolled off the bed, pitching her heavy feather pillow at his face. He batted it aside with his sword, and the skewered case fell behind her, belching feathers everywhere. He waved them away from his face, and jumped off the bed after her.

Alannys grabbed a potted plant and hurled it at his head. He ducked, swinging out with the sword low in front of him, but she was already too far away. By the time he recovered his posture, Alannys had her hand on Songstrike's handle.

She yanked it from the sheath, ignoring the painful protest of her shoulder, and whirled to face him in a panting Ready posture. They circled each other warily.

She remembered vividly how things had gone last time she fought this man—her shoulder throbbed, as if making sure she couldn't forget. She could afford no more mistakes. She watched him move critically, looking for any weak points, when a sudden noise from the door distracted her.

Raman stood in the doorway, sword in hand, kicking the little table out of his way. She had never been so glad to see him. "Alannys! Watch out!"

She whipped her head back around just in time to see the dark swordsman, closing in to attack. She ducked and rolled away to the side, narrowly avoiding the curved blade.

He recovered quickly, but now Raman was charging in to join her. He met the cloaked swordsman blow for blow, driving him backward. "I don't know...who in the Seven Hells you are," he grunted between swings, "but this is the last time...you attack Lady Alannys!"

Raman's last strike swung wide. The swordsman ducked under the swing, and charged Alannys. She gave ground, dodging, holding her left arm as still as she could, aware this was a losing fight for her.

Bellowing, Raman ran at them. The swordsman leaned hard to the side, dodging the strike, and slipped his blade under Raman's outstretched arms, deep into his chest. He pulled back his sword and stepped back, hissing.

Time seemed to stand still as Raman slid to the floor with a small, inarticulate moan. Alannys's hands felt suddenly cold. Her vision blackened, and her brain seemed numb. Her attacker stood over Raman's bleeding form, bouncing on his heels.

It seemed like someone else who took two bounding steps toward the swordsman, someone else who brought Songstrike down in a slashing strike with a roar of fury. She couldn't feel her arms, or even her wounded shoulder.

She could only see the cloaked swordsman's eyes over his dark scarf, wide with surprise and fear. He managed to move just in time to keep his hands attached, but she knocked his sword out of his grasp. It flew from his hands, and landed spinning on the floor.

It spun right to her. Alannys bent and scooped it up, carrying it in her left hand while Songstrike blazed in her right. The swordsman took a small, hesitant step backwards.

"Now," she said, "I sing your doom."

The cloaked swordsman turned and ran out the door.

Alannys dropped her weapons, and knelt at Raman's side. She could not have made good on her threat to sing, not with Raman in such bad condition. She would have killed him long before she hurt the swordsman.

Raman had lost a lot of blood. She snatched a blanket off the bed and wadded it up, then used it as a pillow under his head. He moaned and his eyes fluttered open when she hauled him up on the makeshift pillow. "Oh, thank heaven," she gasped, unable to voice even to herself what she was afraid of now.

The torn and empty pillowcase lay on the floor near them. She balled it up, and pressed it hard against Raman's chest.

He groaned, and his white hand crept up to cover hers. His labored breathing was a sickening wet wheeze. Even his hand felt cool on hers.

Alannys was terrified, and she didn't have time for terror. "Raman?" She put her face down near his ear. "Raman, I have to go get help for you. Can you hold this while I'm gone?"

His eyelids fluttered and he squeezed her hand. She slid her hand out from under his, and ran out into the hallway. Somehow, some way, Raman was still alive.

It was up to her to keep him that way.

♫

Alannys never could clearly remember the rest of that night. She didn't know who she found in Mirendasith Hall to help her, or what she had told them, or what they made of her disjointed, hysterical state.

She remembered Brynth racing into the room, white and strained, no longer looking much like floating. Each footstep pounded clear and distinct in her jumbled impressions, a frantic sort of metronome vainly attempting to impose some order on the nightmare.

Lord Arik arrived a moment later, looking uncharacteristically stern. She heard him directing a complete search of the grounds, but it was all just words to her. The guards left, and Arik's gaze landed on her. "Great Muses — have you been kneeling there on the floor all this time?"

She thought she nodded. It was possible she made no response at all — how could the question matter, when Raman was bleeding to death in front of her?

Lord Arik leaned back out into the hallway. "Bring a robe, a heavy one. And wine, warm and spiced. Hurry!" He was muttering to himself when he came back into the room, and even in her state Alannys had to wonder if he was just trying to distract himself from the crippling worry that consumed them all.

She held Raman's hand while Brynth worked with the salve and the powder and needle and waxy thread, and with her face close to his ear, she sang to him. She sang songs of wellness, songs of strength, to keep him going. Would he make it? *Could* he make it? She wasn't sure. She had seen the way Brynth shook his head when he'd pulled back Raman's shirt. Alannys was no healer, but even she knew that this wound should be fatal. She clearly remembered the triumph in the cloaked swordsman's eyes when Raman fell — he, too, knew a mortal blow had been dealt. It was all up to her now — her, and whatever power she had through her music. Songstrike had not stopped glowing since the fight—she could see the blue light, even now, escaping around the mouth of the sheath she wore over her nightgown. So she knelt there on the floor, with the grip of her sword in one hand and Raman's cooling hand in the other, and she sang, while Brynth worked his careful stitches.

Lord Arik dropped a velvet robe around her shoulders. Had she looked cold? She didn't remember feeling cold, but her hands were clearly trembling. He offered her a goblet of wine, and she stopped singing long enough to coax Raman into swallowing a few sips between gasping, gurgling breaths. Brynth finished his ministrations, patted her shoulder, and left the room.

But he was still shaking his head.

"You cannot keep this up," Lord Arik said gravely.

"Help me move him, my Lord. Please. He shouldn't have to lie on the floor."

He eyed her sternly. "You cannot just ignore me, Lady Alannys, and you will not distract me."

"I—I know. But we can't just leave him on the floor. Please, help me."

He sighed in something that sounded very much like defeat. "As you wish. But I do not think it would be wise for us to move him alone and risk aggravating his condition. Allow me to summon assistance."

Three servants helped them make Raman as comfortable as possible on the big bed, and brought a chair to the bedside for her. She had settled herself onto the chair and taken Raman's hand back in her own before Lord Arik spoke again.

"Alannys," he said, and his tone held a warning. "I meant what I said. You can't keep doing this, it isn't safe. It will be a miracle if you aren't sick by morning."

"A miracle," she murmured, regarding Raman's waxy

hand lying limp in her own. "Do you realize that's just exactly what he needs? It'll be a miracle if he's still *here* in the morning. And I have some experience working magic that is almost miraculous."

"Alannys, I don't think —"

"I have to do what I can. You see that, don't you? I can't just stand by and watch him die. I have to do what I can, and I don't have time to argue it."

She started singing, but she didn't really relax until she heard Lord Arik snoring behind her. She glanced over and found him slumped against the arm of the sofa, asleep.

She didn't know exactly how long she sat singing like that. Servants came in offering food, drinks, and blankets, but she just shook her head and kept singing. Brynth came to the bedside, examined his patient and left, shaking his head, but she ignored him and continued to sing. Hours passed, and still she sang. Lord Arik jerked awake, and eyed her narrowly. "Alannys, have you been singing all this time?"

Alannys sat up straighter in her chair, flexing her fingers. "I have to." Her voice sounded muffled and distant, even to her own ears. "I have to help Raman. I have to —"

Arik caught her when she fell out of her chair, unconscious.

♫

Alannys woke up sprawled on a couch, with a robe spread over her like a blanket. She felt stiff and sore. Her throat hurt, and every muscle in her body ached as though she had used it up. And worst of all, she had no idea where she was or why she felt so awful. She had slept a long time, and the fact of it seemed to reproach her, but she didn't know what for.

She sat up on the couch, and saw Lord Arik at the other end, sleeping uncomfortably against the arm. It all came back to her then — dinner at Mirendasith Hall, her late-night visitors, the midnight attack —

Raman!

She pushed herself off the sofa, stumbling as fast as she could manage toward the bed, cursing herself for sleeping, for giving in to Muse's Fever. She didn't think she could bear to find out he had slipped away in the night while she lay useless on the couch.

Her chair was still pushed up against the bed. She sat down in it, and took his hand in hers.

It was warm.

Tears filled her eyes, unbidden. She could see the rise and fall of his chest as he breathed, quickening now. He was waking.

"Alannys?" The raspy word was barely audible.

She squeezed his hand. "Yes, Raman, I'm here."

He rolled his head around to look at her. "You're alive."

"Yes." She smiled at him. "And so are you."

Raman grunted, wincing. "Barely."

"I know — you were wounded pretty badly. The healer had his hands full. He — we...we were afraid..."

He regarded her again. "You sang. All night. I remember your voice, but nothing else. How could you sing that long?"

She patted his hand and looked away. "Rest, Raman. Rest will do you more good than anything."

"You, too." He managed a faint smile, but on his pale waxy lips it looked ghoulish and unsettling. "You look terrible."

"Ha, ha. I'm serious, Raman."

"Me, too." He looked as if he might like to press his point, but he couldn't quite find the energy. He heaved an exhausted sigh, and his eyes fell shut.

Alannys! Alannys, are you all right? Dorramon's voice sounded in her mind, clear and anxious. The sound of it, so immediate and unexpected, washed over her with a rush of emotions she couldn't control. Quite suddenly she could feel every minute she had been away from the palace, every mile that separated them, as if each one was a physical presence in the room with her.

She swallowed hard. It took her a moment to compose herself enough to answer, even in her mind. *I — I think so. I've had Muse's Fever.*

So I gathered. His tone was wry, and she remembered that whenever she suffered Muse's Fever, the mindlink stayed wide open and uncontrolled. *You don't sound very good at all, Alannys. What happened?*

She didn't really want to tell him. How many times had she had to bring bad news to her friends since coming to Ravanmark? But she watched Raman's bandaged chest rise and fall with each ragged breath, and she knew she had to tell him. Besides, with the mindlink open after she collapsed, chances were good that Dorramon already had some suspicions of his own about what had happened. *Listen, Dorramon, last night...the cloaked swordsman came back. He attacked me in my room here in Mirendasith Hall. Raman came in to help me. He was — Dorramon, he was wounded.*

What? How badly?

It's — not good. She hung onto Raman's hand, wishing desperately that she could hold Dorramon's the same way. *It's pretty bad, actually. I don't think Lord Arik's healer expected him to survive the night.*

Dorramon swore. *So that's how you ended up with Muse's Fever. Alannys, I can't see you two. But I know what you did was horrifyingly dangerous. So answer me straight, and don't sugar-coat anything. How are both of you today?*

I'm fine, she said immediately. *Songstrike — when it glows, it helps me a lot — so this was like any other Muse's Fever. I don't think I would have survived that.*

Then let us be thankful that Songstrike is with you. And

Raman?

She could hear the urgency in his mental voice. She bit her lip, looking at Raman's gray face, wondering how much Dorramon already suspected. *It isn't good. I'm not trying to sugar-coat, but I don't think I can stand to be blunt. He's not well. He can't travel on. That wound – it should have been mortal. It would have been, I think, without everything the healer and I could do.*

I see. He sounded calm, calmer than she could have managed in his place. Raman had to be crazy to think she belonged in the royal family. *I was against this from the start, you know that. Still, I hate to see it end like this. I will send Grayble with half a dozen Royal Guards to escort you back.*

She took a deep breath, steadying herself. *You'll have to send them for Raman. I'm not coming back. Not yet.*

The sudden, short silence seemed to crackle with shock. *What?*

I've only barely gotten started out here; I can't quit now.

Alannys –

Look, I don't know what reason Raman gave you for coming with me, but he really believed in my mission out here. More than I realized. He's stood up for me, Dorramon, he protected me and he kept me going when I wanted to quit. Now this happens – don't you understand – on top of everything else, I have to keep going for him. Because he very nearly gave his life to give me the chance.

I understand how you feel, Dorramon said gravely. *I do. But I can't accept this. This was really too much for both of you to handle together. For just you to go on, by yourself, with that madman after you...* His voice cracked. *It's too dangerous, Alannys. It's suicide, there's no other word for it. You have to come back.*

Coming back won't change anything, she said gently, *for either of us. If I rode back tomorrow, what would you do? How would you fight against the Dark Alliance? How would you defend yourself against Lord Malrec's smear campaign?*

Damn Lord Malrec, and damn the Dark Alliance. I've issued proclamations revoking all of their titles. Lady Etherra rules Brookeshire Holding now, and Orinthal Holding belongs to Baroness Lae. For Glennayre – well, obviously it can't go to my sister. I've sent a nobleman with troops to replace both of them. You don't have to do this.

But I do, she said. *You can't really believe that will be the end of it – that they will disband all their forces and surrender because you revoked their titles. They will move ahead with their war on the Talents and on you, and who can you send in my place who will do what I'm doing?*

There was a long, long pause. *I understand what you are saying, Alannys. But I can't approve of this, not for any reason. Don't try to get me to say this is all right, because it isn't. Please, let me send Captain Grayble for you. Hell, I'll ride out myself if you say you'll come back with me.*

I can't. She wondered fleetingly if he could tell, if he had any idea at all, what it cost her to say those words to him. *It would be bad for you, and bad for Ravanmark. And you can't say things like that, Dorramon. You are the king, and your people need you in the palace running the country, not rescuing some musician who got in over her head.*

I know. I know you're right, and Raman would tell me the same thing, given a chance. But...would it be wrong if I said I almost don't care? You just said you're in over your head, Alannys – would it be wrong if I said there isn't any price I wouldn't pay to save you – even Ravanmark itself?

She sat there speechless, all the words knocked out of her by the unbelievable impossibility of what she'd just heard. She stopped worrying about what this conversation was costing her, and for the first time wondered what it had cost Dorramon to speak those words—what it might cost him yet. Such a sentiment had to be unforgivable, uttered by the king himself. And yet, she could not reject it.

For all her noble words, she felt the same way about

him.

I'm sorry, he said. *Forget I said that. It isn't right for me to say such things, and it's even less right for me to saddle you with them.*

Dorramon, I —

No — don't. You're right, Alannys, you're right about everything you've said, and I need to grow up and accept it. I know this isn't easy for you, and I'm not making it any better, carrying on like this. I've already told you, you should do whatever you feel you must. Just know that there is always a place for you here, should you decide to return.

Dorramon... She cast about for the right words to say to him. His sudden reversal left her feeling as though an opportunity had passed, and she had to wonder what might have happened if she hadn't turned him down.

Only — only that was crazy thinking; *nothing* would have happened, because nothing *could* have happened, and they both knew it. The specter of Princess Varilyn hung between them even now, and neither of them could deny the futility of their feelings.

So why did it *hurt* so badly?

Dorramon, I love you, she said finally, aware that it wasn't enough.

And I you. I only wish I had the freedom to show you just how very much. The overwhelming sadness in his voice brought tears to her own eyes. *Be safe, Alannys.*

It took everything she had not to cry in the lonely silence that filled her head with the closing of the mindlink.

♫

Brynth knocked at the door before Alannys had quite finished composing herself. "Forgive me, but might I come in?"

"Of course, Brynth," Alannys called, scrubbing at her eyes. "Come right in."

Their exchange must have woken Lord Arik. He rose

from the couch, and came to stand next to the bed, beside Brynth.

"He sleeps," Lord Arik observed in his gravelly voice. "It is good for him to rest, I think."

"I don't know," Brynth said, reaching to check Raman's pulse. "He feels very warm. I don't like this much time without waking. It implies a sleep that never wakes."

"He woke," Alannys said quickly, anxious to stop that kind of talk. "Only a few minutes ago."

Brynth glanced at her sharply. "He woke? Are you certain?"

"Quite certain. He spoke to me."

"He *spoke* to you?" Disbelief was plain in Brynth's voice, but he didn't push her. "He knew you? He was not delirious?"

"No, he recognized me. And he seemed to remember what had happened."

"I see." Brynth leaned over the bed, and carefully pulled back the dressing to inspect the wound.

Alannys turned her head away. She remembered all too well how horrible it was. She couldn't bear to see it again.

"He lives," Brynth pronounced. "Your songs have worked wonders that my medicine could not. He is stronger and the wound is better than I could have imagined."

"Wonderful," Raman croaked. "Alannys and I can't stay very long. I need to heal as quickly as possible."

They gaped at him in frank, open-mouthed shock. "We —didn't realize you were awake," Alannys said, postponing the inevitable.

"Obviously," Raman replied, with just a glimmer of his old sarcastic humor. He looked at Brynth. "How soon can we leave?"

"Lady Alannys can leave at any time," the healer

hedged.

"And?" Raman prompted impatiently.

Brynth looked helplessly to Lord Arik. Arik stepped closer to the bed. "I'm sorry, Raman. We have done all we could. We were here all night—Alannys sang until she dropped. But you are in no condition to travel."

Raman stared at him. The shock written on his pale, haggard face was painful to see. "What?"

Arik shook his head. "I'm sorry. But you need time to recover, far more time than Alannys has. We have a carriage outside the forest walls that can take you back to the Great Palace. We can have you home in under two days."

"But...but..." He turned to Alannys, as if hoping she could intercede on his behalf.

"Oh, Raman, I'm sorry. But they are right. We've done all we can do. I won't risk your health any further. I have to go on alone."

"*Alone?* With him after you? Alannys, you have to come back with me. You'll be killed!"

She couldn't meet his eye. Everyone in the room was looking at her now, and she couldn't look back at any of them. She took Raman's hand in hers. She couldn't tell him he was wrong, and that brought suddenly home to her exactly how big of a chance she was taking. *It's suicide, there's no other word for it.* "Maybe. We'll just have to hope I can make enough of a difference to save Dorramon before that happens."

Raman gripped her hand tighter. It seemed that no one could speak.

♬

A horse pulled Raman through the narrow, living tunnel that led out of Mirendasith Hall, on a wooden stretcher with wheels and a feather mattress. Alannys rode with him, sitting at the top of the stretcher with his head in her lap. Lord Arik followed behind them on his own horse.

"Dorramon is going to kill me for abandoning you," he said.

She looked down at him. "I doubt that. You don't exactly have a choice. He's not happy about any of it, but I think on some level he understands. You saved my life. We're both grateful, more grateful than I can say."

The stretched bumped over a rock, and Raman grunted.

"I know." Alannys glanced around at the creepy forest surrounding them. "We're almost out. It won't be long now."

A big carriage with four horses awaited them. One of the wide cushioned seats had been converted to a makeshift bed, with feather pillows and heavy quilts. Brynth waited in the carriage to ride with the arch-prince to the palace.

Lord Arik, Alannys, and Brynth managed between them to get Raman into the carriage and on the bed. She settled him in on the pillows, and tucked the quilts around him.

"This doesn't feel right, leaving you," Raman grumbled.

"Just rest," she told him. "You'll be home before you know it. Thank you, Raman. For everything."

Lord Arik helped her up behind him on his horse, and they watched the carriage rumble away. She waved until she couldn't see the carriage anymore, trying hard to hold back her tears. She was mostly successful.

Arik turned his horse back toward the forest. "He will be fine, Alannys."

"I hope so."

"I am certain of it. He may have saved your life, but you saved his as well. No amount of healing could have done what your songs did."

The tunnel closed around them, tight and airless. It made conversation an effort. Several minutes passed before Alannys could bring herself to break the silence. "I'm sorry for bringing this trouble to Mirendasith Hall."

"Sorry? Lady Alannys, you have nothing to apologize for. You have brought nothing to Mirendasith Hall but hope and friendship. There is but one person responsible for bringing this trouble, and he has escaped."

"Again," she said sourly.

"Yes. Again." He exhaled in a puff. "I would not see you leave this way, alone and pursued. There must be some way I can protect you. Please reconsider — we would be happy to keep you here."

She hated to disappoint him. "I do appreciate the offer, Lord Arik, but I don't really have any choice. I can't stay anywhere very long, but especially not someplace that was mostly friendly anyway. I have to keep moving. It's the only way I have any chance of succeeding."

They came out of the tunnel into the placid tranquility of the clearing. The big pond reflected the patches of sunlight in speckled patterns; to Alannys's surprise Lord Arik made for the pond, not the hall.

"I understand," he said. "What you are doing for our king is noble. It is also difficult and dangerous, with little chance of success. You are hunted by a most tenacious and dangerous enemy. If you cannot stay, at least allow me to send some of my guards with you."

"I'm sorry. I appreciate what you are trying to do, I really do. But I've already seen so much death — I can't allow anyone else to risk their life for my cause. Besides, I'll be faster moving alone, and harder to catch."

"I see. I confess I suspected you would answer this way." He didn't sound convinced, though. They stopped near a white gazebo, surrounded by flowering plants, with ivy crawling up the posts. He helped her to dismount.

"Still, I wanted to speak with you before you leave. I have something for you."

Alannys followed Lord Arik into the gazebo, and sat down on a white bench that faced the pond. He sat down on the railing across from her. "Because you carry Songstrike, I assume you are aware that all relics of Soth are inevitably associated with the Redeemer."

Alannys nodded. The idea had never been expressed to her in so many words, but she understood.

Arik looked out over the pond. "I have but one relic myself. Naturally, I consider it yours." He reached around his neck and pulled over his head a heavy gold chain, with a huge pendant that framed a single enormous stone. Everything about the piece seemed oversized, like it was made for someone much bigger than mere mortals like her. Arik handed it to her, and its weight in her hands was impressive. "I do not know if this will prove useful to you or not. It is the Seeing Stone."

Alannys held the stone up and watched the light play across it. It was heavy and massive—probably four inches tall by two inches wide—and it was oval shaped, in an ornate golden setting. The stone was cabochon cut, with a highly domed top. It glowed a watery blue, shot through with gleaming tendrils of gold and red, violet and green. She couldn't seem to tear her eyes away from it. "The Seeing Stone," she echoed. "What does it do?"

"These days, maybe nothing. Back in Soth's day, he could use it to see the woman he was mindlinked to—his wife."

"I see." She watched the stone spin slowly on the end of its chain.

"The Seeing Stone is not as well known as Songstrike, but to those who understand its significance, it will be another sign."

She cupped the stone in her hands. It cast colored

ribbons of light on her skin. Looking at it made her inexplicably happy. The stone was a sign, all right—a sign that she posited herself as the Redeemer—but it was also a sign of something else. The stone was Arik's, and by letting her be seen with it now, he also made it a sign of his support. If she failed in her mission, she would be letting down more than just herself—just how much more seemed to grow with every stop she made on her journey. "I—I don't know how to thank you."

Lord Arik shook his head. "No thanks are necessary, Alannys. I only hope it brings you some comfort. I wish I could do more to help."

"You've done more than you know," she assured him. She gazed out over the pond. The truth was that no one could help her very much. And as for comfort—she doubted she could find that anywhere. What had to be done could only be done by her alone.

And she would do it, or die trying.

♫

Alannys rode west from Mirendasith Hall. She hoped the cloaked swordsman would expect her to continue riding north, and possibly lose her trail for a while.

But she couldn't fool herself into thinking she could lose him forever.

The bad news, according to the large parchment map Lord Arik had given her, was that she would be crossing into Brookeshire Holding before sunset.

Brookeshire Holding. The place was inextricably linked in her mind to Lord Diabon, even though Dorramon had told her Lady Etherra now ran it, and she couldn't help but expect the entire holding to reflect his special brand of crazy. And honestly Lady Etherra, with her visionary dramatics, wasn't much better. Just riding in Brookeshire Holding was enough to make Alannys feel uncomfortable and on edge—as if she might run into the two of them at any moment. She knew it wasn't rational, but that didn't step her growing sense of unease. Between that and the cloaked swordsman, she kept one eye over her shoulder. She rode all day, hoping to put as much distance between herself and her pursuer as she could.

Sunset found her riding into a village, little more than a cluster of tiny cottages huddled at the foot of a rocky, jagged hill. It wasn't even marked on her map. The homes she could see had thatched straw roofs, and gaping open holes for windows, covered with mismatched fabric curtains. Brown, wilted plants littered the gardens like the corpses of giant, spiny insects.

At the first tiny house she passed, a woman stood in the doorway, watching the sunset with her hand shading her eyes.

"Good evening!" Alannys called to her. "Can you tell me where I might find an inn, or — "

The woman disappeared inside and slammed the door. Alannys could hear the heavy thump of a bar falling into place across it.

That probably wasn't a good sign.

Alannys sighed and rode on, hoping for the best while fearing the worst. The next person she came across was a stocky man in a straw hat, patiently working over a dusty field with a hoe. She slowed, but hesitated to speak to him after her warm reception earlier. If there was trouble to be found in this town, it would have to find her. She would not go looking for it.

The man stopped his work, leaning on his hoe to regard her. "Big day for visitors in our tiny town."

Alannys reined up. "How's that?"

"Ashendowne don't see many visitors." He pushed his hat back on his head and favored her with a wide grin. "We ain't on what you might call a main road. Most folks what do ride through are on their way to somewhere bigger and don't so much as slow down. But today — why, today we've had two young women blow into town, the likes of which we don't usually see around here."

The back of her neck prickled, and she smothered an urge to glance behind her—again. "Two?"

"Why, yes. Just earlier today we had a red-haired lass come tearin' into town, yellin' and hollerin' that we was all about to come face to face with the very devil, in the form of a woman carryin' a sword and callin' herself the Redeemer." He tipped the brim of his hat to her. "I 'spect that'd be you, miss."

"I don't know that I would call myself the very devil," she said dryly, "but I do carry a sword and I have been invested with the title of Redeemer, yes."

The man laughed out loud, then glanced quickly around, as though remembering where he was. "No, you don't seem much like the devil to me, either, miss. Tell me, you planning to stay in Ashendowne?"

She looked up the road in the rapidly fading light. "I had considered it. I don't see an inn, though."

"Oh, there's an inn—of a sort. Not a fancy inn like you'd see in a big town, but Cruthers has a couple rooms he lets out for half a dozen coppers a night."

"Cruthers?" she echoed.

He flinched as though she'd said a dirty word. "Yes—if he's even in town tonight—he may be out at his place. But you'd be best off not going there. Anywhere but there, really. Be glad to have you here, actually."

She looked at him in surprise. "Are—are you serious?"

"Sure am. Right serious. Cruthers...he ain't right, if you ken. Mind's been twisted by the poison Lord Diabon spews—and maybe worse things, too. Not sure you'd be safe there, if I can be blunt. But if you don't mind three kids under your feet, we'd be happy to have you."

"Well, thank you, Mister...?"

He laughed his booming, infectious laugh again.

"Name's Hardred, miss. No need for 'mister.'"

"And I'm Alannys," she said, though she suspected he already knew that. "What happened to that red-haired lady you mentioned, Hardred? Did she leave town?"

"She ain't a friend of yours, I take it? No, I don't believe she did. Last I saw, she was taking to old Cruthers. Maybe she needed a room too!"

He guffawed at his joke, but Alannys frowned. "Didn't you say he was not so nice?" The idea of one person who hated her joining up with a twisted old man who hated her was enough to make her look over her shoulder again.

"Now, don't worry, Alannys. Surely a feisty young lady like that would know better than to get in with someone like him. And Cruthers — well, he can't really be as bad as all that, right? It's just best that you stay away. And you are, so nothing to worry over, right? Now let's get that horse of yours settled in the barn. Ain't much, but it'll be a roof over his head."

She followed Hardred toward the tilted little barn, hearing him chatter on without really listening. She could remember only too well Raman's ominous words about Elossa meeting up with the wrong sort of people. Cruthers sounded very much like the wrong sort of person to her.

And 'nothing to worry over' couldn't have been farther from her mood.

♫

Hardred's family lived in one of the smallest houses in a village of small houses. The room Alannys stepped into behind him served as kitchen, dining room, and living room, all at once. The near side of the room had a stiff, threadbare couch. The air was heavy with the scents of sweat and sheep and baking bread. The slight breeze from the uncovered window openings didn't seem to do much to dissipate the smells, or the stifling heat from the fireplace where the bread was baking. There were two doors on far wall, both closed.

A toddler stood near the big wooden table in the kitchen, his fingers crammed into his mouth. His face was round with baby fat, his nose flat and snub. He looked at Alannys standing in the doorway and said something—it may have been words, but it was impossible to tell with his hand in his mouth that way.

A tall, lanky, teenaged boy leaned toward the fireplace with mitts on his hands, wrangling the covered iron pot off of the hook. "That's right, Parnell," he grunted without looking up. "Da's home." He placed the pot on a flat stone on the table, and turned toward the door.

The smile on his face froze when he saw her, and he stepped protectively in front of the toddler. "Da? Who's she?"

Hardred grinned at his son—but it was a mischievous grin, the kind that would make Alannys check the seat of her chair before she sat down. "I am sorry, Lady Alannys. My wife joined the Muses two years back, and Kerlin's turned a bit mother hen since."

"Mother hen?" Kerlin sounded offended. "That ain't hardly fair, Da—*someone* had to—wait. Lady Alannys? Did you say Lady Alannys? This is—you're the Redeemer?"

"The very same," Hardred said, still sporting that unnerving smile. "Better pray she don't sing you to oblivion for being so rude."

Kerlin's face paled. "I'm—I'm sorry!" He pulled the mitts from his hands, revealing shirt sleeves that fell several inches short of his wrists.

"No, please, don't apologize," Alannys said, embarrassed, and she frowned at Hardred. "That wasn't very nice."

Hardred laughed out loud, letting her irritation roll off of him with no visible effort on his part at all. "It's good for him. Boy's gotten too big for his britches—needs a reminder once in a while that he ain't the be-all."

"If you say so. But you don't make things any easier for me when you encourage people to fear me. More than enough of them already do."

One of the doors swung open, and a little girl staggered out, scrubbing at her bleary eyes. "What's going on out here? Gran can't sleep like this." The high, lilting voice sent an electric chill up Alannys's spine. The girl had long, curly blond hair and couldn't have been more than eight or nine. But she could sing—whether the child knew it or not, she had Talent. Alannys could feel it shimmering in the air when she spoke.

"We didn't mean to wake you," Kerlin said. "But Velya, look! Da brought her home. And just look who it is!"

The little girl's eyes flicked over her with interest. "Someone new? I don't recognize you. My name is Velya."

"It's nice to meet you, Velya. My name is Alannys."

"Alannys..." Velya echoed quietly, to herself. "Alannys..." She finally shook her head. "I'm glad to meet you too, Miss Alannys."

Kerlin snorted with laughter, sounding suddenly very much like his father. "Not Miss Alannys. Lady Alannys."

"Lady Alannys?" Velya's eyes flicked between them, suddenly wide. She took a hesitant step backwards, as though she was thinking about bolting back into the bedroom. "Why is she here?"

Her sudden change of attitude bothered Alannys. She tried to think of a nice way to ask about it, but Hardred was already speaking.

"Now just you remember your manners," he said gruffly, "what manners you got, anyway. I'm washing up for dinner." He disappeared into the room behind the other closed door.

"Guess I better get dinner set out, then," Kerlin said, looking from Velya to Alannys like he was afraid to turn his back on them. "You should talk to her, Vel." His overtly encouraging tone was hard to miss, and judging by her frown, Velya hadn't missed it. He went back to the table and busied himself laying out plates, with Parnell following at his heels.

"You have a very nice family," Alannys said, seeking some way to break down the barrier she sensed in front of Velya now. Everything had been fine until the girl learned her title... "Is your grandmother in the other room?"

Velya took another step backward, her huge round eyes fixed on Alannys. She might have been expecting to be pounced on, the careful way she moved. "Yes. She says not to talk to strangers."

"I'm sure that's wise advice, but we've already met. Does she say that because you can sing?"

"No!" Velya's denial was immediate and intense. "Don't know what you're talking about."

Alannys frowned. There was no mistaking the Talent in the little girl's voice—was it possible she didn't know? Kerlin continued setting the table, shaking his head—and Alannys knew Velya was lying to her. But why? "You've never sung?"

"No! People in Ravanmark can't sing, you should know that."

"I see. It seems like you've heard a bit about me, Velya. You must know you have nothing to fear from me—you must know I don't persecute the Talented."

"I—I—" Velya swallowed hard.

"Velya," Alannys said, as gently as she could. "You can tell me the truth."

Velya burst into tears, sobbing and gasping, her hands balled into fists at her side.

Alannys stared at her in shock. Maybe she should have taught elementary school—her work with older children had not prepared her for this. "Velya..." She stopped and tried again. "Velya, I'm sorry, I—"

The bedroom door behind the crying little girl suddenly flung open again, and a wiry, hard-faced old woman darted out. Her eyes were dark, gleaming like a snake's eyes in the wrinkled skin of her face. She took in the situation in a glance, and latched onto Velya's arm with a grip that seemed too hard to be comforting. "Mind telling me why you're making my granddaughter cry?"

Alannys blinked at her. She hadn't been prepared for hostility.

"No excuse? Then how about you explain what in the Seven Hells you are doing in this living room?"

"Tryle!" Hardred was suddenly there next to Alannys, glaring at the old woman, his face almost purple. "Keep a friendly tongue in your head, you hear? This is—"

"I *know* who she is, Hardred. I asked what she is doing here. Surely you know Lord Diabon tells us she's Soth come again? No righteous family would let this person in their home. Surely you weren't planning to *feed* this creature?"

"Tryle, that's enough. She's our guest, and if you keep insulting her, you're crazy as Lord Diabon yourself. Both of you'd do better keeping your yaps shut."

"Says the man who listens to Lady Etherra!" Tryle's shrill, angry voice hurt Alannys's ears, and she shifted to put more distance between them. "This abomination has bewitched her. Lord Diabon preaches the truth. Cruthers preaches the truth. And the truth is that this person is evil! I won't share my table with her!"

"Then you won't eat, Tryle," Hardred snapped. "I let you stay from respect for my dead wife. But you're her mother, not mine, and I don't owe you nothing."

"But Hardred—"

"No, enough!" A vein pulsed in the side of his forehead, visible proof of his apoplectic rage. "It's my house, my table, and my food, and I'll share it with anybody I want. And if you don't like it, go find yourself somewhere else to live!" He turned his back on her, storming back to the table. He never saw the hatred, the pure venom, in the hostile glare Tryle aimed at his back before she turned and dragged Velya back into the bedroom, slamming the door behind them.

But Alannys did, and as she stood there staring at the closed door, hearing the sound of its slam echo in her ears, she couldn't help but think that hatred that intense had to find an outlet.

What was Tryle's outlet? And what would it do to them all, when she finally released it?

♫

Alannys had enjoyed some happy, festive dinners during her time in Ravanmark, but her dinner at Hardred's house was nothing like that. Tryle's outburst left a dour pall hanging over all of them, like a thundercloud. They ate quickly in the awkward silence. Parnell fell asleep halfway through the meal, his round little face mashed against the wood, a chunk of bread squashed in his chubby fist.

She kind of envied him, honestly.

Eventually, the uncomfortable meal dragged to an end.

"I'm headed out to put up the sheep for the night." Hardred stood, not quite making eye contact with her. "Kerlin, please clean up in here."

"I can do that," Alannys said quickly, before he could turn away. "I'm afraid I made your dinner late—it's already dark. Kerlin can help you, and I'll take care of the kitchen."

For the briefest of moments, something flickered in his eyes—hesitation? Hardred was actually considering rejecting her offer, and she had to wonder why. But before she could say a word, his concern seemed to evaporate, and the wrinkle in his brow smoothed over as if it had never been.

"Thank you, Lady Alannys. We'll try to hurry." His glance flicked behind her, to the closed door, then shied away.

She pretended not to see. A basin filled with water stood on a wooden cabinet in the corner, and she busied herself rinsing the dishes and putting them away on the shelves. The silence of the empty kitchen relaxed her, and she hummed as she worked, making a deliberate effort not to think about Cruthers or Elossa or any of the mischief they might be planning.

The slight creak of a door caught her attention, and she turned to see Velya, staring at her, frozen in surprise.

Alannys spent a couple of seconds trying to arrange her own expression into something a bit less frozen. "Hello, Velya. Are you hungry? Shall I get you something to eat?"

"No." Velya shook her head, backing up, her eyes never leaving Alannys, like she was backing away from a poisonous snake. "I—I didn't come out to eat."

"No? Why did you come out?"

Velya looked at the basin, then quickly back at Alannys, eyes wide. It might have been funny under other circumstances—she looked like she expected to be eaten, or worse. "I help Kerlin clean up when Da goes out to the animals." Her gaze turned suddenly resentful. "But then you came. Now everything's changed."

"Not all changes are bad." Alannys wondered if Hardred had agreed to take Kerlin hoping—or fearing— just this sort of thing might happen. "Maybe you could help me instead."

"I don't want to help you." Velya crossed her arms, regarding Alannys stubbornly, but she didn't go back to her room.

Alannys turned away, sloshing a cup through the

water, wiping around the rim with a worn dishcloth, pretending she had nothing on her mind beyond cleaning the kitchen. Why did this little girl's hostility matter so much? "I'm sorry I've disrupted your routine, Velya. It's only for a little while; I'll be gone before you know it."

"Why?"

"Why?" Alannys echoed. "Why what?"

"Why are you leaving soon?" Velya sounded impatient, like that should have been obvious. "Gran says you came from the Great Palace. Isn't that a long way?"

"Yes," Alannys said, past the sudden lump in her throat. "It is a long way away." *And feeling longer all the time...*

"So why come all that way, then just leave? Where are you going?"

"That's — kind of a hard question to answer." Alannys dried another cup and put it away. "I'm going as far as I can get, I guess. I have a job to do in Ravanmark."

"A job?" Velya cocked her head. Alannys couldn't tell if Velya just wanted to challenge her, or if she was legitimately curious.

"Well, yes. A job for the king, but also for myself."

"What kind of job?"

Alannys laughed. "You go for the hard questions, don't you?"

Velya did not laugh. She didn't even smile.

Alannys sighed. "An important job. It has to be done, and it has to be done now, and no one else can do it for me."

"Because you're the Redeemer." The words were sour, almost bitter — Velya spat them at her as if they tasted bad. "You, and no one else."

"Many people believe that." Alannys tried to tread carefully, wondering what could have prompted that tone.

"But someone's trying to kill you. So not everyone

believes that."

Velya spoke matter-of-factly, but her words carried a sting. Her grandmother kept her uncommonly well-informed. Alannys turned to put a plate away, buying herself some time.

"No," she said finally. "Not everyone believes that." Velya's lip curled — it made her look strangely triumphant, and Alannys wondered about that, too. "But here's the thing. It doesn't matter. I have to do this not because I'm the Redeemer, but because I see the problem, and I know that I can help fix it. You don't have to be the Redeemer to do that. It's every person's responsibility to help where they can."

Velya didn't look triumphant anymore. Her eyes were downcast; her slight shoulders drooped. "But the Redeemer is the only one who can use Talent. Everyone else gets in trouble."

"They do now, but I'm working to — "

"It won't matter." The words were flat, falling like melancholy stones into water that didn't even ripple at their passing. "You can't change it. In everyone else, Talent is bad. Unholy."

Alannys frowned. Now that was a strange word to be summoned up by a girl her age. Who had been talking to her, and what sort of things had they said? "Is that why you deny your Talent, Velya?"

"No. No, I — " The words were too quick, her eyes too wide. "It's just...the Redeemer — I hoped the Redeemer...could be — could be — "

"Could be what?"

Velya stared at her, her scared eyes seeming too big for her pale face. Her lips moved soundlessly. Alannys leaned in to hear her —

And Velya turned and ran headlong toward the bedroom, disappearing behind the slamming door for the second time that day.

♫

Alannys sighed and turned back to the dishes, the sharp slam of the bedroom door still ringing in her ears. It had been too much to hope for that Velya might open up to her—clearly someone here was filling her head with some backward thinking, and there was no way a stranger could undo that in an evening.

Still, it rankled to know there was nothing she could do. A little girl shouldn't have to be ashamed to admit her Talent. She shouldn't have to dream about being the Redeemer just because she thought it was the only way to be Talented and *not* be unholy.

She shoved another plate into the cupboard with a clatter that bespoke the anger she was trying to suppress. Trying unsuccessfully, it seemed. She stared at her own white knuckles, clenched around the edge of the basin, and made a conscious effort to calm down.

The bedroom door creaked open again, and slight footsteps approached her. She exhaled in a puff and turned around, figuring Velya had thought better of running away. She put herself in her best frame of mind, ready to do whatever she could to help.

So she was completely unprepared to find Tryle standing there, glaring right in her face, close enough that she could count every wrinkle and line in the old woman's grimace. She did her level best not to jump, but she jumped anyway. She couldn't even kid herself that it was too small to notice.

Tryle didn't show any reaction at all, regarding her over crossed arms, stony-faced. "My stupid law-son invited you here. I can't for the life of me ken why. I can't change it. But it don't make you one of us, and it don't give you leave to meddle. You ken me?"

"Do I...ken...?"

"Leave my granddaughter alone."

Alannys blinked at her in surprise — surprise that was probably stupid. Tryle's hostility exuded from her like heat from the sun, and it had since the moment they'd laid eyes on each other. *Someone* here had to be responsible for the prejudice poisoning Velya, and at a guess, Alannys could only imagine one person that could be. "I *ken* that you're no friend of mine, Tryle. But I have to admit I never expected this sort of attack just for talking to Velya. It seems a little extreme, don't you think?"

"Muses, woman! Do you figure we're so backwards we don't know nothing at all? Even out here we heard about the things you done — the things you're still doing. 'Just talking' is about the worst thing you could do to that girl!"

Alannys pulled a clay plate out of the water and dried it, clenching it as if she wanted to grind it to dust. "I disagree." How could her voice sound so calm, when Tryle's ravings made her feel like her brain might burst into flame? "Velya has Talent. Like it or not, you can't change that. She needs to know. She needs —"

"Seven Hells!" Tryle exploded, spraying spittle in her fury. "You think she don't know that? Nothing in this world can stop a body finding out they harbor the seeds of evil. She done her best not to let them sprout. And then along comes you, with all of your *talk*."

"Tryle, you're crazy." The declaration was flat, the words sharp and insulting, but even as Alannys said them, she knew they weren't the answer to her problem. *Harbor the seeds of evil?* Tryle may have been administering this poison to Velya, but it was pretty clear someone else was producing it. Something moved in darkness here, something just beyond what she could see. "Having Talent doesn't make a person evil."

"No," Tryle shot back, waving a gnarled finger right in Alannys's face, "but using it sure does. Look, it's clear you come here to turn Velya unholy. And I'm here to tell you to back off. I won't stand for it, and I won't warn you again."

The old woman withdrew her threatening finger, turned her back and stomped back into the bedroom, leaving Alannys alone in a room that suddenly felt cold.

♫

Wind howled through Ashendowne after dark, dragging in cooling nighttime air and filling the town with it, probing doors and shutters for any opening where it could be forced inside. Hardred's drafty house fared poorly against the night wind's determination. Alannys lay under two heavy quilts listening to the hollow wail of the wind swooping around the house, hearing it sniff like a live thing at the loose places in the construction. She wasn't as comfortable as she should have been. The sounds made her feel hunted, as though the wind ravaged the town looking for her.

She hadn't anticipated just how much her presence would disrupt the household — Tryle and Velya slept in the bedroom they shared, as usual, but Hardred had abandoned his bed for her, taking up an uncomfortable-looking attempt to sleep on the couch. Kerlin dragged his cot from his father's bedroom to a place near the couch, leaving her alone and discomfited. Would she have accepted Hardred's offer, had she known how much trouble she would cause? It took her hours of anxious fretting, listening to the moaning of the restless wind, before she finally fell asleep.

It felt like she had only just closed her eyes when a frantic voice dragged her from sleep. Words floated into her consciousness, blurry and indistinct, having no context and no meaning.

"...and tell me if they said anything weird — either of them. Lady Alannys, are you listening to me?"

"No," she said groggily, the word little more than a thick croak. It took far too long for the shape in front of her

169

to resolve itself into Hardred. "I mean yes — yes, of course. I was just — asleep. What's going on?"

"It's Velya. She's gone."

"Gone?" Alannys pushed herself up against the feather pillow. "What do you mean?"

"Just what I said. She ain't here."

"But — Velya's too little to leave by herself."

Hardred threw his hands up in the air, as if he had been attempting to make that point for some time. "Just so. But she ain't by herself — my damned law-mother's gone too."

"Tryle?" Alannys knew she was doing a rotten job of keeping up with the conversation, but she wasn't sure what she could do about it. Her sleep-addled brain just didn't seem to be capable of very much at the moment.

"Yes! I know she don't much like you, Alannys, but I don't guess she'd hold back speaking her mind. I need to know if she said anything strange to you. Anything that might help me figure where she went."

"No," she said, "nothing." She could see Kerlin staring at her over his father's shoulder, his freckles standing out starkly in his pale face. It made him look sickly — sort of like she felt. "I'm sorry."

"Nothing?" Hardred pressed, raking a hand through his hair. "All evening, while we was out tending animals — she never said a word?"

"Not about leaving, anyway. Nothing like that." She scooted back against her pillow, casting a glance at the burlap curtain fastened tight over the square opening in the wall that served as a window. The blackness was unrelenting; it must still have been the middle of the night. It certainly explained the sluggishness of her thoughts and the heaviness of her bones. "I only had one conversation with Tryle this evening, Hardred. And it was short, and confrontational. She was only trying to run me off. She seemed to think that I was her to convince Velya to use her Talent—to turn her unholy, she said."

"Unholy?" Hardred's face was suddenly as white and waxy as his son's. He grabbed her arm, gripping her tightly enough it was painful, but she could feel his fingers shaking. "That's what she said? She used that word—unholy?"

"Well, yes." Alannys tried to pull her arm away, but he seemed disinclined to release it, and she didn't want to agitate him further. "Velya said the same thing, earlier. I thought that was a peculiar choice of words for a child of her age."

"That's because it ain't her word." He finally turned loose of her arm, pinching the bridge of his nose between his thumb and forefinger, looking for all the world like a man desperately holding onto his last thread of control.

Kerlin laid a hand gingerly on his father's shoulder. "It's all right, Da. She didn't take Velya to Cruthers. Gran may be off kilter, but she ain't crazy."

Alannys could practically feel her ears perk up. "Cruthers? The same man Elossa went with? Tryle knows him?"

"Aye, that's one manner of sayin' it." Hardred's shoulders were shaking.

Alannys climbed out of bed, raking her hands through her hair, trying to feel more awake. "Hardred," she said sternly, trying to sound more confident than she felt, "try to stay calm. We haven't lost yet. Tell me about this man Cruthers. What's he like? Why are you so worried?"

"Oh, Lady Alannys. If you heard Tryle talk, you already know a fair bit of him. Every idea she got came from Cruthers. He's a twisted, bitter old man what carries such a hatred for Talent, even my law-mother can't match it. He was going to marry Tryle, you see? Till he found out her granddaughter was Talented. If she takes Velya there now..." He swallowed hard, clenching his big hands into fists and fighting for control. "He says he can drive Talent out of a person. Like it's a disease, or a demon."

Alannys felt sort of dizzy, as if her brain was spinning. Or maybe the world was spinning around her, and she was trying to stay still. She caught up her swordbelt and strapped it on, checking Songstrike in its scabbard with fingers that felt numb. Cruthers *exorcised Talent?* She couldn't see how that could even be possible, but she could easily imagine how he could hurt a Talented person trying. Or even... "Where does Cruthers live?"

Hardred shook his head. "A fair bit out of town, in them rocky hills. It ain't easy, getting there."

"It don't matter!" Kerlin sounded panicked; his voice broke in evident distress. "She didn't take Velya there. She wouldn't. Bet they gone to the inn."

"The inn," Hardred muttered, frown lines creasing his forehead. "Maybe."

Alannys looked back and forth between them, trying to separate actual probability from wishful thinking. "Didn't you say Cruthers owns that inn?"

Hardred glanced at her in sharp surprise. "Well, yes." She couldn't tell if he didn't remember saying so much, or if he just hadn't expected her to listen. "Could be they went there for the night—could be they won't see Cruthers till tomorrow."

"If they see Cruthers at all," Kerlin interjected.

"All right, then," Alannys said, grabbing her cloak. "We still have time. You two go to the inn. See if you can find them there. I'm going out to Cruthers's house, in case they headed that way."

"You sure? It ain't easy, and it might could be dangerous."

"I'm sure." The grimness in her own voice made it sound like a stranger's. "I don't claim to really understand all the reasons why this has happened, but it's pretty clear things wouldn't have degenerated this far without me. I don't want to see anyone else getting hurt trying to fix it."

Hardred nodded absently, but his eyes looked distant and she suspected his response would have been the same no matter what she said. He told her how to find the path that led out into the rocky hills, and she listened with half of her attention, while the other half pondered what she would find in the hills, and how different these people's lives would have been if she had never come here.

♫

The cold night wind prowling Ashendowne didn't feel any nicer than it had sounded from inside Hardred's house. Alannys kept her leather cloak pulled tight around her as she walked through the little cluster of dark cottages that constituted the middle of town, listening to her own slight footfalls on the packed, dry dirt. The barest trace of a single moon hung high in the sky, casting a weak and altogether insufficient light. She inspected every crevice, every shadow around her, as though she expected attack. But nothing stirred except the restless wind.

The path was there, winding off into the trees, right where Hardred had said it would be. It took her a bit to find it, not so much because the spot was difficult to find, but more because it didn't really look much like a path. A man lived at the other end of that path, a man who worked in this town and presumably walked that path most days. Alannys would have expected a path like that to be worn, easily distinguished from the landscape around it—to look, in short, like a path. But this...if she had not been specifically directed where to look, she would never have found it. It seemed to her a snake slithering across bare rock would have left more of a trail. Cruthers must have gone out of his way to leave no sign of his passage.

She wondered about that.

The flat, clear land of Ashendowne rapidly turned rocky and steep, and footing was difficult to ascertain in the smothering blackness that was barely nicked by the crescent moon. Alannys stumbled and staggered, slipping as much as she walked. Coyotes yipped and cried off in the night, and the wind that had felt uncomfortably cold leaving the warmth of Hardred's house now seemed insufficient against the exertion of the hike. She worked her way up the hill, too busy to worry too much about what she'd gotten herself into, which was probably for the best. Hardred had warned her the place could be hard to see, set back against the face of the rock as it was, and half grown-over with vines and scrubby brush. In the dark, it seemed likely she could walk right by it and never see it, especially if Cruthers really was as secretive as she thought him to be.

She reckoned she was halfway up the rocky hill when she first heard the voices ahead. She hurried on, her heart hammering in her ears so loudly that it took her some distance to realize she wasn't hearing *voices* – she heard one voice, young and frantic, tossed on the tempestuous wind.

Velya. The desperation in the voice sent warning flares of anxiety through Alannys, and she did what she would have sworn to be impossible a moment before – she scrambled up the rocky, loose trail even faster. So they *had* come this way – what had they gotten into? Why didn't she hear Tryle? Had the old woman abandoned the child here?

She skidded around a switchback in the path, only to find the way forward completely blocked by fallen rock. Half the mountain looked to have crumbled to pieces and fallen onto the trail, scattering debris and choking dust everywhere.

And pinned under the mini-mountain of stone was the

slight, unmoving form of Tryle.

Velya knelt next to her grandmother, sobbing and pleading and — to Alannys's utter shock — trying to get a song through her tears. She never managed more than a word or two at a time, gasping and shuddering painfully in her grief, wobbling where she sat, but there could be no doubt — she was trying to *sing*.

"Stop!" Alannys grabbed Velya by the shoulders, dragging her back away from the fallen rock. "You can't do that!"

"Gran said...the same thing," Velya sobbed brokenly. Her little chest heaved — it hurt just to watch her cry like that.

"Well, see, she's worried about you, too. You could kill yourself doing that. You've never practiced; you aren't strong enough."

"It's not that," Velya howled. "She don't want my Talent touching her!" She collapsed into a wailing heap of dirt and tears.

Alannys left her there and went to stand near the blockage in the path. Crying wouldn't hurt Velya, but Tryle's situation was an emergency.

The old woman was pinned but good. A big, discolored lump swelled from the side of her head, and blood trickled from her nose and one of her ears. Her arm bent sharply at an unnatural angle. Her shallow, erratic breathing sounded loud in the quiet night.

Alannys gingerly touched the pile of stone. It was far too much for her to move by herself — Tryle couldn't wait that long. She couldn't free the old woman alone, but she couldn't leave her like this, either.

"I need to stabilize her first," she muttered, and knelt there on the rocky ground. Taking the cool, wrinkled hand in her own, she drew a breath and began to sing. "Oh Muses, holy and high—"

"Protect us from this wicked abomination." The voice was behind her, reedy and tremulous, the words spoken so quickly they seemed to run together. "Cast it from your sight, and protect the innocent from its unholy taint."

"What?" Alannys whipped her head around to find a stooped, grizzled old man stepping out of the shadows of the pine trees and the scrubby brush. His back was bent with age, and his fingers curved painfully from arthritis. He regarded her balefully through one cloudy eye and one that seemed only to open halfway, and Alannys knew she had to be looking at Cruthers.

She thought he looked very much like his name sounded.

"She would not want that." He raised his hand to point at her with one shaking, claw-like finger. "You do wrong to curse her with your foul, unholy music."

Alannys gaped at him, dumbfounded. Hardred had warned her, but even so, she hadn't been prepared for this. "Are you serious? I'm trying to save her!"

The old man said nothing, making a peculiar smacking sound with his lips.

Alannys frowned, taking in his demeanor and the tattered, dirty rags he wore as clothes. Was he even sane? "Look, you're Cruthers, aren't you? Stop rambling and help me move these rocks. We can still save her!"

Cruthers planted the end of a twisted, gnarled walking stick in the ground in front of him and leaned heavily on it. "You shouldn't be here." He still spoke too quickly, but they might have been discussing the weather for all the inflection in his voice. "You should leave, now. You and the demon child both."

"She's not a demon," Alannys snapped, turning her back on him. "If you aren't going to help, then leave. I have no use for you."

"High and mighty she is now, yes," Cruthers crooned,

as if to himself. The reedy whisper scratched its way through her ears, impossible to ignore. She shivered, wondering if he even realized he was speaking aloud. "High and mighty, mighty and high. But one day she'll meet the mistress of us all, and her attitude will change, change like the wind. The winds of change are coming for the woman, yes."

"Go away." Alannys could hear her own voice trembling—the old man was unnerving her. "You're raving, old man."

"Raving, am I?" His chuckle was even worse than his whisper—it grated, like the dry scraping of old bones. It made her ears itch. "The wind is not mine. Even now it begins to blow. Your red-haired friend has gone to her already."

"Who?" Alannys demanded. "Elossa has gone to who?"

"*Her.*" A gruesome, toothless smile stretched Cruthers's face when she twisted back around to regard him. "She who commands us all. Even now, hidden in the darkness, her power grows. And when she is ready...no power in this world will save you."

With a truly disturbing cackle, the old man turned and hobbled back into the shadows, leaving Alannys gawping after him in cold shock.

♫

A sudden touch on her shoulder jolted Alannys from her dismal reverie.

She turned and found Velya standing there, sniffling. The girl's white face seemed to glow in the pale moonlight —except for her eyes. They were puffy and red.

But for what might have been the first time ever, she was looking right into Alannys's face, with no hint of malice. "You made him leave."

Alannys shook her head, darting a quick glance at the impenetrable darkness behind them. "I think he just got tired of bothering me."

"No one's ever made him leave before. Can you save Gran?"

"I don't know. I think I could, if I could get her out of these rocks. But I can't do that on my own."

"I'll get help." Determination made her sound suddenly very grown up.

"Velya, I don't think—"

"I can *do* this, Alannys! Let me help!"

She couldn't argue. What else could she do, after all? "All right. Hurry, Velya, and be careful."

"I will!" She ran down the trail lightly, gazelle-like in her flight, her blond hair streaming behind her until she rounded the sharp turn and disappeared from sight.

Alannys sighed and turned back to Tryle, wondering if she was doing the right thing. It didn't really feel like it. But then, she had to admit nothing had really felt right for a while, not since—

Not since she'd left the Great Palace.

The thought brought with it an unexpected stab of pain. She blinked back tears she didn't have time for, hoping against hope that things would work out all right.

For all of them.

♪

It felt, to Alannys, as though she spent quite some time drifting between places. Some of them, like her room at the Great Palace, made her smile just to see them again. Others, like Crinn, curdled her smile. She spent a long time revisiting places she'd seen in Ravanmark, but it all seemed to be over so fast.

So when she pried her heavy eyelids apart, and her blurry vision showed her a rather fuzzy rendition of Hardred's living room, she felt confused and disoriented. She lay there on the hard sofa trying to remember how she had even gotten there.

"Lady Alannys?" The voice was somewhere between

that of a boy and that of a man; when she turned her head she found a teenager watching her, rather anxiously. "You awake?"

"I think so." Her voice sounded muffled, blurry, the same way the room looked. It sounded like she was hearing herself talking from another room. But how could that be, when both her mouth and her ears were on the same head, and it was right here? "Who are you?"

His eyes widened in alarm. "Kerlin. Hardred's son, Kerlin. Don't you remember?"

"Of course. Yes, I remember now." She frowned. "But I didn't remember a minute ago. What's wrong with me? How did I get here?"

His eyes flicked to the kitchen, then back to her. He hesitated, biting his lip. It looked like it hurt. "Don't know how much to tell you. Da figured we should let you recollect for yourself." He studied her frown. "But we reckon you had a touch of Muse's Fever."

"Muse's Fever." It was as if the words unlocked something in her brain, and she remembered it all, in a rush—sitting with Tryle, singing every now and then to help her through, hefting rocks with Hardred and Kerlin while Velya did her best to help, stumbling back down the mountain while Hardred carried Tryle.

She put a hand to her forehead, grateful she was lying down—the sudden onslaught of memories made her dizzy. "Yes. Muse's Fever. I remember now."

"Do you? That didn't seem so bad, from what I heard tell about the fever."

"Yes, I do. I was careful, that's all." She swung her feet off the couch and sat up, ignoring the sudden pounding in her head. "Where is your father?"

"Da?" Kerlin's expression was odd. "Kitchen. Be best if you stay put, though. You're just talking on different stuff all random, ken?"

She pushed herself up from the couch. "I'm fine. It all makes sense to me, anyway. We're all just very tired."

"If you say so."

She swallowed a grouchy retort about respecting one's elders and turned away, heading for Hardred.

Hardred was busy at the fireplace, baking eggs over the fire into something that looked a lot like a casserole.

Kerlin came in from behind her and took a seat at the table, where he'd evidently been slicing apples before his conversation with her. He picked up his paring knife and went back to work, ignoring both of them.

"You're up." Hardred didn't turn to look at her. "How you feeling?"

"I'm up," Alannys said. "It's good enough for me."

"I can't thank you enough," he said. He kept his back to her, fussing with the iron pot on its hook. She wondered if his words made him as uncomfortable as they made her. "Savin' her—it was all down to you."

"Everyone helped," Alannys protested.

"But 'twas you found her. You sat with her, kept her going. Without you...she'd be dead."

"We may still lose her." Alannys turned around, and found Kerlin slumped over the table, asleep. She reached over him, slipped the knife out of his hand, and sliced up an apple while she talked. "I don't know. She doesn't look good, Hardred."

"I know." He sighed and finally turned to look at her. She had to avert her eyes. The stress of the night had carved itself into the lines and valleys of his face, in the deep purple hollows under his eyes that had not been there before. "Don't blame yourself for that. No matter what happens. Figure it this way—without you, we'd lost her for sure. And maybe Velya, too."

"Maybe..." Alannys looked around the room, frowning. "Where is Velya, anyway?"

Hardred's bloodshot eyes cut to the closed bedroom door. "With Tryle. Ain't moved since we come back. Worries me, Alannys. Thinks this is all her fault, she does, and she can't help fix it. Can't even talk to her—it's like she don't even hear me."

Alannys stood up from the table and clapped him on the shoulder. "I don't know what I can do, but I'll talk to her." She popped an apple slice into her mouth and headed for that closed door.

She found Velya sitting at the bedside, holding her grandmother's hand in both of her own. Her face was smooth and expressionless, but her cheeks were damp and tear-streaked. She didn't even look up when Alannys pushed open the door and stepped into the room. "Gran, wake up. Please wake up. I couldn't take it if you...if you...if you didn't wake up, because of me. You got to wake up—please."

"Talking to her is good," Alannys said, and walked into the room, sitting on the edge of Tryle's bed across from Velya. It only took her a couple of steps to cross the tiny room—it barely fit the two small beds.

Velya turned her expressionless eyes to Alannys, but showed no surprise and said nothing.

"It shows her that she's missed, that you care about her and want her to come back. But there's something even better that you can do for her."

Velya's expression—or disturbing lack thereof—did not change. "Something better..? Oh. You mean singing." She shook her head, unloading a massive sigh. "I tried that. You were wrong. I couldn't help her—I guess it's true that only the Redeemer can help people with music."

"No—you've got to understand, Velya, Talent isn't everything. You have the ability, sure, but it takes practice to know what you can do and how to do it."

"Practice?" Her face certainly had an expression now—

it was covered in doubt. "I always thought Talented people were born knowing how to use it. That only I didn't...because there was something wrong with me."

"No. There's an old saying from a famous man where I come from — even if you're on the right track, you'll get run over if you just sit there."

"On the right track? What does that even mean?"

Alannys shifted uncomfortably on the edge of the hard bed. "It means that a good start isn't enough. Having Talent is a good start, but no one's ever shown you how to use it properly. You've never strengthened your skills; you don't even know what to do. It isn't your fault it didn't work, and it doesn't mean you can't do it."

For the first time, interest flickered in Velya's eyes, regarding Alannys over pursed lips. "Really? It doesn't?"

"It doesn't. But let me ask you something. Do you still think that only the Redeemer should be able to use Talent?"

Velya hesitated, glancing at Tryle. "I don't know," she hedged. "I thought so. But then those rocks fell, and Gran was stuck...and I sang. She hollered at me to stop, said she'd rather die than be saved by a song. I still sang — or tried to." She hung her head. "So I guess I don't really believe that after all."

Alannys scratched her nose to conceal her smile. "Don't say it like that. It's a good thing — you tried to save your grandmother. Nothing wrong with that. And what's more, you just saw that your own actions didn't match what you thought you believed. Most adults can't do that."

Velya looked up at her, but she wasn't smiling. "It don't feel like a good thing."

"Of course not. Most changes don't feel good, because they're different. Different is always uncomfortable, at least at first."

"If you say so." Velya sat silent for a long moment, watching Tryle's chest rise and fall in deep, even breaths. When she spoke again, it was in a voice so low, Alannys almost couldn't hear her. "Will you teach me?"

"What?"

"How to sing—how to help Gran. Teach me? Please?"

"I don't know, Velya. That's really dangerous, and—"

"Please!" The sudden ferocity in the little girl's tone made Alannys jump. "I can sing on my own, if you make me. But I'm asking for your help."

Alannys thoughtfully regarded Velya's stubborn visage over crossed arms, trying to find a resolution to this that felt right. It *was* dangerous. But was it as dangerous as diving headfirst, alone and unguided? "Look, Velya, the first thing you need to understand is that singing can kill, and not just other people. If you try to do too much—even help too much—singing can kill you. And even when you don't do too much, it'll make you so sick you'll feel like you're dying. So you have to be careful. Always. Do you understand?"

Velya nodded, her eyes wide and round. "Gran's talked about the punishments of the Muses before."

Alannys frowned. "I don't know if I'd call them punishments, but they are real and very dangerous. As long as we're clear on that, I suppose I can help you. The first thing I want to do is give you some limits."

"Limits?"

"Yes. The best way to make sure you don't get hurt is to limit what you do and how long you do it. So I don't want you to ever sing more than two lines at a time. And keep what you're asking for as small as possible."

"Small? I don't understand. What do you mean, what I ask for?"

"That's a good question. I've never tried to teach anyone this stuff before. When you sing, you're trying to make something happen, right? Otherwise, you wouldn't be singing. The words you sing will be about what you want to make happen."

"Oh—I ken. But I know what I want—I want Gran to be all better. Why waste time asking for small things?" She drew a deep breath, puffing out her little chest.

"Stop!" Alannys clamped a hand over Velya's mouth. "Don't you dare sing yet. That is exactly what I'm talking about. Asking for her to just recover is way too big."

"Mm nmmph?"

Alannys pulled back her hand. "Yes, absolutely. Look, when you sing, the things you make happen don't come free. You pay for them out of your own energy."

"But how do you know how much energy it will cost?"

"That's just it. You don't know. You sing, and then you find out. And if it costs more than you have, you will die. Just from singing. So always sing for small things. Sing two lines at a time, then stop. If you don't feel tired, you can do it again. As soon as you feel tired, even a little bit, quit. Wait a few hours, then you can try again."

"I ken." Velya looked from Tryle to Alannys. "That how you do it, when you sing?"

"Well, no. And when you're grown, you won't have to do it that way, either. You'll have a better idea of what you can do and how much is too much. But you'll always have to be careful. It never stops being dangerous. Any musician who isn't careful is dead."

Velya nodded. Her expression was pensive, and Alannys wondered what the little girl made of all this. So much different than her own music lessons—she couldn't imagine what she'd have done if any of her teachers had solemnly explained that music could kill her.

"So," Alannys said, "given all of that, if you were to sing for your grandmother, what words would you sing?"

Velya's forehead creased into a serious frown. "Well,

making her all better is too big. But I might could sing for her to wake up?"

"I think that's a great place to start. You can try it if you want to. But remember, only two lines, then stop."

Velya nodded solemnly. She swallowed several times, squeezing her grandmother's hand with one of her own hands, and fluttering the other in front of herself in apparent agitation.

Alannys understood. Talking about all of this was one thing — actually *doing* it, knowing the risks and the consequences, was something else altogether. It wouldn't have surprised her if Velya backed out and didn't sing a note. She still felt like chickening out herself, every single time.

"Wake up Gran,
I miss you."

The little song was short, the words sung so fast they tumbled over each other and the whole thing was over almost before Alannys realized it had begun. Velya used only two pitches — one a step above the other.

But Velya turned to her with flushed cheeks and eyes that sparkled with excitement. "I did it! How was that, Lady Alannys?"

Alannys bit down on her tongue for a moment — hard — to keep herself from laughing. "It was perfect, Velya. Nice and short, and you asked for something small. Do you feel tired?"

"No! I feel great!" She turned breathlessly back to her grandmother, and her little shoulders slumped. "But it didn't work. I did it wrong."

"No, not at all. You don't usually make things happen the first time you ask this way. It's all right to sing it again if you want, since you're not tired. And maybe a bit slower this time. It always helps, even if you can't see it."

"I ken, I ken." Velya nodded earnestly, then closed her eyes, took a deep breath, and sang her two-line song again, slower.

Alannys paid close attention this time, and she could hear the strain in Velya's inexperienced voice—the unintentional warbles, the hurried breaths taken at inappropriate times, the way she sought all around the pitch with every word, and sometimes never quite found it.

And yet, there was such *potential* there! All she needed was some practice, some lessons, and she would make a very fine singer. The thing that frustrated Alannys was that she knew that was impossible. Velya would have to keep her abilities secret—which ruled out regular practice—and where in this world could any Talented person find any sort of training?

"That was very good," she said out loud. "Even better than the first time. Do you feel tired?"

"A little," Velya said. "Not much though—hardly at all. I could sing again?"

"No. No, it's very important that you stop as soon as you are tired at all."

"But—but Gran's still sleeping."

"And that's okay. Sleep makes her better. Don't push too hard, Velya—you could hurt her and you. You can try again this afternoon."

Velya nodded. "Thank you, Alannys. I didn't know how to do any of this."

"Not yet, but you would have figured it out on your own. Maybe we just saved you some trouble later. You should probably take a nap now yourself."

"I will."

Alannys stood up from the bed, and as she turned to go, she saw Tryle's free hand twitch on the quilt. It was an encouraging sign, and she felt sure Velya was responsible for it.

But she had to wonder, as she walked toward the door, if Tryle would thank either of them for what they'd done — or if Cruthers's poisoning of her mind was too complete.

And if it was, what did that mean for her chances in the rest of Ravanmark?

♬

Alannys stepped out of the bedroom, still looking back over her shoulder at the old woman and the little girl, and nearly ran into Hardred.

"Oh, sorry," she said reflexively, and turned to face him. The glare he directed at her stopped her in her tracks.

"You should be, seems to me." He stood planted like a boulder in her path, arms crossed. "Care to explain?"

"Explain...?" She blinked at him in confusion, blindsided by this unexpected hostility. "I don't understand. I told you when I left I was going to talk to Velya..."

His face flushed bright red. "That weren't *talking* I just heard, Alannys!"

"Hardred — calm down." She turned to pull the bedroom door closed behind her. "Talk to me. I'm new to Brookeshire Holding, you know that. Is singing forbidden here? Have I broken the law?"

"Law? That ain't the point, I—"

"Have I?"

"No." He clearly didn't like the question or the answer. "No, there ain't no law against singing, it just...it just *ain't done.*"

"Just not done," she echoed. He couldn't hold her gaze; his eyes kept twitching away from her. "I feel for you. But right now we all need to be strong, you maybe most of all. Look, Hardred, without music your law-mother would have died. You know that, don't you?"

"I know." He sounded honestly miserable, and she

couldn't muster any anger at him. "But if there was singing needed done, you could've did it yourself! Why bring Velya into it?"

"Bring her into what? She was born Talented. I didn't bring that to her."

"You didn't bring her Talent, but you sure as anything taught her to use it!" Hardred threw his big hands up in frustration. "Now she's a target, you ken? And this...this singing, it's dangerous. Even I know people been killed. That really power fit for an eight-year-old?"

In the kitchen, Kerlin sat up in his chair, his face red and puffy from sleeping on the table. He sat blinking at them with wide eyes, and Alannys knew this conversation would be repeated—maybe many times. She pursed her lips, choosing her words as carefully as she could. "I didn't make that decision, Hardred, and neither did you. She was born with that power. I did teach her how to use it. Like you said, she'll be a target. What you don't seem to understand is, she already was. People who hate Talent don't care whether you know how to use it or not. And with someone like Cruthers around, she needs to have some way to defend herself, don't you think?"

Hardred just stared at her, speechless.

"But I didn't teach her battle songs. I tried to teach her how to use her Talent to help someone who needed help, without hurting herself. Isn't that something worth knowing? Isn't that a good place to start?"

Silence.

"Look, she would have started singing on her own someday anyway—especially after the rockslide. And when that happened, you would have had no control over what she did first, or how she chose to apply it. Isn't it better that she starts in a good direction now, guided by someone who's been there? The most important thing I taught her was limits, and that's meant to keep her safe."

Hardred's gaze fell to her feet. "I'm sorry." He raked a hand through her unkempt hair. "You're right. I just—I'm worried about her, Alannys. I'm a fair sight more worried now than I was afore you got here."

Alannys sighed. "I know. I am, too. I know it must not seem like it, but I'm trying my best to help. I know there are many who fear the Talents, and people who have them. I know there are those who take...drastic action against people who dare to use their Talent—or even people who have it and never use it at all. With your permission, I would like to make Velya one of my Redeemer's Stewards. It would give her official permission to sing when she needs to sing, and it should help protect her from any backlash."

Hardred considered it. "Single her out, wouldn't it?"

"I suppose that could be possible." Alannys frowned. "I don't generally announce these appointments. If you think it would help, I could publicly announce it, or we could keep it secret. I would give her a silver medallion that proclaims her status. She could show it when it would help her, and hide it when it would not."

"I ken. Guess that'd be all right, then. Breakfast's on the table." Hardred seemed almost grateful to turn away from her.

She understood—that conversation hadn't been much fun for her either. She shook it off, and moved toward the table.

Show it when it will help you, and hide it when it will not.

The similarity of the words she'd just spoken brought Dorramon's voice ringing in her memory, carrying with it a stab of pain so sharp she nearly missed a step. If there was anything she wouldn't have given to be with him right then, she sure couldn't think of it. But her path kept leading her farther away, and for the moment, the only companion she would have was the pain.

♪

Alannys knew she had to keep moving. And after their conversation before breakfast she found it uncomfortable to look Hardred in the eye.

And on top of all that, she was pretty sure didn't want to be in Ashendowne when Tryle woke up. She may very well have changed her opinion of her granddaughter—but her opinion of Alannys was unlikely to ever change.

So after breakfast she sat with Hardred and Kerlin, and explained to them the limits she had given to Velya. Then she held a little ceremony that she made up on the spot, naming Velya a Redeemer's Steward while her father and her brother looked on. After some goodbyes, and a teary-eyed hug from her new steward, Alannys rode out of Ashendowne just before noon, with fog in her head and grit in her eyes from Muse's Fever and most of a night of sleep missed.

She camped that night in a little clearing in a sparse forest she figured was about halfway between Ashendowne and the seaport city of Garrant, judging from Lord Arik's map. The half-day of riding had felt more like a week. She couldn't remember when she'd ever felt so tired. She'd stopped regularly through the afternoon so Quicksilver could rest, eat, and drink, but for herself, she'd done nothing but think.

Ashendowne hadn't exactly been the high point of her journey. Of course, when she looked at it that way, she couldn't really think of *anywhere* she would call the high point of her journey. But Ashendowne certainly hadn't been the low point—she had left the town standing, after all, and she hadn't seen any dear friends home sporting wounds they might never fully recover from. Still, her time there had left her oddly unsettled.

The winds of change are coming for the woman, yes.

The voice made her ears itch, even when it spoke only in her memory. What on earth could he have been talking about? He had seemed half crazy, but aware enough that she would have expected *some* sense somewhere in all of that ranting. But she couldn't figure out what could have made sense in what he'd said.

He had mentioned her 'red-headed friend,' clearly knowing that Elossa was not her friend at all. So they had met, as Hardred had said. What happened after that? Where had Cruthers sent her?

...the mistress of us all...she who commands us all...

That certainly seemed a dramatic way to refer to any woman, no matter how powerful. Could he — could he have been referring to one of the Muses?

Could that creepy old unhinged man really have been a creepy old unhinged murderer?

Or serial killer?

Alannys shivered and flopped down in her makeshift bed of blankets. That kind of thinking was getting her exactly nowhere. Her saddlebags lay on the floor next to her, the flaps open. She regarded them indifferently. Everything she could call hers now she carried in those bags — blankets, oilcloth and tent poles for her camp, a set of battered tin dishes, a flintbox. She couldn't remember everything she had packed, but she thought that covered it. She thought with longing of her luxurious rooms at the Great Palace, with the plush rugs and the enormous soft bed and the huge tapestry of the royal family on the wall, with the gossiping maid and the queen-mother who hated her, and the king who loved her.

She must have been crazy to leave, really, and even crazier to have stayed gone. Even now she continued to ride out toward the coast of Ravanmark, the opposite direction from where she really wanted to go, so things weren't looking any better where her sanity was concerned.

A glimmer in the top of one of the bags caught her eye.

Now what was that? She didn't remember packing any jewels. Oh, wait—of course. That was the relic Lord Arik had given her before she left Mirendasith Hall. The Seeing Stone.

It seemed to call to her, tempting her, testing her sadly deficient willpower. Lord Arik had told her the stone could show Soth the person he was mindlinked to.

She had avoided using the mindlink at all since that day at Mirendasith Hall. Dorramon had nearly broken that day, and so had she. It didn't seem wise to tempt fate by talking again so soon. Besides, she didn't think she could stand any more homesickness. Right now, though, she was lower than she could remember being since she came to Ravanmark, and a glimpse of the king would be a very welcome thing indeed.

She pushed herself up on her elbow and reached out, gently lifting the chain from the bag. In the dim moonlight that filtered into her tent, the domed blue stone glowed as if it was electric. She sat up and huddled over the stone, cupping it carefully in her hands. What was she supposed to do?

She concentrated on Dorramon, allowing every memory she had of him to come into her mind. She focused on those thoughts, and her vision narrowed to encompass only the glowing stone in her hands. The gold veins began to pulsate, throbbing faster and faster as her concentration grew, and she could tell she was on the right track.

Alannys closed her eyes. She remembered Dorramon the last time she had visited him in the Great Hall, sitting in the elaborately decorated golden throne, wearing his jeweled crown. She froze the moment in her mind, carefully inspecting and perfecting her vision of the king until every detail was in place. In that moment she didn't really want to open her eyes to check on the stone; she would have been content to sit like that forever, seeing Dorramon in her mind.

A blinding blue light seared through the little tent, hurting her eyes even though they were closed. It melted her vision of the king into nothing, and when she opened her eyes in sudden fear, all she could see was the afterimage of that light.

Darkness and quiet surrounded her; the light had not been an intruder or an attack. Slowly her eyes adjusted once again to the blackness of the night, and she held up the Seeing Stone.

It glowed from within, soft and blue. She could no longer see the golden veins of the stone — they were obscured by something she couldn't quite believe. Floating somewhere between the flat veined back and the highly domed top was an incredibly detailed, vibrantly colored, three dimensional image of Dorramon. The frozen image sat in his chambers, looking directly at her through the stone. His face looked sad to her, carrying lines and hollows she did not remember. His thick, black hair was ruffled, as though he'd just run his hands through it — she'd seen him do it so many times it made her smile to realize that was what she was looking at now. She had an urge to smooth his hair for him, so strong her fingers twitched around the stone.

But it was his eyes that drew her into the stone, his eyes that made it almost impossible for her to look away. The same blue eyes she had seen every day since he rescued her from Castle Glennayre, right up until she'd left the palace, twinkled back at her now.

Her eyes welled with stinging tears, faced with the one she wanted more than anything but could never have. She wanted to go back so badly it hurt, but she knew there could be nothing for her there.

Alannys?

For a moment, she could only stare at the Seeing Stone in dumbfounded shock, wondering what she had done.

Then she realized the voice came not from her stone, but from her mind.

Alannys? Are you all right? I felt something – strange over here.

I'm – I'm fine. I'm sorry, Dorramon, I didn't mean to worry you. I was just playing with a relic Lord Arik gave me.

A relic? Dorramon sounded the same, but she could tell he was working it out. *From Lord Arik? Do you mean he's given you the Seeing Stone? The Seeing Stone? Soth's Seeing Stone? Do you really think it's a good idea to play with something that belonged to him? We don't understand what most of those things do, or how they do it. What if it hurts you somehow?*

Oh, it's hurt me all right, she said darkly.

Pardon?

No, it's nothing. I'm sorry, I didn't mean to worry you. She was beginning to feel like a broken record. *I guess 'playing' might not have been the best word. I was trying to figure out how the thing works, that's all.*

Are you sure? I don't really get the feeling you are all right. You sound...sad, or upset, or something.

I'm fine, she said, forcing a mental smile.

Alannys –

I said I'm fine! She sat there in stunned silence, unable to believe the way she'd just lashed out at him. *Oh, Dorramon, I'm sorry! You're right, I'm not very fine at all. This entire trip has been an unmitigated disaster. Nothing has gone right, nothing at all. You must have heard.*

I've heard a few things, he said guardedly, *but nothing I would call an unmitigated disaster.*

Really. Alannys was aware of the cutting sarcasm in her tone, but she couldn't seem to stop it. *You can't have heard about Crinn, then. Or how I dragged an assassin right into the heart of Mirendasith Hall. Or the sick and the dead in Falhill.*

Why, just today I put the power of life and death in the hands of an eight year old girl!

Calm down, he lilted, and she felt peace wash over her in a wave. It surprised her—she never knew it was possible to speak-sing through a mindlink. She wanted to resent it, but she couldn't—she missed him too much. *I confess I don't know all the details of those things. But I know they weren't your fault. Lord Arik spoke glowingly of you, from what Raman tells me.*

Raman, she groaned. *Now there's another disaster you can put to my account. He nearly got killed because of me — he never would have been hurt at all if he hadn't been traveling with me.*

Stop that, Dorramon said sharply. *You know he doesn't blame you for anything, and neither do I. If you insist on taking the blame for every single thing that happens in your vicinity, you'll make yourself gray. Look, you know you are welcome back here anytime — nothing would make me happier than hearing you're on your way back right now. But you left the Great Palace for a reason — you wanted to improve public opinion of Talent, turn back that tide to give us a chance to win this thing. Have you done that? Any at all?*

I don't know, she said. *I certainly don't see it.*

That's because you're focused on the things that went badly. You mentioned Falhill. What about Kiarin? There's one young man who is now free to do what he can for those around him — without fear of being called out as a false Redeemer, and without the burden of a role that was never his to fill. Isn't that worth something?

I suppose so. But —

And what about Falhill itself? Dorramon pressed on, ignoring her objections. *There's an entire town that would have sided with Malrec against us before — they thought they already had the Redeemer, so you must be false, and I a fool. Now they support you. You can't put a price on that.*

That's true, she said. *But...but I just...*

Just what? Why are you so determined not to acknowledge

anything positive about what you've done? He waited through a long, silent moment, then sighed. *Tell me about this eight-year-old girl. I assume by 'the power of life and death,' you're talking about music. You taught her to sing.*

Yes, Alannys said, giving away nothing.

Well, tell me why you did that. What happened?

She sighed. *She thought music was unholy – that having Talent made her unholy. There are...some seriously backwards people in that town – including her grandmother. But then her grandmother got hurt. Badly. She tried to sing, to save her, but she's never practiced, so she didn't know how – so I taught her.*

Well, then. Her grandmother might have died, but she didn't. How is that a bad thing?

Nothing's certain, Alannys said, inexplicably irritated by his sunny optimism. *She might still die, and then I'll just have given this girl hope for nothing. And she'll think it's all her fault.*

Hmm. So the fact that failure is possible means that we shouldn't even try.

Alannys said nothing.

Alannys, I don't understand. This kind of defeatist thinking isn't like you. What's wrong?

I don't know. The unfortunate thing was, that was true. *I just...I feel like maybe there's something big out there, Dorramon, bigger than you or me or both of us together, and it's moving against us where we can't even see it.*

Of course, he agreed immediately, sounding confused. *We knew Lord Malrec and his Dark Alliance would do everything they could to stop us.*

Not the Dark Alliance. Maybe even bigger than the Dark Alliance – maybe even worse. This crazy old man in Ashendowne said some things to me...I can't get them out of my head. It could be worse than Malrec, worse than civil war.

Or it could be the senile ramblings of a crazy old man. Right? Or have you seen evidence of this thing for yourself?

No, she said. *I suppose you're right. Everything sounds so different when you talk about it. I just — I don't want to protect my feelings at the expense of the truth. Maybe I have been dwelling too much on the negative.*

Maybe, Dorramon said, with just a hint of wryness. *I don't think I've said anything that was not true. Look, I know this hasn't been easy for you. It hasn't been easy for me, and I'm not even* <u>there.</u> *But I don't think you ever really expected it to be easy, did you?*

No. But I have to admit I didn't expect anything quite this bad.

Well, then. He sounded thoughtful, and it made her nervous. *You have a decision to make here, and no one else can make it for you. You can forge ahead, hope for the best, and keep doing what you're doing, taking the good with the bad. Or you can turn around and come straight back to the palace. You know you'll be welcomed back with open arms.*

She knew. And for a moment the image of that was all she could see, and the loneliness and longing it brought with it would have easily been enough to have her breaking camp and riding for the Great Palace that instant.

Only...only it also brought involuntary thoughts of his engagement to the woman who had a prior claim on his heart, of the as-yet-faceless Princess Varilyn who would be usurping her place at his side, of the royal wedding looming in his future that she could not be part of.

She squashed all of those thoughts, frantically, hoping he hadn't gotten a glimpse of any of them.

Alannys, I —

You're right, she cut him off. What could either of them say now that would make any difference, in the end? She'd already pushed him perilously close to breaking once before. She would not do it again. *There's nothing for it but to go on, or go back. And how can I turn back, if I'm making any difference out here at all? Despairing won't solve anything.*

Alannys... He sighed. *Alannys, I'm not trying to push you on with this. Honestly. I just don't want to see you give up if you're going to regret it later.*

I know. Thank you for talking it out with me.

You're very welcome. Talking isn't much, but it seems it's all I can give you. The bitterness in his tone surprised her, but she understood how he felt. *Good night, Alannys.*

Good night, Dorramon.

All of their conversations lately had seemed so sad. It made sense; she understood it, but she still hated it.

She knew it didn't matter what she thought or how she felt. Going back was the only thing that would make it better.

And there was no going back for her, for more reasons than she cared to acknowledge just then. So out here she was, and for now, out here she would stay.

No matter how much it hurt.

She bundled up in her blankets and cupped the Seeing Stone in her hands, staring into it for the interminable hours before she fell asleep.

♫

Alannys had another long ride the next day in the sparsely populated backcountry of Brookeshire Holding, through the rolling prairie plain that seemed never-ending. The wind blew across her, whipping her cloak around to her side until she lost patience, took it off and stuffed it in her saddlebag. She passed fields where the grass swayed in the wind, taller than Quicksilver's legs. She passed other fields where the grass had already been cut and raked into piles of long, golden hay. But she never saw any houses, or people.

In short, it was a miserable and lonely day's ride.

About the time her stomach started to seriously clamor for dinner, she started passing houses. They were widely spaced, with large gardens, amid big open fields. She started to feel like maybe she was entering civilization again, and she was grateful.

The houses grew closer and closer together. She began to see people, and livestock, and children playing. The dirt path turned to dirt road, then to cobblestone.

She was in Garrant.

The city was incredible, utterly unlike anything she had been in before. Garrant was huge, sprawling towards the sea in a haphazard stretch of cobblestone roads and brick buildings. The buzz of conversations, the clatter of horses's hooves, and the rattle of carriages all blended together into a cheerful din that made the place seem bustling and alive.

Sailors loped by her in crisp linen, heading for the ports with a uniformly peculiar stride that bespoke a familiarity with rolling decks. Women in long, fancy dresses with beaded bodices hurried past in short strides, their heads held high, barely acknowledging each other with slight nods, and acknowledging her not at all. A boy raced across the cobblestone street in a blue top and knickers, running scrolls.

A baker passed slowly by her, pushing wooden a cart whose shelves and bins were full of breads and rolls, cakes and pastries. The delicious smell of warm bread washed over her, and she twisted in the saddle to watch him. The man was what she might politely have called portly, his fleshy jowls wobbling as he called out a steady cadence of items and prices.

After the experiences she'd had lately, Alannys watched all around her, half holding her breath, expecting at any moment for a cry to go up, for the happy faces around her to turn angry.

Two adolescent girls walked down the other side of the road, their heads close together, giggling and stealing glances at a boy about their own age, who paused to buy a roll from the baker. He finished his business and wandered off, and the girls giggled after him, and the baker continued on his way.

And nobody seemed to notice her at all.

She sighed in a puff of relief, then turned Quicksilver sharply and reined up near the cart. "I'd like a roll, please," she said, dismounting.

He showed her a toothy smile. "Certainly. Two coppers."

She dug the coins from her pouch, deposited them in the baker's sweaty palm, then carefully plucked a roll from the cart. It was as big as a grapefruit, and it still felt warm in her hands. "Thank you. This smells wonderful."

The baker inclined his head, and his grin got even toothier. It was kind of creepy, really, and she fought the urge to back up. Quicksilver stomped behind her, and snorted.

The baker was looking at her now, his eyes glinting from deep in the fleshy folds of his face. "Need something else, miss?"

"No," she said immediately, scrambling for an escape, "no, I—actually I could use some help. You wouldn't know where I might find an inn, would you?"

"An inn." He settled back on his heels and regarded her a moment, taking in her riding attire and the sword hanging at her side. "There are many inns in Garrant, but I can think of only one suitable for such a fine young lady as yourself." Something about the way he leaned on the words seemed peculiar, but he didn't give her a chance to ask any questions. He pointed down a lane intersecting the road she had come in on. "Follow that, take a left at the brick building with the red shutters. It'll be the second place on your right."

"Thank you," she said, and started to leave, then turned back. "Forgive me, but can you tell me the name of the place? So I know what I'm looking for?"

For just a moment, as she turned, Alannys thought she

caught a glimpse of something twisted and unpleasant on the baker's sweaty face. If it had ever existed at all, though, it was gone by the time she faced him, replaced by his customary conciliatory, if toothy, smile. "A thousand humble apologies, miss! But I swear I do not remember."

Why was she suddenly so certain he was lying to her? She pushed the thought aside; it didn't really matter. The man had been only helpful, if also somewhat creepy, and did not deserve her suspicion. "Thank you," she said again, and mounted back up, glad to leave the baker and his toothy grin behind.

♫

It didn't take Alannys five minutes to locate the inn. It was exactly where the baker had directed, second place on the right. It was a two-story plank building, with a wooden shingle roof. The sign swaying under the eave said "The Inn of the Abandoned Lord." Small wonder the baker hadn't been able to recall the name; she'd never seen an inn with a name quite like that. It seemed sad, somehow, and at the same time it gave her a shiver.

She tide Quicksilver to the hitching post out front, and went inside. A young fellow with shaggy blond hair sat behind the tall counter, reading a little leather-bound book. That surprised her—she imagined books were handmade and very expensive here. And if she wasn't mistaken, most people couldn't read anyway. His head jerked up at the clatter of the wooden spoons tied to the door.

He stared at her, and all the color drained from his face. His book slid off of his lap to the floor, but he didn't seem to notice. He stood up and leaned over the counter, rubbing his eyes and peering at her.

"Hello?" she said, taken aback by this reaction.

The young man stood up straight again, and his eyes fell on Songstrike. He stumbled, and caught himself on the counter. "My—my Lady," he choked, "words cannot express how happy I am to see you here. Welcome to the Inn of the Abandoned Lord!"

She frowned, watching him closely, wondering what could be behind his behavior. "Thank you."

He smiled at her brightly. It looked odd, really — such a bright smile stretched across a complexion that looked about two breaths away from fainting. "This really is amazing, my Lady — just imagine, you, visiting the Abandoned Lord! They'll all be talking about this for weeks — months!" He finally seemed to notice her confusion. "Can I...help you with something, my Lady?"

Her frown deepened. "Well, I had hoped to get a room."

"A *room?*" His eyes bulged and all at once he was spluttering again. "You mean — do you really mean to say — you want to — *stay* here?"

If her frown got any deeper, she didn't think she'd ever be able to relax her face again. "The baker in the main street sent me here."

"He did? That's a bit of a surprise — but you *agree?*" The young man was frantic with excitement.

Alannys held up a hand. "Look, what's your name?"

"Corran, if it please thee, my Lady. Corran! I can't believe *you* took the time to ask for *my* name, I — "

"Look, Corran. This is an inn, right?"

"Yes, my Lady."

"And you have rooms available?"

"*Yes,* my Lady!"

"Then I would like a room. What do I need to do?"

"*Nothing,* my Lady! Nothing at all! I will take care of everything!" He fumbled under the counter and handed her a brass key. "Here you are, room twelve. Second floor, back of the building." His smile seemed etched into his face the same way her frown was etched into hers.

"Thank you," she said, turning the key over in her

hand. "How much do I owe you?"

"*Owe* me?" He sounded honestly scandalized. "I would never *dream* of charging *you* for a room! Stay as long as you like—there is no charge."

She looked from his earnest face to the key in her hand, and back again. She was missing something. She had to be —but she couldn't fathom what. "I—I see," she said, even though she did not. "Thank you."

She could feel Corran's eyes boring into her back as she left the room.

♫

Alannys found room twelve at the top of the creaky wooden staircase, at the end of the long, musty hallway. The lock on the door made worrisome clanking noises when it turned over, but the door opened when she tried it. She wondered how long the room had sat vacant—the air that rushed out was even mustier than that in the hallway.

Inside she found a small sitting room and a smaller bedroom. A large, worn couch with a scarred coffee table filled most of the sitting room, and in the bedroom she found a big bed with a sagging middle, and two small end tables with giant, smelly, tallow candles on them. A chest of drawers stood against one wall, filled with heavy quilts.

The place seemed comfortable enough. But Corran had unsettled her—she didn't feel right leaving her things behind, so she went down to dinner still wearing her cloak and sword.

The tavern was on the first floor of the inn, in the back. As soon as she walked in the door, an unnatural hush fell over the room, and every person there turned to regard her. None of them seemed hostile, but still...there was something creepy about the silent attention of that group. She attempted a weak smile, then ducked her head and went to a corner table to sit down. Maybe once she was out of the way, things would return to normal.

The scrape of the wooden chair on the floor was loud and jarring in the quiet tavern. It creaked like the indignant squawk of a live thing when she sat down, and the grating, protesting sound it made scooting up to the table set her teeth on edge. She sat there in the acutely uncomfortable silence, staring at her folded hands on the tabletop, thinking how much easier it would be if the floor would just swallow her.

For a moment, people continued to watch her sitting there, as though they expected strange and wonderful things from the Redeemer of the Realm sitting down to eat. After a few minutes, though, they began to turn back to their companions and return to their conversations.

She closed her eyes and heaved a huge sigh of relief.

"Nosy lot, ain't they?" The voice was loud, and right in her ear.

Alannys sucked in her breath and jerked around to find the owner of this strange voice. Without consciously intending to, she dropped her hand to Songstrike's hilt.

"Whoa, now, calm yourself! Old Lomak ain't gonna harm you!" The man who stood before her held his hands up, a metal mug in each. His skin was withered, and his long gray hair hung greasy and unbound. "I brought you a drink. Welcome to the Abandoned Lord, Lady Alannys."

"Sorry," she said, forcing herself to relax. He set one of the drinks on the table in front of her with a thump, then sat down across from her. "I don't know why I'm so jumpy. I've never seen so many people so happy to see me."

He waved a dismissive hand. "Ah, it's understandable. People out there are either don't know what you're here for, or they do and they hate it. What can you expect?"

She picked up the mug and took an experimental sip. It was a dark, foamy ale. The first taste nearly choked her, but after that it wasn't so bad. Something about the old man's words didn't sit right with her, but she couldn't put her finger on what it was. She was finally getting some recognition, some positive attention from people who knew who she was. Why didn't she feel good about it?

The ringing sound of a spoon hitting the rim of a metal cup silenced the conversations and laughter in the little tavern. She looked up and saw Corran standing on the bar, his arm raised. "My friends!" he cried. "You've heard the rumors—I'm pleased to tell you they are all true. Lady Alannys, Redeemer of the Realm, has this very day visited the Inn of the Abandoned Lord!"

Cheers went up around the room, and mugs were raised. Alannys flushed and sank lower in her chair, drinking ale as if she hoped to hide behind the mug.

"But now," Corran continued, as though he could spontaneously combust from sheer excitement at any second, "now I can bring you even more glorious tidings! Lady Alannys is at this very moment *in this very tavern with us!*"

He gestured with outstretched arms to her, and even louder cheers sounded in the crowded room. Every person in the tavern raised their mug to her. She had to admit it, for all his oddities, Corran could really sell it.

She just wished she knew, in this particular circumstance, what exactly 'it' was.

She gave her mug a halfhearted wave in the general direction of the crowd. "Yes, hurray for me," she muttered.

Lomak smiled and winked at her.

"So drink up, my friends, and eat and laugh! Tonight we celebrate! Our Abandoned Lord Soth has at last returned to us!"

♫

The tavern erupted into cheers around Alannys. Somebody let out a cat whistle. Others shouted "hear, hear!" and thumped their mugs on the tables.

Alannys sat suddenly upright, stiff and cold. A tingling chill raced down her spine. She had a bad, bad feeling she'd just found out what 'it' was. "What? What did he just say?"

"Don't worry, my Lady," Lomak said, wiping foam from his mouth with his sleeve. "You're among friends. We understand the truly divine nature of Soth the Demented. Lord Diabon tells us that you are the great Lord reincarnated. What more can we ask for?"

She blinked at him. These people thought she was Soth — and they *celebrated* that? "I don't understand," she said in a small voice. "Are you telling me that you still regard Soth as the Muse's chosen one?"

Lomak thumped his mug down on the table, his face flushing with sudden anger. "The Muses! Spiteful, jealous creatures, they are — who would take such a gifted, powerful man — their finest creation! — and cast him down! They've shown their nature. Our Abandoned Lord is high above the Muses."

Her brain felt numb. These people worshiped Soth. They *worshiped Soth!* She stared at the crowd of revelers, all glorying in the idea that the devil had returned to Ravanmark.

"Say now," Lomak said, "why are you asking about the Muses anyway? Seems you should know their deceit better than anyone."

"Me?" Alannys looked at him in sudden fear and forced herself to laugh. It was a tinny, hollow sound. "I was just — you know — making conversation."

"Conversation? About your sworn enemies?" Lomak's face darkened.

The fake laughter was getting hard to keep up. She was attracting odd glances from other people near them. How could she get out of here? "Well, sure, I mean — what can it hurt?"

Lomak worked that through and then he laughed, a good deal more genuinely than her. "That's right—don't that beat all! You sure showed them, coming back like this!"

She was beginning to sound sick, so she stopped laughing, and stood up. "I think I'm going to go lie down for a bit."

"What? Don't you want something to eat?"

"No—no, thanks. I've had all I can stand."

He eyed her dubiously. "Are you sure?"

She backed away from the table, clumsy in her haste, wanting nothing more than to be away from this place, these people. "Positive. Thank you."

"As you wish, my Lady. I'm going to go celebrate. They will all want to speak with the one who shared Soth's table!"

"You do that," she said, but Lomak was already gone. She feared that leaving the crowded tavern would be difficult, but strangely the people were too busy celebrating to pay much attention to her—the supposed reason for their celebration. She edged out the door, and into the hallway.

Then she ran. She took the stairs two at a time, and pounded down the hallway to her room. She could barely manage to fit the key in the lock with her shaking hands. But she made it in, and she slammed the door behind her.

She leaned back against the door, panting raggedly. What could she do now? Hide in her room for the rest of the night? She didn't really want it spread around the kingdom that she had stayed with Soth-worshipers. That kind of support she did not need.

There was only one thing for it, then. She had to leave, and the sooner the better. Coming here had been a mistake, and it was only compounded with every moment she stayed.

She gripped the key tightly in her hand, and let herself out of the room. The stairs creaked and groaned as she hopped down them, but the hallway was thankfully deserted.

Once again, she had jumped without thinking things through all the way. She was still trying to figure out how to explain her sudden departure when she walked into the office, and Corran jumped to his feet behind the counter. "My Lady!"

"Corran! Tell me, have you stabled my horse yet?"

He couldn't hold her gaze. "No, my Lady, I am sorry — I hurried to spread the news in the tavern. I'll do it right now."

"Don't bother," she said sharply, freezing him in place, turned halfway to the door. She slapped the key down on the counter. "Thank you for the room. But I'm afraid I won't be needing it."

"Wh — what? I don't understand."

"I'm leaving, Corran."

"What! My Lady, Lomak told me you were feeling unwell. I deeply apologize if it's something I did — perhaps I should not have made the announcement."

"No. I am not who you think I am. I am not Soth, or his reincarnation. I will not accept hospitality intended for a man I despise."

Corran stared at her as though she'd slapped him. "A man you...why did you come here, if that is how you feel?" His face clouded with anger, making him seem strange and threatening. "Did you come to mock us?"

"Not at all. I came, I am afraid, from ignorance. But now that I know the nature of this place, I cannot stay. I trust you will announce my renunciation and departure with the same fervor with which you announced my arrival."

"You can count on it," Corran said grimly, looking at

her with a hard expression, as if he intended to stare her down. "You must know this will not be forgotten."

She didn't know what to say to that. She wouldn't forget this either, no matter how much she wanted to.

She left the key on the counter and untied Quicksilver from the post. With a clatter of hooves on cobblestones, the Inn of the Abandoned Lord disappeared behind her.

♫

Now that she knew Soth-worshipers existed in Ravanmark—and were active in Garrant—Alannys resolved to exercise more care in choosing her next inn. On the last street before the beachfront, she saw the Sand and Sea Inn and Tavern. It was a tidy brick building, with a carefully tended yard and a stone walkway. Any other time, she would have walked right in.

But today, she'd just fled from a crowd of manic people trying to make her the devil. She rode past the place twice, carefully inspecting the building, the surroundings, and the people walking in and out.

She couldn't see anything that looked like a warning sign, so she went in. She knew it was no guarantee, but at least she'd done what she could.

The office was home-like, and the middle-aged couple behind the counter were friendly, but not unduly interested. She got an upstairs room, and it was a relief to walk through the door feeling like she would actually stay the night this time. The room had a writing desk on one wall, and heavy curtains covering another wall. A featherbed waited against the far wall, piled high with pillows.

It was already getting dark outside, so she didn't bother checking out the view behind the curtains. Half a mug of ale and a roll had done little for her hunger, so she dropped her cloak on the bed and went down to the tavern to get some dinner.

A barmaid glanced up at her when she walked in, then

went back to cleaning the counter. A fellow with a foul-smelling pipe sat at the counter, drinking something from a tall cup and blowing smoke rings toward the ceiling. Alannys took a table in the corner of the room, as far as possible from the bar and the people.

A serving girl came immediately to the table, wiping her hands on her apron. She wore her thick brown hair in a braid that hung past her waist, pulled tightly back from her face in a manner that accentuated her high, sharp cheekbones. "Good evening!" Her gaze took in Songstrike at Alannys's side, and her eyes narrowed knowingly. "Ah, yes. Welcome to the Sand and Sea. What can I get for you, my Lady?"

Alannys sat up straighter, not exactly comfortable. She knew it wasn't unusual for people to recognize her—people who were not Soth-worshipers, even—but she was still jumpy. "Stew and bread, please, with berry juice."

The girl nodded once and left.

Alannys sat back in her chair, trying to relax. Except for the smoker at the bar and herself, the tavern was empty, so there was little chance of trouble here.

She actually began to doze off. The long ride and the excitement at the Abandoned Lord had taken their toll on her, and the room was warm and quiet. She probably could have slept all night right there in the chair. But the smell of hot food roused her, and she opened her eyes to see the serving girl placing a deep bowl of steaming, chunky stew and a platter of bread in front of her. A pitcher of cold berry juice and a cup sat in the middle of the table.

"Thank you," she said, reaching for the spoon. "That was fast."

The serving girl laughed, a cynical sound with a hard edge. "You didn't have a lot of competition. You're in pretty late."

Alannys nodded, stirring the stew around in the bowl, wondering idly what sort of meat was in it. "I'm sorry about that. I hadn't planned on coming in this late. This is actually my second stop. The first inn I went to was...well, it left some things to be desired."

The girl laughed again, and again it struck Alannys how little true joy there was in the sound. "You don't have to apologize to me, my Lady. 'Tis my job—sailors, thieves, and Redeemers, I serve them all. Everybody's got to eat, and everybody's got to sleep. What you do past that is your own lookout." She scooped up the pitcher and dumped berry juice into the cup with a careless motion, but not a drop splashed out onto the table. "Tell me, where did you go first?"

Alannys hesitated, considering the girl's knowing eyes and jaded laugh. She knew she was opening herself to ridicule. "The Inn of the Abandoned Lord."

To her surprise, the girl did not laugh. "I see." She swept the nearly empty tavern with a glance. "My name is Thera," she said, as though revealing a weakness of her own. "Do you mind if I sit down with you?"

"No, not at all."

She sank into a chair across from Alannys as though her strings had been cut, wiping her hands down her apron again. "Thanks. You seem nice, Alannys." Her eyes looked expectant.

"Thank y—"

"It's not a compliment here. It's really not. Garrant is a huge place, with a big seaport constantly bringing people in and hauling them out again. Things move fast here, and a nice person like you—well, it's like you just fell off the turnip wagon, as they say."

"I—I see." Alannys reached for a slice of bread to cover her embarrassment.

"Now don't get me wrong. I just met you and I already

like you—you seem friendly, and nice. I'm just warning you, that could get you into trouble here."

"I think it already has."

"I don't doubt it. I don't think there's anywhere else in Ravanmark where so many ideas come together so fast. In Garrant you'll find people who believe in the benevolence of the Muses. But you'll also find people who think the Muses are just a pretty fairy tale left over from a time when people didn't know any better. Some people believe that Soth the Demented rules over the Seven Hells on the shattered pieces of Cilahar Island, working to ensnare us all. Others believe there is no Cilahar and never was—and no Soth, either, only tales invented by the monarchy to frighten people so they crave the protection of a ruler. You'll find people who do not believe in Muses or Soth, but still fear the danger of the Talents. And then there are people like those at the Abandoned Lord—those perverse people who find in tales of evil something to admire."

Alannys stared at her, the soup spoon hanging useless from her hand. "I—I had no idea."

Thera shrugged and stood up. "How could you? The Great Palace is a wonderful place—regal and steeped in tradition, fitting for people who've ruled for centuries. But it's also slow-moving and out of touch, and I don't think anything about it can prepare you for a place like Garrant. I think you mean well. But I'm not sure you or your message have any place here."

Alannys swallowed past a hard lump in her throat. For all of her bluntness, Thera did not seem unfriendly, and that worried Alannys even more—with no reason to doubt, she had to assume everything Thera said had been true.

And that scared her most of all.

♫

After dinner in the tavern, Alannys wandered back towards the stairs. The big comfortable bed waiting upstairs called to her, and she had no thought of doing anything but sleeping for tonight.

Until she noticed the small room next to the stairs with a handwritten sign over the door that said "Laundry." At that moment, having her filthy riding clothes cleaned suddenly became the most important thing in her life.

She leaned in the door. A middle-aged woman sat by a steaming wooden tub, scrubbing an apron up and down a washboard. The cluttered little room smelled heavily of lye soap, and the roaring fire kept it sweltering. "Excuse me?"

The woman pushed her damp hair out of her face, and glanced at the doorway. "What do you want?" Her tone had an edge.

Alannys blinked, taken aback. "Can you tell me if there is a place near here where I might buy some clothes? I'd really like to have my things washed, but I don't have extras." In truth her single complete change of clothes was somewhere out in the stable with her saddle and bags, but it seemed easier not to go into detail.

The laundress dropped the apron back into the sudsy water and stared at her. "What sort of person travels with only one set of clothes? Well, to each his own, I suppose, even if it's stupid. There's a tailor's shop two doors down from the inn."

"Thank you." Alannys forced the words past gritted teeth, determined to remain courteous in the face of this woman's rudeness. "It shouldn't take long. Will you still be here?"

"I'd hardly be anywhere else. This is my job, you know. And I can't tell you what a delightful job it is, what a joy it is to serve people without the decency to arrive at a civilized hour."

Alannys bit back a rude response and pulled her head out of the laundry room. Had that woman been so unpleasant because she recognized Alannys, or was she that way with everyone?

It didn't matter. Alannys pushed the thought aside and went out through the inn's little lobby. The laundress had not mentioned which side of the inn the shop was on, but thankfully light spilling out from an open door illuminated the sign. She couldn't make out the words, but the large picture of needle and thread was enough.

Lanterns hung around the room, providing a warm, cheery light in the shop. The floor was a maze of tables and bins, filled with different styles of garments. The tailor himself stood behind a little counter, regarding her with narrow eyes over a long nose, and a mouth drawn down at the corners.

"Good evening," she said. "I've come to buy some clothes."

"Well, you've come to the right place." He had a reedy voice, and his words were short and clipped. "You could certainly use them." He sniffed, and looked back down at the needle he was threading.

Alannys stared at him. Again? Was everybody in this town nasty, or did they just dislike her in particular? The laundress she could have excused as coincidence, but after the baker sent her to an inn full of Soth-worshipers, and now this tailor — apparently Garrant in general had no use for her. She remembered Thera's warning, and wondered if this was all related. Maybe she really *was* outclassed here, and maybe none of these big city people would ever give her a chance.

No. That was defeatist thinking, and she resolved not to give in to it. If Thera thought she couldn't win here...well, she'd just have to prove Thera wrong. She squared her shoulders and went to the nearest table. She had to go almost all the way around the big room, but in the end she selected three pairs of leather riding breeches, three linen workshirts, and a pair of riding gloves — Quicksilver's reins had rubbed her hands raw. She dumped her selections on the counter in front of the tailor.

He looked down his skinny nose at them, then at her. "I see that your taste has not improved, then."

Her face burned, and she struggled to control her temper. "Yes, apparently not. But a person riding a horse should be able to wear riding clothes, don't you think?"

He made no answer, flipping through the little pile and tallying up the price. "Two golds and a silver," he said shortly.

She dropped the coins on the counter, scooped up her purchases, and headed for the door, eager to leave before she lost control and vented her true feelings. Back in her room, she changed into a set of clean clothes, and took her old ones back down to the laundry.

The woman was every bit as pleased to see her as she had been the first time. "Are you sure these aren't better suited for burning than washing?"

Alannys heaved a long-suffering sigh. "How much, please?"

"Three coppers. But I'll toss them in the fire for free."

Alannys paid her, and left before any of her frustration could work its way out. Garrant seemed to be brimming with unpleasant people. Perhaps it shouldn't have surprised her that the best part of her day was pulling the covers up over her head and going to sleep.

♫

The curtains in her room turned out to conceal a balcony, and a gorgeous view of the ocean. She opened them the next morning, and found she could see the piers, with little fishing boats tied to them, and the big docks, where the enormous sailing ships rested. The shore bustled with activity; stevedores hauled goods on and off the ships, grunting and cursing, and women trailing children in their wakes shopped at the seaside merchant stands, raising a busy, happy chatter. And behind it all, the deep, azure, undulating sea cast salty breezes over the town the way the fishermen cast their nets.

Alannys dragged a chair out onto the balcony and sat there, just watching the seashore. She liked Garrant better this way, observed from afar, with no sharp words or cutting glances.

Still, as much as she would have liked to, she couldn't sit on the balcony all day soaking up the sun and the sea. Ravanmark's clock was ticking—and so was hers.

So she strapped on Songstrike and her beltpouch, threw her riding cloak over her shoulders, and hopped down the staircase, doing her best to summon up a positive attitude.

The tavern was busier this morning, with a constant din of conversation and clattering dishes that she could hear before she even opened the door.

"Well, now, good morning to you, Redeemer," came Thera's wry voice as soon as Alannys stepped through the door, cutting cleanly through the noise of the room. "So you survived your first night in Garrant after all."

All of the conversation in the room fell silent for a moment, as every person there turned to look at Alannys. Her face burned and her heart beat double-time; all of her experiences had taught her that being called out in public was not a good thing.

Ever.

They looked at her for a long, uncomfortable moment. Were they sizing up a threat, expecting promises, or excuses? She couldn't tell. There were too many people, and any time she tried to look at any one of them, her nerves got the better of her and her eyes shied away as if of their own accord. Still the silence dragged painfully on.

"Hi," she said finally, lamely.

One by one people lost interest and turned back to

their meals and their companions, as if the act of speaking had proved her human after all, and there was no longer anything interesting to see. She exhaled in a relieved puff and headed for her table in the back, Thera following close on her heels. "Why did you do that?" she asked, as quietly as she could manage.

"Do what?" Thera's confusion sounded at least as genuine as anything else she said — the jaded cynicism that permeated every syllable she spoke made it hard to tell when she was being sincere. "I said good morning. Should I pretend I don't know you?"

"You called me the Redeemer!" Alannys was trying to stay calm, but it was difficult with all the adrenaline dumped into her veins by a nervous system just beginning to figure out that she was not actually under attack. "In front of all these *people!*"

Thera frowned. "I'm sorry, I didn't know it was a secret."

"It's not, it's just..." Alannys jerked a chair back from the table and flopped into it.

"You're afraid of a group of random strangers? That doesn't seem quite in line with what you are doing."

"No — it just feels like nothing good ever comes of being called out as the Redeemer in public. Besides, I got the impression that you don't much believe in Muses or Redeemers."

"I don't. I think you're well-meaning, Alannys, but deluded, calling yourself the Redeemer and doing what you're doing. No, I don't believe. But neither do I shy away from what a thing is. I prefer to call a fig a fig, Alannys, and the King of Ravanmark himself held a ceremony naming you the Redeemer. It seems odd that the rest of us aren't supposed to say it."

"I suppose you're right," Alannys said. "Perhaps instead of worrying about hiding it, I should be hoping for the day I can announce it anywhere, without worrying about who's around."

"Yes, exactly." Thera's laughter finally sounded like there was some real humor behind it. "I'm just doing my part to hasten that day." She hurried off towards the kitchen.

Alannys supposed it was possible, given all she'd experienced in Garrant, that Thera was actually playing her for a fool.

But she hoped not. She couldn't have said why — with her cutting sarcasm and street-smart bluntness, it would have been very easy for Thera to be unlikeable. But she wasn't — she was jaded, but she was friendly, and behind all the talk was a person who cared enough to warn her when she first came to town. Alannys had taken it as her challenge to prove Thera wrong.

But somehow, she didn't get the impression Thera minded.

♬

A platter of eggs and bacon and one cup of juice later, Alannys stood up from the table.

"Off to save the world again today?" Thera asked, clearing a nearby table. The remark could have been cutting, but she was smiling.

Alannys couldn't help an apprehensive glance around, even though the place had cleared considerably since she came in. She smiled, but it felt forced. "As much of it as I can manage, anyway."

Thera laughed, but whether it was at her response or her discomfort, Alannys couldn't tell. "I appreciate the effort, anyway. Good luck with your holy quest, Alannys."

Alannys liked Thera. At least, she thought she did. So why did their conversations always make her so uncomfortable?

She visited the stables and fed Quicksilver the apple she'd saved from breakfast, but she did not take him out.

Today she would go on foot—after all, she was here to make friends and influence people.

Alannys walked out into the bustling street, feeling invigorated by the bright morning sun on her face. Then it made her sneeze.

She almost laughed out loud. That was Garrant, after all—no matter how determined you were to be positive, someone or something could be counted on to put you back in your place. All she could hope was that it wasn't an omen.

She still remembered her unpleasant visit to the tailor's the night before, so she started walking the other direction this morning. The street flowed with people—she was continually surprised by the sheer number of *people* in Garrant, and how they always seemed to be out doing things. She was fairly certain the city never really slept, even in the dead of night.

The morning was cool and crisp, and every sound around her seemed clear and distinct. She could hear birds in the treetops, hooves clicking and carriage wheels rumbling on the cobblestone, and casual conversations of people she passed. And then she heard a different sound.

"Fresh breads! Fresh hot breads! Wheat rolls, two coppers! Breakfast rolls, four coppers! Meat pies, jelly pastries! Fresh breads!"

Alannys stopped cold and frantically searched the street. Where was he? She finally caught sight of him, across the street and a few buildings down, at the same moment he saw her. His eyes widened, and his fleshy face paled.

The baker spun his cart around and ran.

Alannys charged after him, dodging people, ducking around carts and wagons, keeping her eyes on the overweight man in the apron and the bright red cart he pushed. Her feet pounded on the cobblestone, and her heart thumped in her ears.

She was gaining on him.

The baker turned his cart sharply down a little alley. She skidded around the corner after him, panting raggedly. He was only a few steps away. "Stop!" she shouted.

He glanced over his shoulder, and his wide eyes got even bigger. He let go of his cart and ducked around it, leaving it in her path.

Alannys swore, and dodged the cart. Where did he think he was going? She pushed harder, and caught up to him in a burst of desperate speed. "I said stop!"

The baker ran on.

Her last thread of patience snapped. Alannys swerved sideways and plowed into the man. He bounced into the brick wall of the building beside him and stumbled.

She grabbed him by the collar and shoved him up against the wall. He stared at her in abject fear, his blotchy red face dripping with sweat. He shook his head and his mouth worked, but he couldn't seem to make a sound.

"Come on," Alannys snapped. "Spit it out."

"D-d-don't hurt me!" The words came out in a pitiful squeal.

"What makes you think I'm going to hurt you? You're bigger than me—what makes you think I *can?*"

His eyes flicked to Songstrike. "You're that woman, the one who sings. The one who says she's the Redeemer."

"So you do know who I am. Is that why you sent me to the Abandoned Lord last night?"

He couldn't hold her gaze. He nodded, bouncing his fleshy cheeks against her hand. She jerked away, and he collapsed into a heap in the trash along the base of the building. She eyed him with disgust. "Is this whole town mean-spirited and rude? That was hardly any way to treat someone who approached you with friendliness." He made no response, and she sighed. "Tell me, baker, what do you think I should do with you?"

He began to shake, shivering like a cowering puppy. "Strike me down with your sword, my Lady, or burn me with your song." He sat up, with his head high, almost—almost as if he was offering his neck to her blade. It was the first spark of courage she had seen from him, and it astounded her.

Alannys looked at him for a long, silent moment. "I will do neither." She offered her hand to help him up.

The baker stared at her. "What?"

She grasped his hand and hauled him to his feet. "I'm not going to do anything to you. I'm sorry I frightened you. I only wanted to ask you why you sent me to that place." She wiped her hand on her breeches.

"I—I am humbled, my Lady. You have shown me mercy, when I did nothing to warrant it. I confess, I'm surprised."

Alannys laughed, but it sounded almost as uncomfortable as she felt. "I don't doubt it. Mercy seems to be a rather scarce commodity in Garrant. Look, you don't need to fear me. I'm trying to save Ravanmark, not destroy it."

"Save Ravanmark?" Skepticism dripped from the words. "From what? The king and the lords will fight the war—not you."

"From fear, my friend. Why do you think Lord Malrec has a chance with this at all? The same sort of fear that prompted you to send me to the Abandoned Lord last night will proved disastrous for the entire realm if we cannot change it."

"Fear? *That's* what you're doing, how you propose to save the realm—going around meeting people so they won't fear you?"

"That's right. Do you have a better idea?"

He dropped his gaze. "No, my Lady. Nothing else will convince them, I'm afraid."

"And do you find me fearsome, now that you have spoken with me?"

"No. No, even though we have—disagreed. I misjudged you."

"Then tell people that. They don't need to fear me, and they don't need to fear my Talent. The Talents are here to stay. If we can't accept them, we are doomed."

"Yes, my Lady. I have heard King Dorramon can sing. But I am still more afraid of Lord Malrec of Glennayre than him."

She put a hand on his shoulder. "Tell people that, too. If Lord Malrec prevails, we will all have a lot more to worry about than Soth-worshipers. A benevolent person with musical Talent is nothing to fear. A malicious person who can paint, though...that's a different matter. A different matter indeed."

"Indeed," he echoed, and turned back to his abandoned bread cart. "This isn't going to be easy for you. I wish you luck on your holy mission."

She stood frozen in place as he wheeled his cart out of the alley and left. His words struck a cold chill in her, reminding her suddenly of Thera's words earlier that morning. Thera, who thought she was tilting at windmills. *Well-meaning but deluded,* Thera had called her.

What would Thera call her when she found out she had run a man down and manhandled him? Was *that* a valid means of changing minds? Hadn't she put herself on the level of Lord Malrec here?

Could she really call it a victory, won by means such as that?

♫

Alannys emerged from the alley firmly resolved to do better. The baker was thankfully nowhere in sight—either she had stood back there grappling with her moral failings longer than she'd realized, or he had really hustled out of there.

She wandered on up the street, watching the people of Garrant walking, talking, shopping, eating—generally going about their daily lives. It all seemed so far removed from the concerns that drove her—and they thought so too, judging by the sidelong glances she was getting. With so many people, how could she hope to sway enough of them to make a difference in the time she had? Even in Falhill—a fraction of this size—it had taken a catastrophe.

A couple of teenaged boys loafed in front of one of the shops she passed. A partly unloaded wagon sat nearby, it and its load of crates ignored as they leaned against the wall, evidently preferring gossip to work.

Unfortunately, from the way they were pointing, it seemed pretty clear they were gossiping about her.

She wondered what they were saying. 'Hey, there's that well-meaning but deluded woman who calls herself the Redeemer.' Or maybe, 'I hear she keeps company with Soth-worshipers.'

Or even, 'Oh, her—she's the one who chases down people who don't agree with her and roughs them up.'

She sighed, walking on past the boys. If she didn't like that perception of herself, it was up to her to change it. But how? Just exactly how was she supposed to go about changing people's minds about music when there was nothing for a singer to do? A woman brushed by her with a hard, unfriendly stare, and Alannys sighed again.

Look, Muses, she thought, *I don't know if you can hear me, or if you're even real. But everyone thinks I'm working for you, and I think you want me to succeed. And I want to succeed. But I need a start—just a little crack.* She closed her eyes and turned her face up to the mid-morning sun, hoping its warmth would lift her spirits. *Give me a hint, here—some kind of sign. What am I supposed to be doing?*

She opened her eyes, hoping for blazing letters across the sky, or an angelic vision to point the way. She would have settled for a single sunbeam, illuminating the destination she couldn't seem to discern.

What she got was the cold, gray dimness of the sun hiding behind a cloud, and the distant silence of celestial voices that refused to provide the barest hint of divine guidance. Not even a tiny glimmer of a clue.

"So much for being the Muses's chosen one," she muttered, and then someone crashed into her back, sending her staggering.

"Stop that boy!" The cry came from somewhere behind her, shrill and desperate. "Stop, thief!"

Stumbling, trying to keep from planting her face in the cobblestone road, Alannys looked up and saw one of the gossiping teenagers she'd seen earlier. Only now he was running, panting and glancing behind him, clutching something that glittered in his hand.

She launched herself forward, chasing after the kid with everything she had. He glanced back and saw her, and she heard him utter a word she felt was completely inappropriate for a youth. "Do you kiss your mother with that mouth?" she hollered at him.

His retort made her ears burn. She had hoped to catch him off guard, recovering so quickly from the push he had probably expected to sprawl her on the ground. But now that he had seen her, he was really putting on some speed. Her only hope, as far as she could see, was the sheer number of people in the street, slowing him down. As long as she stayed in his wake, she had an edge.

But it didn't take her long to realize she'd underestimated him. This kid was agile, and his reflexes were good. He shoved people out of his way, dodged carts, and jumped over obstacles with a smooth grace that made his whole flight seem rehearsed.

She had been kidding herself. There was no way she could outrun a teenaged boy, even on a crowded city street. He was already pulling away from her, and there was nothing she could do to close that gap. Probably it would be best for her to give up now, before she winded herself any further.

"No." She hadn't intended to say the word out loud, but hearing it helped to steel her resolve. "I'm not letting this little punk win. I'm not giving up until there's no chance at all!"

She really opened up then, pouring everything she had into running, her arms and legs pumping like pistons, propelling her forward and blurring the world around her. She could hear her heart thumping in her ears, could feel every pounding step in her bones. She was running as she'd never run before, flying as though she had no concern for life or limb or planting her face among the stones that made up the street.

But it wasn't enough, she could already see that. She was giving everything she had, and he was still leaving her behind.

And just at that moment, when despair overcame her and she was about to give up, when the thief she pursued looked back and laughed at her, a red cart thrust out in front of him and sent him sprawling.

Alannys dove onto his back, pinning him. "Got you!"

"Dammit, lady—let me up!" A crowd instantly formed around them, watching and waiting to see what she would do.

She ignored them. A shadow fell across her, and she looked up to see the baker smiling down at her, standing next to his red bread cart. "So it *was* you!" she exclaimed. "Thank you!"

The baker touched his hat in a sort of salute. "Happy to do what I can to help our Redeemer. I'll just go bring the reeve, shall I?"

His words sent excited chatters through the crowd of people looking on, but for the first time she found she didn't mind being called the Redeemer in public.

An elderly woman pushed through the crowd, searching wildly until she found Alannys sitting on the teenager. "Oh, thank the Muses! You caught him! I can't thank you enough. This young rapscallion stole my mother's necklace."

Alannys could see the golden glimmer of that necklace in the kid's hand even now. "I think we'll just let him hold onto it until the reeve arrives."

"Oh, thank you—you're my hero, young lady."

"I just did what anyone would have done." For just a moment she was gratified, almost ecstatic, thinking that she had finally made a difference, finally found the crack in Garrant's hard exterior.

Then she realized that what she had said was true—it really wasn't anything special, just something anyone could have done. And the old woman hadn't even realized who she was.

She hadn't made a difference at all. She was right back where she started.

♫

By the time the old woman had her necklace back, the reeve had the young thief in custody, and the whole affair was settled, it was time for lunch.

Alannys didn't always eat lunch, but after all of the running she'd done that morning, she felt like she needed it. And she wasn't in the mood to contend with an unfamiliar place—she was wallowing in her failure. So she headed back down the street to the tavern at the Sand and Sea.

Either people in Garrant didn't favor lunch, or the Sand and Sea was not a popular place for it, because the tavern was not nearly as busy as it had been that morning.

That suited Alannys. She wasn't really up for crowds, or company, or anything.

Thera was across the room, serving another customer. "Well, now," she called, "if it isn't our friendly neighborhood holy warrior!"

Alannys raised a hand, but she didn't speak or smile. She made a beeline straight for her usual little table all by itself in a dark corner. She dropped herself into a chair, and found that being alone in the dim light suited her so well she wasn't inclined to leave.

Perhaps she would spend the rest of her day parked right here. Maybe all the rest of her time in Garrant.

Thera brought over a cold pitcher of berry juice and a cup. "I take it things haven't gone well in Redeemer land."

Alannys flopped her head down onto her arms. "I suppose you were right, Thera. I don't think I can succeed here. All the Redeemer has done today is scare a baker half out of his mind."

"I do love a good opportunity to say 'I told you so,'" Thera said, shifting her tray to prop it against her hip, "but I'm not so sure this is one, you know? Wasn't he the one who sent you to that inn full of Soth-worshipers?"

Alannys raised her head and cracked an eye at Thera. "How did you know that?"

"Oh, honey, you hear everything in a tavern." Thera grinned broadly, looking quite pleased with herself. "You think the palace is the only place with a flowering grapevine? Ravanmark's covered in them. It sounds like all you did was chase this fellow, since he was seen selling bread like usual a few minutes later, and he wasn't bruised or battered. Personally, I'd say he could have done with some dusting up."

"Thera! I can't make progress by beating up people who don't like me."

"Sure you can. Make it a lot faster, too, seems to me."

"No. That's not the way to effect lasting change. You can't just force people to bury their disagreement—that lingering resentment will sink you later."

Thera's grin broadened. "Well, then. Seems to me you should be happy, Alannys—you took the high road. No lingering resentments. Right?"

"Ah, but the primary goal isn't just avoiding resentment—it's effecting change. And that's where I seem to be failing pretty spectacularly." She dropped her head onto the table again.

"Well, now, that's strange." Thera pulled out a chair and sat down, ignoring the customer over at the other table, who was trying to call her back. "I just had a woman in here not ten minutes ago who seemed pretty impressed. Word on the street is that you ran down a thief on foot. She saw it happen. Wasn't that you?"

"Sure," Alannys said, "but anybody could do that! I don't see how that helps me."

"I don't see how it *couldn't* help you," Thera retorted. "Anybody could have done it, but you're the only one who *did*. If you had done what everyone else did, a criminal would have gotten away."

"I guess."

"Alannys, be reasonable! You're trying to show people you aren't all bad, right? Doesn't helping people in need do that? Or does it only count if you're doing some big, superhuman thing with music? I mean, I know that's important to you because only you can do it, but is it really all that matters?"

Alannys stared at her, completely dumbfounded. She remembered, as if it had happened years before, meeting Cedrick in the market at the Great Palace. Talking, there in the leathersmith's tent, with Raman beside her, all of them laughing, Cedrick bringing them all dinner in the guardhouse later that evening—the very first time she could remember changing a critic to a supporter...to a friend. She'd been so excited, so *happy* to have made that one friend—such a simple thing, really, but what consequences it had set into motion...she still felt a pull at her heart when she thought of dear Cedrick.

When had she lost sight of that? When had she become so focused on the destinations that she'd stopped enjoying the journey?

How could she hope to make a difference if she was so intent on changing people's *minds,* she'd forgotten to care about the *people?*

"You're right," she said, finally understanding it, finally *feeling* it, like dawn breaking in her soul. "Damn me, you're *right.* I've been so focused on the forest...thank you for showing me the trees."

Thera laughed. "I didn't know I did, but you're welcome all the same."

"You did. You did, and it's just what I needed to see. I was ready to give up, and I haven't even properly started. It's no wonder I haven't made any progress, I've been doing things all wrong." She tossed some coins on the table to cover her untouched berry juice, and turned for the door. "You'll see a different me at supper, just wait."

"I'll look forward to it." Thera was still laughing. "Make me proud, Redeemer."

Alannys pulled the door shut behind her, feeling truly excited for the first time since coming to Garrant. She felt like she could win over all of Ravanmark.

And she would do it, if she had to do it one person at a time.

She would do it.

♪

Before she ventured back outside, Alannys stopped by the laundry room again. She made a conscious effort to put yesterday out of her mind and start with a clean slate as she leaned around the door. "Good afternoon!"

The laundress never looked up from her work, pushing clothes around a tub of hot water with a wooden pole. "Well, now, you're just a bright ray of twice-blessed sunshine, aren't you?"

The woman's dry, cynical delivery made it pretty clear that this was not a compliment, but Alannys smiled nonetheless. She imagined this was hot, thankless work, and it wasn't hard to understand how it might make a person feel prickly. "I do try."

The woman did glance at her then, and it was an unfriendly, cutting glance. "Then why don't you try shining somewhere else?" she snapped.

Alannys folded her arms and watched the woman for a moment. For her part, the laundress seemed content to ignore Alannys entirely, presumably waiting for her to leave.

"Look," Alannys said finally, "I can see we've gotten off on the wrong foot. I don't know what I did to offend you, but I'm sorry. Let's try starting over, shall we? My name is—"

"I know who you are," the woman cut her off shortly. "Go away."

"And you are?"

"Not interested in talking to you. Go *away*."

Alannys took a deep breath, smothering her irritation. Her new resolution wasn't going to carry her very far, if all it took was one grouchy woman to throw her off. "Okay, so you don't like me. Is it me in particular, or just the whole Redeemer thing in general?"

"It isn't you," the laundress said, still not looking at her. "It's those damned Muses you work for."

"I don't work for anybody," Alannys said immediately. "What I do, I do for the king, for Ravanmark, and for myself."

The woman shook her head, but she didn't even glance

up. "That's what you say. That may even be what you believe, but it doesn't change the truth. Muses are tricky creatures."

"Tricky," Alannys echoed. She'd heard that sentiment before. She could hear Captain Grayble's low, rough voice clearly in her memory. *What's the only thing trickier than a woman?*

"Just so. Mark my words, if you're the Redeemer, you're doing their bidding, whether you will it or no."

"I—I see," Alannys said. "What if I really am acting according to my own will, and it happens to coincide with something the Muses want?"

The woman laughed out loud, a short, barking sound that seemed more pained than amused. "You sound just like my husband."

"Your husband?" Alannys prompted as neutrally as she could manage, sensing that they were getting to the heart of the issue.

"My husband," the woman sighed, stopping her work to stare up at the ceiling. "Finest man I ever met. He ran a little chapel, just down the road from here, just for sailors. A rescue, he called it. Sailors, he said, see so much...it's easy for them to lose faith. And to hear him talk, well, seeing that sailors kept their faith in the Muses seemed like the most important thing in the world."

"It does sound like a very noble thing," Alannys said.

"Does it? It certainly did to me. He laughed that off, though—he said it was the least he could do. And he did, for all the years we were married, he ministered to those sailors. He gave it everything he had, and he always seemed so *cheerful*. Just like you, really."

The laundress fell silent, staring into the steaming, murky water that was beginning to bubble, now that she wasn't stirring it.

The silence felt contemplative, and sad. Alannys knew

it was a compliment to be compared to the woman's husband, but it only increased her sense of dread. "What happened to him?"

"Dead," the woman said shortly, shoving the wet clothes roughly around the tub with her stick. "He went to sea to help rescue some sailors lost in a shipwreck. They brought the sailors back fine. My husband washed overboard and drowned, not far from port. You can see the spot from the docks."

"Oh—I'm so sorry," Alannys said, knowing it wasn't enough.

"Don't be. The Muses look after their own, in the end, and leave the rest of us to muddle along however we can. Some things remind me of that—like you—and that makes things harder for a while. Makes it seem like not so much has changed, really—makes me feel like swimming out to that spot, just to see what I'd find. Could be the Muses'd look after me, too."

Alannys stared at her in mute shock.

"Why are you here?" The laundress sounded suddenly old, and very tired.

"I—just—to pick up my clothes."

"What, those things you dropped off last night? They're not ready yet."

"Oh, I'm—sorry to bother you," Alannys said lamely.

"They'll be ready this evening, I expect. I'll have them delivered to your room. Might be easier for me if I don't see you. Muses never brought anything but death and destruction to Garrant, and I don't figure you'll be any different, acting in their stead."

"I—I'm sorry." Alannys wanted to defend herself, but there was nothing she could say. "I...I hope one day I can change your mind."

She held her head high, but she left the room with a sinking heart.

Because she knew there was nothing she could do, either.

♫

After her encounter with the laundress, Alannys went down to the docks. The pointing and whispering on the street bothered her more now, and she couldn't help but look at each building she passed, wondering if it used to be the mission for sailors. The keeper of that particular chapel was beyond her help now — he'd lived and died doing what he felt important, and whether the death was fair payment for the life was not a subject for his concern.

But his wife was still here, still broken, beyond all possibility of help, at least from Alannys. Trapped here, she slowly marked out the years of her bitter, lonely life. The street, the city, even the sea all seemed to her but monuments to her destruction, and now Alannys saw them that way, too. So she hurried out of town to the sea coast, as if seeking escape in the open, salty air. Perhaps she was. Beseeching the Muses themselves for answers had certainly not provided her anything but a headache.

Many of the big ships Alannys had seen that morning from her balcony were gone, but others had already come in to take their places. Cargo was loaded, and unloaded, and the air was full of the greetings and laughter, grunts and curses, of working men. Past it all the sea rippled peacefully, glittering a deep, impossible blue. Small breakers rocked the ships and boats at the docks, and overhead, seagulls circled and coasted, their calls so familiar that if she closed her eyes, Alannys could have believed she was on a beach back on Earth.

A market of tents and stands lurched haphazardly across the sand in front of the boardwalk and the docks. If Alannys had hoped, in coming to the beach, to find solitude, she had been doomed to disappointment — this market seemed even more popular than the shops in town. Already Alannys could see a shopper elbowing the young man carrying her things, talking quickly and nodding in her direction.

Well. That wasn't great, but what could she do about it? People had to know she was there, after all, if she was to have any chance of success. *You have to take the bad with the good — you can't only be recognized when it suits you,* she told herself, and headed for the market.

The place was pretty amazing — just walking through the stalls, she saw seashells the size of dinner plates, tiny seashells threaded onto string to make jewelry, and seashells carefully cut to make candle holders. She saw fine, flowing silk robes from Duranth, and glittering, razor-sharp daggers from Tibado. Dried spices and bottled oils tickled her nose. She even passed a stall selling exotic reptiles, although she wasn't sure if the creatures were intended as pets or food.

She came to a tent filled with rocks, displayed on tables and shelves. Some gleamed in the light, polished and shiny, while others sat rough and jagged. All of them were originally gathered from the ruins of the Spire of Glory, according to the sign outside the tent.

If it had to do with the Spire of Glory, Alannys was interested. She stopped, and went inside.

It didn't take her long to wish she hadn't. This particular merchant favored a strong, musky incense that made her dizzy and nauseous. The tent was completely closed up, except for the front opening, and the air was heavy and stale with the sickening scent. It made her brain feel stale and heavy, too.

The variety of stones in the shop surprised Alannys. There were big, shaped rocks that could be used as seats, or small tables — rocks that would take several men to move. There were rocks meant for display; rocks the size of a grapefruit, or a man's head, some polished, some left rough. Some tiny, polished rocks had been worked into jewelry, and there were some clearly meant to serve practical functions, like door-stoppers and spoon-rests.

But the ones that interested Alannys were highly polished stones spread on a velvet-covered table at the back of the tent. These small stones, scarcely bigger than coins, were intended to be carried as talismans, offering protection from a variety of hardships, according to the cards displayed with them.

Alannys picked up a round, flat stone with a pinkish hue, tilting it this way and that on her palm, watching the way the low light skimmed across its surface, catching tiny sparkly bits she hadn't even noticed. The stones were carved with strange symbols she had never seen before, almost runic in appearance. She had no idea what they might mean. She started to ask the merchant, but—

"Oi! Don't 'andle the merchandise, eh, luv?"

Alannys looked up in surprise to find the merchant standing right there in front of her, on the backside of the table. "Oh, I—I'm sorry." She placed the stone back on the velvet.

"Sure, luv." The merchant smiled, but it was a cold smile, almost predatory. The spider might have smiled like that when he issued his famous invitation to the fly. "Can't be too careful these days. I've 'eard there's *undesirables* come to Garrant."

She watched him a moment, while his unpleasant smile broadened and sharpened. It was possible the man was harmless, just odd and off-putting.

Of course, it was also possible the man was amusing himself being deliberately insulting to her.

"That so?" she said, keeping her tone carefully neutral. "These stones are all from the ruins of the Spire of Glory?"

"That's what the sign says, luv. No shortage of rocks on Mount Mouseion, as I expect you know well enough."

"I beg your pardon? I've never been to the place."

He cackled at her. "Place just toppled of its own accord, did it?"

Alannys stiffened. "You're misinformed. I am not Soth, and I never — "

"I'm going to stop you right there, luv. You can save your stories for someone who might believe them. For me, though, I suggest only that you go back to the Spire of Glory."

Completely against her better judgment, Alannys took the bait. "Go...back?"

"Sure, luv, sure — the place killed you once. Maybe we'll get lucky again!" He doubled over with unkind laughter. The seal-like bark of it followed her out of the tent.

She stood there in the row of shops a moment, listening to her heart thump in her ears and trying to regain her composure. It seemed she had miscalculated when she spoke to Thera earlier — her attitude was, after all, only half of the equation. Before her newfound resolution, it seemed most of the town had no use for her.

And now, after her great revelation, they *still* had no use for her.

And there didn't seem to be anything she could do to change that.

♪

After her visit to Garrant's sprawling seaside market, Alannys walked out to the immense boardwalk that connected all of the many piers that jutted out over the water.

There were lots of people out here, too — sightseers, mostly, strolling along the boardwalk, or leaning on the rails and staring out over the water. Most of them paid her no attention, save for the occasional hostile look. Sailors hustled along the walk, single-minded, without a glance left or right.

A couple of sailors walking close together knocked into

her, shoving her into the railing.

"Watch it," one of them said, "the docks ain't no place for ladies or Redeemers."

"That's all right," the other said, "she ain't neither."

One of the sightseers guffawed.

Alannys figured the most important thing she had done in Garrant was learn to let things like this roll off her back. She righted herself and moved on down the boardwalk without a word, or even a dirty look.

But her ears still burned.

At the far end of the boardwalk she found a large observation deck, built far out over the deep water. Wooden benches were spread generously over its surface, but she passed them by, preferring instead to lean on the high railing and look out at the water. She couldn't remember a time she had felt quite so lonely. She wondered, in her melancholy, how many times the laundress had come to stand in this very place. She gazed out at the sunlight reflecting and sparkling on the water, and wondered if she might be looking, right now, at the very spot where—

"'S beautiful, isn't it?"

The voice startled her. She spun around and found a grizzled sailor settling himself onto one of the wooden benches. He looked older than anybody she'd ever seen, and something about his wild white hair reminded her of Tryn. Her reaction seemed to amuse him. "Don't mind me, missy—I just like to sit down every now and again on something that ain't swaying with the water." He lit up a pipe and watched her watching the sea. "Something on your mind, m'Lady?"

She shook her head.

"Oh, come now. You can tell old Ern." He puffed on his pipe a moment in silence, inspecting her countenance. "Let me guess, then. Nice young lady comes to Garrant as she's traveling Ravanmark, with no expectation beyond seeing some sights and talking to some folks. Only, they haven't been nice to you at all. Nasty lot of rutters. Is that it?"

Alannys looked at him in frank surprise.

Ern gestured at her with his pipe, showing her a grin that was missing most of its teeth. "Ah! See, I knew something was troubling you." He leaned back against the bench. "Missy, you can't take them people personal. Garrant is a real sea town. Mostly sailors, or families of sailors. Living by the ocean, a body sees things other folks don't. Sometimes horrible rains come in and drown everything that grows. Sometimes no rains come to shore and nothing grows. Sometimes the sea gets ugly and wrecks homes, sinks ships—and where is the justice in that? Who decides which man gets swept overboard and which man remains? Some faraway Muse singing a pretty tune?" He shook his head. "Sorry, but after you've lived with the sea, that don't cut it. Muses is just a bunch of pretty nonsense."

"I see," Alannys said, and she thought that maybe she did. What the old sailor said made sense, even as it saddened her.

He nodded at her. "Course you do. Folks who ain't got no use for Muses, ain't go no use for a Redeemer. Most people in Garrant don't really believe music has power anyway. And those who do, don't believe anyone with that power would use it for anything but their own personal benefit."

She regarded the wrinkled old man. "What about you, Ern? What do you believe?"

He gave her that toothless grin again. "Ah, that's the question, ain't it? I've sailed all over this great big world, missy, and I've seen more than I can remember. I once sailed out to Mount Mouseion and saw the ruins of the

Spire of Glory. You ever been out there, m'Lady?"

Alannys shook her head.

Ern crossed his arms and spoke around the pipe hanging from the corner of his mouth. "There ain't nothing like it. Nothing like it anywhere else in the world. It's enormous, missy, grand on a scale nothing in Ravanmark can match. And the foundation—it's solid. Stout as the floor of the world. That rutter was built by people who knew what they was doing, and it was built to last the ages."

He paused, letting his description sink in. Alannys tried to imagine those massive rocks, tried to imagine how small he'd felt, looking on them.

"And yet it fell. Rocks that big, that well shaped, that expertly set—they don't fall of themselves. Something or somebody had to make them fall, and it's beyond the power of anything and anybody I've seen in this world to make it happen." His glance fell away. "So yeah, I believe in your Muses, missy, even though most in this town don't. It's the only explanation I can accept for what I saw."

"Thank you, Ern." Her voice sounded hoarse; the sound of it in her own ears surprised her.

He looked surprised himself. "Thank me? For what?"

"For restoring my faith. Garrant has been...a bit difficult. You've just reminded me that it is all for a purpose, that there's hope after all."

"Don't thank me yet, m'Lady. The Redeemer has to go out there to Mount Mouseion, and fix the things in our land that are broken." He pointed at her with his pipe. "You do that, you'll restore *my* faith."

She grinned at him. "Then I suppose we will be even."

Ern put his pipe back in his mouth and grinned back. "Aye, I suppose we will."

♫

Alannys went to bed early. She wanted the solitude of

her room, and the comfort of the big bed. Her thoughts chased each other in restless circles, getting her nowhere.

She needed to be moving on. She knew that. But she didn't feel like she'd made much of a difference in Garrant —she wasn't even sure she *could* make difference here. She sifted through all of her experiences here—everything she'd done, each person she'd spoken to, looking for some clue as to what she should do next.

Unfortunately, sleep found her before she found any answers.

A sharp knock at the door woke her. It was dark as death in her room—the curtains were open, but the sky was so thick with clouds, not a single star could be seen. She sat up in her bed, scrubbing at her eyes with the heels of her hands, wondering who could possibly be knocking at this hour of the night. Maybe she'd just imagined it. Maybe she should just go back to sleep.

"Redeemer! Wake up, Alannys, you've got to let me in!"

In her groggy state, she couldn't put a name to the voice. But she remembered it, and she knew she couldn't ignore it. She threw back the quilts and staggered to the door, grumbling.

Thera stood in the hallway in the dim light of the oil lantern she carried, looking as disheveled as Alannys felt. Her long brown hair hung loose and rumpled over a shapeless linen gown. Her eyes were puffy from sleep, but her crooked smile was the same as always. "Well, you're in a fine state."

"You're one to talk," Alannys said. "What's got you up in the middle of the night?" She frowned, noticing all at once the way the lantern shook in Thera's hand. "Really— what are you so upset about?"

For a moment, it looked like Thera wasn't going to answer, which seemed insane considering she had come here in the middle of the night to say whatever it was.

"Tidal wave!" she finally blurted.

"Wh — what? Now? Coming *here?*"

Thera nodded.

Alannys couldn't seem to think fast enough. "But how do you know?"

Thera wrapped her arms around herself, like she was trying to stay warm, or keep herself together. The light of the lantern flickered around them, looking somehow ominous. "The reeves are going door to door. Sounds like a ship that just made it in warned them."

Alannys grabbed her sword and her cloak. "We've got to get out of here!"

Thera shook her head. "I'm sorry, Alannys, there isn't time. The wave will be here before we could make it out of town."

Alannys stood there staring at her, holding Songstrike and her cloak like she wasn't sure what she should do with them.

"It's huge — beyond anything we've ever seen before. The entire city will be destroyed."

"So...we're doomed here, and we can't escape." Alannys looked from her cloak in one hand to her sword in the other, wondering why she was still holding them. "Then why did you wake me?"

Thera bit her lip. "Don't rightly know. Maybe — maybe I just wanted you to have a chance to make your final peace with those Muses of yours. One last chance to kiss your aft end goodbye." She smiled, but it looked forced. "At least, that is what I would have said, if this was happening three days ago. But now...damn me, but I think I really came to ask you for help. And I can't even explain why — I can't conceive of a single thing you could do about a tidal wave. But here I am."

Alannys wasn't completely convinced that she could

trust her ears just then. If what she had just heard was true, well—it felt like a bright ray of sunshine had just broken through the storm clouds, to think that someone as cynical as Thera could come around. She buckled on her swordbelt, threw on her cloak, and clapped Thera on the shoulder. "I don't know what I can do, either. But I'm ready to find out."

"You're—taking a sword?"

"Yes." Her hand fell to check Songstrike in its scabbard as though it had a mind of its own. "It's lucky, you might say." She pulled on her boots and headed for the door.

Thera followed her. "Wait! I'm sorry, Alannys—I shouldn't have bothered you. This is madness, you're going to get killed out there!"

Alannys couldn't help but grin. "I'd get killed if I stayed in here, too. If it's die in here or die out there, I would prefer to be out there, doing whatever I can, even if all I can do is holler at the water to go back. You're a quick thinker, Thera. Thank you for waking me." She didn't turn around, but just kept moving down the hallway, as fast as she could.

Thera followed her down the stairs, her oil lantern casting a warm light that seemed almost alive, the way it bounced and danced around them. "I'm coming with you."

"You sure? It's not going to be any fun."

"You think I don't know that?" Thera sounded like she'd found some of her old spark. "You want to be out there doing what you can—so do I, even if all I can do is be there while you do it. You don't have to do everything alone."

"Thanks, Thera."

If Thera noticed the peculiar break in her voice, she didn't let on. "Don't thank me—just you try making me stay behind." Her laugh had a nervous, strained sound.

"Only...do you think those Muses of yours might come along too?"

"I hope so," Alannys said grimly, stepping out into the darkness of the street. "I don't know if we can survive this alone."

♫

The wind whipped Alannys's riding cloak, stinging her arms where it lashed her. Her hair blew in a frenzy around her face, and the driving wind made it hard to breathe — it seemed to alternately steal all of the air from her, and drive it into her face too fast for her to handle. It tasted salty and damp.

She held onto the boardwalk railing to hide the way her hands shook as she looked out over the tumultuous ocean. It had seemed so peaceful earlier, but right now she could really *see* it for the first time as a force capable of destruction. The water looked dark and foamy. Short, choppy waves rocked the boats lashed to the piers, and some even splashed up onto the boardwalk, soaking her boots.

She figured she would have bigger problems than wet boots, soon enough.

"Are you sure about this?" Thera stood next to her at the railing, still clutching her lantern, although Alannys didn't see how it could last long in the tempestuous wind. "I've got a bad feeling about it."

"Me, too," Alannys said. "But there's no way to feel good about it — it's a tidal wave. We're both crazy for being here." She pried her fingers loose from the railing, and clapped Thera on the shoulder. "The good news is that we aren't risking anything that wasn't already forfeit."

She turned away, and headed out to the end of the closest pier alone. It felt like the longest walk she had ever taken, and the howling wind and violent sea did little to settle her misgivings. This attempt could kill her. She did not want to die.

But if she didn't try, she *would* die, and so would most of the rest of Garrant. She could not allow an entire city to die, while she stood by and did nothing. Their salvation could be within her power. She had to try.

She glanced back over her shoulder at the boardwalk. She could still see the light of Thera's lantern, flickering precariously in the wind. It heartened her, seeing that warm light and knowing she had a friend, here at the end of everything.

The water under the boardwalk disappeared. The sea was pulling back, in preparation for the massive wave that would strike in mere minutes. Alannys could see the foaming crests even now.

Her heart pounded against her ribs. Her blood ran like ice, and yet it seemed to burn in her veins; she could no longer feel her hands or feet. She had never been so scared in her life. The sea spray, driven by the relentless wind, had soaked her hair and everything she wore. She could hear a rumbling, low but intense, as though the very foundations of the world were shaking. She could feel it in her bones, could hear it even over the roar of the wind in her ears.

Her time had run out.

The tidal wave was taller than anything she had ever seen, a wall of water, an unimaginable solid mass, rushing toward her with a speed she could not have conceived of. The visceral urge to run that washed over her then dwarfed every other fear she had ever experienced. Drawing on courage she hadn't known she possessed, Alannys faced the doomsday wave.

"Nothing to it but to do it," she muttered.

Standing small and alone before the massive gray wall of water, Alannys stretched out her arms, closed her eyes, and sang.

Chapter Four

KORTHA

"*I*'m telling you there has been no change. We can't work with all these interruptions. You're going to have to leave."

The voices floated in the formless black mist that surrounded her, brushing by her, meaning nothing.

"I'm not going to ask you again to keep your voice down. I will notify everyone as soon as there is any change."

The voices were buzzing bees, annoying her. She pushed them away.

"We are doing all we can, I promise you. The rest is up to her. Now please step outside, we need quiet."

The voices kept coming back. She tried to follow them to the surface, but pain like sheet lightning tore through her, shredding her consciousness. She floated back down, into the darkness and quiet, defeated. It was too much — it hurt too much — might as well give up. She floated deeper, farther away from the voices and light.

Alannys, don't do this. Don't give up. Come back, you can do it. Alannys...

She could not deny that voice. She pushed through the pain, broke through the black mist. She sat up, gasping, reaching out into the emptiness in front of her, covered in cold sweat and clutching the Seeing Stone in her other hand. "Dorramon!"

The stone was warm against her skin.

A woman in plain blue robes ran to her, took her arm, and helped her to lie back down on the bed. "Kelvan! She is awake!" Her brown eyes were wide with concern, but her voice, though urgent, was quiet and controlled. "Please, my Lady, you must lie still. Do not tax yourself further."

A young man wearing identical robes rushed up beside the woman. "I am here, Misha. What do you need me to do?"

Misha felt for Alannys's pulse, and laid a hand across her forehead. "Bring cool cloths. And some warm broth. And for the love of the Muses don't let anyone in!"

Kelvan nodded once, and disappeared through a door behind Misha.

Alannys scrubbed at her gritty eyes, trying to clear her blurry vision. She ached all over; just raising her hands to her face hurt. She groaned, and dropped her arms back to the bed. "I have to go back."

"Go back?" Misha's tone of polite confusion sounded polished; no doubt she had tended many disoriented people before.

"Dorramon—I heard him. I've been away too long, I have to go back!"

"Dorramon? Do you—do you mean the king?" Misha reached down and pried Alannys's fingers off the Seeing Stone. "I am afraid there is no one here but you and I, my Lady. And you've been nowhere but this room. I know Muse's Fever can be difficult. Don't try too hard—just rest."

"What happened?" The words burned her throat, and her voice sounded like gravel crunched under boots.

"You survived," Misha said simply. "You collapsed on the boardwalk. Thera from the Sand and Sea brought you here. We weren't sure you would make it."

The boardwalk. Thera. The flickering lantern. Singing. A wall of water...

Alannys clutched at Misha's arm. "Garrant—the tidal wave. Did I do it? Did I turn back the water?"

"Shh, my Lady. Don't distress yourself. You are safe, and so is Garrant." She smiled like sunshine. "You succeeded."

Alannys fell back against the pillows. Relief brought stinging tears to her eyes. She had done it. She could relax.

For the first time, she looked at the room around her. She was in narrow bed, next to a little table full of bowls holding crushed herbs. The room was small, and the only other furniture was a chest of drawers on the far wall, next to a wooden door. Somebody had pressed leaves and flowers, framed them, and hung them around the room.

"Where am I?"

Misha smiled. Her cheeks were plump, and her face was pleasant. "You are in the Healing House, my Lady. It is my great pleasure to finally welcome you."

Kelvan came back in then, with a damp washcloth in one hand and a bowl of broth in the other. He spread the cloth over Alannys's forehead, while Misha fed her broth.

"Healing House?" Alannys echoed. The broth was very nearly clear, with a few vegetable slivers floating in it, but it seemed to have more flavor than any soup she'd ever eaten.

All at once she was ravenous. She couldn't get to the spoon fast enough.

"Easy there!" Misha laughed. "You've got to take it slow! Yes, this house is devoted entirely to healing. I and three other healers work here, along with two apprentices. Kelvan is my apprentice."

Alannys slurped more broth from the spoon. A house filled with healers — what better place to be when suffering Muse's Fever? She thanked Thera, silently but fervently.

"You don't know all the healers, my Lady, but they all know you. We've been tending you for six days."

"Six days? I was unconscious for six days?"

"Yes, my Lady. It was a very brave thing you did for Garrant, a very noble thing. A miraculous thing. But it nearly cost you your life to do it."

Alannys sank back against the pillows. Misha wasn't kidding. She had never been sick that long with Muse's Fever. It was a good thing she didn't have to make a habit of turning back tidal waves. She sighed. "Thank you for taking such good care of me. After a couple of days in Garrant, I was beginning to think nobody here cared about me at all."

Misha gifted her with another kindly smile. "How do you feel? Do you think you can stand?"

Alannys sat up, and carefully swung her legs out of the bed. "I think so."

"Let me help you." Misha took her arm, and helped her to walk to the closed wooden door on the far side of the room. Her linen shirt and leather pants felt stiff and strange rubbing against her skin.

Kelvan waited by the door, and opened it as they approached. Misha helped her out onto a balcony with a high iron railing.

Before Alannys was even completely out on the balcony, her ears rang with a deafening roar. What on earth was that sound?

And then she stepped out to the railing, and she saw them. The little cobblestone street overflowed with people, big and small, elegantly and shabbily dressed, alone and in families. They carried flowers, and gifts, and cards.

And every one of those hundreds of people was

cheering for her.

Alannys leaned heavily on the railing, tears welling up in her eyes. The people of Garrant recognized her sacrifice. And they were grateful. She raised a shaking arm to wave, and the shouts grew louder still.

This time, she called it victory.

♫

Alannys stayed in the Healing House for two more days before Misha pronounced her well enough to leave. She stayed in bed for two days, but she was not resting.

A constant stream of people flowed in and out of her room. The line of people who wanted to thank her and shake her hand seemed never-ending. And yet it was quiet and orderly; the people of Garrant were content to wait as long as it took to have a chance to speak to the Redeemer. Every person in town had been a potential victim of the tidal wave, and they all knew it. The healers did their best to ensure her privacy when she needed it, but that afternoon when she woke from her nap, she found a stack of her own clothes folded neatly on the table next to her bed. On top of the clothes were three copper coins and a carefully lettered note:

This one's on me—delivered to your room as promised. Looks like I was wrong about you and Muses—you brought something good after all.

Today I'm going to go look at the sea, and think about how lucky I am to be here.

Thank you.

Alannys smiled, and tucked the note into her beltpouch.

One of the young men who waited patiently in the line was not from Garrant. His breeches and boots were clearly intended for riding, and a royal medallion hung around his neck, glimmering like unshed tears in the light of the recovery room, impossible for Alannys to ignore. It was a match for the one she wore even now. It was odd to see it on someone else — in her time away from the palace, she'd come to regard it as her own personal token of Dorramon. Strange to see it on this young man, and remember they were used for official palace business all over Ravanmark. It made her feel...distanced somehow — even more than she already had.

"Greetings on behalf of his Royal Majesty, King Dorramon of Ravanmark. I bring tidings to the Lady Alannys of Gale, Redeemer of the Realm, from the Great Palace."

Alannys just stared at him, eyes wide. It had been so long since she'd heard that particular high pattern of speech that flourished at the palace, she couldn't even formulate a decent response.

The royal rider inclined his head, as if excusing her breach of etiquette. "His Majesty extends unto you his congratulations for your heroic rescue of the city of Garrant, his gratitude for the services you have rendered unto Ravanmark — and this, a token of his great esteem. Please accept these things from me on behalf of his Majesty."

"I — I do, of course," Alannys said, feeling more befuddled with every word the man spoke. "Thank you."

He inclined his head again, and handed her a paper packet. It was plain brown paper, with no sign or seal, but it set her heart to pounding the moment she touched it. "Then I shall take my leave. I wish you a speedy recovery."

Misha showed him out of the room, and closed the door, leaving Alannys with a few precious moments of privacy to open her parcel.

She was ridiculously nervous. She knew it was stupid, and it embarrassed her, but she couldn't stop it. Just a few days ago—a matter of hours!—Dorramon himself had touched these wrappings, had prepared whatever lay inside. It was the closest she'd felt to him since leaving the palace.

Inside the packet, she found a thick, folded piece of parchment. There was no greeting, no signature, nothing that might connect the package to her or to him.

Perhaps a medallion is insufficient...if even half of the tales I have heard are true, you are not making the use of it I might have hoped.

I beg of you to wear this as well. It should prove more difficult to hide, I think, and I'm quickly coming to the conclusion that there is no such thing as too much protection when it comes to you. The words 'careful' and 'safe' must have altogether different meanings for you than for me.

That said, I cannot conceal how very proud I am of you. I think you must surely be able to see the good you have done this time. I doubt anyone else could have survived it. It will be the stuff of legends one day.

Just...please be careful. And wear this. I beseech you.

Alannys reached to the bottom of the packet, and lifted out a gold bracelet. Each link in the bracelet was cast in the shape of a shield, enameled half red and half blue, with a pair of battling stags in the center.

The royal crest. She remembered seeing it on the flags at the top of the palace keep, caught high in the wind, bright against the sky. Her breath caught in her throat, seeing it now. She didn't understand all of the details associated with the crest, but she knew its usage was carefully controlled — you had to have a signed document granting you permission to display it in the market — even if the royal family regularly patronized your shop. There was probably only a single smith in Ravanmark permitted to have the molds to make these links.

This bracelet had to have been commissioned especially for her, then — she'd certainly never seen anything like it before, not even on the Queen Mother Farrine, back when she had been Queen of Ravanmark herself.

She held the bracelet up in the light, and swallowed a lump in her throat. "I'll wear it," she said, even though she knew he couldn't hear her. "I promise." She could have contacted him through the mindlink, but she was afraid to.

She didn't trust herself to talk to him just then without crying.

♪

Alannys heard raised voices at the door before she had quite recovered herself. She managed to wipe her eyes before the door crashed open and Misha tumbled in, flapping after a very imposing man.

"Sir!" she squawked. "I am sorry, but as I told you, the Lady Alannys is not receiving visitors right now!"

She might as well not have spoken at all. The unannounced visitor didn't acknowledge her, didn't even slow down — by the time she finished her sentence, he was already leaning uncomfortably over the bed.

Misha sighed. "I'm sorry, my Lady. I tried."

"Don't worry about it," she said. She wasn't sure how best to respond to his mind-boggling rudeness, so she ignored him for the moment. "Help me with this?" She held up the bracelet.

Misha's eyes widened. "Certainly, my Lady." She pushed in next to the man at the bedside and fastened the bracelet, but she said no more, and asked no questions.

Alannys understood. This man's attitude had already secured her dislike as well, and she didn't feel inclined to give him any information either. The man was almost unnaturally tall and gaunt, with a long face that gave him a dour, disapproving aspect. He wore long, featureless, white robes, and he looked at Alannys with an expression that clearly said he would rather be looking at anything else.

"Good day, Lady Alannys. I trust you are recovering well." He spoke quickly, with precise diction and careful pronunciation, but almost no inflection at all.

Alannys found it creepy, really. On the whole, this strange, skeletal man gave the impression of being more dead than alive. "Very well, thank you. And you are?"

"I am pleased to hear it," he said, evidently as good at ignoring as she was. "You'll be leaving with me. Today. Prepare your things."

"Wait, what?" Alannys looked from her strange visitor to Misha, but the healer seemed as gobsmacked as she was. "Who are you?"

"That is of no concern to you." His words sounded even more clipped than usual—she supposed in a man like this, that probably signaled great irritation. "You must hurry. I haven't time to waste on trifles."

"Excuse me," she shot back, "but this is no trifling matter. You clearly expect me to leave with you, and you must think I'm insane if you believe I would do that without knowing just exactly who the hell you are!"

The corners of his thin lips twisted sharply down, and he held his nose higher in the air. "Such cheek. I fail to see why I should be required to tolerate such a ridiculously dramatic display. You may take as a reflection of the serious nature of my intent the fact that I am still here. I am a personal emissary of the most glorious Lady Etherra of Brookeshire. You may call me Jarran."

"Lady Etherra," she echoed in a horrified gasp.

"Just so. Your presence is commanded at Brookeshire Castle, at your earliest convenience. I will be escorting you hence, and I am here to make sure that your earliest convenience is *now*. Begin your preparations. We depart in one hour."

He swept from the room, leaving Alannys staring after him with her mouth agape, all of the fight drained from her at the mention of Lady Etherra. She had so hoped to slip through Brookeshire Holding without attracting her attention!

Misha watched Jarran leave the room with a clear expression of doubt, and moved to the bedside. "I am sorry. I tried to keep him out." She lowered her voice to a whisper. "I could go tell him you're not well enough to travel."

Alannys laughed nervously. "I appreciate the offer, Misha, but I don't think it will help. I'm afraid nothing but a declaration of my death would stop Jarran—with *proof*."

"My Lady!" Misha sounded scandalized, but she laughed.

Alannys did not laugh with her. She couldn't do anything about this unplanned journey, but she had a very bad feeling about it. Brookeshire Castle was just about the last place in Ravanmark she wanted to go just then.

But she would be setting out in an hour, come hell or high water. And that thought gave her a shiver.

Because with Lady Etherra around, Alannys expected both.

♫

Brookeshire Castle was nothing like anywhere Alannys had ever been before—and quite honestly nothing like anywhere she'd ever *wanted* to go. In spite of its name, it did not look much like a castle to her eyes—the whole place had a cold and forbidding aura that reminded her very much of Lord Diabon. It had been a long, hard ride, but there was no relief in arriving at a place like this.

The building loomed immense before her, three stories tall and lined with arched windows. Long balconies connected each row of windows. A massive vestibule jutted out in the center of the building, with an arched entry that stood two stories high by itself. Gorgeous stained glass surrounded it. Behind the vestibule, a tower soared up at least another three stories. The tower held a set of enormous arched doors that opened out onto the top of the vestibule, which was railed and evidently used as a balcony. Alannys could easily imagine Lady Etherra or Lord Diabon giving their evangelical speeches from up there, and the thought gave her a chill.

At the very top were nine towering spires. Each of the spires bore a different decoration; a crown of ivy, a lyre, a veil, a golden crown, a scroll, a tragic mask, a staff, a crown of roses, and the unmistakable shape of a flute. The spires evidently represented the nine Muses, each marked by her icon. Calliope's golden crown graced the largest spire, the one in the center of the tower.

Alannys reined up a few yards away from the enormous entrance. A line of solid white extended completely across that massive arch, flummoxing her. Jarran reined up next to her, but judging by his bored expression, he didn't find the display unusual. It took her a moment to realize she was looking at people, in voluminous white robes that dragged the ground, with large bell sleeves, and hoods that draped down over their foreheads and hid most of their faces from view. Each one wore a long sword. They stood with their hands folded together in front of them, so that all she could see was the sleeves of their robes meeting. The only flesh visible was lower jaws. They looked like monks, but menacing, somehow. Like warriors. Warrior monks.

Creepy.

Alannys cleared her throat nervously. What should she say? She had no idea what she was supposed to do now, and Jarran wasn't helping.

"Lady Etherra welcomes the Redeemer, Lady Alannys of Gale, to Brookeshire Castle." The entire line of robed figures spoke simultaneously, with identical inflections. Her skin crawled. These people were seriously weird.

A lone figure in a white robe approached her. Behind him, off to the left of the massive castle, she could see the stables. Another figure stepped forward to collect Jarran's mount.

"Your horse, my Lady?" The man's voice sounded like the rustle of dry leaves. It made her ears itch. She did not want to leave her horse with these people.

She dismounted, but as soon as she tried to hand the reins to the cloaked man, Quicksilver jerked his head away, snorting.

"That's odd," she muttered, and tried again. Quicksilver reared up, whinnying, pulling the reins from her grasp. "Hey! Easy there, boy!" She patted his nose, and stroked his mane, and he calmed. Still speaking softly to the horse, she handed the reins to Brookeshire Castle's unique version of stableboy.

This time, Quicksilver went without complaint. Shaking her head, she turned back to the castle. She wondered what Quicksilver knew about this place that she hadn't figured out yet.

Jarran waited a few steps ahead of her, saying nothing but wearing a look of pure impatience. She moved to catch up with him, but she didn't particularly hurry. It gave her a juvenile pleasure to see his aggravation.

Smoothly, with a minimum of motion, the solid line facing them broke into two lines, one at each corner of the entrance, creating a lane for them to pass through. No one acknowledged her as she followed Jarran into the enormous vestibule, and when she looked back the line had closed over the archway once more.

No, she had never been any place like Brookeshire Castle before.

Jarran led her through a series of quiet, narrow corridors. They went up two different sets of stairs, and just when Alannys's eyes had completely adjusted to the low light inside, they came out into the blinding light of the large railed deck she had seen from the ground. The massive doors leading into the tower were shut, but as they approached four more people draped in white pushed them open.

The enormous room inside the tower had nine white pillars stretching from floor to ceiling, positioned under the spires she had seen on the roof. Carved into the pillars were the images of the Muses themselves, each holding the icon that represented her on the spires. The tops of the high walls were filled with stained glass, and beautiful, multicolored beams of light angled through the hall.

At the far end of the hall, on a raised platform, sat Lady Etherra in an elaborately carved white throne. The nine Muses were carved into the base of throne as well.

Alannys stared. What were the implications of a ruler sitting on the gods? Who did these monks really worship —the Muses, or Lady Etherra, in her own creepy little cult?

Lady Etherra sat in the enormous throne, dwarfed by

its sheer size, wearing a sparkling white gown with an attached cloak. The gown had huge bell sleeves that draped to the floor, and the cloak trailed the ground. A prettier, higher-class version of the robes her monks wore — that was how Alannys saw it. Etherra sat perched on the edge of her seat, watching Alannys approach, fidgeting with her hands in her lap.

Something about Lady Etherra always put Alannys on guard.

Alannys and Jarran stopped before the immense white throne. "Presenting the Lady Alannys," Jarran said, as clipped and formal as ever. He bowed once, and stepped away from them, waiting by the wall.

Lady Etherra rose from her throne, ran down the steps from the platform, and threw herself on her knees at Alannys's feet. "My Lady! I cannot tell you how honored I am that you have deigned to call on me." She sounded breathless, and she would not look Alannys in the eyes. "I thank you, my Lady — I am eternally grateful you have accepted my humble invitation."

"What?" Alannys stumbled back a step, clumsy in her surprise. "Lady Etherra, please get up. This isn't necessary. You're embarrassing me."

"I beg your forgiveness — I dare not! I am not worthy to stand in your glorious presence! The Muses would strike me down!"

Alannys shook her head. She should have expected something like this. She glanced at Jarran, but he just stood there, leaning against the wall, watching them as though this was the single most boring thing he had ever witnessed.

She figured she should have expected that, too.

"Lady Etherra," she said finally, "if you do not get up off the floor, I'm going to leave."

Still Etherra did not move. Alannys turned, and took

two steps away from her before she heard the rustling sounds of the voluminous white gown. "No! I beg of you, do not grace us with your blessed presence only to take it away so soon!"

Alannys rolled her eyes. In Ravanmark, Etherra was considered a visionary. Where she came from, they would have called her a drama queen. She turned back around. "Lady Etherra, I—"

Etherra's shrill scream cut her off. "I cannot see! I am struck blind by the sight of one so heavenly!" She collapsed back to the floor in a whimpering, shivering heap. "Forgive me, my Lady. I should not have been so bold. Jarran, help me!"

The white robed figure moved away from the wall. Alannys held a forbidding hand out to him. "Stay where you are!"

Jarran bristled. "Do you dare to suggest that I ignore my Lady's plea?"

"I dare to suggest that if you come any closer, I'm going to gut you! Listen to me for once, and don't encourage her!"

Jarran gawked at her, his lips working silently. "The outrage!" he finally managed, and fell back into position against the wall.

Alannys stomped over to Etherra, grabbed her by the arm, and hauled her to her feet. "This is ridiculous. You have got to stop carrying on like this. Etherra, you know who your gods are. There are nine of them. They live in the Valley of the Muses. What are their names?"

Lady Etherra stared at her, wide-eyed, unblinking. Alannys could almost believe she really was blind. She made no attempt to answer.

Alannys shook her arm. "Come on, you can do this. What are their names?"

"C—Calliope."

"Right. Keep going."

Etherra swallowed hard. "Clio. Erato. Euterpe, Melpomene, Polyhymnia, Terpsichore, Thalia. Urania."

Alannys released her, and stepped back. "Right. Nine Muses, nine names. And nowhere in there did I hear of a Muse named Alannys."

Lady Etherra blinked at her. "What?"

"I am not a god, Etherra. You've got to stop treating me like I am."

Etherra nodded slowly. "I shall attempt to do as you ask, my Lady."

Alannys sighed. That was probably the best response she was going to get from Etherra. She glanced around the empty hall, eerily devoid of courtiers or servants, except for Jarran's glowering presence. "Why did you summon me here?"

Etherra looked away. "I wanted to ask you to sing."

"What, here? Now? You can't be serious."

Lady Etherra grabbed her arm. "Please, Lady Alannys, I *beg* of you! Nothing in this world brings us closer to the Muses than your songs. The ecstasy of your music is like none I have ever known—none! I beseech you—do not deny me this!"

Alannys extricated her arm, eyeing Etherra warily. "I can't, not right now," she lied. "Surely you heard of my collapse at Garrant?"

"Oh, your deeds at Garrant will be legend, my Lady! It was a most heroic thing."

"Yes, well, that most heroic thing cost me six days in the Healing House with Muse's Fever. I'm only just now really recovering. I couldn't risk singing again, especially after the long ride."

"Oh!" Lady Etherra was instantly solicitous. "How stupid of me! Of course, of course, I won't trouble you any longer today. Jarran, show Lady Alannys to her room. Be sure that she is provided all that she needs. Remember, she is the Redeemer of the Realm. Her word is our law."

"Of course, my Lady." Jarran's delivery was as dry as ever, but something about the steep arch of his eyebrow made her think she was witnessing his version of sarcasm. He bowed low to Lady Etherra, and led Alannys from the room.

"Jarran, I can't stay here. I've been too long in Garrant already. I simply cannot afford to—"

"That's enough." His clipped, precise words cleanly cut her off. "I tolerated what you did earlier only because we were in front of Lady Etherra. But now...she has said you will stay, so stay you shall. And if you think you are good enough with that blade to gut me, I invite you to try."

"But—but Etherra said—"

He rounded on her suddenly, his long face twisted with rage into something ugly and unrecognizable. "Just who do you think runs Brookeshire Castle? Lady Etherra? She is a visionary, Lady Alannys, a dreamer. She hasn't got the practical, critical focus to keep things in line." He took a step towards her—only a single step, but it felt like a threat. "*I* run Brookeshire Castle, and while you are here you answer to *me*. I do my best to keep things the way my Lady would want them, if she spent more time in this world, and less in the ones in her mind. And what she wants is you, here. So I suggest you accept that fact right now. You aren't going anywhere, not unless and until Lady Etherra says you are."

Alannys swallowed hard, looking into Jarran's stony face. His eyes were hard and cold, like flints, and she didn't doubt that he meant what he said. She was stuck here until she fought her way out or sang her way out, and on her first day out of the Healing House, she didn't feel confident in her ability to do either one.

So she bit back her objections, and followed Jarran

deeper into Brookeshire Castle, wishing she was anywhere else.

♫

The tiny bedroom Jarran showed Alannys into did not improve her impression of Brookeshire Castle. No place she had ever stayed had been so spartan. The men in white really were monks, and the castle was their monastery.

A single, narrow cot, low to the floor, sat along the back wall of the room. It was a simple wooden frame with a blanket over it. There was no pillow. A short two-drawer chest sat against another wall. It held only an extra blanket. A small chamber pot at the foot of the bed completed the room's sparse furnishings.

The room's single window was an open slit in the stone wall almost as tall as she was, but it was so narrow she could not have slipped even her head through.

Jarran stood in the doorway, watching her survey the room, grim satisfaction evident on his face. "Do you require anything else?"

A short moment passed while she considered all of the possible responses she could give to that question, remembering with longing her suite at the Great Palace. "No," she finally sighed, "I don't think so. Maybe some supper."

He bowed, his hands folded in front of him inside the huge sleeves of his robe. "Of course. I live only to serve."

Alannys turned to contemplate the dismal bed. "How much of this is Lady Etherra, and how much is you, Jarran?"

He looked at her with an exaggerated expression of surprise. "Why, whatever do you mean?"

She waved an arm in a gesture that encompassed the room. "It seems a bit...sparse, don't you think?"

"Perhaps. It certainly doesn't meet the standards of excess observed at the Great Palace, if that is what you are getting at. In any event, it is only a lifestyle of self-denial that leads one closer to the Muses. I believe Lady Etherra would agree."

"You may be right," Alannys said, her tone non-committal. "And Lady Etherra, does she observe this lifestyle of self-denial as well?"

"I should say not! Lady Etherra has a very delicate disposition. It would be a cruelty to impose such things on her. Besides, if she were any closer to the Muses, she would leave us entirely, don't you think?"

"I—I see," Alannys said.

"We do not ask that Lady Etherra deny herself, and we do not deny her, either. Do you understand? I was most disappointed that you chose to refuse her request earlier."

Alannys looked at him, then looked again, certain that she must be missing something. "Jarran, you understand she was asking me to sing, right? To *sing*. Right there in front of both of you."

He shrugged. "I am certain a musician of your caliber could have performed in a manner that would have posed no danger."

"*Danger?* Do you still not get what she wanted me to do? She wanted me to sing to make her feel...ecstatic. To use music like a drug—to *abuse* music."

Jarran looked a little shaken, but he recovered quickly. "Still, I fail to see the harm—if your songs can lift my Lady's spirits..."

"Lady Etherra's spirits are not my concern. What you are talking about is creating some sort of...of music addict. And I don't see any way in the world that can *not* be a bad thing."

Jarran frowned. "Your feelings don't matter. This was my Lady's request, and my Lady's requests must be honored."

"Not this time. Not by me. I'm sorry, but I refuse to go

along with this. You can do a lot of things, but you can't force me to sing. Even killing me wouldn't force me. I will not sing for purposes like these."

"I see." Jarran's face might have been chiseled from granite. "Then I am afraid I shall have to refuse you as well. You shall find no dinner, nor any other sustenance, here."

"So be it. I won't sing for her, Jarran." She laid down on the hard, uncomfortable cot and turned her back to him.

But she didn't relax until she heard the door close behind him.

♪

Alannys took off Songstrike, her cloak, and her boots, and put them on the chest of drawers, hoping she could finally get comfortable on the cot. It helped, but only marginally — the wretched thing was too hard to be really comfortable no matter what she did. She wondered if she might be better off on the floor.

Against her every expectation, she finally fell asleep. Her dreams were tortured and erratic, resonant with the sound of thumping footsteps. But it wasn't footsteps that woke her up.

It was the clashing of swords.

She sat up in bed, gaping towards her open door. She had just woken up, but she was sure it had not been open when she had fallen asleep. There was no lantern in the little room, and the only light was what spilled in from the dim corridor.

A dark shape whirled inside her room, battling four white shapes. His fluid spinning gave the dark shape away — it was the same man who had attacked her twice before. The four white shapes were some of Lady Etherra's warrior monks, dressed in their flowing, hooded white robes. As they fought, ducking and dodging, turning and striking, their voluminous robes wound up and furled out, know."

Alannys laughed sharply. "It seems to me that your ego is plenty healthy enough to survive it."

"Alannys." He sighed. "I don't like this wall you're putting up. Why won't you talk to me?"

She flinched. "It's not you, Chen. Really. It's just...what you said...and what you did...reminded me very strongly of something someone else once did, back when I first met him. The words...the rose..."

"Someone...else?"

"Yes." She side-stepped the implied question. "I did appreciate the party. Really. I guess I've just been feeling a little lonely lately."

He watched her fidget for a long moment. "Well, you're in the right place. It's hard to feel lonely with three hundred people around." He stood up, and she thought maybe she was finally off the hook. "Come with me. You left before we could give you your present."

"Present?"

"Just come with me." He took her hand and led her away from the tent, to the ring of wagons that surrounded the camp. He opened the door to a big wagon she did not recognize, and gestured her up the wooden stairs.

Inside a lantern burned, casting a warm light over the room. There was a narrow bed, piled high with quilts, and a little desk against the far wall, where the lantern sat. A tall chest of drawers and a wooden chair completed the room's simple furnishings.

Alannys turned back around. "I don't understand. This —this looks like somebody's home."

Chen grinned at her. "Welcome home."

She scanned the room again. "I—I don't understand."

He sat down on the little chair. "I spoke to the Council of Elders after we got back from Pinevale. I meant what I told you earlier—I don't think the *kortha* of the tribe should have to sleep on the ground in a little tent. The elders agreed. So," he shrugged, "we cleared out this *mol* for you. We had been using it for storage space, but it wasn't really needed for that. All of the things in it fit easily enough into our other storage wagons."

"I don't know what to say. Thank you. This means a lot to me."

"Don't thank me. It was no trouble. And I would have moved out of my own wagon before I let you go on living in that tent."

Her eyes welled up with tears. She had been going around with a chip on her shoulder, begrudging these people the inconvenience she judged them to be. And yet they cared about her, and troubled themselves to see that she was comfortable. And Chen — doing this for her, after everything that had happened...

She looked away, hoping to hide her tears, and dragged her sleeve across her face. She didn't want to explain any more than she already had. "This is wonderful, Chen. It's perfect."

To her surprise, she found him watching her with sympathy in his dark eyes. "Not yet it isn't. Let's go get your things and bring them in."

She felt oddly exposed. How much did Chen already know? How much had he guessed?

She pushed the unsettling questions aside and followed him back out of the wagon — her wagon. She still couldn't quite believe that. What had she done to deserve such kindness?

She didn't know. But she vowed to try her hardest to be worthy of the Singari in the future.

♫

Dinner at the camp was early that evening. They gathered around the great campfire, passing around platters piled with meats and vegetables, drinking and laughing.

Alannys left her wagon and joined them, making a deliberate effort to be more involved with the Singari. Their hearty welcome humbled her. She had been holding the entire group at arm's length, but they included her wholeheartedly in everything they did.

Quite a few people she had never met came over to where she sat with Chen and introduced themselves. When she found a few moments of quiet, Alannys excused herself and went to find the elders.

She found them sitting together at a table in the shadows, away from the crowd. She wondered if they kept to themselves voluntarily, or if the other Singari stayed away. She couldn't say she was any too keen on approaching them herself, actually. It seemed as though all of her interactions with the elders were negative. She hung back in the shadows until Chira gestured her forward.

"Come, come, child. You needn't stand on ceremony here; we're just three old people running our mouths. What can we do for you this fine evening?"

Alannys knelt by the table. "I wanted to thank you for what you've already done. I'm honored that you've given me a place to stay."

Bayred snorted. "That's why you're here? It's hardly worth mentioning. That useless boy doesn't have very many good ideas, but I suppose this was one of them."

Chira smiled tolerantly. "Now, Bayred, that is no attitude for accepting thanks." She turned back to Alannys. "It was the least we could do, Lady Alannys. We have place a terrible burden on you, and you have borne it admirably."

"No." She shook her head. "No, I haven't. I haven't really accepted my position here, I haven't really tried. But I intend to start."

Legara frowned ominously. "That kind of talk doesn't

sound appropriate for the Redeemer," she said in her shrill voice.

"What, I'm not allowed to apologize? I'm here to own up to my wrongs, and that's hard enough without anyone making it worse. I didn't understand what I was getting into with Brutagar—I would have done it anyway, mind you, stopping him was worth the price—but then I held the consequences against you. I was angry at you, and treated you unfairly. I'm sorry."

"Stop!" It seemed like a well-done apology speech, right up until Legara's shrill shriek put an end to it. "This is *not appropriate!*"

Alannys stared at her in shock. "What are you talking about? You should apologize when you've acted wrongly. This is basic playground etiquette here."

"Not for the *kortha!*" Legara's face was bright pink. "Even less for the Redeemer. This is just—just *groveling!*"

Alannys gritted her teeth together to forestall an impolite response, and stood up, suddenly eager to distance herself from the elders.

"Now, Legara, that is no way to speak to Alannys." Chira's tone had a hint of an edge. "For your part, Alannys, please understand that behind Legara's reaction is a valid concern. It does not do for a leader to show weakness."

Weakness? An apology was a sign of *weakness?* She thought back to the hours after King Caleb's funeral, back to the shame Dorramon had felt. Shedding tears for your father's death was evidently a sign of weakness, too.

"I'm not that kind of leader," she said. "I don't care to be that kind of leader. I'm not infallible, and I'm not omnipotent. I'm only human, and I won't pretend to be more."

"That's fool's talk," Bayred said. "You know so much now that you can sneer at advice from the *zhotha?*"

"No," Alannys said. "I don't imagine I ever will. But I won't change who I am, either. You put *me* in charge, not someone who doesn't believe in showing weakness. I'm afraid you just have to deal with it now. Unless — you've changed your mind, and I'm free to go?"

"If that's your impression," Chira said, "I'm afraid it's mistaken. You are, of course, free to do as you wish with our advice. But I hope you won't always dismiss it so lightly."

The people around them suddenly began to break up, sparing Alannys from responding. Some cleared away dishes and food, and others disappeared into tents and wagons, only to reappear a few moments later wearing bright scarves and sashes. Horses had been hitched to a bright purple wagon, and as Alannys watched, it filled with men and women dressed in vivid reds, purples, blues, and greens, with faces painted to match.

Alannys jumped at the chance to change the subject. "What's going on?"

Chira smiled, either unaware of her deflection or deliberately letting it go. "Tonight, they dance. The *stortha* are going to Pinevale. It is how they earn coin."

"Ah. I see." Alannys stood. "I'll wish you a good evening, then, and let you get back to you meal."

None of the elders looked very pleased, but she scooted away before they could challenge her further. It wasn't the best way to end a conversation, but at that point, she would take whatever she could get.

She headed back across camp toward her wagon, watching as those around her continued their preparations for the dance. Somehow she had always assumed that the entire tribe went into town to dance, as ridiculous as that seemed now. What would the elderly and the children do? She shook her head. Her assumptions showed the same flaw as the attitudes of the townsfolk; a failure to consider the Singari as people. It seemed to her that the root of all prejudice was that same failing, and it outraged her even more when she saw it in herself.

There had to be a way to change that.

Alannys climbed the stairs into her wagon, and shoved the door closed behind her with a foot. She flopped down on her bed, not bothering to light the little lantern. Darkness suited her mood.

She reached into her shirt and pulled out the Seeing Stone. Since meeting the Singari, she wore it all the time. She knew it didn't make sense, but she felt like the stone supported her—and she could use that support right now. She cradled it in her hands, and it glowed with a soft blue light. Dorramon's image floated there, perfect and clear, somehow separate from the colors and veins of the stone.

Alannys sighed. The tightness in her chest bespoke unshed tears. How in the world had she ended up like this, so far from home, so far from her friends, with so many people relying on her? She could have used the stone again to acquire a new image of Dorramon, but she didn't have the heart to do it.

There was a slight rap at the door.

Alannys wasn't in the mood for company. She ignored the door, figuring whoever was there would go away.

"Alannys?" To her surprise, the door pushed open. "Are you in here?"

"Not big on privacy, are you, Chen? Come on in." She didn't bother to sit up.

She could see him climb the wooden stairs into the wagon, his silhouette strong and sharp against the outside light. He hesitated in the doorway. "I hope I didn't wake you."

"Oh, no. I haven't been sleeping. You aren't interrupting anything."

"Ah. All right." He seemed uncertain, but in the low

light coming in the door, he found the little wooden chair and sat down. "I wanted to talk to you about something."

Alannys rolled over on her side to regard him. "Go for it. What can I do for you?"

He sat back in the chair, looking somewhere over her head. "You said earlier you are trying to bring music back. And we've all heard stories of the risks you've taken to do just that. I've been thinking...we talked once about how strange it is for the Singari to dance with no music. What if...what if we brought the music back to the dance?"

She sat up. This conversation had suddenly gotten a whole lot more interesting. "You mean perform in towns, with music?"

Chen looked uncomfortable. "That's what I was thinking, yes."

"Even I've never thought of anything that bold. Do you think people would really come?"

"I don't know. I think so. Everybody's heard how you saved the king's life with music once, and how you saved Garrant. The nobles of the court even came to hear you sing. I think everybody is going to be curious about it."

"You do have a point." She had to admit his points made sense, but there was still something about it that made her shy away. There was so much risk in proposition—she racked her brain, trying to think of a way to mitigate that risk. Anything at all. "I wonder...if they might be more comfortable with music if they didn't have to see it?"

"See it?"

Alannys stood up, pacing the length of the wagon. "Yes, you know—if they didn't have to watch. Where I come from, auditions are often done behind screens. They do it to ensure impartial judging, but it also can help your nerves, if you don't see the people listening to you. I wonder if it might also work the other way—if it might help the townspeople's nerves if they don't have to see the people making the music."

"You may be onto something there." He seemed to consider it, leaning back in the chair, watching her pace. "We'd need something to hide us. We could probably make something."

"It wouldn't have to be much. Just hanging a sheet would do it. Just so that they don't actually see anybody playing."

Chen grinned at her. "So you think it's a good idea?"

"Chen, I think it's a great idea." She grinned back at him. Now this felt big and exciting—for the first time, she felt like she might have a chance to make a real difference, without a disaster prompting the change.

At least, she hoped their performance wouldn't be a disaster.

♫

Everything in the Singari camp looked different to Alannys the next morning, though she knew it was all the same. It felt as though her new motivation changed it all—as if her secret performance plans colored every thing her eyes touched. For the first time, she walked through the camp with a bounce in her step, excited about what was to come.

Just as everyone was beginning to prepare for supper, Chen collared her and took her out into the forest to show her what he had been working on all day. He was so vague, Alannys knew it had to be related to the performance. She figured he had to be almost as excited as her—he made her walk out into the forest ahead of him, with his hands over her eyes.

"Come on, Chen," she complained, stumbling over a tree root for the third time, "can't I look yet?"

"Now, now, Alannys, the Muses smile upon patience. You can't just *look* at this, you have to feel it, absorb its essence. It must become part of you."

"Wow—that's really creepy. I'm not sure I want to see it now. What have you been doing out here?"

She heard his delighted, musical laughter, and he withdrew his hands. She couldn't have said what she expected to see, but she was pretty sure it wasn't the thing standing in the small forest clearing before her.

It was a wooden frame, maybe two yards square, and pulled taut inside it was a bright purple piece of cloth. The frame was hinged so that it could be folded for transport.

"Wow," Alannys said, lost for a moment for anything else to say. "This is amazing."

Chen gave her a hard, focused look, as though he might have been gauging her sincerity. "You are sure?"

"Positive. Honestly, Chen, I can't imagine how it could be better. This is so much nicer than anything I had imagined."

His stern expression dissolved into a grin. "Terrific. Then you have no excuse not to go with me tonight."

"I—what?"

"The *stortha* return to Pinevale tonight. We can take this along. I have the lute ready. Naturally you'll want to bring your violin..."

Alannys stared at him. "Naturally. You do believe in jumping in with both feet, don't you?"

Chen shrugged. "Once you've decided where you're going, I don't see what you gain by sitting and staring down the road."

"I suppose. Are you sure this is all right?"

Was it just her imagination, or was there something odd in the way his eyes slid away from hers? "You worry too much. I've spoken with the dancers, and they're excited about it. Come on, we need to hurry and get your violin. They'll be leaving soon."

"Chen, I'm not sure that—"

"Less talking, more moving! Do you want to get left

behind?"

He shooed her off and folded up the screen, then followed along behind her back into camp, keeping up a constant stream of excited chatter that almost distracted her from her reservations.

Almost.

They picked up her violin from her wagon, and the lute from the council wagon. They bypassed the bonfire and the food, and went straight to the *storthamol* – the dancer's wagon. Chen helped Alannys into the bright purple wagon. Wooden benches lined the inside, full of dancers in bright blouses and scarves. She huddled on the floor against the wall just inside the door, clutching her violin case across her lap, trying to imagine some way of looking at this situation that made it feel like she belonged there at all.

Chen followed her in, carrying the lute in its wooden chest. She glanced up at him as he sat down next to her. He was dressed like the other dancers, with vividly colored silk scarves tied around his neck, waist, and wrists. She felt very plain by comparison. "Don't think I don't see that look," he said. "Didn't I tell you not to worry?"

"Well, yes," she said, "but—"

The door to the wagon flung open, and silhouetted in the doorway was the irate figure of Bayred. "You!" He hauled Chen up by the collar, with a strength Alannys wouldn't have expected in a man of his advanced years. "Outside, now!"

Chen didn't manage to get a word out before Bayred dragged him to the steps and tossed him down. Alannys stepped around the lute chest and followed, trying to get her head around what she'd seen. Hadn't Chen just told her not to worry? She shook her head, and hopped down the little stairs.

Chen sat there in the grass, dusting off his sleeves with exaggerated impatience. "You'll be explaining that, I should hope. Or apologizing. Or *both*. I don't appreciate being thrown around like a sack of rotten potatoes."

"A sack of rotten potatoes," shrilled Legara, standing across from him, "would be less troublesome."

Chen snorted disdainfully.

Chira stood next to Legara, watching him over crossed arms, shaking her head and saying nothing.

"*Sharast.*" The word ground like a curse from Bayred's throat, heavy and severe. "No other punishment could be sufficient for this."

"Bayred..." Chira was still shaking her head.

"No, wait!" Alannys pushed into the middle of the group. "You can't be serious."

"Chira, you can't possibly defend him this time." Bayred barreled right on as though she hadn't even spoken. "This isn't harmless, and it isn't cute. You can't let this go!"

"Now wait just a minute," Alannys said again, grabbing Chen's arm and hauling him to his feet. He stood staring at the elders, looking completely pole-axed.

The elders paid just as much attention to her as they had the first time she'd spoken—which was to say, none at all. Bayred pressed on as though there had been no interruption at all. "Music, Chira—music! You understand that, right? You know this hooligan, this...this unrepentant blood traitor was planning to take our most dangerous secret out into public and—"

"That's enough!" Alannys made sure they couldn't ignore her this time—her voice was loud and sharp, with just a hint of musical command. "I've had just about all I can take of this. Would someone care to explain what exactly is going on here?"

"Perhaps we should ask you that," Legara said, her

tone snippy and impatient.

"I'm so glad you asked. It looks to me as though you are attacking Chen for something that was my idea."

For just a moment, Chira's mask of neutrality slipped. "Your idea? This was your doing, Alannys?"

"Yes. So if we could all calm down and be reasonable now, it would be much appreciated."

Bayred rolled his eyes, supremely unimpressed. "We are expected to look to you for the standard of reasonable behavior now? This outrageous situation doesn't help make your case, you know. Chira — we must take action on this. An example must be made!"

Alannys crossed her arms. "You want to make an example of me? Go for it. Exile me. I was against this *kortha* thing from the start."

Bayred looked suddenly pale. "One does not," he swallowed hard, "...*exile* the Redeemer. But this — this thing you planned must not go on. It's unthinkable!"

"Unthinkable," she echoed. "Why?"

"It — it's just *not done!*"

"I'd like to ask one question, if an unrepentant blood traitor might be permitted to speak." Chen squeezed her shoulder, and gave her a conspiratorial wink. "I'm pretty surprised to see the entire *zhotha* here — does that mean this is a matter of the old ways? Do our laws prohibit our performance?"

Chen sounded innocent — almost *too* innocent, given the way Bayred's face turned immediately purple. "No," the old man said. It sounded as though the single syllable had been forced out past every bit of resistance he could muster.

"I see." Chen appeared to think this over. "So the *zhotha* is opposing the *kortha* on a matter unrelated to law?"

Even Chira looked shocked, hearing it put like that.

"Now, wait, Chen. That's an over-simplification. We can't go along with this. You know that."

"Well, I know you don't like it. But I also know this is what she's sworn to do—it's part of her mission. And you knew that too, before she even came here."

Chira frowned. "That's true, but—"

Alannys interrupted, suddenly seeing the opening Chen had given her. "And what's more, you agreed to support my mission when you made me *kortha*. Isn't that right?"

Chira sighed in evident defeat. "All right, you win. I had hoped you might pay more heed to our warning, but I suppose we approached it badly." Her sidelong glance at Bayred was not lost on the old man, who turned uncomfortably away. "Still, these things are not done for a reason. We had hoped you might respect that."

"That reason is fear," Alannys said. "You know I'm here to change that. I won't respect it, and I won't kowtow to it. Do you still intend to oppose me?"

"As Chen so kindly pointed out, it isn't our place." Chira held up a hand to silence Bayred, who clearly had objections. "We are here to oversee matters of law. As this is not such a matter, we are powerless to intervene."

"Fine, then." Alannys caught hold of Chen's arm, and turned to leave.

"However," Chira said, perhaps a little louder than strictly necessary, "setting the *zhotha* aside, as an old woman who has seen and experienced much, I beg you to reconsider. Nothing good will come from this."

It might have been a good moment for a snappy rejoinder, but Alannys suddenly found she didn't have any. She watched Chira shuffle away, standing and staring as though nailed to the spot. The old woman's words had cast a curious chill over the clearing.

Chen took her hand and pulled her back into the

dancer's wagon. "Try not to let them get to you."

"Thanks." She settled back into her spot on the floor, pulling her violin case back into her lap, trying to push away the memory of Chira's slow shuffle and haunting words. "Remind me again why I thought this was a good idea."

Chen looked at her in surprise. "Second thoughts?"

Alannys shook her head. "No, not really. I know this is the right thing—I know it's necessary. It's just—just nerves, I guess." She held up her hands, gleaming pale white in the low light. "All of the sudden my hands are cold."

Chen laughed and put his arm around her shoulders. "There's no reason to be nervous, Alannys. Everything will be fine."

She believed him, but at the same time she couldn't help thinking those sounded an awful lot like famous last words.

♫

Famous last words.

It was the first thought through Alannys's mind when she woke up, sprawled uncomfortably on a plain wooden bench in a room of native stone. Her head hurt, and her arms were sore.

For a tingling moment she had no idea where she was, or how she had gotten there. The room was completely empty but for herself and the bench she lay on. The floor and the ceiling were rough, uneven stone, and so were the walls—except for one. The wall farthest from her was composed entirely of thick iron bars, with a gate in the center, secured with a large padlock.

Alannys pushed herself up to sit on the bench, resting her throbbing head in her hands. What on earth had happened? She cast back through her memory, and slowly things started to come back to her. She had fleeting impressions of people she had seen in the Pinevale town square, nodding and clapping. Around the edge of the screen she had even seen a few spectators begin to dance themselves.

Someone screamed. People ran, people panicked. Blows were struck. She handed her violin to Chen and went out into the square to see what had happened, and if things could be salvaged.

Her memories after that were even more scattered. Angry faces, raised voices. The Singari dancers, fleeing to the purple wagon. Two of the men hauling Chen inside. The wagon, rumbling away into the forest.

Alannys groaned. She still had no idea what had really happened last night, but it was plain that their grand idea of bringing back music had gone down in flames. And now here she sat, alone and to all appearances forgotten, in Pinevale's stone jail.

The Seeing Stone still hung inside her shirt. She could feel its weight around her neck. Her royal medallion was in her wagon back at the camp, where it wouldn't do her any good at all. But Songstrike and her beltpouch hung at her side, untouched out of respect or fear. Even her insanely valuable royal bracelet still glimmered on her wrist.

The little cell was solid. The walls were mortared stone, and the irons bars were set deeply into the stone. She would not be leaving this place until someone let her out. She could attempt to sing up a storm large enough to destroy the jail, but the attempt would likely kill her—and the weather itself would kill countless others. No, she was stuck here—her music would not save her.

Through the bars she could see a large open room, with three wooden desks and chairs. As if on cue, the iron-reinforced door opened, and a tall, balding man came into the room. He wore the bronze medallion of a reeve.

The reeve flicked a careless glance her way, and settled

himself in one of the chairs. He pulled a sheet of paper and a quill from a desk drawer, and started writing.

"You're awake." His tone was flat. He did not look up from his work.

"Yes." She stood up and walked to the iron bars on legs that felt shaky and untrustworthy. "Are you going to let me out of here?"

"No."

Alannys backed up and sat down on the bench, taken aback. He hadn't even hesitated, and he sounded completely unconcerned with her. "Can I ask why not?"

The quill paused. The reeve looked over at her out of the tops of his eyes. "You don't know why you're in here?"

Alannys shook her head.

He propped his quill carefully in an indentation in his inkwell. "Well. Inciting a riot. Performing harmful music in a public place."

"Harmful?" she blurted. "We were playing dance music!"

He looked at her expressionlessly. "So you say. I am no expert on the Talents." He folded his hands in his lap. "All I can tell you is that you played, and a child fell gravely ill. The only reason you are still in this cell is because we don't yet know whether to charge you with poisoning or murder."

The world lurched sideways, and she put a hand on the bench to steady herself. "Murder?" Her hoarse whisper felt like it came from someone else. "You mean this child —this child might die?"

He regarded her in hostile silence.

"And you think I did this? You think I came here and willfully poisoned a child?"

He lifted his shoulders in an uncaring shrug. "I can't say. You may only be an accomplice."

"Accomplice?"

"What did you think would come of associating with Singari? Decent people keep their distance from them, Lady Alannys, and there are good reasons why. Your— companion may be good-looking, but you shouldn't have let that fool you."

Alannys stared at him. Over and over she told herself it didn't matter, she had to stay calm or she would never get out of here. But she kept hearing his disdainful tone, seeing his smirk, and her fingers curled into angry fists as her last thread of patience snapped. "Do you mean to sit there and tell me you are keeping me in this cell for no better reason than your own prejudice against a group of people who have done you no wrong? A child gets sick, and you can think of no better explanation than the Singari must have done it?"

He came up out of his chair. "I mean to tell you, my *Lady*, that you had better take a nicer tone with me! You are in there until I decide otherwise, and this is certainly no way to begin securing your release!"

Alannys walked right up to the bars, looking directly into his narrowed, hateful eyes. "I am here, Reeve, until I decide I have had enough of this foolishness! Do you think you can keep me anywhere against my will?"

It was a bluff, but he had no way to know that. His eyes were huge. "Are you threatening me?"

She exhaled in a puff, reminding herself that this man knew nothing about her or what she could do. "I'm giving you fair warning. If you don't start talking sense, and soon, I will not waste time threatening you." She turned away and went back to her bench.

A long time later, she heard him sit back down in the wooden chair. She unclenched her fists, and slowly released a breath she hadn't been aware of holding.

♫

The reeve's door flew open and banged against the

wall in the middle of the afternoon, jolting Alannys from a nap. The smell of chicken and onions still hung in the room from the reeve's lunch. He had not given Alannys anything to eat, muttering about the irregularity of Singari meals and how surely she was used to going without by now.

She pushed herself up off the wooden bench, ignoring the aching protest of her muscles. A plump woman in a brown woolen dress came in, her gray hair wrapped up in a brown scarf. Chen followed on her heels, his shirt wrinkled and his hair limp and mussed. He looked as though his night had been as bad as hers, but he managed to muster a wink and a smile for her.

The woman glanced around the room, her gaze lingering sympathetically on Alannys. The contours of her face were soft, but her eyes as they continued their round of the room turned hard and flinty. "Reeve Turan!"

The reeve jumped up out of his chair, running a hand absently over his thinning hair. "Dame Pria. What can I do for you?"

"You can let Alannys out of that cell!" Chen snapped. "This whole thing is ridiculous, and you've kept her here far too long."

Turan's thin face twisted into a sneer. "I don't remember addressing you, Singari. This conversation is between the healer and me."

Chen threw his hands up in frustration.

Pria put a hand on Chen's shoulder in a motherly gesture. "Control your hostility, Turan. Chen is right. He told you from the beginning that Lady Alannys and the Singari did not cause Lira's illness. Now you have my diagnosis to confirm it."

"Told you so," Alannys said.

Turan threw an angry glance toward her cell. "I am not sure, given your well-known sympathies for these vagrants, that your word can be considered sufficient to release her."

"Merciful Muses!" Pria said. "You have always been a small man, Turan, and you are becoming smaller by the day. Still, I anticipated this sort of attitude from you. Three other healers have examined Lira." She thrust a scroll at the reeve. "Here are their signed diagnoses. You will find that they all agree, and I agree with them."

Turan slowly unrolled the paper. "Three healers...and you...that's every master healer in Pinevale!"

"Yes. I advise you to accept that as sufficient to release the mage, unless you wish to invite trouble with the Healer's Guild."

Turan stared at her.

"Pinevale is fortunate to have four master healers in residence," Chen said conversationally. "It would be a shame if they felt slighted enough to leave, say, if the town reeve felt his opinion was more valid than their diagnoses."

"But..." Turan trailed off.

"I see," Alannys said suddenly, and all of them turned to look at her in surprise. "Would someone mind passing me a quill and paper, then? I've just come from Brookeshire Castle, and I think Lady Etherra might like to know she's got a reeve working for her who lets his prejudice inform his work this way. What do you all think? Would she come down here if I asked?"

The reeve's ears turned pink. "I should have expected something like this. This whole damn country has lost their heads over that woman." He tossed a ring of brass keys onto his desk. "Fine. Open the cell. Just get her out of my town before she does any more damage." He stomped out of the open door.

Pria sighed and went after him.

Chen scooped up the keys and unlocked the iron door.

"I am so sorry about this, Alannys. I had no intention of leaving you last night. I'm afraid the dancers panicked. I took the instruments to the *storthamol* for safety, and they took me with them when they ran." He swung the door open. "Are you all right? Has he mistreated you?"

Alannys came out of the cell and hugged him hard. "Thank you, Chen. I was afraid I was going to be stuck in there until I died or forced my way out with a destructive show of song." She sighed and stepped back. "This place is crazy—I couldn't get Turan to see reason at all. What on earth is going on?"

Chen took her arm and led her out of the building. Nightfire waited outside, next to a stout pony that Alannys assumed belonged to the healer. "A child fell ill at the performance last night. I'm afraid a lot of people jumped to conclusions. There was a riot."

"Turan thinks I did that."

"I know." Chen climbed up on Nightfire, and held out a hand to help her up behind him. In the sunlight, his face was full of lines she had never seen there before—he must have been dead on his feet. "That's crazy, and I think most people in town realize that. At least they do now—last night no one was thinking very reasonably. Hold on to me —Nightfire can be hard to ride when you're not used to him."

Alannys wrapped her arms around his waist, and they started out of town. "Have you been here all night?"

Chen shrugged. "Almost. I came back as soon as I could. Things were out of control—people running around making accusations, fighting each other, destroying things, but nobody doing much of anything to help. As crazy as it sounds, jail was probably the safest place for you in Pinevale last night. Would you believe nobody had even summoned a healer for the little girl, not even by the time I got back to town?"

"What?"

"It's true, I swear. Her father had some kind of breakdown. I found him sitting by her bed with his head in his hands, rocking back and forth. He didn't seem to realize I was there, not even when I spoke directly to him. It's just him and her; she doesn't have any other family. So I went and found Pria myself and brought her there."

The farther Pinevale receded into the distance behind them, the better Alannys liked it. "Thank you, Chen. If you hadn't done what you did, they may never have let me out of there."

Chen said nothing, tacitly agreeing. She tightened her hold on him, thankful he was on her side. It had been a narrow escape.

♫

The Singari remained camped outside of Pinevale for two more days, waiting for Alannys to give some command. She stayed in her wagon, coming out for neither meals nor company. She spent most of her time stretched out on her bed, staring into the Seeing Stone and wondering what the devil she should do now.

Their disastrous failure in Pinevale haunted her. How could she go on leading them when her decisions had led them to that? Her instinct told her they should leave Pinevale, and soon—but her instinct had also told her that the musical performance was a good thing. What would she be leading them into this time, if she was wrong?

At some point she picked herself up off the bed and went to sit at the writing desk. She put the Seeing Stone on the desktop, and its faint blue light was sufficient for her to see. She laid out a few sheets of the heavy paper and the bottle of ink she'd bought in town, and sat there toying with the quill, wondering, now that it came to it, what she thought she was going to write. She had bought the paper thinking to write to Dorramon, hoping it might ease her loneliness. But what could she write to him now? Would she write of her failure in Pinevale? Would she tell him of the night she'd spent in jail? Would she tell him all of Pinevale looked down on her now because she went around with Singari?

No, she wouldn't. She couldn't. But writing about anything else felt false. So she sat there, turning the quill over in her hands, gazing at the Seeing Stone. She was no closer to any answers now than she had been two days ago.

When the door flung open, she was still sitting at the desk, still staring at the blank page. The bright light spilling in the doorway hurt her eyes. She couldn't even tell who had come into the wagon.

"Alannys, you've got to come out of here. You can't keep doing this."

She sighed and turned back to the desk. "Shut the door, Chen. That light is too bright."

He turned back to close the door, then hesitantly stepped toward her. "Muses, Alannys, I can't even see in here. Is this what you've been doing the last two days, just sitting here in the dark?"

She didn't answer. She hoped the darkness would prove too uncomfortable for him and force him to leave, but evidently his eyes adjusted quickly. He stood next to the desk, looking down at her. She saw his eyes flick to the Seeing Stone.

"This isn't good for you. This isn't good for *us*. How long do you want us to sit here, waiting for you to pull yourself out of whatever it is you've sunk into?"

She shook her head. "I don't care. You're a self-sufficient bunch of people, you can make your own decisions. If you are tired of sitting here, pack up, go somewhere else. I don't care. Just go away and leave me alone."

"No. I won't." Chen knelt in front of her chair and put

his hands on her shoulders. "If I wasn't here, you would have your wish. None of the others would come in here and disturb you."

"Then why don't you go back out there with them?" Her words were short and cruel, trying to sting him into leaving.

He gave her a shake. "Because none of them care about you, damn you! As a leader, yes, and as a savior and a political figure. But as a person you are lost on them. And they would allow you to wallow in here until that person is gone. But I will not."

She stared at him. "What do you want me to do?"

"I want you to come out of here. I want you to get back to the things that are important to you. What happened to your mission? What happened to bringing back music?"

She dropped her head in her hands. "It got thrown in jail, that's what. And the Singari got run out of town. And a child is ill. Things are worse in Pinevale now than they ever were before I brought music there."

"So you're just going to give up? Alannys, what happened in Pinevale was not your fault. Those things were out of your control. And it doesn't mean that the whole idea is bad. Look, I know you've experienced a lot of failure since you came to Ravanmark. But haven't you had a lot of success as well?"

Someone knocked at the door.

Chen muttered a curse under his breath. "Go away!"

"I can't." The voice was hoarse and ragged. "I have to see the Lady Alannys."

"What's this?" Chen stood and moved toward the door. "That is no Singari."

The door opened on a short man. His face was haggard and unshaven. His eyes were blotchy and red. Alannys squinted at him in the sudden glare. "Can I help you?"

"Oh, my Lady, I hope so." He wobbled where he stood.

"I am Mago. It's—it's my daughter. She fell ill at the performance—"

"Your daughter was the child who fell ill?"

"Yes, my Lady. The town healers have been with her ever since. But she is not improving. They say there is nothing more they can do." His voice cracked. "You are my last hope."

Alannys grabbed her riding cloak. "There is no guarantee that I can help. Music can not heal all hurts."

The man nodded.

The ride to Pinevale seemed longer than ever, though the three of them pushed their mounts as fast as they could though the steep mountain forest. Alannys had little attention to spare for the beauty of Pinevale, and focused on following Lira's father as he led them to a small, two-story pine log home.

He opened the door and stepped aside to let Alannys and Chen inside. Alannys swept the empty living room with a glance. "Where is she?"

"Upstairs."

Chen took the stairs two at a time. Alannys followed him into a bedroom. She tossed her cloak and sword on the sofa against the wall and knelt by the bed.

The child before her looked maybe four or five years old, and dark hair framed her face in tight curls. Her skin looked thin and fragile, and her lips were pale. Alannys laid a gentle hand on her forehead.

Lira felt cool and clammy. Alannys tried hard not to show any reaction, aware of Mago's anxious eyes on her.

Chen studied her face, then laid a hand on her shoulder and gave it a squeeze. "Come, Mago," he said, turning to the man lingering by the door. "We should leave Alannys to her work."

The door closed softly behind them. Alannys rested her forehead on the edge of the bed, trying to gather whatever courage she had. Loathe as she was to admit it, the healers had been right. There wasn't much more that could be done here.

But she refused to give up. She didn't know what illness had stricken this child, and she didn't care. She would do everything in her power to help. And if the attempt took her own life as well, that was a risk she was willing to take. It was better than living out her life knowing she had allowed a child to die, and done nothing.

That didn't mean she was looking forward to it, though. "Help me out here," she muttered, wrapping one hand around Songstrike's grip, trying not to notice the way her fingers trembled. With a deep breath to steady herself, she reached out to take Lira's hand in her free one.

And she sang.

♫

Alannys lost all track of time. She couldn't have said how many hours she spent kneeling beside the bed, holding Lira's hand and singing. She couldn't feel her legs, and her hands were cold and numb, but she was past caring. All that mattered was the music, keeping the music going, holding open the channel of song. She couldn't have said what words she was singing — was she even singing words? She had gone beyond being able to tell.

The sound of a door flinging open startled her — her definition of the place she was in had not come to include doors or people who opened them. She twisted stiffly around to look at the doorway, but her eyes were so blurry and unfocused she could not tell who was standing there.

"Alannys!" Strong hands gripped her shoulders, shaking her when she didn't immediately respond. "Merciful Muses, have you been singing this whole time? Come away from there. You need a break."

The concerned face in front of her slowly swam into focus. "Chen? Chen, what are you doing here?"

"Stopping you from killing yourself, apparently," he snapped. "I'm serious. Get up off that floor — you can't keep this up."

"I can't quit." She turned back to the bed, ignoring the aching in her bones. "She won't get better if I quit."

"Alannys, *you* won't be able to get better if you push this much farther!" He raked a hand through his hair, looking from her to the sleeping form on the bed. "Look, I'll take over, all right? I asked Mago to bring up some food. You can get yourself something to eat, have a nap on the couch, and I'll do this so you won't have to worry. Will that work?"

"Sorry, Chen." She tried to smile, but she couldn't tell if it worked — the muscles of her face felt creaky. "Can't. If I stop, I'll have Muse's Fever within an hour. Can't stop till I'm done."

Chen puffed out his cheeks in evident frustration. He started to say something else, but the door swung open again, and Mago edged sideways into the room, carrying a tray of meats and cheeses. Behind him was Dame Pria, and a younger lady Alannys did not recognize.

"*This* is your miracle cure, Mago?" The young woman sounded scandalized, and the glance she raked across Alannys was haughty and dismissive. "A Singari, and — and this? You're really desperate enough to let this woman sing for your daughter?"

"Hush, Wylda," Pria said. "These things aren't for you to question. Lady Alannys's song may yet raise Lira — we do not know." Her words were encouraging, but her face looked doubtful.

Wylda sniffed. "Aye, it might, but at what cost? A person raised by music isn't a person at all, if you ask me."

"But nobody did ask you," Chen said, facing Wylda with a hard expression. "Healing someone isn't changing them — I would have expected a healer to know that."

"Sure, if singing and healing were the same!" Wylda shot back. "But they aren't, and if she keeps this up, what climbs out of that bed isn't going to be Mago's little girl."

"That's ridiculous," Alannys said. She was feeling dizzy and having trouble following the conversation, but even in her state she could see that kind of thinking had to be refuted.

"I agree," Mago said. "And I don't think you should be in here bothering her when she's working so hard to save Lira."

"As you wish," Pria said, throwing a hard look at Wylda to forestall any further outbursts. She moved beside the bed, and felt of Lira's forehead and pulse. She leaned in close and lifted the little girl's eyelids, and listened closely to her chest as she breathed.

Through all of this she never made a sound, never spoke a word that Mago could take issue with. But the grim way she shook her head was not lost on Alannys, or the tight set of her lips, pressed together in a thin, hard line.

"We'll take our leave, then," Pria said finally, grabbing Wylda's arm and hauling her toward the door. "Take care of yourself, Mago. Please try not to get your hopes too high."

Mago followed them out without comment.

"Healers," Chen snorted, watching the door swing shut again. "If it isn't the kind of healing they do themselves, it doesn't count. 'Not Mago's little girl,' indeed. It's pathetic. They're afraid of anything they don't understand."

"But everyone is like that, Chen," Alannys said. She knew it was only her imagination, but she swore she could still feel the healer's disapproving eyes on her. "I just hope their assessment was wrong—they didn't seem to think Lira has a chance of making it."

"Of course it was wrong. They don't know the first

thing about music or what it can do. Nothing worthwhile ever comes from listening to people like that." Chen blew out an exasperated sigh. "Look, get up from there. You can stop long enough to eat without triggering Muse's Fever, and I'll keep singing while you do. You've got to do something, Alannys — you really look terrible."

"Okay," she said. She knew he was right. She felt weird — her brain was distant and fuzzy, and her own body felt numb and disconnected. It was entirely possible that she had already gone too far, that she had already put so much of her energy into Lira that there was no turning back for her.

That thought didn't scare her the way it should have, and that was probably a bad sign, too.

Chen looked down at her and arched an eyebrow. "Then why aren't you getting up?"

"I don't think I can. It's like I'm stuck or something. Nothing's moving when I tell it to."

Almost before she'd finished speaking the words, Chen scooped her up off of the floor, cradling her in his arms as though she was made of glass that he feared might shatter. "Nothing except your mouth," he quipped, but his ears were red.

"Of course," she said. "Always energy to run my mouth."

"Yes, well." He put her down on the sofa and ran a hand through his hair, oddly avoiding making eye contact with her. "How about you try feeding it instead, and give me a break?"

"Yes, sir." She reached for some salted beef, and he turned away, going back to Lira's bedside.

For a few minutes she did nothing but sit on the couch and eat. She wasn't hungry, she didn't feel any satisfaction from eating the food — she couldn't even really taste it — but she knew Chen wouldn't be happy until she ate, so that's what she did.

And during that time, she never heard him sing. She didn't know if her sense of hearing was as dulled as her sense of taste, or if he was taking special care not to be heard, singing right into Lira's ear as he was—or both—but she ate in a curious, enveloping silence that seemed to beckon her inward, onward, deeper down.

"Don't you dare go to sleep," Chen said suddenly, sharply, startling her. "I'm not at all sure you'll wake up if you do."

"Don't worry, I wasn't even close to falling asleep," she lied, pushing herself off the couch and hobbling, stiff-legged, back to the bedside.

"Could've fooled me," Chen muttered, sitting back on his heels to watch her.

She pretended not to hear him, putting her hands on the edge of the bed and forcing her knees to buckle so she could kneel beside Lira again.

She started once again to sing, using the same song as best as she could remember. The lifeline opened up again, a yawning, black chasm draining her energy, and she lost everything she had gained from her short meal.

Chen joined in singing with her before she had finished three lines. She knew he couldn't be singing the same words that fast, but she also knew it didn't matter. The effect was immediate, and very welcome—she could feel some of that awful drain lessen.

Chen didn't seem convinced, though, watching her with visible, growing concern. They hadn't sung for more than a couple of minutes before he reached out and took her hand.

With that small motion, everything changed. Music charged like rushing water between them, *through* them, a force bigger than the two of them put together. Physical contact made the music they produced seem almost physical as well, and orders of magnitude stronger.

She had barely adjusted to this new development before something else happened she had never experienced before. She had been able to *feel* Chen's concern for her, an outside force moving through the music he was making, ever since he first took her hand. But all at once her hand grew warm in his — uncomfortably warm, almost unbearably warm — and the concern that had been moving through her suddenly turned *on* her, bringing the healing power of the music with it. She could feel it warming her, lifting her, restoring her energy and reviving her dulled senses.

She jerked her hand free and scooted away from Chen, dropping the song and staring at him through eyes wide with shock and dismay. "Chen, you can't *do* that!"

"What are you talking about?" The set of his jaw looked obstinate.

"You know damn well what I'm talking about," she snapped. She knew she couldn't last for a long argument; she had to settle this quickly. "We'll be lucky if we manage to save Lira — you don't have the energy to be worrying about me, too."

"Energy, hell. You say that like I have a choice. Music is all about intent; you know that as well as I do. You can't ask me to sit here and not care that you're slipping away in front of me."

"I am not slipping away."

"Sure, not *now*. Not since I helped you. But you needed it. You can't argue that."

She couldn't. She let her gaze slide from his, wondering how far she should go before she had to admit defeat. Risking herself was one thing, but was she really prepared to risk both of them, on a case the healers said was hopeless? Was she really *entitled* to risk both of them? She bit her lip, weighing her options and responsibilities, and then her gaze landed on the bed in front of her.

Lira's color was better—her cheeks were pinker, her lips no longer ashy gray. Her breathing was deep and even, audible in the quiet room. The rise and fall of her chest was detectable under the blankets.

And she knew she couldn't quit. No matter what the healers said, no matter what anyone said. And if Chen wanted to help, she couldn't tell him no. Not with these stakes.

"All right," she finally said. "I get what you're saying, just—try not to do that, okay?"

"All right," he said. She couldn't help thinking he'd agreed a little too quickly, and as they went back to singing, she was careful to keep her free hand down at her side. She couldn't tell him no, but she wouldn't help him make the risk to himself any bigger than it had to be.

She had a feeling it was already more than big enough—for both of them.

♪

It was impossible for Alannys to tell how long she knelt by Lira's bed, singing with Chen at her side. Mago brought more food twice—or was it three times?—and they took it in turns to slip away from the circle of song and eat. Pria and Wylda came in, and left again, shaking their heads. But if they said anything, Alannys and Chen never heard what it was. They were too busy singing, supporting each other, and watching the slow but steady improvement in their little patient. Alannys didn't know if the healers honestly couldn't see the change, or if they simply couldn't accept how it had come about.

And then came the moment when Lira's eyelids began to flutter, and she stirred in the bed.

Alannys and Chen fell silent, watching, holding their breath, hardly daring to hope.

But she continued to move, and her breathing quickened.

"Go get Mago," Alannys whispered, "if you can walk. I don't think I can."

Chen squeezed her shoulder, then pulled himself up and staggered out of the room. As miserable as he looked, Alannys still had to envy him—she couldn't even have stayed upright just then. She watched him sway unsteadily out the door, then turned back to the bed.

Lira's eyes were open.

"Oh, thank heaven." Alannys leaned heavily on the bed, positioning herself to see the little girl better. "Lira, can you hear me? How do you feel?"

Wide brown eyes examined her face. "Where's Daddy?"

"My friend has gone to get him. They will be back soon."

"Are you an angel?" Lira studied her face as if she recognized it. "You were with me all this time. I heard you sing. People don't sing."

Alannys laughed. "Sorry, I'm just a person—a person who can sing. My friend also sang, remember?"

"Maybe your friend is an angel, too," Lira said seriously.

"Listen to her," said Chen's cheerful voice from the doorway. "I like the way she thinks."

"Lira!" Mago crashed into the room, rushing to the bed and gathering his daughter into a crushing hug. "Lira...thank the Muses!"

"Daddy!" Lira crowed, throwing her arms around his neck. "Daddy, I missed you!"

Mago hugged her for a long moment, weeping into her hair.

"I don't think he believed me," Chen said, pulling Alannys to her feet, "not really. Not until he saw for himself."

"I wouldn't believe it either, if I hadn't seen it,"

Alannys admitted, swaying where she stood.

"Alannys!" Mago turned to her and hugged her till she thought her ribs would crack. Then he hugged Chen. "This is a miracle," he said, his voice raspy. "There's no other word for it. I owe you a debt bigger than my life. No thanks could be enough for this. Let us—let us come with you. We will join you on your journeys."

Alannys smiled, leaning heavily on Chen, but she shook her head. "I'm sorry, Mago, but we can't accept. The Singari life would not agree with you and your daughter, I'm afraid."

"I see." Mago sounded honestly disappointed to her—she must have been worse off than she realized. "I hope you will reconsider—how can I forfeit a life debt?"

"Don't look at it that way," Alannys said, trying to ignore the way Mago's image was swimming in front of her. "There's no debt here. The best way you can repay us is to keep on doing what you've always done, so Lira will be happy. But for now, Chen and I must leave."

Mago looked at her doubtfully. She didn't know if he had understood half of that; she was slurring her words pretty badly. "But—"

"I'm afraid Alannys is right," Chen said. "We really have to be going." He wrapped an arm around her waist and helped her hobble to the door.

Alannys focused hard on each individual step, and then the next, trying to survive what felt like a grueling journey to the front door. If she could just make it outside, she told herself, just outside, Quicksilver would get her back to camp and she wouldn't have to worry any more. Just outside.

She thought she had probably never been so happy to see a front door in her life as she was to see the front door of that little log house just then. She was holding onto Chen's neck, and his arm around her back was the only thing keeping her upright. She knew she didn't have much more in her, and she desperately wanted to get to Quicksilver before she lost it all.

But as Mago stepped in front of them to open the door, she could already tell it wasn't going to be that easy. Along with the first bright spray of light spilling around the edge of the door came the muttering of discontented people.

"Great," Chen said from beside her. "What's this, now?"

"I am sorry." Mago's face was out of Alannys's narrowing field of vision, but he certainly sounded apologetic. "Not everyone in Pinevale approves of what I have done, it seems."

"Muses preserve us, I should have expected something like this." Chen glanced down at her, and even in her state she could see the worry on his face. "We haven't got time for this. *She* hasn't got time for this. Can you help us, Mago?"

She could hear Mago's heavy sigh — it made her wonder about what he had been dealing with while they were upstairs singing. "I'll do whatever I can. It's me they are really here for, not you."

But as the three of them stepped out towards the horses, it wasn't Mago that was the focus of the hostile attention of the small crowd.

"Wylda was right," someone said. "They actually have the nerve to show their faces."

"Out of our way, please," Chen said evenly. "Lady Alannys is not feeling well."

"Is that so?" This disembodied voice sounded even more sneering, even more hostile than the first one. Alannys found herself glad that she couldn't really see their faces — perhaps it was a sort of blessing after all that she couldn't seem to focus on anything farther away than her own hands. On the other hand, it left her feeling oddly exposed. "Maybe she *shouldn't* feel well, after using music on a defenseless little girl!"

Yes, she was definitely feeling exposed. More so all the time.

Chen pulled her closer to him, and edged toward the horses. "Now, just calm down. We don't want trouble."

"Then you should have stayed in your wagon, Singari! You and that woman ain't welcome here!"

"That's enough." Mago sounded so calm, Alannys could hardly credit it—but then, he wasn't being insulted or threatened. "These two have done me a great service— me, and Lira too. She's awake now, and you lot are liable to scare her. Don't make me summon the reeve."

"Turan?" someone snorted. "Don't make me laugh—he likes these two about as much as we do."

Still, the threat seemed to have some effect—in the ensuing silence Alannys could hear the shuffling of nervous feet.

"It's a pity, don't you think?" Mago continued. "That two people, like this, two people who came here only to help a sick little girl, could be harassed this way. It makes me wonder about Pinevale."

Chen hoisted Alannys up onto Quicksilver, and pressed the reins into her hands. She wrapped the leather around her fingers, trying to stay on the horse and follow the conversation at the same time.

"It makes me wonder about *you*," the heckler retorted, "that you would allow such a thing. Maybe you don't belong in Pinevale."

"Maybe you're right." Mago sounded like he was finally getting angry. He took a couple of steps toward the street, seeming almost accidentally to leave enough room behind him for the horses to pass between him and the house, but he was waving them past behind his back.

"There are plenty of people in Pinevale who see your wrong-headedness for what it is. Your attitude will not prevail here. As for Lira and I, we shall join the Witnesses."

"The Witnesses!" came the gasp from the crowd. Alannys and Chen rode slowly behind Mago and out onto the street. "Are you serious?"

"Very much so. Now if you'll excuse me, I should go tend to Lira. It seems I didn't need to call for Turan after all—I can see him coming this way right now. Good morrow."

It didn't take the crowd long to disperse when they recognized Turan's lanky figure approaching. Mago disappeared back inside his house, and Alannys and Chen started back out of town.

"Do you think he was serious?" Alannys's voice sounded as though it was coming from somewhere else. It was disconcerting.

"I do. If you come to Pinevale next month, I wager Mago will be gone."

The words had an ominous sound that gave her a chill. "What are the Witnesses?"

"You mean you don't know?" Chen stared at her in open astonishment, but she couldn't manage more than shaking her head. "I—I see. The Witnesses are people, Alannys, who travel Ravanmark telling tales of the deeds you've done. There are people from Garrant, Falhill, Mirendasith Hall, the Great Palace—even a few from Crinn, who talk about the corruption that took over the town before you came."

If they hadn't both been in such bad shape, she would have sworn he was having a joke on her. As it was, though, she couldn't imagine he had the energy for pranks. "Are you—are you serious?"

"Dead serious." He looked at her evenly, and she could

see no hint of untruth in his face. "I thought you knew. You've had quite an effect on some people, Alannys. Life-changing."

There was something odd about his tone, but she couldn't spare any brainpower to think about it. She was having all she could do to wrap her mind around the idea of the Witnesses. People who traveled the countryside telling tales of her deeds? It was a blessing she could not have hoped for. She wasn't trying to turn the tide of public opinion alone, after all.

Perhaps there was hope, for her and for Ravanmark.

♪

Alannys and Chen rode straight back to camp without dallying any further in Pinevale. Alannys had no love for the town, and she wanted to be back among friends before the inevitable hit.

Chen kept a close eye on her during the ride. "Are you all right?" he asked her, over and over, and she assured him that she was. Later in the ride, she only nodded, slumped low over Quicksilver's neck.

"Are you all right?" Chen asked again as they rode into camp. She did not respond, and he looked over at her, alarmed. "Alannys, are you all right?"

He slid off Nightfire, and ran over to Quicksilver. He caught her when she slipped sideways off the horse, unconscious.

"I need Nashara!" he shouted, carrying her to her wagon. "And broth, and extra blankets. Hurry!"

He put her carefully onto her bed, and watched the women scurry around the wagon, setting up basins and cloths, bowls of broth, and a chair for the healer who came running.

"It's all right, Chen, dear," Nashara told him, laying a hand on his shoulder, and settling into the chair. "I can take it from here."

"Good," Chen said, and fainted dead away.

♫

Alannys groaned, and struggled to move. Her gritty, sore eyes would not open, and her head was wrapped in something heavy and wet. That made sense. Wet towels would help contain the fire raging behind her eyes. Without the towels, the pillows and the bed under her would surely succumb to the flames.

"Nashara! She's waking!"

The words buzzed around her ears, muffled and annoying, like gnats. She wanted to swat at them, but they swirled away into the distance, leaving her in darkness and peace.

A warm hand touched her forehead, spreading tingling electricity across her skin, startling her. She sat up, staring in utter disbelief. "Dorramon?"

The king smiled down at her. "Alannys. What are you doing here?"

She looked around at the enveloping darkness that pressed against them, painting the king's silhouette in high relief. Where exactly was she? She couldn't remember. "I—I don't know."

"You have forgotten me." Dorramon's tone was heavy, his face grave. His blue eyes were bright, almost unnaturally bright in that darkness—she swore she could feel that piercing gaze burning her.

"No! No, of course not. How could I? I've been out here working, doing just what I told you I would."

Dorramon glanced around them, and the darkness immediately lifted, low light warmly illuminating the inside of her wagon. She was sitting on her bed. In the chair against the far wall sat Chen, napping with his head tipped down against his chest. An unfamiliar woman worked at the desk, crushing herbs in a bowl. She did not seem to notice Alannys or the king.

Alannys watched Dorramon wander the little room, stopping here and there to inspect a quilt on the bed, the little lantern burning on the table, the unused writing paper in its neat stack. Seeing him there hurt her deep in her chest, and watching him move in his familiar manner around the wagon made her want to run back to the palace that instant. She swallowed hard. "I didn't ask for this," she said haltingly.

Dorramon looked up at her. "Ask for what?"

She waved her arm in a gesture that encompassed the room. "Any of this. I didn't ask for any of this to happen at all. I never asked for this wagon. I never asked for the responsibility for these people."

Dorramon finished his round of the room and sat down beside her on the bed. "The thread runs longer than that, I think. You never asked for any of your life in Ravanmark; the power or the responsibility. You never asked to be admired or despised here. You never asked to *be* here at all."

"That's true enough, I suppose. I sure didn't know what I was getting into." She looked over at Chen, sleeping by her bedside. Something uncomfortable stabbed her conscience, and she let her gaze slide on by. "But I'm here now. I can't leave, and I can't change what I am. And these people...they need me."

"All people need you, Alannys." She turned back to Dorramon, and found him still watching her. His eyes looked dark, and his gaze felt somehow sad. She stared at him, transfixed. It felt like forever since she'd seen him this close to her. "Whether they realize it or not, it's true. And you can't change that, either."

She sighed. "Dorramon, how do you do it? How do you wield a responsibility you never wanted, for a group of people who may or may not want you? How do you handle knowing others may live or die based on decisions you make—sometimes without even realizing the importance of the decision?"

Dorramon gave her a crooked smile, and reached out to push her hair back from her face. "I don't have a magic answer for you, Alannys. What you describe is what it is to be a leader."

"But I don't want to be a leader!"

"Those who want to lead rarely make good leaders. Lord Malrec alone should be proof enough of that." He gave a light shrug. The motion seemed somehow philosophical, and she wondered if she would ever manage to carry these burdens with his grace. "Whatever happens, you must always remember this, Alannys: no matter how poor you may feel your leadership is, as long as you are trying, you will succeed. The only way you will let these people down is to give up."

She leaned forward and hugged him hard. "I want to come home. I miss you."

"I know. I want you to come home. I can't even tell you how much. But are you ready to do that? Will you put all of this aside and return to the palace?"

"I can't." She couldn't let go of him, either—she clung to him with a force that betrayed all of the things she felt but could not say. "I can't—I'm not done, and the things at stake here are bigger than what I want."

"You are very strong, Alannys." He leaned back from her, pulling loose from her arms and taking her hands in his. "Stronger than I could be in your place."

"I don't feel very strong. But I'm doing my best."

Dorramon smiled at her, helping her lie back down into bed. "Then I must leave you now. You've much to do, my Lady. As do I." He drew the blankets up over her.

"No! Please, don't go." She clutched desperately at the fine fabric of his sleeve. How could she go back to being without him, with no earthly idea when she might see him again? "Please."

"I'm sorry, Alannys." His smiled softened. "I don't

want to leave you. But we both have our paths to follow. And for now, I am afraid they move in different directions."

"No," Alannys moaned. "No."

Dorramon leaned over her, placing a gentle hand on her forehead, clasping her hand in the other. "I'm sorry," he said again. "I love you." His face drew closer, his blue eyes deep, bottomless wells that seemed to fill her entire field of vision. She tipped her face up and his lips found hers, sending electricity racing between them. She twisted her fingers into his hair, savoring the feel of him, the smell of him. For a long, breathless moment there was nothing in the world but him, and her, and the music only they could hear.

When he finally pulled away from her, she felt as if her heart went with him. How could she love him so much, knowing he could never be hers? She bit her lip until she tasted blood, trying not to beg him again to stay.

His smile looked as pained as she felt, as if he had heard everything she hadn't said. "Stay safe, Alannys." He drew his hand down, over her eyes, and all was darkness. She could feel his warmth receding from her.

"No!" The single word was a desperate shout in the darkness, and it came from her. She could still feel warmth on her hand, and she flung herself upright in the bed, wrenching her eyes open.

The eyes that stared with concern back into hers were brown, not blue. And there was no electricity in the hand that gripped her own. "Alannys? Are you all right?"

"Chen." Tears burned in her eyes, and she blinked them back, unwilling to explain them. The Seeing Stone hung heavy from her neck, radiating warmth against her skin. But for Chen and herself, the little room was empty.

Dorramon was gone.

Alannys pulled her hand away and curled her knees

against her chest, wrapping her arms around them and willing herself not to cry. What could she do now? The physical impossibility of what had just happened did not trouble her. It had been real. She was certain of it. The raw, tingling sensation of lips that had just been kissed, the slight scent on the air, the residual rippling of electricity on her skin — these things did not lie.

Chen watched her a moment, an indecipherable expression on his face, biting his lip. Then he shoved his chair back from the bed and went to lean out the door. "Nashara! Alannys is awake — hurry!"

She buried her face into her arms. She didn't want to see a healer, and she didn't want to see Chen. Somehow she had to find a way to deal with what had just happened. Seeing Dorramon again had brought home to her very clearly how much she had left behind, how much she would lose forever when Princess Varilyn came to Ravanmark and became his queen. She wanted to saddle up Quicksilver and ride, as fast and far as she could, and never stop until she saw Dorramon in front of her again.

But she couldn't do it, she already knew she couldn't. Dorramon was right; their paths were too different, and nothing she could do would change that. Besides, what she was doing was necessary, for both of them and for the entire land. She could not deny this.

And what would it solve, running back to the palace now? Nothing could be changed. The royal wedding would go on, whether Alannys was there or not. And on that day, she wanted to be as far from the Great Palace as physically possible. So why torture herself thinking she could somehow elude the inevitable?

No, Dorramon was right. She belonged here, and she had things to do that could not be denied or postponed. She had faced many dangers to get this far. She would face many more before the end.

But she would see it through to that end. No matter what.

♫

The sword slashed down through the air in a vicious arc, then stabbed forward. Pulling his blade in a tight line to cover him, Raman spun around into a slashing upward attack, coming to rest in a winded Ready position that made obvious the trembling of his sword.

Raman cursed under his breath.

"Not exactly Muse's song, is it?"

Raman swore again, instinctively swinging around to face the intruder, ready to defend himself. The point of his sword came to rest a scant inch from Dorramon's chest.

The king quirked an eyebrow at him. "Heavens, Raman, I don't think things are quite that bad yet, do you?" He pushed the sword tip away gingerly, with a fingertip against the flat of the blade.

Raman flushed and looked away. "You startled me." He jammed the weapon back into its sheath.

"Startled you?" Dorramon swept the Royal Guard training room with a glance, as if he might find the words he sought along the stone walls. "Raman, if you startle that easily during a practice session, I don't think you're quite fully recovered, do you? Is it wise to consider leaving the palace so soon?"

"This again? I thought we agreed I have no choice. All I've thought about since I came back here was getting back on my feet so I could go back to help her. She's going to kill herself out there, Dorr. You heard what happened in Garrant."

"Alannys can take care of herself."

"Look at me and say that again."

Dorramon turned uncomfortably away. "I didn't come here to talk about Lady Alannys."

"No?"

"No."

"Then what did you come here for, if you don't mind my asking?"

"I came here to ask you to give this up. I need you to stay at the Great Palace." Dorramon's clear, direct gaze was unsettling.

Raman pulled a chair over from against the wall, flipped it backwards, and straddled it. "So you have come to talk about Alannys after all. I take it things are not going any better at court?"

"No. Ambassador Thell is still banned from my court, but you can imagine how Cadenda feels about it. They don't want him to come back until he does what he was sent here to do, and they aren't happy with me. So he sits in his ship, anchored in the sea, dispatching messages to them and messages to us."

"And?"

Dorramon shrugged. "And what? Just because he sends me messages doesn't mean I have to acknowledge them."

"It doesn't really help to ignore him though, does it?"

Dorramon shrugged again.

Raman heaved a sigh. They'd had this conversation a hundred times. Dorramon was never willing to discuss the real root of the issue, and Raman didn't have the heart to push him very hard—it was too plain that he was suffering. Today, though, something was obviously wrong. Something had shaken the king, and Raman had no idea what. "You know," he said carefully, "sooner or later you are going to have to deal with this."

Dorramon looked away and said nothing.

No response at this point was probably a good response, so Raman pressed on. "Every day you do nothing is a dangerous day for Ravanmark, Dorramon. If Cadenda takes too much offense, we could be facing a war. Is that what you want; to send our people to war to gain you a little time?"

For a long moment Dorramon didn't answer.

Raman sighed again. "Look, Dorramon, we are already facing a civil war with the Dark Alliance. Do we really want to court international war with Cadenda as well, over Alannys? Do you think she would be pleased with that?"

"That is not your concern." Dorramon's entire attitude became cold and curt in an instant. "I am asking you to stay here, to help me with the court. I really need your support."

"But Alannys needs me more. She's out there all alone. She needs protection, and I—"

"Alannys is already protected," Dorramon said shortly, baffling him. "And she is not alone." He turned and swept out of the training room without another word.

♫

Alannys craned around in the saddle, watching the snaking trail of horses and wagons behind her, then turned back around to regard the narrow, rocky trail ahead. "So this is Eversnow Pass."

"The start of it." Chen rode alongside her on Nightfire, looking no worse for the wear of a bout of Muse's Fever that had kept him bedridden for a day, a couple of days before she had awakened. "The pass itself is very long, and it climbs all the way to Cloudytop Lake. It will take many days to cross."

Alannys nodded, considering that. Perhaps it explained the dubious expressions she'd seen when she had announced the route. "Have you ever been through Eversnow Pass?"

"Once, I think, when I was small."

She frowned. That might not be a good sign, if people as well-traveled as the Singari rarely used this crossing. Still, time was of the essence. And Chen did not seem particularly apprehensive, riding along beside her.

"Lady Alannys!" The shout came from behind them, but it was catching up fast. Alannys twisted around in the saddle, and saw a heavyset, dark-haired man urging his horse around the sloppy caravan line, yelling for her the whole time.

"Watch yourself," Chen told her quietly. "That's Mortan. He's one of the most influential men in the tribe, and one of the most outspoken, too. I doubt he's coming to congratulate you."

Alannys could see — even from her distance — the hard set of the man's jaw, the grim line of his mouth, turning sharply down at the ends. "No, I don't suppose so."

"Lady Alannys," Mortan said again when he finally caught up to her, panting as though he had been hurrying instead of his horse. "I won't waste your time. I've come to ask you to turn back."

"Turn back? It's a bit late for that — the wagons are already on the move."

"It's not too late, though. Not too late to stop you from making a mistake."

"A mistake." Alannys didn't look at his face — the sight of that hard, disapproving expression close up could only make it harder to stick to her decision. "Tell me, Mortan, where would you have us go instead?"

"Instead?" The question clearly surprised him. "Back the way we came, I suppose. Does it matter? Eversnow Pass is dangerous!"

"Dangerous," she echoed. "I don't doubt it. Crossing the Cloudytops this time of year is bound to be treacherous. But it does matter, a great deal. I have to keep moving forward. I can't go back to places I've already been — it doesn't help my mission. I've looked at the maps, Mortan. Eversnow is the only way across the mountains from here. Skirting the range for another crossing could take days, and the crossing we find could be just as dangerous. I don't have that kind of time."

"Your mission." Mortan's words were clipped and short. "The king's mission, you mean. It is not right to risk Singari on a quest to serve a king who is not theirs."

"King Dorramon does not enter into this discussion," she said sharply, feeling a stab of pain just speaking the name. "The mission is mine, and I have vowed to complete it. While I lead the Singari, they must support that mission as well."

"Alannys—"

"Thank you for your concern, Mortan," she cut him off. "It has been noted. But we continue through Eversnow Pass."

For a long moment, Mortan glared at her. She refused to look at him, riding with her eyes straight ahead, as though he wasn't even there.

Without another word, he turned and rode away.

"Good for you," Chen said under his breath.

She didn't respond. She had been pushing the episode in her wagon out of her mind ever since it had happened, but she hadn't come out today prepared to have the king thrown in her face. The dull ache in her chest bespoke unshed tears—she felt as though she'd torn open a wound that had only barely begun to heal.

Alannys sighed and looked down at her hands on the reins. In the day that had passed since Dorramon's visit, she had rediscovered her purpose, and led the Singari back out on the road again. But she felt more isolated and alone than ever. The mindlink hadn't so much as twitched since Dorramon left. His silence stung. What had she done to offend him?

The long, slow climb into the Cloudytop Mountains continued for three grueling days. At times the trail became so narrow the caravan had to move single-file up the mountainside. It was a miserable, tiring trek, but one thing kept them all pushing forward.

Fear.

Snow powdered the rocks and grass around their feet, edged the needles of the evergreens as delicately as frosty breath on pane glass. Their climb was slow, but hour by hour the changes around them were apparent. Already snow was on the ground. And the dark, rolling clouds looming over them only promised more. The sharp bite to the cold air brought one thought to every mind: Winter was coming. And with it, the legendary blizzards that made Eversnow Pass infamous. And if that soft, killing snow trapped them here, so many days and miles from help of any sort, what then? No one voiced the knowledge that gnawed at them all: no amount of music would save them then. Only Alannys was skilled at using music for specific purposes, and Chen had the barest amount of experience at her side. The two of them would not be able to save themselves, let alone the rest of the tribe.

The Singari considered the Redeemer to be one of them. Most of them considered her to be the Redeemer. She knew that was the only thing that held them now, kept them toiling together farther up the indomitable pass each day. But fear worried at their minds, nibbled at their sleep, and chipped away at their faith in her. She could hear it in the whispered conversations that suddenly hushed when she came near, could see it in the widened eyes that flitted away when she looked their direction.

Fear hunted them, stalked their footsteps like a predatory beast. One day it would catch them, and the stench of panic would prove stronger than the gaunt courage that united them for now. Eventually, it would happen. Their control would fail.

She could only pray she could get them over the mountain before that day came. Anything else meant certain death.

For all of them.

♫

At the summit of Eversnow Pass was Cloudytop Lake, an enormous freshwater lake, framed by snow-capped peaks and glistening in the high-mountain sun. The caravan stopped and made camp at its shores, partly because the direct sun kept the snow melted back to a tolerable level—making for the first decent campsite they had seen in two days—and partly because Chen doggedly insisted that they needed to stop at the lake. He refused to tell Alannys why, but he was adamant and she relented. It was, after all, a beautiful place, and all of them needed the rest.

They made their camp in the late morning. Alannys unsaddled Quicksilver and rubbed him down, found him a spot where the melting snow had exposed some brave spindly grass, and went to her wagon. After two days of napping on horseback, a few hours of sleep on something that wasn't moving sounded like heaven.

No sooner had she shut the door behind her than there came a knock. "Alannys?"

She sat down heavily on the bed. "Yes, Chen, come in."

He did, acting little tentative, she thought, carrying something half concealed under his arm. He looked apologetic, but said nothing. She was instantly on guard. "What's on your mind?"

He looked at her a moment, then his gaze wandered uncomfortably around the wagon. "I told you it was imperative that we stop at Cloudytop Lake, Alannys, but I don't believe I told you why."

She looked at him wryly. "I'm sure you didn't tell me why. I asked you several times. You were very insistent about it."

"Yes, well—I wanted to have this in hand before we talked about it." He handed her the leather folder he had been carrying.

"Hmm." She flipped it open, and found pages covered with Ravanmark's cryptic musical notation. She hadn't seen any of that since leaving the Great Palace, and it felt unexpectedly sentimental. "Sheet music? Chen, what's this for?"

He sat down in the desk chair, and stared down at his feet. She couldn't figure his strange attitude, but it was making her nervous. "Alara's baby has not had his *marzhabray* — his naming ceremony — yet," he said. "Alara and the elders think we should do it here."

"Why here? And why 'we'?"

"There has to be water, you know. He was too small at Pinevale. But now, we have Cloudytop Lake."

"Cloudytop Lake? But it's freezing! It isn't safe to put a baby in water that cold."

Chen fixed his gaze somewhere over her left shoulder. His neutral expression seemed carefully arranged on his face. "I know. We all know, Alannys. But we also know — well, the pass isn't going to get any easier. Much as I hate to admit it, Mortan's warnings weren't for nothing. Some of us may not be coming down on the other side. If — if something should happen, we want the baby to be named first. The Muses don't recognize the unnamed, even in death."

She swallowed hard. It still sounded like madness to her, but the ceremony clearly had deep religious significance. And Alannys had learned not to underestimate the Muses. "I understand. What do I need to do?"

Chen sighed, as if a great burden had been taken off of him. "The *zhotha* will be there. They will decide whether to accept the baby into the tribe."

"What? He's already here — how could they not accept him?"

"You must understand, a lot of the ceremony is ritual.

Of course there isn't any question that he will be part of the tribe. It's just how the ceremony is done."

"Oh. Okay, I see." It wasn't that different from some functions of the court, when she thought about it. "So the council will decide whether to accept the baby. Then what?"

"Then, assuming their decision is positive—which it will be, there's no possible way they'd let the child of a Singari woman slip out of the tribe—you will sing this song, supplicating to Terpsichore to accept and protect him. Terpsichore is the patron Muse of the Singari, and all of our ceremonies are addressed to her."

"I see." She glanced down at the music in her lap. "You mentioned the elders wouldn't let a Singari woman's child slip away. What about children of Singari men?"

"Well, Alara's baby is both, of course, but...Talent flows strongest in the maternal line. That is why an outside man wanting to marry a Singari woman serves a seven year indenture, but an outside woman wanting to marry a Singari man must serve twelve years. Bringing in outside women dilutes the Talent line in the tribe a lot more."

"I see. Well, I suppose I had better start learning this song."

He stood, keeping his eyes oddly averted from her. "Yes. I need to prepare as well."

She looked up at him in surprise. "You're in the ceremony too, Chen?"

"Yes—well, this is an exceptional case. The father must accept the baby and present him to the council. This baby's father is, of course, no longer in the tribe, so a stand-in is necessary."

"And Alara asked you? That's wonderful! She must think very highly of you." Alannys put on a falsely cheerful tone, attempting to cover a stab of something that felt an awful lot like jealousy. But it couldn't have actually *been* jealousy—that would have been laughable, given her situation.

"No—she didn't ask me, not exactly. It's sort of...customary."

"Customary? For you to be the stand-in for a baby's exiled father?"

He ran a hand through his hair. "You certainly aren't making this easy. It's customary for the *markortha* to stand in where necessary. And in this case, that's me."

"*Markortha?*"

Chen's face reddened. He couldn't even seem to look at her. "Roughly translated, it would mean leader's consort."

Alannys stood up, dumping the music onto the floor. "What? Is that what you've been telling people—that you're my consort? *Bragging*, like some kid in a locker room?"

Chen stared at her. "I have no idea what you are talking about, Alannys, but I certainly never told anyone anything of the sort. We've never had a *kortha* who was unmarried before. There is no provision for a stand-in when a consort is unavailable. I'm the only chance this baby has for legitimacy. And to be honest, I don't see why you are so upset."

"Upset? Upset doesn't begin to cover it, Chen. I'm humiliated and embarrassed—to think, the people I'm supposed to lead have nothing better to do than stand around conjecturing about me and what I might be doing with you!"

His nostrils flared. "Embarrassed to be associated with me, is that it? Don't worry, Alannys, you won't ever have to suffer it again!"

He slammed the door when he left, leaving her in the silence with sheet music scattered on the floor.

♫

Alannys spent two hours stewing in her wagon, occasionally working on the song, but mostly stomping around feeling frustrated. She knew she wasn't being reasonable, but it didn't help to calm her down. Chen wasn't responsible for the rumors among the tribe. There wasn't much reasonable about the way she had acted around Chen from the moment she had met him, and that upset her more than anything he'd said.

She finally ventured out and knocked on Chen's door, but he wasn't there. She had no idea where to find him, and in her state, it wasn't a good idea to wander through camp looking for him—she thought she had rumor problems *now*. In the end she went back to her own wagon, repentant and depressed, and sank down on her bed and cried.

When the sun was highest in the sky, there came a gentle tap on her door. She raked her fingers through her hair, scrubbed at her puffy eyes, and opened it.

"Chen!"

"Alannys, you've been crying." He stepped quickly inside, and shut the door behind him. He wore the same scarves he had worn to Pinevale. He looked dashing, and it didn't make things any easier on her. "Are you all right?"

She tried to laugh, but it came out as a strangled sob. "I'm surprised you even want to ask. I wasn't very nice to you earlier."

"Ah, Alannys." Chen sat down on the edge of the bed, and pulled her down next to him. "I wasn't very nice to you either, I'm afraid. I'm sorry. It was silly for both of us to get so worked up. I think you just misunderstood me."

She shook her head. "I think I just wasn't listening. You were pretty clear."

He put his arm around her shoulders. "Alannys, honest as Muse's song I never tried to make anyone think anything was going on between us. But like it or not, that's their impression. We are together an awful lot. And it isn't hard to tell how I feel about you."

She couldn't hold his gaze. Her eyes flicked to the Seeing Stone on her desk, casting its soft blue glow in the low light of the room.

Chen followed her gaze and frowned. "Alannys, I love you. Surely that must be obvious by now. Can you look at me and honestly tell me you feel nothing?"

Alannys looked up into his face, and back down at her hands. "No. I can't. But that isn't the problem, Chen. I—I'm on a mission here. I can't abandon that for anything or anyone, not even you."

"I'm not asking you to. We're on this mission with you, remember? I support you in everything you do, and that's never going to change."

"Chen—you don't understand."

"Apparently not. Explain it to me."

"I can't, I—" She looked at the Seeing Stone again, fighting a strong urge to go pick it up. "My heart...is with another."

Chen regarded the stone thoughtfully. She could see the faint blue light reflected in his dark eyes "Right. The king."

"Wh—what?" Hearing those words, that calmly, hit her like a physical blow.

"It's no secret, Alannys. Everyone knows you two were involved—even Singari. But Alannys...King Dorramon is engaged. Has been since he was born. You know that, right? There can be no real future for you there."

"I know. I can't help it, I just..." She sighed, and tears welled up in her eyes.

"No, no, don't cry. I'm not asking you to do anything. Just—don't shut me out, all right? Think about what I've said. Give me a chance." He leaned over and kissed her cheek.

She had no idea how she should react, or even how she

wanted to react. Chen was warm and caring, and the slight kiss felt soft and kind. She couldn't calm her fluttering heart.

But there was no tingling electricity between his skin and hers, and its absence made her want to cry. She would never hear Chen's voice in her mind.

Chen seemed to sense her ambivalence, and smiled at her, patting her shoulder gently. "And now," he said, "whether we like it or not, it is time for the *marzhabray*."

She stood up, and went to the desk. He watched her put the Seeing Stone back around her neck, but said nothing. She picked up the leather music folder to take with her. When she finished, he took her hand and led her out into the blinding sun toward the lake shore.

"We'll have to start out again in the morning," Alannys said, deliberately turning to light conversation, eager to put her inner turmoil behind her.

Chen nodded. "Yes. But it is good that we have this break. The other side of the pass is harder, in its own ways, than the climb. The descent will be steeper, so we will be leaving the snow behind sooner, but the trail will be narrower. And the snow will get deeper on the other side, until we do get low enough for the temperature to help us."

Alannys shook her head. "I see now why the Singari so seldom use this pass."

Chen glanced at her sidelong, and squeezed her hand. "Would you have done it differently, had you known?"

She considered it. "No. I didn't think I had much choice, and I still don't. Mortan did warn me, after all. This has been a slow, grueling climb, and it will be a slow, grueling descent—but it's still far faster than any alternative we had."

Chen nodded without comment, and led her to join the Singari near the water's edge. Alara stood holding her baby, with the elders gathered around her. Much of the tribe had turned out to watch, and enjoy the sunshine.

A few gazes lingered on Alannys and Chen, and she blushed burning red and let go of his hand. He looked at her in surprise, but said nothing. Alannys went to stand next to Alara, whose long, brown hair shone in the sun, full of golden highlights Alannys hadn't known were there. "You look great, Alara," she said. "I've never seen you without your headscarf before."

Alara beamed at her. "You've never seen me unmarried before. My marriage to Brutagar has been dissolved, and I no longer wear the *braytha*."

Alannys wasn't sure whether to offer condolences or congratulations on the loss of the scarf, and so she said nothing.

"My dear friends." Chira's voice, trembling with age, was raised to carry across the crowd at the lakeshore. "We are gathered here today for a most joyous occasion: the naming of a new member of our tribe." She turned to face them solemnly. "Alara, you may present the baby to his Muse-father."

Alara's smile suddenly seemed strained, her face unnaturally pale. She turned stiffly to Chen, and held the blanket-swaddled bundle out to him. "Chen of the Singari, Muse-father of my child, I present to you our baby, who is named Mylan."

Chen reached up and untied one of the bright scarves from his neck. "Alara of the Singari, I stand before the elders and the Muses and accept this child. With this token, I recognize my Muse-child." He wrapped the scarf around the baby, and took him from his mother. His hands, Alannys saw, trembled. It had to be some kind of record — Chen being serious twice in one day. He obviously understood the solemnity of this occasion, and earlier, back in her wagon...

She pushed that thought aside, and focused with effort on the ceremony. Chen in his white shirt in the bright sunlight, decked with scarves and holding a baby, was an oddly arresting sight. It took an effort of will not to let her mind wander back to just the subjects she was trying to avoid.

Chen turned to face the three elders, holding the baby out toward them. "*Zhotha* of the Singari, I beseech you to recognize this child, who is named Mylan."

Chira dipped her head low toward Chen. "Chen of the Singari, we the *zhotha* recognize this your Muse-child, who is named Mylan. Alara of the Singari, we the *zhotha* recognize this your child, who is named Mylan. Alannys of the Singari, *kortha* of this tribe and Redeemer of the Realm, we the *zhotha* ask you to supplicate unto the Muses on behalf of this child. Will you do this?"

Alannys swallowed hard. "I will." Her own hands were suddenly shaking at least as much as Chen's. She had not had time to memorize the hymn, so she held the open folder as steady as she could, and sang.

"O Terpsichore
who delights in dance
who guides the Singari from afar

Hear us now
we beseech unto you
hold this young child near to your heart

Help him
protect and guide him
and be with him in all that he does."

No one moved until the last note finished ringing off the mountain peaks, and faded away into silence. Chira dipped her head in Alannys's direction. "Thank you, Lady Alannys. Alara, you may now cleanse Mylan and yourself in the water."

Chen handed the baby back to Alara. She looked from Chen to Alannys with wide, fearful eyes, then clutched the little bundle to her chest and started resolutely for the water's edge.

Chen came to stand next to Alannys, and she leaned toward him. "Is Alara going in the water too?" she whispered.

"She has to." His voice was low, close to her ear. The rich, masculine sound of it made the skin on the back of her neck prickle. She tried hard to stand still and look impassive. She was mostly successful. "It will wash away the impurities of birth. Her seclusion will end today."

It made sense, with what Alannys had learned about Singari concepts of cleanliness and impurity. Still, it was with barely concealed dread that she watched Alara wade out into the bitterly cold water, until it covered both her and the baby completely. She couldn't have rationally explained why, but it brought to mind her initial, Second-Sight-fueled impression of Alara's wagon, an impression that had never really faded...

Death was coming among the Singari.

And soon.

♫

"So tell me, my dear," Lord Malrec said in honeyed tones, a false smile on his face that he hoped would carry into his voice, "what news?"

For a long moment nothing moved in the painting before him, its shimmering surface depicting the dimly lit inside of a wretched wooden wagon. A slight woman sat huddled under a patched quilt on a thinly padded bed in a dark corner of the cold little room, nursing a baby and not daring to raise her face to regard the gray blur she must have seen hovering in midair. Malrec tapped his long fingers impatiently on the arm of his velvet-upholstered chair.

"I—I have no news, my Lord." Even in the silence, he could barely hear her.

He clenched the arm of the chair with white-knuckled fingers and counted slowly to ten before he spoke. "I'm sorry, my dear, it seems I must have misheard you. Did you say you have no news for me?"

She swallowed audibly. "That's right, my Lord. The woman is not here." She still did not look up. Something about her posture was odd...she slumped as though she lacked the energy to hold herself upright—Malrec wondered idly if she was entirely well.

He pushed himself out of his chair and began to pace in front of the easel in short, angry steps. "So. You have no news for me. The woman is not there." He paused and glanced at the painting. "And yet...and yet, my *faithful* servants have brought me other tidings. Brutagar is gone, it seems, the victim of a most unusual curse...and I have heard other stories as well...of music in Pinevale...of a most unusual prisoner and a most miraculous cure..."

Her hand clutched convulsively tighter, gripping the edges of the quilt.

"And yet you say nothing! Tell me, how is this possible? Who brought you hope when all others had failed you? Who gave you that which you desired more than all else, the only reason you claim to continue to draw breath? Who risked life and limb to bring you that happiness that sustains you, even now? Tell me, woman, who has ever shown you greater kindness than I? And yet you dare to lie to me! Perhaps you think, since it is over, that you owe me nothing now?"

Her face drained of color in an instant, stark and sickly pale in the dark room. Her eyes were wide and ghostly. "N-no, my Lord, of course not. I owe you a debt which can never be repaid."

"See that you do not forget it. I am quite unreasonable when I am provoked. I may decide to revoke that which I have given you."

She gave a sort of strangled gasp. "No, my Lord, please!" Her eyes fell to the blanket-wrapped bundle in her lap. "It is possible I was mistaken in my original report."

"Is it?" Malrec sat back down in his velvet chair, rubbing his hands together. "That is a most promising development, my dear. So the Singari have welcomed their Redeemer at last?"

He couldn't keep the sneer from his voice. The woman flinched, then spoke haltingly. "Yes, my Lord. I—you see, Brutagar was beating me when she found us. She fought him with music, and laid upon him the curse you mentioned. He fled." She grabbed a handkerchief from somewhere in the blankets next to her, and sneezed into it. "The elders applied the rules of succession to her, since naturally the Redeemer is one of us."

"Naturally," Malrec spat. "And now she leads you. Tell me, do you really believe this alien creature is the Redeemer?"

"Oh, yes!" The woman's face, Malrec noted with displeasure, was rapturous, even with her deathly pallor. Alannys had done her work well, it seemed. "She is a good leader, my Lord, and wise."

"I did not come here for a listing of the woman's charms!"

A tense moment of silence passed, broken only by the ragged sound of his own breathing.

"I am sorry, my Lord," she said at last. "I did not mean to offend you."

She did not sound particularly sorry, but he chose not to pursue that now. "Where then has your great and wise leader led you? What has she been doing?"

It might have been his imagination, but he thought she hesitated. "She joined us just before Pinevale. You've already heard about that, it seems."

"Yes, quite," he said shortly. Her faith in Alannys annoyed him. "Jailed her, didn't they? For poisoning a child?"

The woman's cheeks burned red in the low light. "That wasn't Lady Alannys, that was fever. Things were fine till then."

"And where are you now? It seems rather chilly."

She muttered something indistinct.

"What was that, my dear?" Lord Malrec was doing his best to be patient, but getting useful information out of this woman was proving to be incredibly difficult.

"Eversnow Pass." She couldn't seem to look at him.

Lord Malrec laughed aloud. "Eversnow Pass!" He slapped the arm of his chair. "This proves it, what I have been saying from the start. The woman is mad."

The Singari woman did look up then, and her eyes blazed. "She is not! Lady Alannys is the best *kortha* we've ever had!"

Lord Malrec paused. "Is she? It would seem to be madness, leading a group of people — women and children, even — into such an unforgiving place, at such a dangerous time of year. But perhaps it is brilliance, misunderstood. Tell me, then, how does your great leader intend to get you all safely out of there? Surely she must know something about that pass that I do not."

She looked down and shook her head.

Malrec snorted in frustration. "And still you would claim your people do well to follow her! This is madness, whether you would hear it or not. And if you will not be swayed from this path, I am afraid there is little left for us to discuss. The woman is leading you to your death, and the deaths of all you love. So be it. Farewell!"

The woman squirmed in agitation, clutching the baby to her chest. "You are wrong! Lady Alannys is the Redeemer. She will lead us through, and she will save us all. You are wrong, Lord Malrec!"

Malrec threw drying powder at the painting, his lips a thin, angry line.

"Damn that woman!" He brushed his hands together and ran them down the front of his robe, leaving long powdery white streaks on the fine velvet. He sighed heavily, massaging the bridge of his nose between his thumb and forefinger. "Damn her!"

A hand, gentle and timid, fell on his shoulder. "I am sorry, my Lord."

Princess Delline. He had forgotten she was in the room. He straightened with a shuddering sigh. "A thousand pardons, my dear, for allowing you to see me in such a state! I am afraid for those people. It grieves my heart, what is happening to them. She will lead them to their deaths."

"And yet they will insist upon following her," Delline mused. "Perhaps she has bewitched them."

Malrec lifted his hands eloquently. "The Singari? She has no need to bewitch them. She has Talent, and she has Songstrike. What do the Singari live for, but to serve the Redeemer?"

Delline sighed. "Truly the Singari are simple and ignorant people. And she is pandering to their deepest beliefs."

"Yes. And she must be stopped, or she will destroy these people." He placed his hands on Delline's shoulders and regarded her solemnly. "If there is any way, any way at all, that completion of the Collar of Silence can be hastened, my love, I beg you to tell me. The lives of the Singari—perhaps the lives of us all, depend on it."

Delline's wide eyes glistened. "I wish that it were so, my Lord. But the skin must age for the full six weeks, or the collar will not work. There is no shortcut for this. But Lord Malrec, the collar is not the most efficient way of dealing with Alannys. Why seek to control her voice when we could simply eliminate it? A town healer with a knife could silence her—"

Malrec jerked his hands off her shoulders and turned away. "Why do you insist on coming back to that, woman? She is no use to us without her voice."

Delline folded her arms over her chest, her wedding ring glittering in the low light. "And that is your only interest in her, Lord Malrec? As a weapon?"

Malrec sighed, eyeing her balefully. They had only been married six weeks, and already the woman was often more trouble than the benefits her position provided were worth. "This again? How many times must we go through this? She is not *a* weapon, she is the ultimate weapon. We need only keep her voice intact, as I have grown extremely weary of reminding you!"

Tears welled up in Delline's eyes. "Then you need no further counsel from me. There is no way to rush the collar. Kill her, or wait. The decision is yours." She turned and left.

"Damn it!" Lord Malrec turned and dealt the easel a savage kick. His pulse thumping hotly in his ears, he watched the easel collapse into a pile of spindly wooden legs, the painting of the Singari wagon lying crookedly on top. The destruction made him feel somewhat better.

"I suppose I had better go smooth the royal feathers," he muttered, kicking the mess into a corner of the stone floor.

And after that, it sounded as though he had a decision to make. Should he let the music mage live to face the Collar of Silence?

Or would it be more efficient to kill her now?

♫

Alara lay in her bed, sweating with fever and moaning with delirium. Alannys worked at her bedside, sponging her forehead with cool cloths and pushing her damp, matted hair out of her face. She still remembered how striking that hair had been, gleaming in the sunlight two days ago. Seeing it now, limp and tangled on the pillow, saddened her.

The door creaked open, and Nashara came quietly in, with her leather bag of healing supplies. Her curly gray hair was pulled back in a manner not much neater than Alannys's; it seemed Nashara had time for very little outside of tending her patients. She felt Alara's pulse and looked at her eyes, making small, disapproving clucking sounds the entire time.

Alannys watched her anxiously. "Well? Do you see any improvement?"

Nashara turned to her almost too quickly, as though the words had been startling, like maybe she had forgotten Alannys was even there. She smiled a gentle, practiced smile that Alannys felt certain had concealed a lot of bad news over the years. "I don't want to disappoint you, my Lady. You've worked so hard."

Alannys sighed, scrubbing at her eyes with the heels of her hands. "That sounds like a 'no.' Don't try to spare my feelings — this is my fault. I never would have let us continue through the pass all day yesterday if I had known she was ill. She wasn't in any shape to travel."

"That wasn't your fault. She didn't tell anyone. I myself did not know until early this morning."

Alannys shook her head. "I'm the *kortha*. It was my job to check before giving the command to move out." She dipped the cloth into the bowl of cool water by the bed, wrung it out, and draped it over Alara's forehead. "I should have said something before then, back at

Cloudytop Lake. I should have stopped her."

"Do you think Alara didn't know the risk?" Nashara looked at her seriously. "She understood what that ceremony might cost her. She did it to secure the best possible chance for herself and for her baby, should something happen like—well, like this."

"But if she hadn't gone in the water, this wouldn't have happened! She did it for nothing!"

The angry words hung in the air between them. In the silence that followed, Alara's uneven breathing seemed unnaturally loud.

"You can't know that," Nashara said finally. "But even if what you say is true, can you guarantee she and her baby would both have survived the rest of the pass?"

"I..." Alannys clenched her hands into frustrated fists. "I..."

"Alannys, none may know the minds of the Muses. Not even you. Alara did the best she thought she could with what she had. All we can do now is honor her the best way we can with what we have."

Alannys stared at her. "You're talking like she's going to die."

"Mylan is well." Nashara looked away. "He sleeps; I think his mother's milk has helped to protect him from this fever. That much is good, at least."

"Nashara! Alara isn't going to die! Tell me she's not going to die!"

"Alannys." Nashara sighed, looking from her to Alara. "You know that promise is not mine to make. All I can tell you is that it would be wise, right now, to be prepared."

"No." Alannys's anger abruptly bottomed out, leaving her with a scared sort of desperation. "Should I—should I sing? Do you think that might help her?"

"Now you're thinking again. I don't see how it could hurt. I've done all I can—perhaps you can do what I could not."

Alannys wasn't so sure. Still, if there was a chance, she had to try. She got down on her knees beside the bed, and took Alara's hot hand in both of her own. With a deep breath for courage, she began to sing.

"Oh Muses, we beseech you—"

Alara screamed. Alannys dropped her hand and stared. It was a bloodcurdling scream that lasted until her breath was entirely gone, then she hitched in breath to scream again.

Nashara put a gentle, wrinkled hand on Alara's forehead. "Alara, dear..."

Her eyes never even opened. Her head tossed head back and forth on the pillow. "Alannys—help me. Help us. Lord Malrec, I am sorry. The woman is not here. Not here!"

Alannys glanced over at Nashara, baffled. "Lord Malrec?"

Nashara frowned, and shook her head, but said nothing.

Alara fell still and silent on the pillows. Nashara hurried out, discomfited. Alannys sat alone by the bed in a room that was suddenly cold.

♪

Alannys dared not sing again. She sat by the bed, wetting and wringing the cloth, and dripping boiled willow bark infusions into Alara's mouth at regular intervals. Nashara came, shook her head, and left again. Alara's fever grew hotter, and hotter still. Alannys worked with a terrible, frantic desperation, but nothing she could do seemed to make the slightest bit of difference.

But she couldn't give up.

Chen came quietly in and sat next to her. A familiar middle-aged man followed him in, and stood at the bedside with his graying head bowed.

Chen leaned towards Alannys. When he spoke, it was so softly she could hardly hear him, even though his mouth was next to her ear. "You remember Mortan. He has come to represent his family in paying final respects."

She stared at him. "Final respects?" she mouthed.

Chen reached for her hand, but said nothing. She watched helplessly as Mortan stood quietly for a long moment by Alara's unmoving form. She knew what final respects were where she came from, but she hoped they were something different in Ravanmark.

Because she hadn't given up, damn it.

She squeezed Chen's hand and shut her eyes tight, trying to keep from lashing out. These people were only doing what they thought was right.

When she opened her eyes again, Mortan stood right in front of her, regarding her solemnly. "Alannys. I have not always agreed with you, or supported your actions, but I am sorry to see your suffering. My family sends condolences for you, and for Alara's family."

Chen seemed to sense her loss for words. He squeezed her hand. "Thank you, Mortan. We will convey your condolences to Tor."

Mortan nodded, and left the wagon. Before the door closed completely, it swung open again, and Yeff came into the little room.

He stomped the snow off his boots, keeping his eyes carefully averted from them. "Pesia couldn't make it," he said. Alannys had a sudden vision of Pesia's eyes, narrowed in hate, and understood.

Everything in the room seemed too small for Yeff. He stood for a few awkward moments by the bedside, working his hat through his hands. His shoulders were hunched as if he feared a blow.

Finally, he turned from the bed and faced Chen,

looking somewhere over his head. "Condolences to Tor," he said stiffly.

Chen nodded, but said nothing, and Yeff let himself out of the wagon without a look back.

Alannys watched the door swing shut behind him. "Chen, what is going on here?"

Chen couldn't hold her gaze—he looked at her, then quickly away again. "I'm sorry, Alannys. Alara is dying. Nashara has made the announcement, and now it is just a matter of time, I'm afraid."

"Nashara made the announcement, did she?" Alannys pulled her hands into her lap and balled them into fists. "Without talking to me?"

Chen sighed. "You've got to understand—I know you are *kortha*, but medical issues are Nashara's domain. She's just doing what she's supposed to."

"No," Alannys said sullenly. "I haven't given up. She knows I haven't given up. Alara's not going to die, do you hear me? I won't let her."

"Alannys, you are going to have to accept this. Nashara wouldn't have announced it if she wasn't sure. There's nothing you can do." He placed a gentle hand on her shoulder, offering support she did not want.

Alannys shook his hand off of her. "I think you're forgetting who you're talking to. There's always something I can do."

"Alannys, no!" Chen's voice was colored with pure panic, and he clutched at her arm. "She's too far gone— you'll kill yourself!"

Alannys ignored him, grabbing Alara's hand and pulling in a deep breath.

"Alannys? What in the world are you doing?"

The confused voice was weak, feminine, and definitely not Chen's. Alannys looked down in utter shock to see Alara sitting up, dark eyes regarding her strangely.

"Alara? You're awake?"

Alara's gaze wandered for a moment, then settled on her again. "Lady Alannys. I am glad you're here. I need to talk to you."

"No—no, Alara, you aren't well. Lie back now, you need to save your strength." She leaned down, trying to help Alara back down to her pillows.

"There isn't time for that." She sounded impossibly calm. "My time is nearly spent, Alannys. But I have to tell you—you must know."

Alannys sat back down with a thump. "What do you need to tell me?" She couldn't argue it anymore. Nashara and Chen had been trying to tell her all morning, but looking at Alara now, her small, frail movements and her pale, translucent skin...there was no way to deny she was dying.

Chen reached over and took Alannys's hand without a word.

"I have been in contact with Lord Malrec." Alara paused, drawing a breath as though it hurt. "Please understand, this is not something I am proud of, nor did I completely understand what I was getting into when it happened. But Lord Malrec has asked about our movements, and I have kept him informed."

Alannys stared at her. She didn't have any words—it felt like her brain was frozen. That explained Alara's outburst earlier. But how had she ever ended up spying for Lord Malrec in the first place—especially among the Singari, who were so adamant about contact with outsiders? "How—how did this happen?"

Alara seemed to look through her to something nobody else could see. "Many months ago, before you came to Ravanmark, the tribe was working our way slowly through Glennayre Holding. I was about three months pregnant with Mylan. We were camped outside of the town of Glennayre itself one night when Brutagar flew into one of his rages. He gave me a terrible beating.

"Afterward, I discovered I was bleeding."

Alannys gasped, but she dared make no move to comfort her, not while she had that otherwordly look in her eyes. Her scream from earlier that day still echoed in Alannys's ears.

"I was terrified. I didn't want to lose Mylan, but I didn't know what to do. I waited until Brutagar was asleep, and crept out of the wagon..."

♪

The heavy snores from inside the wagon covered the slight sounds of the latch as Alara eased the door shut behind her. She pulled her shawl tight around her and hurried through the dark camp, past the smoldering remains of the fire, stepping lightly past the tents. Nashara's wagon was completely on the other side of the camp from hers, and Alara cursed that happenstance a hundred times during the anxious journey.

She tapped on the door, nervously shifting her weight from foot to foot. Long minutes of silence passed before she worked up the nerve to knock again, louder this time, glancing anxiously around.

The door flung suddenly open. Nashara, still in her nightgown, gave her a hard look. "Alara! What are you doing out without your *braytha*, child? Why, think of the shame if you, a married woman, were seen out like this..."

"I don't care! I don't have time to worry about headscarves," she said, ignoring the older woman's scandalized gasp. "Nashara, I'm bleeding."

"Bleeding? Merciful Muses, child, come inside, come inside!"

It took only a short and uncomfortable physical examination to confirm her worst suspicions. Alara couldn't stand to look at the healer, couldn't stand the pity in the old woman's eyes. "I'm losing the baby?"

"I'm sorry, child. There is nothing I can do. The bleeding will cease, or it will continue, as the Muses have sung."

It seemed like someone else who gathered her shawl around her shoulders, as though she could ever feel warm again; someone else who numbly left Nashara's wagon on that cool spring night. Inside she was frantic, inside she was screaming. How could this happen? How could Nashara be so uncaring about the death of her baby?

This couldn't be right. This *couldn't be right!* There had to be something she could do. Somebody, somewhere, had to be able to stop this.

There was only one answer, then. But she couldn't believe it, even as she started walking out behind Nashara's wagon, into the woods that surrounded the camp, she couldn't quite believe she was doing this. Contact with outsiders was strictly forbidden, that had been drilled into Alara her entire life. If anyone found out that she had snuck to town—if anyone found out she had allowed a *sharo* healer to examine her...

She would be exiled. Permanently exiled.

Sharast. She swallowed hard at the thought. But still, what else could she do? This was her baby, her entire reason for living since her marriage had turned into a nightmare. She would risk everything for the chance to save the child, and she would never look back.

She found a healer on the Glennayre town square. An outsider—a male outsider—examined her immediately. She would never recover from the shame. He turned to the bowl and pitcher on the counter behind him to wash his hands. And when he turned back around to face her, she knew before he spoke a word, and she started to cry.

"I'm sorry, miss, I really am. But there isn't anything I can do."

"But surely," she said, heedless of the tears on her face,

"surely there is something, anything, that might save my baby."

He looked away from her. "There is an herb. But it is rare, and very expensive."

"I'll pay anything! Anything you ask!"

He shook his head. "I'm sorry, miss—it isn't a matter of money. There just isn't any to be had. It doesn't grow here, you see? We won't be getting another delivery for about a week. And you need help right now." He looked at her with pity in his eyes. "I'm sorry."

She staggered out into the street. The bleeding was heavier now, she could feel it. She didn't know how she could even make it back to camp like this, and what did it matter if she did? She would be exiled for what she had done, and she would be alone. Childless.

She had gambled everything, and she had lost.

Her sobs came so hard and fast she almost couldn't breathe. Alone and destitute in a strange town, she fainted.

When Alara awakened, she was in a gray velvet chair in a strange room. Someone had propped her feet up on a footstool, and it had helped to slow the bleeding.

A tall man stood with his back to her, covering up a painting with a black velvet cloth. His hands shook, and his skin looked pale. A fire in a nearby fireplace took the edge off the chilly evening. She wondered frantically how long she had been asleep. How much time had she lost?

How much time did her baby have left?

"We haven't much time, my dear," said the tall man suddenly, turning to face her, "so I'll get right to the point. You are miscarrying. The town healer probably told you there is an herb that can help. He probably also told you there is none to be had right now."

Alara nodded.

"He was only partly correct, as it turns out. None is to

be had by normal means. I, though, am a man of extraordinary means. I have already procured the herb which can save your child." He held up a few sprigs of a green herb, with long slender leaves that came to a point, and tiny purple flowers.

Alara gasped. "Please, sir, I beg of you..."

He held up a hand, silencing her. "I will help you. I require only one service of you in return. It is small, a pittance, really, for so great a favor."

"What do you want?" Her voice sounded small.

"There is a woman, my dear, who will soon be coming to Ravanmark. An outsider, who has some measure of Talent. I don't expect that she will ever leave Castle Glennayre. But if she does, and if she should somehow end up among the Singari, I would like you to let me know. Can you do this for me?"

Alara stared at him. An outsider, among the Singari? A woman of stature enough to live at Castle Glennayre, coming to live among the Singari? Obviously this man was insane. There was no way she would ever be called upon to fulfill such a debt. "What is this woman's name, sir?"

"Alannys, my dear. And I am Lord Malrec of Glennayre. Have we a deal?"

The whole thing was entirely crazy. So why couldn't she shake the feeling she was making a horrible mistake? "We do, my Lord."

The smile on Lord Malrec's face made her shiver in the warm sitting room.

♪

"You don't hate me, do you? Please, Lady Alannys, tell me you don't. Ever since word began to spread of the Redeemer in Ravanmark, I have seen why Lord Malrec asked of me what he did. But at the time, I thought it a harmless request for so great a favor.

"Of course," Alannys said, "how could you have thought otherwise? I don't blame you at all, Alara."

Everything about Alara's experience rang familiar for Alannys, and it was all too easy to imagine how she had been manipulated into such a promise.

"Then—you forgive me?"

"Alara, there's no need for—"

"Lady Alannys, please—you don't understand. I have betrayed a friend. I have betrayed a life-debt. Most of all, I have betrayed the Redeemer. Do you forgive me?"

Alara's eyes looked farther away every minute. Alannys sighed. "Yes, Alara, I forgive you."

"Thank you." The two words were barely audible, like a sigh, and they were the last words Alara ever spoke. She slumped back against the pillows, and moved no more.

Alannys came up out of her chair and checked Alara's pulse. She was gone.

Alannys glanced over at Chen, and found him staring at her in shock. "I don't care what you heard," she said flatly. "I don't care what the old laws might say, or what the *zhotha* might decide. Nothing that was said here ever leaves this room."

"Alannys..." Chen glanced at Alara, then back to Alannys in a hurry. "Are you sure about that?"

"Did I hear you right? Are you seriously suggesting that we rat her out?"

"Now calm down." He held up his hands in a placating gesture that only made her angrier. "Alara was right. She betrayed a life-debt, and she betrayed the Redeemer. She betrayed the entire tribe, feeding information on us to Lord Malrec."

Alannys glared at him. "He tricked her! You heard the story. I've met the man—I don't doubt he's capable of it."

"Would you mind not making such a scary face? You could cut stone with that, you know. I'm not criticizing Alara, may the Muses bless and keep her. I'm simply pointing out that things were done, serious things. Hiding that is nothing to sneeze at—we could face some pretty stiff consequences ourselves, if we were found out."

"The only way we'll be found out is if you tell somebody," she said, "because I'll take it to my grave. What do you say, Chen? Will you turn me in? Or will you help me?"

Chen sighed. "As if you even need to ask. I'll do anything if it gets you to trust me."

"I already trust you." Her voice was barely audible, even in the quiet room. "I wouldn't ask you if I didn't."

A heavy, awkward silence fell over them.

"I've got to go tell Tor," Chen said finally. "He's been watching Mylan—Alara made him promise. I'll need to take over for him, so you may not see me for a while."

Alannys nodded. "Do whatever you need to do. I'll be here. I wouldn't feel right leaving her alone."

He patted her shoulder, and turned for the door.

"Chen," she said, suddenly unwilling to see him leave, "thank you."

He stopped for just a moment, but he didn't turn back around. "You don't need to thank me, Alannys. I know I'm not much account—flighty, irresponsible, just out for fun...I'm the Singari kid who never grew up. But I'm doing my best to help you, to be what you need. Just...let me keep trying. Don't shut me out."

The door closed softly behind him.

Alannys sat in the wagon, alone with the mortal remains of the first Singari friend she had ever made, crying, and trying not to think about all the reasons why.

♫

It felt like hours later when the door creaked slowly open, and Tor dragged into the room, moving as though everything hurt. She remembered him well, happy and spry, after the *zhothast* had acquitted Alara. It was such a stark contrast—she could not have imagined him laid low like this, back then.

"Oh, Alannys—I'm glad you're still here. Chen said you would be, but I'm honestly never sure whether I can believe that boy. I wanted to ask you if you would help with the preparations. It's traditional for all the female relatives to participate, and Alara really did think of you as a sister, after you rescued her."

Tears welled up in her eyes. What could she say? She didn't really trust herself to speak, so she just nodded.

Tor smiled. It was a pale ghost, a faint echo, of the hearty smile she remembered. "Thank you. I know Alara would be pleased." He glanced at the bed, then looked quickly away, blinking fast. "My law-sisters will be here soon. They will be bringing the oils and linen you'll be needing."

Alannys shook her head. She couldn't imagine actually preparing Alara for her funeral, it just seemed too horrible. She scrubbed at her eyes with her fists, trying to force back tears.

A gentle hand fell on her shoulder. "Alannys, you mustn't think of this as something terrible. Alara had a hard life, I suppose you know that as well as anyone. But it was not a wasted life. And death is never an end."

Alannys stared at him.

"It may be difficult to understand, coming from a different background, but among the Singari death is a cause for celebration. She has moved on to a joyous, musical life with the Muses. What could be happier? Our only sadness is for ourselves, that we are separated from her, until we may join her again when our own times come."

Tor patted her shoulder and left, but she could still see that sad smile, keeping her company while she waited for the others.

Alara's aunts brought several yards of undyed linen, and clay jars filled with aloe, sandalwood oil, myrrh, and balsam. The four women worked most of the night, rubbing the oils into Alara's skin, and wrapping her in the linen. They all slept there in the wagon.

In the morning, they sat with Alara in the wagon while a pyre was built outside. Alannys, Tor, and Alara's three aunts carried her out and placed her on the pyre. The Singari gathered around, wailing and tearing at their hair.

The elders came out from the *zhothamol*, dressed in the scarves they would have danced in when they were younger. "People of the Singari!" Chira spoke in a voice that carried through the pass. Her tone and inflection suggested that this speech was ritual. "Why do you grieve? Your sister is ready to make her final journey to the Valley of the Muses. This is a glorious day!"

Bayred carried a torch to the pyre. "Let the heat of these flames free Alara's spirit to fly to the Valley of the Muses. Let her join in joyous dance and thankful song with Terpsichore and her sisters in that hallowed realm that knows no sorrow." He held the torch high, and with a theatrical gesture, set the pyre alight. A cheer went up through the tribe, and suddenly Alannys was in the midst of a celebration.

The dancing and feasting lasted most of the night. Alannys watched for awhile, then retired to her own wagon. She envied the Singari their joyful attitude toward death. For herself, it was not that easy. She couldn't really find any cause for celebration in Alara's death. Every death to her was just one less life, and loss of life was never a good thing, whether it came through illness, or at the hand of a sworn enemy.

Or even at the end of a cloaked assassin's sword.

She tried to imagine any of her friends celebrating at her wake the way the Singari were celebrating at Alara's now. She just couldn't envision it, it was just too strange. The only person she could imagine dancing around her funeral pyre was Lord Malrec — probably with Princess Delline.

And that notion didn't provide any comfort at all.

Chapter Five

AVALANCHE

On the far side of Cloudytop Lake, Eversnow Pass snaked between rocky cliffs that towered out of sight, and around tall, wide, lumpy sedimentary rock formations that Alannys eyed dubiously. What had deposited those huge rocks, way up here in the peaks of the tallest mountains she had ever seen, and what was the likelihood of it happening again?

She didn't know, couldn't guess. It didn't matter anyway. She was dead, and so were the people she led, all of them. Snow lay thick around them, treacherously deep in places. Footing was uncertain, and very few dared to ride. Alannys and Chen slogged through ahead of the train, sitting horses that struggled for secure footing. Even over the sound of her own ragged breath, Alannys could hear the jagged cliffs above her groaning under the incalculable weight of the snow and ice. Behind her trudged the Singari, hollow-eyed and exhausted, putting one foot ahead of the other more from habit than anything else.

They didn't stand a chance.

These people had a will of iron, though, she had to give

them that. She didn't see what else could be keeping them going. It certainly wasn't faith in her; the muttered conversations that stopped when she approached were proof enough of that.

She sighed, her head dipping toward her chest. The pass stretched inexorably out before them, she was unutterably tired, and there was no end in sight. She couldn't even look forward to the slight relief of a campsite; the deepening snow and groaning cliffs convinced them all it was not worth the risk.

It seemed only a few moments later when she jerked her head back up, but the late-evening light in the pass told her it had been a couple of hours. In a sort of panic, she found that she and Chen were no longer at the head of the train — they were riding almost a third of the way back. What kind of leader was she?

Chen's gentle hand fell on her arm. "It's all right. You were sleeping, so I fell back and let some others go on ahead. May as well have alert eyes at the front."

She forced a weak grin. His logic made sense, but she couldn't pretend to be happy about it. She was *kortha*; she should have been the alert eyes out front.

Chen glanced at her sidelong. "One person can't do everything, Alannys. I should think you would know that by now."

Alannys puffed out her cheeks. "You're right. I'm sorry. I guess I'm just worried about what I might be leading your people into."

"You wouldn't be a very good leader if you weren't," Chen pointed out.

He was right. But that didn't make her feel much better.

"If you don't stop frowning," he said conversationally, "you're going to get worry lines all over your pretty face."

She looked over at him, startled, and he laughed.

"There," he said, "that's much better."

Alannys turned away in a hurry, trying to hide her burning cheeks. The breeze through the pass was stiff and cold, and so constant that she no longer paid attention to it. Now, though, it began to puff snowflakes in her face.

She cursed under her breath. The first break in the snow they'd had since leaving Cloudytop Lake, and it didn't even last a whole day. The snow was blowing at them from the direction they were going.

Suddenly she was a whole lot more worried about what she was leading them into.

"Stay here," she said, and nudged Quicksilver a little faster.

"Now hold on!" Chen called after her. "Where are you going?"

Alannys shook her head. "I'm just going to check on our line leaders," she told him, and rode on ahead, moving toward the front of the train.

She could feel his eyes still on her back as she approached the two men riding point. She appreciated his concern, but sometimes he felt like a mother hen. It was nice to have someone looking out for her safety, but at the same time it seemed he had forgotten that she'd been traveling Ravanmark on her own for a long time now.

The two men nodded deferentially to her when she rode up beside them. She recognized Drigo and Grald, two of Chen's closest friends. Of course, he would only have chosen people he trusted to guide the group in her absence. "I hope you have rested well," Drigo said to her.

"Very well, thank you," she lied. "How goes it here? Have you noticed anything unusual?"

"No, my Lady." He frowned. "Are you expecting something?"

"No. Not exactly. I just have a—a really peculiar feeling."

The men exchanged unsettled looks. If they had brushed her off, she might have ignored her intuition. But now...

"Look," she said, "I'm going to ride on ahead and scout the pass for a little way. You two just keep doing what you're doing. Okay?"

"Well—very well, then. If you're certain. We could go on ahead while you lead."

"Thanks anyway. I'll be fine."

A flick of the reins, and Quicksilver left the wagon train behind. He seemed as restless as she felt.

Snow fell softly in the fading light, absorbing sounds and making the world seem muted. She strained her ears, but couldn't catch a single sound out of place. The pass snaked between the jagged cliffs at one of its narrowest points here, and there was no cover on the trail floor where anyone could hide.

So why did she feel so certain something awaited them out there?

She wasn't alone. Quicksilver snorted and tossed, sidestepping and stomping. Something had the horse spooked—she hadn't seen him act like this since Brookeshire Castle.

The sun had dipped behind the mountains, reducing visibility in the pass to almost nothing. Every bit of scrubby brush poking up out of the snow, every shadow stretching black across the ground, needed careful inspection to ensure that it was what it appeared to be. She went slowly and cautiously, eyeing everything on the trail floor.

A streak like dark lightning rushed at her, flying from a ledge on the cliff face and crashing into her. It knocked her off her horse, and she rolled over and over, struggling with the dark shape.

When they stopped rolling, she came out on top,

straddling her attacker. She didn't need to see the black scarf pulled high up under his eyes to know it was the cloaked swordsman. She balled her hands into fists and rammed them into his face, right then left, over and over, her leather riding gloves cushioning her hands. He held his arms defensively over his face, but he could not hold her off or deflect her blows. Months of fear and anxiety welled up in her and were unloaded onto the man sprawled below her.

His arms dropped limp to the ground. He seemed stunned. She stopped swinging, resting her hands on her thighs, panting raggedly. Before he could recover, she reached for the scarf on his face.

The man's knees rammed into her back, sending shards of pain screaming up her spine. Damn him! She'd fallen for his ruse, and let down her guard. He twisted sideways, dumping her off into the snow.

Alannys couldn't stand, couldn't sing—she couldn't even seem to catch her breath. Searing pain tore through her chest with every small movement, and her vision wavered. The cloaked swordsman circled her ominously, twirling his viciously curved blade from hand to hand in a display that did little to restore her hope. It seemed she had made it this far in Ravanmark on nothing but luck—luck that had now at last run out. There was nothing she could do, no last trick she could pull from her hat to avert the dark fate that had finally caught up with her. She couldn't even pull her mind together enough to open the mindlink. What a miserable end to her grand adventure. What would become of the king? What would happen to all of those people who had believed in her? What about the Singari? What would become of all of Ravanmark, with Lord Malrec as king?

She had failed them all, failed them utterly. This was not the end she had imagined for her story. It was all so wrong, and yet there was nothing she could do to change it. Even the jagged cliffs under their enormous burdens of snow groaned for her. "Sorry," she muttered, turning her face to the side.

"Yes, I daresay." The swordsman's voice was as rich as chocolate, heavy and seductive in her ears. "You have not made this easy, my Lady. But all things must dance to the tune of the Muses in the end, as they say in these parts. 'Once the Muses most beloved, now their most despised,' or so I am told."

She drew a small, shuddering breath. "Spare me the religious rhetoric," she gasped, "and get it over with."

His eyes crinkled. "Defiant to the end. It is a pity we had to meet like this—I could have quite enjoyed you, I think. In its own way, my Lady, this has been a pleasure. But the bigger pleasure by far will surely be having this whole miserable affair over with."

She closed her eyes and turned her face away. She hoped her end would be sudden and swift, and she didn't want to see it coming. Her right leg burned against the snow—she must have injured it in the fall from Quicksilver. Not that it mattered much now. All of her problems were about to become someone else's.

She squeezed her eyes tightly shut, bracing herself against what was to come. She was determined not to give her mysterious attacker the satisfaction of a cry of pain.

"No!"

The startling shout was fearful, yet forceful, ringing through the pass with an air of command that could not be refused. There was music in that single word. And it had not come from her.

She whipped her head around, and caught a moment that engraved itself into her memory like a flash of lightning, intense and perfect.

Chen sat astride Nightfire atop the ridge, painted in

high relief by the last fading rays of the dying sunlight, one hand stretched out toward them. His superhuman shout of fear and rage echoed off the cliff faces. The cloaked swordsman froze, his curved blade high in the air above her.

The heavy, unnatural silence made another sound obvious; at first barely audible, but building to a thundering roar.

Avalanche!

Sudden fear choked Alannys. She had prepared herself for a quick, clean doom at the business end of a sword. Smothering, slowly freezing under an impenetrable blanket of thick snow would be a death neither quick nor clean. This was not how she wanted to die. She swallowed a lump, struggling to sit up, reaching out towards Chen. She could not face this.

She had no choice. Her fate was upon her, even as she watched her attacker bound away and leap, catlike, up a series of small ledges in the far side of the pass. The roaring, thundering wall of snow barreled over the cliff, and the world turned white and cold, then black and silent.

♪

The blackness lifted suddenly, leaving Alannys awake and alert, but profoundly exhausted in every molecule of her body. She had no idea where she was, and she didn't have the energy to open her eyes and find out.

Just lying there with her eyes shut, merely existing, was a swirling torrent of agony. Pain knifed through her chest with each breath, even under the tightly wrapped bindings she could feel squeezing her. Her head hammered. Dull flames radiated up her right leg. She was in absolute misery, and she couldn't even remember why. She sifted through her memory, searching for some clue to the reason for her suffering. Things had started to go wrong, it seemed, about the time she saw the gray blur on her office wall. Maybe she should have taken a job flipping burgers after all.

"Now listen, damn it, Trago, and listen good, because next time you open your mouth I am going to answer you with the leather of my boot. I don't care who you are. I don't care what your gripe is. No one sees the Lady Alannys. *No one*. Now if you think you are man enough to take me, then have at it. Otherwise you can clear your carcass off this stoop."

The voice was barely recognizable as Chen's. It shook in rage and frustration, and she wondered if she heard fear there as well. It was a disconcerting notion—she had never seen Chen afraid in all the time she had known him. What had happened?

A door slammed. The confrontation was evidently over. Where was Chen? Had he left her there alone?

A floorboard creaked. So she was not alone. Where was Chen? What was he doing? She held her breath, listening for any more slight sounds.

A hand fell on her face, stopping her heart. She sucked in a surprised gasp, sitting up in bed, and met Chen's startled gaze. For just an instant they stared at each other, wide-eyed and speechless.

The next instant Chen sagged into a wooden chair at her bedside, his face in his hands, weeping.

Alannys stared at him, aghast. "Chen! What's wrong? What happened?"

He could not seem to look at her. "I'm sorry, Alannys. It's just...these *people*...they never quit. The demands, the complaints, there's never a moment's rest. And then I came in...and you weren't breathing...and...I thought you were *dead*." He drew a long, shuddering breath.

"And you're crying because I'm not?"

Chen laughed, a strained, strangled sound a lot like a bark. "Oh, Alannys, I'm so glad to see you awake again I don't care if you tease me. I was just...so *worried*." He leaned forward and scooped her into a crushing hug.

Alannys closed her eyes against the pain that tore through her like sheet lightning. But at the same time, it was comforting to have warm arms around her again. She had never seen Chen like this before—she could only imagine what he must have gone through. She managed to get her arms up and around him. "Hey, Chen, it's okay. I'm still here. I'm just—how long have I been unconscious, anyway?"

Chen released her and sat back, avoiding her gaze. "About a week."

She stared at him. "What?"

Chen took her hand in both of his, focusing on her fingers as if he spoke to them. "I'm not sure how much you remember about what happened that evening. It took us eighteen hours to dig you out of the snow. The avalanche brought down rocks with the snow, and it dropped one of them on an outcropping next to you. You were in the little crook between the slab of rock and the ground—that's probably the only reason you didn't smother under the snow. But you were still unconscious, in the freezing cold, for all those hours. You had broken ribs. By the time we got to you, you also had a fever. And some frostbite. We did the best we could. Nashara's been working non-stop, I even sang, but—it's a miracle you survived."

She couldn't seem to get her mind around it. Eighteen hours buried in the snow, a week unconscious, and she was still alive? It really was a miracle.

Her work here, it seemed, was not finished.

Alannys shivered in a sudden chill.

Chen looked at her in sudden sharp concern. "Are you all right?"

She sat back against the pillows, dodging his gaze and

trying not to wince. "I'm fine. Just a little tired, I think."

"Hmm." He didn't sound convinced. "I'm going to call Nashara back anyway. She should never have left to begin with. Nothing in this camp is as important as tending to your health."

She quirked an eyebrow at his obvious annoyance. "Chen, where is Nashara now?"

He looked at her in surprise, then quickly looked away. "Don't worry yourself about that, Alannys. I'm going to go get her. You just rest. She'll be here before you know it."

The door clicked softly shut behind him, and she closed her eyes. She really was tired, and the brief conversation with Chen had taxed her more than she had realized.

What exactly was it he was hiding from her? His attitude about Nashara seemed strange and he certainly did not want to talk about it. He had fled the wagon in a hurry as soon as she'd asked him.

But she'd been unconscious for a week. A week! Who knew what had happened in the tribe in the last week, cold and alone in Eversnow Pass? Chen's feud with Nashara was probably the least of her concerns.

The door creaked open, and soft footfalls crossed the wagon. Alannys opened her eyes to find the healer peering at her, the wrinkled face compressed in an expression of concern. "Hello, Nashara."

Nashara released a pent-up breath. "And hello to you, Lady Alannys. I am happy to find you alert. When Chen said you were awake, I have to admit I thought he was trying to trick me back here."

"Trick you back here? Why would he do that?"

A small, careful silence passed while Nashara felt her pulse. "You know your health is of utmost importance to me, Alannys. I would not leave you if you needed me and I could help you."

Alannys nodded. Nashara's single-minded devotion to her duty was never in question.

"Having said that, I also have to say that I understand completely where Chen is coming from. But still, I think it a little excessive to demand that I remain here constantly, when all I can do is sit by your bedside and there are so many others who need help." Her nervous eyes flashed to Alannys's. "You understand? I would not leave if I could help."

"Of course not. I understand."

Nashara sighed. "Well, that's settled, then. Not that I hold anything against Chen. We all do what we feel we must. What more can anyone ask of us?" She turned to the writing desk on the wall, crushing herbs in a bowl.

"Indeed." Alannys's mind churned. "Nashara, what happened? Why do so many need help?"

The pestle clattered onto the desktop. Nashara turned back to face her with wide eyes. "Chen has told you nothing?"

"No. I was hardly awake before he went to find you."

"I suppose I am not surprised." She sank heavily into the chair at the bedside. "Lady Alannys, you were beneath the snow for eighteen hours. Eighteen hours of people digging in teams, through the dark and the cold, digging with whatever was close to hand." She averted her eyes. "A reasonable man would have ridden back immediately for help after the avalanche. You may have noticed, though, that Chen is incapable of reason where you are concerned. He left his horse and dug in the snow with his bare hands until we caught up and found him there. We couldn't get a clear story of what had happened—he couldn't even tell us what we should do to help. Mortan took command when we realized that Chen could not." She sighed. "I have heard some whisperings of late—I know you must have heard them too. In the moment the snow came down upon you, the whispering was forgotten. Every Singari who was able came to dig. An incredible amount of snow and rock was moved."

"There were accidents." Alannys said the words dully, but she did not doubt them.

Nashara nodded. "Yes. Twice snow and rock slid back in on those digging. It did not take long to get them out, but the rocks caused a fair amount of injury. Mortan was killed outright by the falling rock."

Alannys sucked in her breath. Mortan...gone? Such a thing seemed utterly impossible. A fifty-something, big, strapping man, outspoken but fair—gone? It didn't seem like it could be real.

"A few others have died, from fever or from injuries. Mortan's daughter Mirenne died, trying to save her father. Chen has had quite a job, looking after you and turning away the constant stream of people coming to your door. Some are well-wishers, come to check on your progress. But most are relatives of those who have died, or been sick or injured. And I doubt they are bringing flowers."

Alannys shook her head. "That's terrible."

"Yes. But Chen's biggest headache has probably been me. He believes that as the healer for the tribe, I am obligated to stay at the bedside of the *kortha*. But there have been many others who needed my help." She flashed Alannys a quick smile. "And with Chen here, I can assure you that you have not lacked for attentive care."

"Of course." Alannys couldn't respond too intelligently; she was having trouble processing what she had heard. "So we are still camped—near the avalanche?"

"Yes." The healer sounded almost apologetic. "You must understand, after the avalanche, the way ahead is not yet passable. A few people have gone out during the day—they dig tunnels into the snowbank and burn great fires, helping to melt back the snow. No organized effort has been made though; Chen is just not up to leading us, and no one else has come forward."

"I see."

Nashara stood, wiping her hands down her apron. "Well, Lady Alannys, you seem to be doing very well. I'll just have a look at your leg, and I should be finished with you."

Her right calf throbbed as the healer carefully pulled back the blankets. Clucking softly to herself, Nashara emptied a little water into the herbs she had ground, and soaked a loose-woven cloth in the mixture.

Alannys pushed herself up off the pillows to look at her injured leg, dreading what she might see. What kind of break could cause this sort of knifing, splitting pain, even a week later, even with no weight placed upon it?

The outside of her calf was swollen and misshapen in a long, narrow wound, wide at the top. The skin was oddly bumpy, as if someone had buried their assorted marble collection underneath. *As if something was trying to get out,* she thought, and the idea chilled her. Blackened and blistered, oozing from deep, angry cracks, the wound turned even her own stomach.

"That's not a break," she said in some surprise.

"Indeed, my Lady. It is a burn, and a bad one at that." Nashara's gaze flicked to Alannys, then back to the cloth. She wrung it out, then dipped it back in the solution in the bowl.

"A burn?" Alannys looked from the festering wound to Nashara, and back again. "How did I manage to get badly burned under all that snow and ice?"

"It is a difficult thing to imagine," Nashara admitted, glancing at her sidelong. "I was hoping you could tell me. There is no question; that is a very bad burn."

Alannys stared blankly at the old healer, then frowned at her leg. "It's sort of a funny shape, isn't it? Almost like..." She broke off suddenly. "Nashara, where's my dagger?"

If Nashara thought the question odd, she gave no indication of it as she opened the writing desk's single drawer and withdrew the dagger in its familiar embroidered leather sheath. She held it next to the burn.

"That's not possible," Alannys breathed.

The wound followed exactly the shape of the dagger against her leg. There was no question what had burned her, but how?

Nashara sank into the chair, turning the dagger in her hands. "Lady Alannys, is there an enchantment upon this blade?"

"I don't know," Alannys said, trying to remember everything that had happened when Raman gave it to her. "It was a gift, bought for me from a weaponsmith's tent at the market of the Great Palace. I didn't know weapons could be enchanted."

"Weaponsmithing is a craft—a Talented weaponsmith can do many things others cannot. Of course, I don't think anyone knows how to do it anymore. If what I suspect is true, this blade is far older than any of us. The weaponsmith may have sold this, but he certainly did not forge it."

"What sort of enchantment do you suspect?"

"A seeking spell, that would alert you when a certain person is near. There was a time when many swords and daggers had such spells. But to activate that spell, this dagger would need to have tasted his blood." She raised her eyes slowly to regard Alannys. "Has this blade drawn blood?"

Alannys swallowed hard. "Yes. As a matter of fact it drew the blood of the same fellow who attacked me before the avalanche."

Nashara nodded as if that was just what she had

expected. "That explains it, then. This blade has a seeking spell forged into it, and that spell has been tuned to your attacker. When he comes near, the dagger will grow warm. If he is attacking, it can get hot enough to burn."

"Obviously," Alannys said sourly, looking at her charred calf.

Nashara smiled gently. "It is a very valuable blade, my Lady, and I am sure you will find it very useful." She laid the dagger gingerly on the desk, as if knowing about its enchantment made it fundamentally more dangerous. "Now as for that leg, I have something that might help with that."

She turned back to the desk, squeezed out the cloth in the little bowl, and tied it around Alannys's leg.

Alannys heaved a long, grateful sigh and fell back against the pillows. "That feels wonderful, Nashara. Thank you."

"You are welcome, my Lady." Nashara stood, and moved uncertainly toward the door. "Well, I think you are going to be fine. You need some rest and some time, neither of which I can make for you. You are recovering well, my Lady. I hope I will not offend you if I go now to assist others who are not doing as well."

"Of course not."

Nashara smiled and quietly let herself out. Alannys tipped her head back against the pillows, drinking in the cool relief of the damp, medicine-infused cloth pressing against her leg. It was dripping from the edges, making quite a little mess in her bed, but she didn't care. The comfort it provided was well worth the cost.

She relaxed in the quiet, and closed her eyes. Pain and discomfort aside, after what she had been through, she was grateful to be alive. It seemed a wonderful gift just to be there, lying in a soft bed with a cool cloth on her burned leg. What more could she ask for?

The wagon door creaked open. Soft footsteps entered, hesitated, then crossed to the little chair.

Alannys didn't open her eyes. "Hello, Chen."

"Alannys! I thought you were asleep."

"I know. But I'm just resting."

There was a small, awkward silence. "Well—that's good," Chen finally said. "You need your rest."

Alannys had nothing to say to that. She stretched in the bed, wincing when the motion aggravated her sore ribs and back.

Chen was immediately at her side. "Are you all right? Should I go get Nashara?"

"No—I'm fine, just sore." She finally looked at him. "Chen, why didn't you tell me what happened?"

He shifted his eyes away from her uncomfortably. "Damn Nashara, I told her not to talk to you about that."

She frowned at him. "That does nothing to make me feel better, you know."

Chen sighed. "I wasn't trying to hide anything from you, Alannys, not really. I would have told you, you must know that."

"When?"

"When you were ready for it!" He threw up his hands in a dramatic show of frustration. "Look, Alannys, in case it has escaped your notice, you were in a near-fatal accident. You're lucky just to be here. I don't think you need to be burdened with tribal affairs yet, do you?"

Alannys sighed. "You can't coddle me forever. In a day or two I'll be on my feet again, and—"

"A day or two!" A vein pulsed ominously in Chen's temple. "I should say not! Have you missed the point of this entire conversation? *You need your rest.*"

"There isn't time for resting, Chen! I'm *kortha* of this tribe, and they need me. We have to start making coordinated efforts to open the pass."

"I don't care. I will pull everyone together to work on the pass. You are not getting up from that bed for at least a week. You were unconscious for that long, and we are still here, muddling through as well as ever."

"Except that people have died. I might have been able to save them. I might still be able to save others if I go now." She reached out to him with a shaking hand. "Help me up, will you?"

Chen took her hand, kissed the back of it, and carefully tucked it back under the blankets. "No. You are not strong enough yet."

"Chen, if I don't go out there, people will die!"

"If you *do* go out there, *you* will die. Look at yourself, Alannys, you can't even stand up without help. You are in no shape to sing. Do you think you could survive Muse's Fever like this?"

"That doesn't matter. Listen to me — "

"No, you listen to me!" His handsome face, usually so easy-going, was hard with anger, and his dark eyes blazed. "This does matter, Alannys. You are the Redeemer. Nothing matters more! Eight Singari gave their lives to save yours. Is tossing it away any way to repay their sacrifice?"

She stared at him, stung. "No."

Chen flopped back into the chair, exhaling in a noisy puff. "Well, I'm glad we agree on something, anyway. Now go back to sleep. You need your rest."

She didn't appreciate being told to go to sleep like a child, but what could she do? The sudden, unwelcome reminder of those who had died on her behalf had stolen her will to resist. Maybe Chen was right. It seemed everything she did here was wrong.

She rolled over to face the wall, tears burning the backs of her eyes.

♪

"Damn it!" Alannys dropped the half-mended sock in

her lap and jammed her left index finger in her mouth, blinking back sudden tears, more of frustration than pain.

Chen glanced apprehensively over at her from the writing desk, where he had spread out some type of game, played with small carved wood tiles. "Are you sure you ought to be doing that?"

She glared at him. "I am perfectly capable of darning a sock, Chen." She peered at her finger, found it still bleeding, and squeezed it with her other hand. "I just haven't gotten used to these long needles yet."

Chen swept the tiles off the table into a matching wooden box. "I'm not saying you aren't capable, Alannys. I'm just saying it seems sort of a—waste, perhaps, for someone of your abilities."

"Of course it is!" Alannys exploded. "There are sick and injured people in this camp, but instead of helping them I've spent the last two days flat on my back in this bed. We're finally working together to open the pass, but instead of helping I'm lying here, darning socks! Of course it's a waste! And who do you suppose you have to thank for that?"

Chen snapped the lid on his wooden box, seeming unable to look at her. "Now calm down, I wasn't being critical. I think it's wonderful that you want to help."

"But?"

He threw his hands up. "But you are not ready to get out of that bed yet, and you are certainly not ready to sing!"

"Why don't you let me be the judge of that?"

"No. You'll get up when Nashara says it's all right, and not a moment before. Speaking of which..." He looked around suddenly as though the thought had just occurred to him. "I wonder where she is? It is long past the time she should have come to check on you."

He wandered out of the wagon, and the door fell shut

behind him.

Alannys threw the half-darned sock at the door. She did not doubt that he would hunt down Nashara, and she knew he would not rest until he had dragged the healer back. But she also knew that the real reason he had left was that he was simply unwilling to discuss what was bothering her. Chen did not like to argue with her, but he refused to back down on this.

"Nashara!" The shout, slightly muffled, was still clear to her inside the wagon. Evidently the door had not fallen completely shut. And poor Nashara had not been hard for Chen to find.

"What is it, Chen?" Exasperation was clear in the healer's voice.

"I was just in with Alannys. It's past time you checked on her, don't you think? Just because she's done well so far doesn't mean we should become complacent —"

"Chen! Just who is the healer here? I assure you I have not forgotten the Lady Alannys. But at this moment I am off to my *mol* to tend to a young man who is in truly dire shape, a young man who may not be with us by nightfall. So you'll forgive me if I put his needs ahead of someone who is recovering quite well, and doesn't need any help from me *or* you!"

Alannys felt numb. She had never heard Nashara so angry, had never heard her admit so flatly that one of her patients might die. This man had been growing steadily worse, his survival now in grave doubt, while she sat on her rump darning socks?

No more. She'd had enough of this nonsense. She didn't need Chen or Nashara to tell her she could leave her wagon. She drew a deep breath and swung her feet over the side of the bed to touch the floor for the first time in ten days.

She wobbled when she stood, and her vision speckled

with bright pulsing stars. She grabbed the chair for support, and breathed deep until things looked normal again. She was still in her shapeless linen nightgown, but she lacked the energy or the will to bother with dressing. A man's life was hanging in the balance. What did it matter if she wore a nightgown?

Alannys peeked around the edge of the door, afraid she would find Chen still standing there. Stubborn as she was, she was still in no shape right now for an argument with him, and there was no time for that.

Fortunately, he was nowhere to be seen.

She lowered herself carefully down the few stairs, already aware of the pain in her leg, of the shortness of her breath. It was a very good thing for her that Nashara's wagon was only the second one down from her own. She'd been doing nothing but resting for ten days. How could she still be this weak?

By the time she'd dragged herself across the few yards to Nashara's wagon, she was limping, gasping for breath. Muse's Fever was bad, but she had been soundly thrashed by nature's fury.

Nashara could not have looked more surprised if Soth himself had walked in. "Alannys! What are you doing out of bed?"

Alannys looked from Nashara to the young man whose forehead she was sponging. "Forgive me...for eavesdropping," she said, trying hard not to sound as short of breath as she was. "I overheard how bad his condition is...and I thought...maybe I could help..."

"Oh, of course!" The healer stood up out of her chair and hurried over to help Alannys to the bedside. "I know I should not allow this, but he is in such bad shape...Alannys, if there is anything you can do, I beg you to try. My efforts will not save him."

Leaning heavily on the wall by the bed for support,

Alannys took a few deep breaths. The Singari man on the bed before her looked pale and drawn, his skin tinged with gray. She summoned all her remaining strength, gripped his arm, and sang.

♫

The bed was soft, but the sheets were stiff and uncomfortable with dried sweat. Alannys's hair was plastered to her head, and the bedclothes stuck to her, so she imagined she had been the one doing the sweating. She tried to open her eyes and sit up, and she heard a moan.

She was the one doing the moaning, too.

Alannys gave up on sitting and settled for opening her eyes. She was in her bed, in her wagon. Standing beside the bed, glowering, was Chen.

"Do — you — have — any — *idea* — what — you — have — done?" His voice was clipped and controlled, his face tight with tension, but his eyes bored holes in her. She had never seen him look at anyone like that — least of all her.

Irrational fear welled up in her. She fought it down and glared back at him with everything she had, which admittedly at that moment was not much. She could take anything he dished out — she had saved a life. "I did the only thing I could do, Chen. A man was dying. I had to try to help."

"Are you mad? Or just suicidal? You could have died!"

"I had to do it, Chen."

"Had to do what? Risk yourself needlessly?"

"It wasn't needlessly! A person was dying! I had Talent that could help. It is my duty to do what I can to help those around me."

"Horseshit," Chen snorted, turning away from her. "For what it is worth, there are those in this tribe who agree with you. There are those who have been beating down the door ever since we got you back from the avalanche, demanding that you come and sing to help this or that person."

"Well, then, you see—"

"They're full of horseshit too!" His angry shout cut her off cleanly.

She stared at him a moment. "And all this time, I suppose you've been doing nothing at all—never leaving my bedside, never singing to help anyone?"

Chen flushed bright red. "Of course not. I did what I could. Mostly, I sang to help you."

"And I am grateful. But how could you ask me not to do the same?"

"It isn't the same at all! Alannys, your life is worth more than mine. Worth more than anyone in this whole tribe, worth more than everyone in this whole tribe! No one else can do what you have to do. If something happens to you, all hope is lost for Ravanmark. Forever. You can't take foolish chances!"

Alannys gritted her teeth and pushed herself up against her pillows. "But I wasn't taking foolish chances! I saved someone's life!"

Chen just stared at her, a stricken look in his eyes that pained her.

"What?"

Chen's face fell, his eyes suddenly soft. "No, you didn't. I'm sorry, Alannys. He died last night."

The news hit her like a physical blow. How had she failed so miserably? She fought to remember, but everything after arriving in Nashara's wagon was a blur of pain and blackness. "What happened?" Her voice sounded hoarse.

Chen sank into the chair beside her bed and took her hand. "It wasn't your fault. You just weren't up to singing, Alannys. Nashara said you managed to sing maybe two words before you collapsed. She wasn't able to wake you. I helped her move you back here. She fretted the whole time, telling me over and over that she should never have asked you to help."

"It wasn't her fault. She didn't ask me to go there."

"I know. There was nothing you could have done."

Nothing she could have done. Only because she was so frail at the moment—any other time she could have saved that man, she knew it. She could feel it. "I could have saved him, Chen. If I wasn't sick. I *could* have." She sighed. "If only there were more of me."

Chen gave her a small, sad smile and brushed her hair back from her forehead. "There is only one, Alannys. As I do keep reminding you."

She couldn't argue, and she wouldn't agree. So she sat there in silence, feeling the softness of his fingers stroking hers, until her fatigue overtook her and she fell asleep.

♫

If only there were more of me.

Alannys jammed the long, unwieldy needle through the sock in her lap again, knotted the thread, and savagely bit it off. She tossed the finished sock into the reed basket by her bed, and dragged another out of the pile beside her.

If only there were more of me.

She knotted the thread on her needle, and started again. The Singari certainly were hard on socks. At this rate, she didn't see how anybody got anything done except mending socks.

If only there were more of me.

Of course, probably nobody worried about socks. That was probably why she had so many to keep her busy now —socks were just not a high priority for the Singari. You darned socks when you had nothing else to do, or if you were a bedridden, recovering Redeemer who was able to do nothing else.

If only there were more of me.

Alannys put the sock and needle down, and rubbed at the bridge of her nose. The thought was not going away. It was a useless thought, fit for a useless Redeemer like herself. Of course there weren't more of her. How could there be? As everyone seemed determined to point out, there could be only one Redeemer. And so far, it seemed she was the lucky winner.

But...but that young man had not needed a Redeemer.

That perfectly obvious realization seemed to knock the constant chatter in her mind silent for a moment. She had to acknowledge the truth of it. He had not needed the Redeemer.

He had only needed a singer.

And she was surrounded by people who could sing.

It was a revelation. She wanted to jump up and scream it to the heavens, but she couldn't seem to move. She just sat there, wordlessly realizing that there *were* more of her. This whole tribe was full of people who could sing. And some could play.

All she had to do was teach them.

♫

Chen wasn't sure what to think when he walked into the wagon. Something had changed here, that much was obvious. Yet he had no idea what might have changed, or how, when Alannys had been here alone in the wagon. He had only been gone an hour or so—what could have happened? It didn't make sense.

And yet, there was no denying that something had happened. The socks Alannys had stubbornly insisted on darning for the past four days were scattered on the floor next to the bed. Alannys sat back against the pillows with a quill and her stack of writing paper, scribbling furiously.

She stopped and looked up when he came in, graced him with a radiant smile, and went back to her writing.

Chen sat down in the chair next to the bed, glancing around for some clue about this sudden change. "So...I see you've given up the darning."

Alannys laughed. "Yes. I've found a much more

worthwhile pursuit."

"Well, that's good to hear." He waited, but she said nothing. "So—what are you doing now? Penning a manifesto?"

Everything he said, it seemed, made her laugh. "Of a sort." She put her papers aside and turned to him. "People with Talent should be able to use it. Do you agree with that, Chen?"

"Well, naturally." He hesitated, wondering where she was headed with this. "If this is about your Redeemer's Stewards, I think that was a really good idea, and—"

"No. No, I actually was thinking of something else."

He waited, but she fiddled with her blanket and said nothing. "Can I ask what?"

Alannys looked up at him. "I'm sorry, I'm not trying to be difficult. It's just that, well, I'm not sure how to approach this."

She could practically see his guard go up. He met her gaze, but his eyes seemed wary. "I usually find," Chen said, "that directly is the best way to approach most anything."

"Okay." She hesitated a moment longer, nervous, then just blurted it out. "Chen, do you think the Singari would mind if I taught them music?"

Chen stared at her. He didn't even blink. The question, it seemed, was highly offensive.

"I'm sorry—I didn't mean to upset you, I just—"

"Upset me? *Upset* me?" He shook his head. "Alannys, you know me. I don't have words to tell you how fantastic I think that would be."

"So—it would be okay?"

"Sure, if you ask *me*." Concern was plain in his brown eyes as they searched hers. "But have you thought about what you'd be opening yourself up to? The elders especially have not reacted well when we've played in the past. *Sharast,* remember? They wanted to make an example of us."

"The elders," she mused. "No, I suppose they wouldn't like this much. The elders are very resistant to change, until that change is right in front of them and unavoidable. I kind of think of that as their job. But they aren't unreasonable."

"If you say so."

She smiled at him affectionately. "You're just grumpy because you're their problem child, Chen. I'll take care of the elders. I was worried more about how everyone else would take it. Do you think it would be all right?"

"Oh, yes. That would be more than all right."

Alannys beamed. "That's great! Judging from you, I expect the Singari will have excellent results singing for effect. Who knows, maybe you could actually use that on your travels—you could heal and help—you could even charge for it if you wanted."

Chen had clearly never thought along those lines before. "Wow."

She grinned at him. "Yeah. But we're getting a bit ahead of ourselves there. Right now I have an important question for you. Who is the best woodworker in this camp?"

"Well, we have a few, but if you want the best, that would be Lorimar. He's a bit odd, though."

"That's okay, so am I. Can I ask you a favor?"

"Me? Anything, Alannys, you know that."

"Wonderful. I need you to grab my violin case out from under the bed."

He looked a bit dubious, but complied. "All right, here it is."

"Now help me out of this bed. We're going to see Lorimar."

♫

Grizzled with age, thick cataracts completely obscuring

both eyes, Lorimar sat at a scarred wooden bench in the middle of a wagon whose walls were lined with hand tools. Kerb, his apprentice, worked in a corner, whittling a replacement part for a broken chair sitting next to him. A small lantern propped in the seat of the chair provided the room's only light.

Alannys and Chen stood just inside the doorway a long moment, waiting for their eyes to adjust to the darkness. Even leaning heavily on Chen, Alannys had been winded by the walk, and she hoped she could recover her breath before approaching the master woodworker. As she grew accustomed to the darkness, Alannys could see that the shelves hanging on the walls near her were filled with carved wooden statues of the Muses. They beamed at her with soft, joyous expressions so expertly crafted, they seemed alive. A three-dimensional mural hung nearby, composed of each Muse's icon, each rendered in a different type of wood. She had been right to come here— the man's skill was obvious in everything he did.

Kerb glanced up from his work. "Hello, Chen, Lady Alannys."

Lorimar cocked his head, rubbing his hands down his worn leather apron. "Well, well—Chen and the Lady Alannys. What can an old man do for you this fine day?"

Alannys put her violin case on the edge of the workbench and flipped it open. "I wanted to ask you a favor, Lorimar. Say I have something—a handcrafted, wooden thing—and I need another one. Would you be able to copy it for me?"

The old woodworker pulled a rag from his apron pocket and rubbed at his hands with it. "I'd be a pretty poor master if I couldn't. Just bring by this thing you want copied."

Alannys grinned, and lifted her violin out of its case. "As a matter of fact, I have it right here." She placed it in his hands.

The color drained from his face as she watched. He ran his hand over the back of the violin, around to the front. When his fingers touched the strings, they jerked back reflexively.

Alannys frowned. "Is something wrong?"

"This—this is an instrument. A *musical instrument!*"

"Yes, it's my violin." She glanced at Chen. He stood next to her, arms folded, kneading his thumb with his teeth. He caught her eye and shrugged. "Is that a problem?"

Lorimar put the instrument gently down on the workbench. "My Lady, I cannot construct such a thing as this."

She regarded him a moment in silence. He was still shaking his head, his fingers stealing toward the violin, but shying away when they encountered it. Kerb watched them intently from his chair. "Cannot?" she finally asked. "Or will not? The skill is there, I think."

"No—no!" Lorimar shook his head vigorously. "My skill is not sufficient for this, Alannys. No man could duplicate the instruments of the Muses."

The pain in her leg made it difficult to concentrate. She glanced around the room, and saw a three-legged stool against the wall. She nudged Chen and gestured at it. "This is not an instrument of the Muses. This is an instrument of men, made by men and played by men."

He looked exceedingly unconvinced. "I—I don't know, my Lady, I just don't know."

Kerb abandoned his knife and came to the workbench. "You must do this thing, Lorimar."

Lorimar whipped his head around to face his apprentice with an expression of perfect outrage. "That is no way to speak to your master!"

Kerb's ears reddened. He stepped closer to the old

woodworker. "True. But this is no way for you to speak to the Redeemer! You cannot deny her, Master. Especially for something this important. Bringing back the lost instruments—it is a wonderful opportunity!" He smiled at Alannys in a way that made her own ears redden.

Chen appeared at her side with the stool. He gave Kerb a sour look, and solicitously helped Alannys up onto the stool.

Lorimar touched a finger to the violin in front of him, then pulled it back. "But—"

"I don't doubt your skill, Lorimar," Alannys interjected.

Kerb nodded sharply. "Nor do I. You are the greatest woodworker there is—perhaps the greatest there has ever been. I know that you can do this. But will you?"

Lorimar picked up the violin and turned it over in his weathered hands, running his fingers over the glossy varnished finish. "Bringing back the lost instruments," he echoed. "There can be no higher calling, I think, if the Muses have willed it. But if not...there can be no bigger betrayal of them. Am I betraying the Muses, Lady Alannys, if I listen to you? This is no small thing you ask."

"How can you even ask that?" Chen said angrily. "You can't betray the Muses by helping Alannys. She—"

"Chen." Alannys held up a hand to silence him, and turned back to Lorimar. "My time is growing short," she said. Until that moment she had not known it, but it was true. The words had come from her flaky Second Sight. "Soon all will be decided, for weal or for woe. You all know my task here. The undertaking is bigger than all of us, and it may yet consume me."

Kerb averted his eyes uncomfortably. She heard Chen's painful gasp, but she could not afford to spare any of them —even herself.

"If that happens," she continued, her even voice

betraying none of her inner turmoil, "or if those who seek to destroy me should succeed, I would not have music in Ravanmark die with me."

"Alannys, don't." Chen's tone tore at her, and his dark eyes glistened moist in the low light.

"I'm sorry, Chen," she said, and she was. "But I don't have any guarantees, so I can't make any. I might be here for the next fifty years, or I might fall to the cloaked swordsman tomorrow. Either way, what we have started here must continue. When I am gone, it will be the Singari who spread music throughout Ravanmark. And you will do it on instruments you have made yourselves, under Lorimar's instruction. One day, those instruments will be in the hands of Talented people who will have no need to hide them."

An awful silence fell over the wagon. Kerb could not seem to look at her, Chen could not look away, and Lorimar seemed completely absorbed in the violin in front of him.

Alannys cleared her throat. "My violin should give you a good starting place. I expect as you make a few and learn what works and what doesn't acoustically, you'll make changes that suit you. Perhaps you'll invent new instruments entirely. But none of that can happen without this first step. Can you do it, Lorimar? Can you take that first, most important step for the Singari?"

Lorimar brushed his fingers across the smooth, varnished surface of the violin, and ran them down the length of its silver-wound strings, muttering to himself the entire time. Finally, he gave a strained, forced smile. "How can I refuse the Redeemer?"

Kerb whooped triumphantly and ran to Alannys, throwing his arms around her. "I knew you would convince him, I just knew it!"

Alannys could feel her face redden, and she struggled

to keep her balance on the stool. "I—well, that is—"

Chen caught him by the shoulder and regarded him with an expression like a thundercloud. "You and Master Lorimar must surely have a lot of work ahead of you," he said pointedly.

Kerb quickly withdrew to the other side of the workbench.

"Yes, yes," Lorimar said, taking up the violin and heading toward the back of the wagon. "Come, Kerb, we should get started. There is much to do before we can begin work on such a project."

Alannys turned to dismount her stool, and distinctly heard the old man mutter, "And may the Muses forgive me."

She whipped back around, but the two woodworkers were at the back of the wagon, their heads close together as they held a quiet discussion about precision of measurements and types of wood. She frowned, watching them. Had she just imagined that?

And if so, why did it give her such a chill?

♪

"Alannys? Are you all right?"

She twisted around on her stool by the workbench in Lorimar's wagon, and found Chen frowning at her. "Of course, I'm fine. I just—I hope we've done the right thing."

Chen looked at her in surprise. "What do you mean? I thought we were agreed that bringing back music can only be a good thing."

"We were. We are. I just wonder—bringing back instruments, it's a big step. And perhaps it wasn't for me to decide when that step should be taken."

Chen smiled at her tolerantly and took her arm, helping her off the stool. "You worry too much, Alannys. You are the Redeemer. Who else could make a decision like that?"

She sighed, shutting her eyes tight against the sudden

stab of pain that came with standing. "A violin makes as good a starting point as any, I suppose. Perhaps they will learn to copy the lute, as well."

Chen reached out to open the door for her. "That might work out. I suppose we'll want to see how this one turns out before we plan anything else."

Alannys lowered herself gingerly down the few steps, watching her feet and leaning heavily on Chen.

"Well, now, look who has ventured out of the wagon on this fine day."

The sarcastic cut of the voice whipped her like a lash, and she felt Chen's hand tighten on her arm before she even knew who had spoken.

"You're looking well, for someone Chen assures us is walking the path to the Valley of the Muses."

Alannys straightened with effort, and found herself facing a small, angry, Singari mob. Five or six people stood in a knot, silently supporting the jeering man in front of her. His complexion was unnaturally pale, and his face was tight, with high patches of color burning in his cheeks. His reddish hair hung longish and shaggy, his beard longer than Singari men usually favored, and untrimmed. He did not look as though he had slept in days.

"Trago, you look unwell. Perhaps you should retire to your home." Chen's tone held a warning.

"My home? My home? My *empty* home, you mean — cold and dark and empty thanks to the woman you hold on your arm. How can you desert your people, Chen, and coddle this outsider?"

"Outsider?" Chen had never looked so outraged — at least, not in front of her. "That's a fine thing coming from you, ungrateful *sharo*."

"Ungrateful? You dare..." Trago stiffened and pointed a shaky finger at Alannys. "I served seven years indenture to Mirenne's uncle, Chen. I had the ceremonies. This—this *woman* did nothing but force herself into the middle of Singari affairs, pretending to be one of us. She's done nothing but endanger us, forcing us closer to outsiders, bringing us here, getting us killed! Getting Mirenne killed! For this I should be *grateful?*"

Chen stepped between Trago and Alannys, and she suddenly realized how tall the red-haired man was. "Ceremonies are not necessary for the Redeemer, you know that. Not for the Redeemer."

Trago's dismissive snort expressed very clearly his opinion of Alannys as the Redeemer. "I've had enough of this Redeemer nonsense. Mirenne believed, and look where it got her. This woman wishes to display her Soth-sent Talent, and the only way she can safely do that is to claim to be the Redeemer of the Realm. Do you really think we are too blind to see this? Redeemer, my eye!"

The group behind Trago grumbled in sullen agreement, and Alannys had a sudden, chilling vision of a stormy night in Crinn. *There can be only one end for a false Redeemer...Stone the false Redeemer!* This situation had to be defused, and fast.

"My friends," she began, and Trago shot her a glare that stopped her words short.

"Alannys..." Chen gave her a warning look and shoved her behind him. But how could she talk to these people if she hid from them? And how could she change things without talking to people? Left to themselves they would fester in their hatred, whip up support among the malcontents, and eventually kill her or tear the tribe apart trying. She couldn't let that happen. The Singari deserved better than that.

Even these Singari.

She pushed past Chen, and pitched her voice to carry. "Look, Trago, I know things have been difficult. And I know I am no kind of a *kortha*. It saddens my heart to hear of your wife. So many good Singari have lost their lives, and it is a debt I can never hope to repay.

"And yet I would try. I can't give up, I can't turn away from the Singari or my mission. To do so would be to dishonor those who have died because of me, and I can't do that." She took a shuddering breath, and extended her hand. "Will you help me, Trago? With your unique views, you could help reshape the world. Can you do this, to honor your wife?"

Trago stood silently facing her, knotted cords of tendons standing out on his fists. His jaw trembled, and as she watched his left eye began to twitch.

Slowly he unballed his hands, and reached out to take hers. She smiled and grasped his hand, and he pulled her toward him.

"Alannys, no!" She heard Chen's panicked shout, but before it even registered a giant fist crashed into her face, and she staggered backwards, stumbled, and fell flat on her back.

Trago followed her. "You heartless bitch!" He fell on her, fists flailing, his face a dead white. "You speak your pretty words...you *smile* at me! You dare to speak of my wife — you *dare*...to ask my *help*...for my *views*..." He spoke in vicious snaps between sharp, short punches to her face, her belly, her arms, anything he could reach. She could make out Chen behind him, pulling for all he was worth, but he could not break Trago's blind fury. "This is my view," he hissed, panting. "You can *die!*"

Her vision was splotched with red and black, and it seemed a fiery glow surrounded Trago. It took every bit of her meager remaining strength just to stay conscious, to continue to exist. She could not answer him. She could only hope, pathetically, for some kind of divine intervention. She tried to breathe, and shards of agony shot through her chest.

Dying might not be such a bad thing after all. She closed her eyes and waited for it.

The blows stopped falling. For just a moment her mind was bathed in a silence as thick as any of Nashara's balms, then a woman's shrill shriek splintered the silence to bits.

Alannys's eyes were too swollen to open fully, but she cracked them enough to see what was happening. Chen had hauled Trago off of her, his arms around the bigger man's neck. Trago clawed at Chen's arms, trying to break the choke-hold. His lips were beginning to turn blue. A plump, dark haired, middle-aged woman beat ineffectually at Chen's shoulders. "Let him go, you beast! You're choking him!"

"Beast?" The look Chen shot at her could have burned stone. He threw Trago to the ground, and pointed at Alannys with a shaking hand. "Do you see that? Do you, Majari? Look at what your precious law-son did to a woman. Look!"

Majari's frantic gaze flicked in Alannys's direction, touched her, and jerked away.

Chen snorted. "You can't even look at her, can you? There is a beast here, woman, but it isn't me." He gestured at the crowd behind her. "All of you should be ashamed! Turning against your own people for this animal! Brutagar was exiled for less than what has happened here today."

Trago pulled himself to his knees with a strangled cough. "Leave them alone, Chen. These people have nothing left except me."

"I can't believe—"

"Chen." Alannys couldn't imagine that Chen could possibly hear her choked gasp, but he immediately turned toward her. "Leave them. Please."

He stared at her, and for a long moment she was afraid he would argue with her. "Fine, Trago," he finally said. "I leave them to you, and may the Muses sing mercy for all of you."

He turned his back on them and knelt beside her, and the little mob might have ceased to exist. "Oh, Alannys." The look in his eyes frightened her—she could see there exactly how bad off she was, and it was really bad.

"Chen, I—" She tried to push herself up on her elbows, but collapsed back with a gasp.

"No, don't move. You can't walk like this." He gathered her up as easily as if she were a rag doll, and cradled her against her chest, carrying her away without a backward glance.

♪

Alannys lay back against her pillows, trying to focus on the soft comfort of her bed instead of the million places where she hurt.

Nashara sat on the edge of the bed, dabbing a cool, greasy salve around Alannys's eyes. "I don't understand, Chen. You say *Trago* did this?"

Chen nodded without taking his eyes off Alannys. That concern, that horrible pity, had not left his face. If she looked anything like as bad as she felt, she could understand why. "Yes. He was an animal, Nashara, a murderous, savage animal. I have never seen anything like it."

The healer shook her head. "I would not have believed it."

"Me either. But I was there, I saw it with my own eyes."

"So this is not typical of Trago?" Alannys's voice rasped.

"No." Chen's answer was immediate. "No, I should say not. He was the kindest, gentlest husband you could ever hope to see. I don't believe he ever raised so much as his voice to Mirenne."

"She was his world," Nashara said simply, with

sadness haunting her eyes.

"Still, I can't believe he would sink this low," Chen said. "And Majari, to just stand there and do nothing..."

"What else could she do?" Nashara said. "Mirenne and Mortan are dead. With her husband and her daughter gone, she has nothing left but her law-son."

Chen shook his head. "Still, I would think that—"

"This was not Majari's fault," Alannys croaked, cutting across their bickering. "And it was not Trago's. It was mine."

"Alannys!" Chen gasped.

"No, it's true. That man is being consumed from within by grief and anger. But I don't think he came out today intending to physically attack me. I think he just wanted a chance to vent his feelings, to tell me personally how I've wrecked his life. You tried to keep me back, Chen, and if I was smart I would have listened. But I didn't. I believed I would find the right words to reach him, and instead I pushed him right over the edge."

"Alannys, I don't think you should blame yourself for this," Nashara said.

Chen nodded. "Yes. The blame is entirely Trago's, and he shall answer for it."

"No!" Alannys tried to sit up, and fell back against the pillows. Her ribs were wrapped so tight it was difficult to get a good breath. "Chen, you've got to leave him alone. Can't you imagine what he must be going through? On top of everything else, he's got to live with this now. If he is the kind of man you say he is, that won't be easy. I've already pushed him to do something horrible to me. I don't want you pushing him to do something horrible to himself as well."

Before Chen could say anything back, the door to the wagon flew open with a crash. All three elders hurried in, as flustered as she had ever seen them.

"Alannys!" Chira's hair was mussed, and she panted raggedly. "We came as soon as we heard."

"I'll just...be on my way," Nashara said, glancing around the crowded wagon, and disappeared out the door.

Chen stood up, frowning. "I'm not sure she's really up to this yet. Perhaps— "

"Nonsense. This needs to be handled right away, young man, I should think you would see that." Chira's voice had an iron edge to it that Alannys had never heard there before, not even when she threatened to sing in the *zhothamol*.

Bayred pushed past Chen and settled into the chair. "Trust me, we had no desire to disturb you. Either of you."

Alannys looked around at all of them in a numb sort of amazement. "What are you all doing here?"

"We came to see you, dear." Legara sat down at the foot of the bed. "We heard that you were attacked." Her shrill voice was unusually kind.

"We heard, but we did not imagine it was this bad!" Chira turned toward Chen. "You should have come to us immediately. We should not have heard of this through rumor. This should not have been permitted to go so long unpunished."

"No," Alannys interrupted. "Chen did nothing wrong. I do not wish any punishment for Trago."

Chira stared at her as though perhaps she had misunderstood. "Alannys? Surely you wish to see justice served?"

Alannys shook her head, and slumped back against her pillows. "Of course, Chira. But punishment would not be justice, not this time."

Chira folded her hands over the top of her walking stick. "Your inclination to mercy is inspiring. I have to warn you, though, a certain level of discipline is absolutely vital. Whatever motives you may have for doing so, I urge you not to let this pass. To do so would be to encourage similar outbursts, and that is a thing we must not have."

"We'll deal with any others as they appear."

"And how will you support punishing them for their infractions, if you have let this one go without consequence entirely? Men have been exiled for less, as I am sure Pesia will remind us."

Alannys shook her head. "I don't know. Look, would we even be having this conversation if I was a man? I don't think he intended to attack me, at least not at first. But I can't forget the look in his eyes when he talked about his empty home, Chira. Punishing him will only hurt him more, and drive him farther from us."

Chira considered it. "You are saying that Trago is not responsible for his own actions."

"I suppose I am, after a fashion. He is too distraught, and I provoked him."

"Anyone might provoke him, them, with the wrong words at the wrong time."

Alannys wondered where she was going with this. "It would seem so. He is unpredictable."

"But he will recover," Chen interjected, with more force than the conversation seemed to warrant. "He is grieving, Chira. He will recover — you must not pronounce him *pratha*."

Chira regarded him with raised eyebrows. "Such cheek! You tell us you are not *markortha*, and yet you presume to advise the council on what they must or must not do."

Chen dropped his gaze. "I apologize, Chira."

"Apology accepted." She smiled. "And we are not unreasonable, Chen. We had only considered a declaration of temporary *pratha*, until Trago has worked through his loss."

Chen stared at her. "You mean, you came here with this verdict prepared? And yet you made Alannys defend her position, to reach a conclusion you had already decided upon?"

"Not exactly. We had anticipated that Alannys might not wish to pursue punitive action, that is all."

"And I thank you." Alannys did not take offense at this the way Chen evidently expected her to. Chira was right, some basic level of discipline was necessary to maintain order. They only disagreed on what that level should be in this case. "What is *pratha*?"

The elders looked to Chen. "*Pratha* is — well, literally I think it would be best rendered as 'tainted'. It is not the same as unclean — it's more like an illness. An illness of the mind. And until the illness is cured, Trago will be sequestered."

"And if he refuses?"

"Refuses to be sequestered? I don't think such a thing has ever happened. To refuse to obey the decision of the Council of Elders would bring exile. Even Trago would not do this, I think."

Alannys considered that. Chen was probably right. Trago obviously blamed her for his wife's death, and he wanted vengeance; he wanted her ousted from the tribe. But he held no grudge against the tribe itself, and if he wanted to leave he was free to go. But he hadn't. "And who will decide when the illness has passed? When the sentence of *pratha* can be lifted?"

"The Council of Elders would decide that, upon Nashara's advice."

"Does this sound acceptable?" Chira seemed sincere. "Matters of law and punishment are the domain of the council, but we do not wish to alienate you, Alannys."

"Yes, yes, that sounds fine. Thank you for considering

my input on this." In light of all that Chen had told her about the Singari balance of power, this was probably a very unusual move.

Chira inclined her head. "You are quite welcome, Alannys. We would not lightly go against your wishes. But there is more at stake here than just the Singari. You must be protected."

With that solemn reminder, Chira and the elders left the wagon.

Chen sat back down in his chair, shaking his head. "I can't believe you defended Trago. How can you be so concerned for him? He just tried to kill you!"

"I don't argue that, Chen. And I appreciate all that you did to save me, I really do. But what happened back there was not his fault. Even if I had said nothing to him, I'm not sure it would have been his fault. Can't you see where he is coming from, what he is going through? You've said what kind of man he is, Chen, not that different from you. Can you imagine the loss, the grief it would take to drive that kind of man to what you saw today?"

Chen looked into her eyes for a long moment. "Yes," he said, and his voice cracked. "Yes, I can."

Alannys dropped her gaze and slumped down into the bed, worn out. Chen sat at her bedside, watching her sleep.

♪

Alannys felt even worse in the morning; stiff and sore, with a dull thumping headache that made it hard to concentrate. She rubbed at her temples, and pressed experimentally on the skin around her eyes. She was still pretty swollen, but she could touch her face without jumping out of her skin, and that was an improvement.

"Don't worry. You'll be better before you know it." Chen sounded impossibly cheerful.

"You're still here?" It was no wonder people had ideas about them. She couldn't remember the last time she'd woken up in an empty wagon.

Chen sat back in the desk chair, stretching. "Yes. Nashara just left. She wanted to check on you, and to scold me for allowing the *zhotha* to pester you while you're recovering."

"Ah. You have my sympathy. For what it's worth I think you did the right thing. Chira was right, there has to be a certain level of discipline if we're going to get through this. We have got to get moving again, Chen. We're all going crazy, stuck here like this."

Chen nodded. "Trago would certainly have fared worse without your intervention. Surely that will mean something to him, even in his current state."

"We can always hope." Alannys sighed. "Chen, right now it isn't a problem, because we are trapped here until the pass is cleared, but what happens when we're moving again? Trago and Mirenne shared a tent, didn't they? How do you confine a person to their house when their house travels on the back of a horse?"

"Ah. Yes, Trago lives in a tent. So do most of the Singari in the camp, actually. That is what the *prathamol* is for."

"*Prathamol*," Alannys repeated slowly, working out the meaning. "A wagon for mentally ill people?"

Chen grinned at her. "You're getting good, Alannys. Pretty soon you won't even need me. Yes, we have a community wagon for sequestering. We have to, really. Even if everyone in the camp lived in wagons, you can't really confine someone to their own wagon. You need something you can lock, that they can't unlock. The *prathamol* bars from the outside."

It made sense, and it shouldn't have surprised her. Didn't the Singari have community wagons, after all— didn't she have firsthand experience of the *zhothamol*? Hadn't her own wagon once been a community storage wagon? She sighed and shook her head. When would she ever learn to accept the Singari as a living people with a fully formed society, and drop her own stereotypical expectations of them?

Chen eyed her sharply. "Something wrong?"

"No. I mean, I—"

A rap at the door interrupted her, surprising them both.

"Don't you dare get up," Chen admonished her. "I'll get that."

She sank back against the pillows, happy for once not to argue.

"Drigo!" The welcome in Chen's voice was genuine. "Come in, come in!"

Chen came back into the room, followed by a dark, lanky young man, ducking his head in the narrow entry. He smiled warmly at Alannys. "My Lady, it is good to see you looking so well. We have all been worried."

Alannys smiled at him. She personally doubted that she looked well at all, but she did appreciate the sentiment. "Thank you, Drigo. It's really good to see you, too."

He inclined his head to her graciously. It always confounded her where Drigo had acquired his good manners and rather cultured speech, with parents like Yeff and Pesia, and an older brother like Brutagar—it seemed Drigo's whole family tended toward the crass.

"Well, what news?" Chen demanded, rubbing his hands together. "I can only assume you did not come just to exchange niceties."

Drigo looked between them and folded his hands. "As you know, I have been supervising the efforts to reopen Eversnow Pass these last days."

"And?" Excitement was plain in Chen's tone.

"And I am pleased to announce that our efforts have

been successful. The way is now open again."

Alannys sat up, pushing against the pillows. "Drigo, that's wonderful news!"

Drigo beamed at her. "The digging crews are quite pleased as well, my Lady, to have such good news."

"And so fast!" she marveled.

"Too fast, really," Chen said, frowning.

Drigo lifted his shoulders in an elegant shrug. "It is rough and narrow, certainly. But it is passable. Of course further cleaning and smoothing will be required before we attempt to take wagons through. But it is progress."

"It's wonderful," Alannys declared, clutching her robe around her middle and swinging her legs over the side of her bed. "Just wonderful."

Chen was still frowning, but now he was frowning at her. "Just what do you think you are doing?"

She wanted to glare back at him. But this was a happy occasion; the best news they'd had in ages. She swallowed her ire and tried to be pleasant. "I'm going to see the pass, Chen. It isn't every day something this good happens. I intend to enjoy it."

"I won't stop you," Chen said, moving slightly so he stood squarely in the path to the door. "But you're going to have to enjoy it from right here."

Alannys sighed. Didn't he ever get tired of bickering with her? "Look, you aren't being reasonable. I—"

Chen held up a hand. "No, stop right there, Alannys. *You* aren't being reasonable. You are in no shape to walk across this room, let alone this camp. Do you really think Nashara would permit you to—"

"That's enough." Alannys pushed herself abruptly to her feet. She wobbled, and Drigo hurried to offer his arm. She leaned on him, grateful for the support, and regarded Chen levelly. "Nashara is a wonderful healer, and I trust and respect her opinion. I always consider her advice. But she does not command me, Chen. And neither do you. I will not allow either of you to 'permit' or 'not permit' me to do things."

"But Alannys..." Chen floundered for words. "I—we only—"

"I know, you are trying to do what you think is best for me. But that isn't for you to decide. I'm sorry, but I'm going to have to put my foot down about this. We can only have one leader here. With everything that's happened, it certainly doesn't help when you argue with every word I say." She sighed. "Dorramon didn't want me to leave the Great Palace to begin with. If the King of Ravanmark himself couldn't force me to listen, why do you imagine your luck will be any better?"

Chen stared at her, stricken. His eyes dropped to the Seeing Stone around her neck and she looked away.

A long, uncomfortable silence filled the wagon.

Alannys took a deep breath to steady herself. "Drigo, I hate to impose, but I don't think I'm strong enough yet to walk to the pass by myself. Do you think you could help me?"

"Certainly." Drigo tightened his grip on her arm and led her toward the door, carefully avoiding Chen's gaze.

Chen was recovering nicely from his shock, if his grumbling was any indication. "Unbelievable. No sense at all...traipsing around camp in this condition..." He pushed the wagon door open for them, and took her other arm in gruff silence.

Alannys released a breath she hadn't been aware of holding. She regretted bringing Dorramon into the discussion. It had obviously upset Chen—it felt like hitting below the belt. She felt like she should apologize, and yet she couldn't quite make herself do it. Her relationship with the king, such as it was, was no secret, and she certainly wasn't about to apologize for it. Everything she had said was true.

So why did it hurt so much to know that the one she'd said it to was Chen?

♪

Alannys walked to the avalanche site in stubborn, uncomfortable silence, leaning heavily on Chen and Drigo. She would never, ever have admitted it, but Chen had been right. She had no business making the long walk, and without her two helpers she would have collapsed halfway there and never moved again. *And maybe we'd all have been better off,* she thought, struggling to hide her labored breathing.

She forgot all of that when they reached the dig site. She stopped short, drawing curious glances from her companions. She had not been near this spot since the avalanche. She couldn't help but wonder why she had come here now. Her skin felt clammy, and electricity darted up and down her neck. Alannys had nearly died here, and some part of her would never forget it.

The world seemed to stop turning. She tried hard to breathe. She could hear Drigo calling to the digging crews, but the words didn't seem to mean anything to her.

A firm squeeze on her arm brought her out of the mental tunnel. She looked around, startled, and met Chen's knowing gaze.

She gave Chen a shaky smile and tried to focus her attention on the pass they had come to see. How did he *do* that? How did he always manage to know just how she was feeling, just what to do to save her — even now, when he must have been so upset with her?

The weather had been on their side — bright and clear with enough direct sunlight to help melt off some of the snow. The sides of the pass jutted up, tall and spiky, but bare rock could be seen.

On the ground, though, the snow was still thick. Crews of a few men each worked in groups scattered through the pass, huddled around fires burning debris, and clutching shovels. Large rocks that had been dragged down with the avalanche into the pass had been hauled to the edges and stacked. It was dirty, messy, slogging work.

But she could see through to the other side of the pass, to the trail where the avalanche had not touched.

Alannys squeezed Chen and Drigo in sudden excitement. "This is wonderful!"

Grald approached them from the nearest camp, using a long, skinny, peeled, almost-straight tree limb for leverage. "Lady Alannys! Lady Alannys, it's wonderful to see you out and about."

She grinned at him. "Not half as wonderful as it is to *be* out and about. I can't thank you enough for the work you've done here!"

Grald handed her the walking stick. "Please, take this. Drigo said you might come today, so we made it for you."

"Thank you so much. Now you can show me everything. I can't wait — now we can get the wagons moving again!"

A look flashed between the three men, warning her. "What?" she said, looking from one to the other of their apologetic faces. "What is it?"

It was Chen who finally answered her. "I was afraid this might happen, Alannys. Progress has been made, yes. Tremendous progress, given the circumstances. But the horses couldn't cross this path alone right now — let alone pulling the wagons."

Her face fell. Chen patted her arm. "I know. It won't be long — a few more days, maybe. But not yet — here, let Grald show us the work they are doing. You'll see."

She didn't want to believe him. Chen was over-protective, after all, and maybe he was holding out for a smoother ride for her sake.

But Grald took them slowly from camp to camp while

she hobbled along behind them, and she couldn't deny it. There was no way the horses and wagons would make it through this mess. It was almost too much for her. Slogging through the debris-littered snow was exhausting, and she was still weak. She struggled to keep up with the rest of them.

Chen glanced back and saw her there, doubled over her walking stick, gasping for breath. "Drigo, Grald, thank you. But I think it is time for me to return the Lady Alannys to her wagon."

Both men stopped and stared at her, and she could feel her face burn with embarrassment. They all hurried back to her.

"My Lady," Drigo gasped, "forgive me — we kept you too long."

"No," she sighed, "It isn't your fault. I really shouldn't have come — I'm just slowing you down. You've done a terrific job."

"Thank you," Grald said, dropping her a clumsy little bow.

"I won't keep you any longer," she said, struggling to get turned around in the snow. Chen stepped up next to her and put her arm through his, and between the walking stick and his support she managed to make it back to her wagon.

But she couldn't make it inside. She stood there, panting like she had been running for hours, and she could not force her legs to take her up the few steps it would take to get inside.

"I'm sorry, Chen," she said, and her voice broke and the next thing she knew tears of frustration were running down her face. "I just can't do it."

"There now," he said soothingly, scooping her up as though she were a small child, "nothing to get upset about." He carried her into the wagon and put her carefully down on the bed. "You're just a little overtired, that's all."

She shook her head. "I'm just a little over-stubborn, you mean. I'm sorry, Chen; I should have listened to you."

He sat down on the edge of the bed. "I do love to say I told you so. This time, though...well, maybe I had a point, but you did too. I'm sorry if it seems like I'm just being difficult. I know you don't think so, but I am only trying to help."

Alannys lay back against the pillows. "You know, this was just one of I-don't-know-how-many things that I could not have done without your help. And Drigo's, and Grald's. It doesn't seem right, that I lean on you so much."

"Why not? I told you before that we've never had a *kortha* before who wasn't married. It isn't a job that one person can do alone, especially a person with as much else going on as you have."

She regarded him thoughtfully. "You know, you are right. I never considered it that way before. In that case, I think we ought to formalize the arrangement."

"Formalize the arrangement?" Chen suddenly seemed pale. "What exactly are you suggesting?"

She looked at him, surprised by his tone. "I need my deputy, Chen, and you need yours. I don't know what the appropriate terms would be, but I think you, and Drigo, and Grald, need official positions. You need to be able to act officially in my stead." She swallowed hard. "And if someday something were to...happen to me...you would be able to continue on without me."

He frowned at her; evidently that was not the explanation he had hoped for. "Stop talking like that."

"No, Chen, I'm serious. I know you don't like hearing it, but I can't be with the Singari forever. Too many people are after me—too many people want me dead. I don't know what is holding Lord Malrec back, but when he decides to move again I could disappear at any time. And his assassin is still after me."

"No," Chen said. "He died in the avalanche."

"I wish that was true, but I saw him. He escaped."

"No one could have escaped that, Alannys." His tone was insistent—strangely so, as though he was concerned for her sanity.

"I'm telling you he did. I saw him." She shook her head. "But that isn't even the point. Even if all of that weren't true, the simple fact is that I am out here working for the Great Palace. And when this mission is done, I'll have to return to the palace. I have to do what I can to help."

"No." His eyes were dark and mesmerizing, and she couldn't look away. It made her heart race almost painfully in her chest. "Why do you have to go back there, to watch him live his life with someone else? You owe him nothing. You belong here with us, Alannys. With me."

She dropped her gaze. "I wish that were true, Chen. I think I could be happy here, traveling with you forever. But they need me at the palace."

"For what? A concubine? Those people are royalty, and they take care of themselves. Always have. Don't believe that they need you—they may use you, but they will discard you in the end."

"No. You aren't being fair. You are judging them by how their ancestors treated the Singari."

"Maybe." He stood up from the bed. "But times haven't changed that much. Royalty are like a force of nature, Alannys. They can't be predicted, and they can't be controlled. He will plow right over you like you aren't even there. Nothing at the palace will change for you. You won't even slow him down."

He turned and went out the door, leaving her alone in a room that felt suddenly cold.

♫

Alannys didn't see Chen again until the next day. It was an unusually long time for him to be gone, but when he came back he bounded happily into the room as though nothing had happened.

"Good afternoon!" he beamed at her.

"What's good about it?" A whole day alone, stuck in bed, had made her mood really foul.

He looked taken aback. "You're here, for one thing."

"Bah. That's no different than any other day."

"You're right, and it makes them all good days." He grinned at her.

Her glare never faltered.

"I see. Well, then, maybe you'll be more pleased to hear that work on the pass is going very well. They are farther along than expected."

She sat up straighter in the bed. "Now that really is good news. When can we start moving?"

"Hey, hold on. They aren't that far along. It still isn't what I would call passable. A couple more days, maybe. They're getting there, but it takes time. It was sunny today, and that helps."

"Helps," she snorted. "Not much, it doesn't. We've got to get moving! Why are you always so over-cautious?"

"*Overcautious?* Why are you never cautious at all?" He threw up his hands, and turned away in frustration. "You always push too hard, too fast—that's why you always land in trouble."

"You'll see trouble if we don't get moving, Chen! We can't keep this up—something has to give."

"And changes are it'll be your health or your safety. It always is. Alannys, if you don't learn to lower the intensity—and soon—you're going to wind up in a scrape I can't get you out of."

She stared at him, willing herself to deliver a snappy reply, but she was coming up empty. There was something cutting in that sentence, something she couldn't defend against.

She just hoped it wasn't truth.

A sudden, urgent rapping on the door startled them both. "Lady Alannys! Lady Alannys, please, let me in!"

The voice was Nashara's. Chen frowned, and went to open the door.

Nashara didn't waste any time. She pushed past Chen and hurried to Alannys's bedside, her face white and strained. "Legara is dead."

Alannys stared at her in dumb shock. "What? How can that be? I didn't even know she was sick."

"She wasn't." Nashara was wringing her hands in helpless agitation. "It's the cold, Lady Alannys—this bitter cold, nobody can keep really warm. And the very young and the very old; well, they are more susceptible to that sort of thing."

"That settles it." Alannys gave Chen a hard stare. "We are moving out tomorrow, come hell or high water. Tell Drigo and Grald. We stay long enough for Legara's funeral, and then we leave."

Chen swallowed hard. "But Alannys—it isn't safe."

"No matter what, Chen. Tomorrow, we leave."

♫

"This is absolutely untenable!" Lord Malrec turned away from the big desk in unutterable anger. He rubbed at his pointy chin, making a concerted effort to calm down. A fit of temper would not help him salvage the situation, he knew that. Still, to come so far, and face failure now, over something so *insignificant*... "There must be another way. There has to be."

"My—my Lord," Baron Prubard said, "we have examined all the scenarios, several times. There is no other way. Every option we have requires two artists."

"Or you could learn to be in two places at once," Lord Diabon put in sarcastically, leaning back in the gray velvet chair and folding his arms. "But there isn't any way for you to open all of the portals we need. The gloss simply dries too fast."

"Seven Hells," Malrec cursed. "What are we going to do now?"

"There is your brother," Prubard said. "If he could be compelled to help..."

"He won't do it," Princess Delline said from the corner. "You couldn't force him, not even if you killed him. Raman will not assist you."

"Such cheek!" Diabon said disapprovingly. "Malrec, I don't know why you tolerate her at our meetings at all. But for her to speak out, as though she has any place—"

"She is right," Malrec said shortly. "The arch-prince is out of the question. We shall have to find a way to accomplish our ends with one artist, because that is what we have. I will leave you gentlemen to your work."

Lord Malrec stormed out of the study before the other men could protest, with Princess Delline following close behind. "Unbelievable," he muttered. "Just unbelievable."

Could this day get any worse? Just that morning he had received word that a band of traveling missionaries was in the Glennayre town square, regaling anyone who would listen with their tales of Alannys's exploits. Even the poisoned child and her father traveled with them.

How did she manage this? How did everything she touched turn to gold? How was the woman even still *alive?* She was still the most powerful weapon in Ravanmark, and she was still frustratingly out of reach. She had been trapped in Eversnow Pass for nearly a month, sick and injured, and he was unable to capture her simply because he lacked a means to control her voice.

And now it looked like even the Alliance's plans to take the Great Palace were in jeopardy. He had sent a rider to the palace, bearing the severed head of the man

Dorramon had dispatched to take Castle Glennayre. It was a fine gesture—and satisfying, too, to see through a painting the young king's face lose all color when it was brought into his court—but it was a meaningless gesture if he couldn't follow it with an attack.

Lord Malrec didn't see how he could take much more.

"My Lord," Delline said hesitantly.

He stopped and turned to her, counting to a quick, silent ten in an effort to rein in his temper. "What is it, my dear?"

"I wanted to tell you how distressed I am to hear of your difficulties," she said earnestly, leaning forward to put her hand on his arm. "If there is anything at all I can do to help, I hope you will not hesitate to ask."

"Interesting you should mention that. The one thing we need more than any other is the music mage. What I need from you is a way to bring her here, now, safely."

She stepped back, taking her hand with her. "What?"

"We need Alannys, here. Now. Is the collar ready?"

"No. No of course not! It should be finished curing tomorrow. And then we have about three more weeks of preparation before we can use it."

He sighed impatiently. "In that case, put the collar aside for now. What other options do we have? We need to control her voice, so that she may only sing when we will it."

"There is no other way. The collar is the only option, unless you want to silence her permanently."

"That is no answer!" he shouted. "You claim to be the expert on these matters, and yet the best you can offer me now is to silence her permanently?"

"Yes!" Delline balled her fists at her side and stood her ground, but her face was strained and white. "You ask for the impossible, Lord Malrec! I cannot give you what you want!"

"In that case," Malrec said shortly, "I wonder why I keep you around at all."

He turned sharply and left her standing in the hallway, shocked and silent.

♫

Chen arrived at Alannys's wagon early the next morning. She didn't mind. She was already out of bed, dressed, and tying her leather cloak around her neck. She was also exhausted. She had never known just changing clothes could be such hard work.

"What are you doing?" Chen asked suspiciously.

"I am getting ready for Legara's funeral," she said, as if she couldn't see where this was going.

"No. No, are you crazy? I absolutely forbid it."

She put her hands on her hips and regarded him. "I thought we discussed this 'forbidding' business. Didn't we just decide we are going to work together?"

"We never discussed working together on killing you! You can count me out of that."

"Chen, this isn't going to kill me. I'm not sick. I'm just weak, and injured. I may get tired, I may need your help, but I won't die. Besides, this is the easy part."

His eyes narrowed. "What is that supposed to mean?"

"Making it through the pass is going to be the hard part." She couldn't even look at him when she said it; she had a pretty good idea how he would take that.

"*What?* Now I am sure you have completely lost your mind. Alannys, there is no way you are strong enough for that."

"I know." She hated to admit it, but she couldn't deny it. "But I don't really think I have any choice, do you? I'm their *kortha*. This is dangerous and arduous and I think they need to see me with them. Don't you?"

It felt like a risk, asking his opinion when she knew he dearly wanted to disagree with her. But she did it, and she forced herself to wait quietly for his answer.

To her surprise, Chen appeared to seriously consider her question.

"Yes," he finally said, with evident resignation. "You are right. They are going to need to see you. We've lost people here...even one of the *zhotha*...I can't remember when we've faced anything quite like what has happened here. They are going to need the reassurance of seeing you lead them through this."

She sank down onto the bed. It worried her how good that felt, how bone-tired she was just from getting up and changing clothes. "I'm nervous about it, though. I don't think I'm strong enough for this yet. How am I going to manage?"

Chen sighed. "I had planned to try to talk you into riding in the wagon. But I can see that isn't really an option." He stood up next to her, and offered her his arm. "For what it's worth, I'll be right there with you. All the way. You can lean on me whenever you need to."

She stood and took his arm with a smile tinged with sadness. "It's worth a lot, Chen. It's worth a whole lot."

He helped her out of the wagon, and she tried to put off her dark mood. It wasn't easy. Chen's solid support next to her kept her going, and she knew that *a whole lot* didn't begin to cover it. It was worth more than she could repay.

And it didn't make her feel any better to know that Chen didn't expect her to.

♫

Alannys tried not to lean on Chen too much during the funeral, because it really was the easy part. Still, it was disheartening how much support she needed just to stand through the ceremony.

After the funeral, the Singari began to break up camp. Alannys returned to her wagon to rest, and Chen oversaw the preparations, with Drigo and Grald.

The peculiar melancholy that had gripped her all

morning still held her. She had meant what she'd said to Chen before—she knew her time among the Singari was limited; she knew they would have to be able to go on without her. Chen and his friends seemed likely choices to carry on in her stead—people in the tribe were already accustomed to seeing the three of them carrying out her wishes when she was physically unable to do it herself.

Alannys figured she'd have half the day to rest; breaking up camp after being parked this long was not likely to be fast. But scarcely two hours later, Chen came back to the wagon.

"Back already?" she said. "There's no way they can be ready to go. Is there?"

"You'd be surprised," he told her. "They didn't need much encouragement. Everyone is ready to leave this place behind."

"I suppose I can understand that. Are we ready to move out, then?"

He nodded. "You're sure you don't want to change your mind about this? You could stay right there in your bed."

"No." She stood up from the bed, and grabbed the walking stick Grald had given her. "I guess there's no point in stalling. The sooner we start moving, the better."

Chen held his arm out to her, and his silence was as close to agreement as she figured she would get. She took his arm, and together they left the wagon.

Quicksilver waited outside, tied near the door. "I'm sorry, old boy," she told him, stroking his nose. "Today isn't going to be any fun for any of us."

Quicksilver snorted and shook his head.

"I know." She untied him and led him by the reins, out in front of the wagon train.

"All right, everyone!" Chen shouted. Even as he spoke, Alannys could see Drigo and Grald working back through the train, relaying his words. "People first, leading your horses if you have them. The wagons will follow. Any livestock should be driven behind the wagons. This isn't going to be easy. Stay alert and don't give up, and we'll get through this. Onward, ho!"

Alannys and Chen plowed into the pass first, with Drigo and Grald close behind. Nightfire followed Chen with no lead necessary, snorting and complaining.

Alannys couldn't blame him. She couldn't remember a more devilish, miserable slog. In some places the ground was frozen hard and crusty, treacherous and slippery. In other places she sank into the snow nearly up to her knees with every step. Without the walking stick she would never have made it through the snow, ice chunks, and rocks.

They didn't make it halfway through the fallout from the avalanche before she did finally stumble and collapse on her face into the snow. At that moment it seemed more than she could do to pull herself back up, so she laid there, cold and wet and utterly unable to keep going. Quicksilver nickered and pushed his nose into her back.

"I know," she sighed. "But I can't do it, Quicksilver. You should just go on without me."

"If she keeps talking like that, you should step on her." Chen's voice sounded close. He knelt down next to her, and lowered his voice. "You know we aren't going to leave you here. I would die first."

Strong hands grabbed her arms and hauled her to her feet. She leaned on the walking stick, wobbling where she stood, while he brushed snow off of her. She hated the helpless feeling it gave her.

"You know," she told him, "I think you would. I really think you would. At some point, you are going to have to cut your losses here. I'm a no-win proposition, Chen. I'll just drag you down with me."

He stood up, looking right into her face, resolute. "Never. I will never give up on you. We will make it through this together, or not at all." He took her free arm, and together they struggled through another few steps in the snow.

"I'm not talking about the pass," she said finally.

Chen didn't look at her. "I know."

♫

Time seemed to stop in the snowy, debris-filled pass. Each stumbling, staggering step was a battle fought and barely won, and it may have taken seconds or minutes to win it. In her exhausted, dulled state of mind, Alannys couldn't have said. Each minute stretched slowly on into the next in an interminable procession that was impossible to track.

Somehow, the Singari finally made it through the avalanche site. When they emerged on the other side, they found that they could ride the horses again.

"Please tell me," Chen said, "that you will go back to the wagon now."

She shook her head. "I can't, Chen. I have to keep going."

"How long?" His voice was low, but agitated. The sound of it made her feel guilty. "Till you fall over?"

"Maybe." She didn't look at him. "They need me. I don't have time to be weak."

He helped her up onto Quicksilver. "If that's what you want, I'll do what I can. I don't have to like it, though."

"No. You don't have to like it."

The pass descended steeply, far faster than the gradual climb on the other side. It made things harder on everyone, human and horse alike, and they were all more than ready to stop when they reached a big clearing in the woods that evening.

Alannys rode among the Singari on Quicksilver as they pitched camp. She offered praise, encouragement, and support where she could. It had been an impossibly long, grueling day, but people seemed in higher spirits than she had seen them in weeks.

She rode by the *prathamol* on her rounds. Nashara was just leaving after her daily visit. She glanced up at Alannys and shook her head, barring the door behind her.

"Perhaps a few more days..." she said, and hurried away.

Alannys sighed. She still felt guilty when she saw the wagon, with its single tiny window, lined with iron bars. Chen reminded her daily that it was Trago who attacked her, not the other way around, but that didn't help. She knew that if she had just listened to Chen and kept her big mouth shut, he wouldn't be in there right now.

She paused at the window as she rode by. "Trago, do you need anything? Is there anything I can do for you?"

It was dark inside the wagon, and she could barely make out his face. What she could see was twisted with hatred.

"Yes," he said. "You can go to the Seven Hells!"

He spat in her face.

She rode away, wiping her face on her sleeve. When would she learn?

She found her wagon on the far side of the camp. Chen was setting the brake on it for her.

"Still on horseback?" He looked up at her, surprised. "I thought you would have given that up by now."

"I would," she said, "but I don't think I'll be able to stand up if I do. It's embarrassing to admit, but I don't think I can get down."

He grinned at her. "Sounds to me like you could use a *markortha*." He reached up and helped her down from the saddle. As soon as her feet touched the ground, she crumpled.

"You weren't joking," Chen observed, laughing,

holding her up. "Let's get you inside." He scooped her up and carried her into the wagon.

"No," she protested, squirming. "I have to take care of Quicksilver. I can't just leave him there like that."

"Don't worry," he told her. He put her down on the bed and pulled a folded blanket out of the chest underneath it, shook it out and spread it over her. "I know a thing or two about horses myself. I'll tend to Quicksilver for you."

"Thank you," she sighed, and sat back against the pillows. "We did well today."

"Yes. To be honest, I wasn't sure we would really make it until we were already through. That was really something. We must be halfway down the mountain now."

Alannys nodded. "That's what I was thinking too. I think we'll make it into Shadowkeep tomorrow."

"Town," Chen said, and for once it sounded like a good word when he said it. "We really need to replenish our supplies."

"Tomorrow we get our chance," she said, and yawned.

Chen laughed. "I'll get out of your hair and go take care of your horse. You get some rest. Big day tomorrow."

He left, and she settled under the covers. She couldn't put her finger on why, but his words gave her an ominous chill.

♪

After Chen left, Alannys napped. She hadn't intended to sleep when there was so much still to be done, but she was so profoundly exhausted it happened anyway.

When she woke up in a panic an hour later, the sun had fallen low and red in the sky. She pushed the covers back and grabbed the walking stick, hurrying for the door.

Outside, she found Chen and Drigo, having a quiet but animated discussion a few steps away from the wagon. They both looked at her in surprise when she came out.

"Alannys! I thought you were sleeping." Chen sounded guarded. "What brings you out here?"

"I need to talk to you," she said. "Is there a Seer here?"

Chen and Drigo exchanged a look. "Well...yes," Chen said. "Why?"

"I need you to take me to her. I need to see her." She looked from Chen to Drigo, and back. "What? What is it?"

"Nothing, my Lady," Drigo said, turning her direction, but still looking sideways at Chen. "It's just...interesting that you should ask that."

"We were just debating whether to bother you with it," Chen said. "Ibira has been asking to see you."

"Ibira?" The name was unfamiliar.

Chen nodded. "She's a Seer."

"And she was asking to see me?" Her brain didn't seem to be working right—maybe it was the nap.

Chen sighed. "Well, really, demanding to see you is more like it. I'm afraid she's pretty upset."

"Me, too. I've had this awful dream, with painting and fire, and—" She swallowed hard. "Can you take me to her?"

Chen looked at Drigo, and both men shrugged. "Sure," Chen said, taking her free arm. "If that's what you want."

Alannys couldn't believe she had never noticed Ibira's wagon before. It was black—black as night, black as tar— so black it seemed to draw in all the light around it. There were flower boxes running down the sides and around the back, with spiny, spindly plants hanging over the edges.

A large sign on the door proclaimed "DO NOT DISTURB" in large, shaky letters.

Chen stepped up to the door and beat on it.

"Can't you read?" The voice was female, sharp and cranky.

Chen rolled his eyes. "Ibira, you are the one who asked to see Alannys. I have convinced her to visit you, and this is the greeting she gets?"

There was a short pause. "What? She's here? What are you standing outside for? Bring her in, boy, are you addled?"

Alannys was starting to see why Chen and Drigo had wondered if bringing her here was a good idea.

But it didn't matter. She had to talk to someone. Chen and Drigo could not help her. Ibira was the only one who might have some insight for her.

The inside of the Seer's wagon was as unusual as the outside. Plants and herbs grew in pots scattered around the room, and the walls were lined with shelves crammed with odd-sized bowls and cups, mortars and pestles, and tools she didn't even recognize. The place smelled strongly of garlic and juniper, a combination that Alannys found made her queasy.

Ibira sat at a wooden table, crushing something in a bowl. She looked older than Alannys could imagine, with paper-thin skin that knotted on the backs of her hands as she worked. Her hair was thin and white and floated around her head in an unruly cloud. She was draped in layers of shapeless clothes, all black. She didn't glance up when they came in, but clucked disapprovingly in their general direction.

"About time you wandered in. Got any idea how much trouble we coulda missed if you just dragged yourself in here a little sooner?"

Ibira's voice was reedy and unpleasant, sour, like the scent of her home. Alannys looked at Chen in surprise; this was not the sort of greeting she had expected.

Chen rolled his eyes at her and shrugged. "From the way you carried on earlier, Ibira, I assumed you had something more important to say to Lady Alannys than that."

The old woman puffed herself up. "Everything I say is

important, Chen. I expect even a young turd like you would know that."

"I'm sorry," Alannys interjected. "It seems I have offended you somehow."

"Offended me?" Ibira's beady black eyes glared in her direction, unfocused, and Alannys realized with a start that the Seer was blind. "You could say that, yes. What kind of *kortha* makes decisions without consulting me first? I know they say you have the Second Sight, but I also know that in you it's broken — not all there. What business did you have leading us into Eversnow Pass without asking me about it?"

"I'm new at this, I didn't know I *could* — wait a minute. Do you mean to tell me you knew all this would happen? The avalanche, the deaths, the — everything?"

Ibira nodded sharply. "What do you suppose it means to be a Seer? I knew as soon as we reached Cloudytop Lake. I could have saved us all of this misery, if only you had asked me. Of course, we'd have other misery, but that's for you to decide, ain't it?"

Alannys didn't know what to say to that. The old woman's pique was obvious, but it also seemed to Alannys that if Ibira had known all this, maybe she shouldn't have waited to be asked about it. And Cloudytop Lake...that was a little late to have saved them — they were already committed to their course by then, which probably explained why Ibira could see the consequences so clearly.

In any event, it was too late to change anything now.

"Is this all you brought us here for?" Chen sounded irritated. "Just to complain, just to tell us about your 'help' now that it's too late to make a difference?"

Ibira sat up straight, glowering. "Ask your woman why she's here, Chen."

Chen flushed. "She's not my woman, Ibira. Keep your

riddles, if that's what suits you. Just don't keep Alannys too long. She isn't well." He folded his arms and leaned against the door, hanging there like an angry thundercloud.

Alannys stepped hesitantly closer to Ibira. "I'm sorry to bother you," she said, which seemed ridiculous to her since Ibira had been demanding to see her, but she couldn't think of anything better to start with. "I had this dream, and—"

"I know why you're here," Ibira snapped, and dropped her wooden pestle on the table, wiping her hands on her clothes. "Didn't I tell you I'm a Seer? You can't judge a Seer by your own bastardized Second Sight, Alannys. You go along, careless, and sometimes you get impressions about things. But most of the time you don't. In a true Seer, that ain't the way of it."

Alannys couldn't imagine an appropriate response to that diatribe that she wouldn't regret later. So she held her tongue and watched Ibira rifle through her shelves, gathering an assortment of items she carried back to the table in front of them.

"I can tell you this," Ibira continued, setting up an apparatus that held a small hammered copper bowl over the flame of her lamp. Her voice was suddenly deeper, more dramatic. "Orinthal is a dark place, foul in bearing and vile in deed. Baron Prubard has twisted this place, and it reflects him more than bodes well for us. Now, though, things are much worse."

"Worse?" Alannys had a hard time imagining much that could be worse than what Ibira had just described. More than Ibira's tone changed when she prophesied; her whole manner of speaking seemed different—more educated, somehow.

The old Seer nodded, uncorking a small vial and dumping a handful of seeds into the copper bowl. "Much worse," she repeated. "Prubard dwells at Castle Glennayre now, aiding the Dark Alliance. Baroness Lae stays at the Great Palace — not that her presence in Orinthal would be of much help; the baron has spent years teaching his people to look down upon her and disregard the authority a baroness ought to hold."

Standing and leaning on the walking stick was beginning to wear Alannys out, and it didn't look as though Ibira was likely to invite her to sit. She finally decided that not passing out was more important than being polite, and pulled another chair up to the table. "So who's driving this thing?"

Ibira picked up a spoon and stirred the seeds around over the flame. "There is no governing force in this place. The Baron's Guard have attempted to enforce order, but their reach is limited and their motives suspect. In other parts of the land the strongest have banded together, looting and raiding and terrorizing the population around them. These groups rival each other and compete for dominance."

"That sounds awful," Alannys breathed.

"Indeed." Ibira tapped the spoon on the rim of the bowl and laid it aside. "The situation cannot continue. If things are left as they are, Orinthal will fall."

"Anarchy."

"Yes. Had anyone bothered to ask my opinion, I would have advised avoiding Orinthal at any cost. Dark things are afoot here, and I do not see what we can gain by wandering into the middle of it."

Alannys took a deep breath, leaning back in her chair. Anarchy could not be allowed to gain a foothold in Ravanmark. If even a single holding fell, the Dark Alliance would win. She didn't know how she could stop it, but she knew she couldn't allow it to happen.

Perhaps the real question wasn't what they could gain,

but what Orinthal could gain from their presence.

"Well," she said, trying to sound more confident than she felt, "we are here now."

"We certainly are." Sarcasm dripped from the comment. The seeds in the bowl started to smoke, and Ibira wafted the smoke towards her face. "So for the moment, all we can do is try to see how much truth there is to that dream of yours."

Alannys shivered. She had been hoping that Ibira would dismiss the dream right away. *How much truth* implied that some of it had to be true, and that was not reassuring.

The seeds in the bowl were small and gray, and they reminded Alannys of poppy seeds. They made more smoke than it seemed like they should, though, and it was a dense, heavy smoke. And the *smell*... Alannys pulled the collar of her linen shirt up and hid her nose and mouth behind it. The heavy fumes were making her queasy and clouding her brain. She saw Chen push the wagon door open a crack, and thanked him fervently but silently.

Ibira closed her eyes, swaying side to side in her chair, waving the noxious smoke towards her face. "Yes, yes...I see..." Her voice softened and took on an almost musical quality, hypnotizing, like a drone. "I see...the return of one thought lost to the mists of time. I see in the darkness of Orinthal, even darker forces build. Those with power await the arrival of one more powerful still. Paint shimmers like a window, and an unwilling one is dragged through."

Between the fumes and the droning speech, Alannys had a hard time keeping her eyes open. The things in the wagon seemed to waver in her vision, and she slumped sideways in her chair. In another second she would be on the floor, and she couldn't seem to do anything to stop it.

Then the wagon disappeared.

It was dark, suddenly, disorientingly dark, and where she lay huddled on the ground, gasping, unable to move, she could hear trees rustling and frantic shouts. She knew things were bad, and she knew it was her fault, and she knew she was about to pay for it. She couldn't move, and the calls of her friends were still much too far away to save her from the doom that hovered over her now.

Her skin prickled, and the hair stood up on the back of her neck, and she knew without even looking that she was being watched through a painting. If she could turn to look behind her, she would see the telltale gray formless blur of the opening the painter had created.

Of course, if she could turn to look behind her, she wouldn't waste time looking. If she was capable of any movement at all, she would be out of there, gone, running for everything she was worth.

But she couldn't, so she laid there, her body as useless as a marionette whose strings had been cut, until rough hands grabbed her from behind and hauled her through the void behind the gray blur, into the painting and away from all her friends and anyone who could possibly help her.

"Alannys—Alannys!"

She became aware of Chen, holding her and shaking her. How long had he been doing that? She couldn't say. The wagon rematerialized around her, still dim and filled with the heavy, unpleasant scent of the burning seeds. Ibira swayed and hummed in the fumes, apparently oblivious to both of them.

That had been her dream. She'd just hallucinated her dream. But why?

"What happened?" Alannys's voice sounded strange to her own ears, as though it came from a great distance away.

Chen shook his head. "Ibira, it is time for us to leave. I

have to take Alannys back to her wagon."

Ibira didn't seem to hear him.

Alannys took his hand and pulled herself heavily to her feet. The floor seemed to lurch unpleasantly underneath her, and she stumbled. "Whoa—what's going on?"

He pulled her arm over his shoulders and half-carried, half-dragged her out of the wagon. "It's the henbane. You'll be all right once we get you outside. But you can't stay in here."

"Henbane?" It was difficult to get the unfamiliar word out. Things weren't working quite like they should—she could feel her feet on the ground but it didn't feel right, like maybe they weren't stuck down good. Maybe, she thought fleetingly, she had magnets in her feet. And they were turned opposite of the magnets in the ground, so that they repelled. Maybe that was why she couldn't quite seem to stand properly.

"It's what Ibira was burning in there. Henbane seeds. Dangerous stuff—henbane is poisonous, even the seeds, even the smoke from the seeds. But it's what Seers have always used to bring on visions."

She let go of Chen's shoulders and crumpled in a heap on the cool, damp grass, sucking in the air that smelled of pine trees and horses. Magnets. Maybe. Or maybe she was just stoned.

"It seems to me," she said, "that maybe the henbane is more responsible for the visions than the Seers. Anybody could use that stuff and see things."

Chen laughed. "You do have a point. But there is more to it than that. Lots of people react very badly to henbane. Some even die. But more than that, you could lock fifty people in a room with burning henbane, and if it didn't kill them, they would all have visions of some kind. But only the ones with Second Sight would come true."

...the ones with Second Sight would come true... She thought of her own vision. As disorienting as it had been, it matched what she had seen in her dream. She shivered.

Chen frowned. "We had better get you up off that wet ground." He took her arm and helped her up again. "Are you feeling better?"

Alannys swallowed hard. "Lots, thank you. That was...interesting."

"Interesting. I suppose that's one way of putting it. What was all that about? Why did you want to see Ibira?"

She couldn't quite look at him. "I had a dream. I needed to know if there was anything to it, or if it was just a dream, and I could safely ignore it."

"I gathered that much. So was there anything to it?"

She shivered again, remembering her vision on the floor of the wagon. "Yes. Yes, I'm afraid there was." She hauled herself up the few steps into her wagon. It felt like she had just run a marathon. She flopped down onto her bed.

"You look terrible. What kind of dream was this?"

She didn't really feel like talking about it. What good would it do? But hiding from it wasn't going to do them any good either. She sighed. "It was a dream, so a lot of the details are fuzzy. We were outside somewhere—somewhere dark, somewhere I didn't recognize, but from what Ibira said, my impression is that it was somewhere in Orinthal. I think there had been fighting. We were separated. You and some others were looking for me. But before you could get there, I was pulled through a painting."

Chen stared at her. "A painting?"

"Yes." The horror on his face matched the way she had felt when she woke up...it was the same horror, the same fear, that had driven her to seek out the Seer. "Look, I know it's upsetting. But it doesn't really change anything.

This just proves what I've been saying all along—I don't have much time. We don't have much time." She shook her head. "Will there be a bonfire tonight, do you think?"

She could see Chen try to put aside his shock. "Yes. Yes, after the way things have been lately, I don't doubt there will be a bonfire. People are eager to return to normal."

"Good. Round up anyone who is interested, and we'll meet a little outside of camp where we won't disturb the others. Those singing lessons I promised start tonight."

"Tonight? Are you sure you're ready for that?"

She leaned back against the pillows. "No. But we don't really have a lot of choice. I never had much time to begin with, and it's slipping away so fast..." She shook her head. "You've had more experience than the others, Chen, singing with me. I'll be counting on your help."

"Sure," he said, but he looked a little nervous.

She couldn't blame him. She was nervous herself. That, along with her constant frail health lately, was why she had kept putting this off. But it didn't look like she could afford to do that any longer.

Lord Malrec was coming for her.

♫

"You must try not to be disappointed," Chen said, holding Alannys's arm as she navigated the uneven forest between the camp and the clearing Grald had chosen for their impromptu master class. "It's our first night out of Eversnow, and people had work and visiting to do. Some would just rather be at the celebration tonight. It doesn't mean they aren't interested."

"Oh, I can't blame them," Alannys said, stumbling as her walking stick caught in a gnarled tree root. "I'd rather be at the celebration myself, if the truth were known. I feel like I have to try to get started, but that doesn't mean everybody else has to drop everything to come with me."

"Doesn't it, though? I mean, if you are teaching and

they are feasting, how does that help?"

Alannys smiled at him. "The wonderful thing about students, Chen, is the way they can also become teachers."

He looked surprised. "Oh."

"I couldn't possibly teach all of you everything you need to know. But I don't have to. I only have to teach one of you, and then he can teach the rest."

"He?" Chen swallowed hard. "I don't know, Alannys —I'm not really cut out for responsibility. I'm more the worthless layabout type, you know?"

She patted his arm. "You're a natural choice, don't you think? You already have more experience than everyone else here, just from working with me. You've even been through Muse's Fever. I bet nobody else here can say that."

He shook his head. "It isn't the same, though. I'm not you. They need to learn from you."

"And I'm here to try to teach them what I can. But I won't be here much longer, Chen--we knew that even before the dream. And then you can carry them on."

She didn't know if he agreed with her or just ran out of time to argue. They stepped into the clearing, where about a dozen Singari waited for them in a restless knot. Drigo and Grald stood off to the edge, as though they expected someone to make a run for it. The thought made her want to laugh.

"Thank you all so much for coming tonight," she said, making an effort to stand straighter and walk more confidently as she moved to the center of the clearing. "I know the feast tonight is tempting, and it means a lot to me that you have chosen instead to come here and start learning how to use your Talent."

She surveyed the little group; half a dozen men, four women, and two twin girls. Where to start?

"First," she said, "I'd like you all to sing and hold this

note." She picked a pitch out of the air and sang it for them.

They looked at each other hesitantly. Nobody seemed to want to be the first to jump in.

"Together?" said one of the twins, looking uncertain. She was wearing leather breeches, with about three brightly colored skirts of different lengths over them. "All of us should sing—at once?"

Alannys frowned. It had never occurred to her that this would be a problem—the Singari's acceptance of music made it easy for her to forget the fear with which it was generally regarded, and the relative lack of practice they all had. "Yes," she said. "I know that may seem strange, but one of the first things we'll need to learn is to sing together."

"Strange?" The word came from a short, slightly-built man near the front of the group, but everyone looked uneasy—she could hear their feet shifting on the forest floor, could see the way they were edging out of the center of the clearing. "Strange doesn't begin to cover it. We aren't supposed to sing together."

"I see." Alannys watched him, trying to think herself a way through her dilemma. "Is this a law, then? It's peculiar that it was never mentioned when we went to Pinevale."

"Sure, and what a great idea *that* was," he said sourly. "It's tradition, which may as well be law. The *zhotha* did try to stop you, didn't they?"

"Here's the thing about traditions—you can always make new ones." Complete silence blanketed the clearing now; they all watched her closely. "You are the Singari; music flows with the blood in your veins. I think your traditions should reflect this."

"As do I," said Chen from beside her.

"I'm not here to force anyone to do anything," she said.

"If you would rather sing only by yourself, that's fine — we can arrange private lessons. But tonight, in the interest of time, we're going to work in a group. If you want to leave, I won't try to stop you. But I hope some of you will give me a chance."

People looked at her, then at each other, as if searching for a clue as to what they should do.

"Our traditions are our identity, this is true." The rumbling, solemn voice from the back of the group, at the far side of the clearing, was familiar, growing steadily louder as its owner approached. Tor emerged from the small crowd, and came to stand by her side. "We must always be mindful of what that identity is, though — these particular traditions came from fear, and that is an identity I do not choose. Do you?"

The naysayer shook his head. "But Tor, surely — "

"Do you still not see?" Tor said. "When my daughter fought for her life, Alannys fought alongside her — with music."

Alannys shifted uncomfortably, remembering how Alara had reacted to that attempt.

"With this knowledge, I could have fought for her as well. Perhaps with more of us, we might have saved her. Will you learn from my fate? Or will you refuse to see, until it is your own loved one whose life hangs in the balance? For myself, I will stand by Lady Alannys."

One or two people left anyway, stomping back through the woods toward camp, shaking their heads and muttering. But most of them stood, watching Alannys and silently waiting for whatever came next. It wasn't a standing ovation, but she figured it was as close to acceptance as she was likely to get, and she decided to go with it.

"So the first thing we're going to learn is how to sing together. I know we're overthrowing tradition here, but we're doing it for good reasons. We don't have as much time as I might wish. We need to move fast, and the best way to do that is to work in groups. For now, I'd like you to sing this pitch." She sang the same note she'd chosen before.

Tor immediately sang with her, his big, deep voice rumbling several octaves below hers. Chen and his two friends moved into the group and sang as well, and slowly the rest of the Singari joined in.

Alannys walked slowly among them, listening intently. It was amazing to her—they all held the proper pitch in steady, clear voices. Even on Earth, where music was common, it would have been hard to find a group of such strong, accurate voices. Here in Ravanmark, where the ability to carry a tune at all was rare...it was phenomenal. All of them were incredible.

Except...her. Alannys stopped in front of the same girl who had first raised objections to singing as a group. She was all over the place, wavering above the pitch and below the pitch, and sometimes her voice would break and there would be no sound at all.

Her face flushed red as Alannys watched her. "I'm sorry," she said finally, looking at her feet. "I can't really sing."

"What's your name?"

"Eleana, my Lady."

"I'm kind of surprised, Eleana—I thought all of you here tonight could sing."

"No." She shook her head, bouncing her dark ponytail off her shoulders. "I—I do something else."

Alannys frowned. Eleana had shown up for music lessons, so she must have had musical talent. But she didn't sing, and they only had the lute, which was rarely played. "What is it that you do?"

Eleana couldn't quite seem to look at her. She reached

into a pocket on her breeches, and dropped a wooden object into Alannys's hand. "I play this."

It was a little hand-carved instrument with holes for pitch, something like a flute. Alannys turned it over in her hands, impressed. "You made this yourself?"

Eleana nodded. Her ears were pink.

"Eleana's weird," her sister piped up, dropping out of the singing. "She can't sing, her clothes are weird, and girls don't whittle."

"Shut up, Leeara," Eleana muttered.

Alannys shot Leeara a sidelong glance. They were obviously twins, and yet Leeara could sing, while Eleana played instruments. This was fascinating, but Alannys didn't know quite how to make use of it. "This girl obviously whittles," she said. "And does a fantastic job of it, too." She handed the little flute back to Eleana. "Can you make more of these? We may have others who need instruments as well."

Eleana nodded. "Oh, yes. I have others already. This is just my favorite."

"That's wonderful. Don't worry about singing. You can play along with whatever the others sing."

Eleana grinned at her, and raised the flute to her lips. Out of thin air she picked the right pitch and played along with the group. The tone of the little instrument was rich and sweet.

"That's terrific," she told the group, moving back to the front. "I know that singing together is new to you. It's important to be able to do that when you are singing for effect, though, because the more people you have making music together, the more powerful the song will be."

"So if two people sing together, the song is twice as powerful?" asked Leeara.

"Almost," Alannys said. "Really, it's more than twice as powerful, from the experiences I've had. A musician working alone is powerful. But multiple musicians working in groups are much more powerful—it even lessens Muse's Fever. And I don't think that is widely known. Such a large group of Talented people, together—it gives you a huge advantage."

"That sounds amazing," Chen said. "Can we try it?"

Alannys was a little taken aback. As surprised as they had been at the idea of singing together, she never expected to encounter such eagerness to experiment. Then again, this was Chen talking. Perhaps he wasn't a representative example. "Sure," she said. "Are there any songs you all know, that you can all sing together?"

Chen grinned, it seemed to her, a little evilly. "Sure," he said back to her. "We may not sing together, but we do sing." He turned to the group and called out a rapid string of Singari words. Alannys thought it must have been the name of a song, but she didn't understand it. The only word she recognized was Terpsichore, the name of the patron muse of the Singari.

Before she could sort it out, the group began to sing, as if following a cue she couldn't perceive.

Alannys had never heard anything like it before. It was enough to make all her hair stand on end.

It was like watching a time-lapsed video of a choir coming together. They were hesitant at first, unsure, singing in breathy half-voices as they picked up the key and the tempo from Chen's strong tenor in the lead.

Alannys had never heard the song. She had no idea what the words meant, but it was obvious the whole group knew the song very well. Within a few bars they were singing in unison in strong, clear voices, with a sameness of pitch and enunciation that would have taken any choir back home weeks of study to achieve.

She stepped back toward the edge of the clearing. It was a good thing they were not singing to any purpose—

who in the world could have resisted their combined song?

And then, before Alannys was quite comfortable with the juggernaut she had unleashed, something happened that was so amazing she couldn't accept the reality of it, even as she stood there watching it.

Without any sort of cue or instruction, the Singari broke into parts — Chen and a few other mid-range voices carried the melody, and Tor provided an earth-shaking low continuo. Leeara sang a soaring high harmony, and the silver notes of Eleana's flute wound through all of it, weaving a counter-melody that was haunting and beautiful.

A shiver ran up Alannys's spine. This was supposed to be their first lesson, but the Singari were schooling her. One thing was already abundantly clear — teaching the Singari was not going to be hard.

The hard part was going to be keeping up with them.

♫

Something is wrong.

The thought tormented Larric, destroyed his peace, kept him up and pacing when he should have been long since asleep.

Darkness enveloped Castle Glennayre; stillness settled upon it like a shroud. Not a sound crept along the corridors. It was quiet as a tomb, quiet as a grave.

And yet Larric had been drawn here with a terrible urgency, finding sleep eluded him entirely in his bed in the stablehouse. Something was wrong, that was all. He didn't know exactly what, but he knew it was here. It was here, and he had to find it.

He had to stop it.

The twin moons were high and full in the sky, and yet the darkness inside the castle was impenetrable. His eyes strained to adjust, to find something familiar.

A tiny glint of light flashed at the far end of the long

hallway; faint and quick, there and then gone again before he could focus on it properly. A reflection, probably – the low light glinting off of metal. The slight sound of slippers against stone reached him.

"Kalyn? Is that you?" His words were barely above a whisper, but clearly audible in the silent castle.

"L – Larric?"

He frowned at the strange sound of a voice that should have been familiar. "Are you all right?"

For a moment there was no reply. He wished he could see her. Something was wrong, all right, and he would wager it was here in front of him.

"You should go back to the stables, Larric. It's very late."

Her voice rang off the stone walls in the darkness, cold and aloof and *wrong* somehow. It sounded like a heartless imitation, like Kalyn had locked herself away and a hollow shell now spoke to him with her empty voice.

"I will," he said in sudden alarm, "if you will come with me."

"I cannot. I have things to attend to here."

His disquiet grew with every word she spoke. Whatever was going on here was not good. This had to be stopped. *"Please*, Kalyn. Come out to the stablehouse with me. I'm begging you."

"Larric..." He could hear her indecision. It hung in the air around him like a chilling mist. Finally she sighed. "As you wish, then. I'll come with you."

He followed the slight scuffing sound of her footsteps into the kitchen. The dim light here gleamed off the copper countertops. Kalyn walked on through the kitchen and outside, her shoulders slumped, her face turned down. The plain shift she wore as a nightgown had to be entirely insufficient against the winter chill, but she didn't even seem to notice. She didn't slow down, didn't glance left or right, but went straight to the stablehouse and let herself in.

Larric followed, gnawing on his lip. He couldn't put his finger on it, but something about her was definitely off. What in the world was going on?

He turned to close the door behind them, scrambling to put his thoughts in some kind of order. "Kalyn," he began, turning back around to face her, "I—"

Kalyn was staring at him, her eyes big and round, her expression vacant. She stood like a marionette hanging from limp strings, as if she had no volition of her own.

She was clutching a knife. The biggest knife from the kitchen, by the look of it. Given the size of some of the animals she had prepared, it was a pretty big knife.

He couldn't even finish his sentence. Kalyn was wandering the castle, alone, in the middle of the night—carrying a knife? It was as if the world had turned upside down around him, and nothing made sense. He just could not process this situation.

"I'm going to kill him," she said bluntly, matter-of-factly. The words, coming from Kalyn, sounded entirely alien.

Larric stared at her. "Lord Malrec?"

The knife twitched convulsively in her grasp. "Yes. And the best time is now, while he is asleep. I need to go. What do you want?"

"Kalyn, I..." He shook his head. He stood between her and the door, keeping a wary eye on the knife. Kalyn usually wouldn't hurt a fly, he knew that. But that knife... "What happened? Why are you doing this?"

Her gaze slid sideways, away from him. "Do you remember when Lady Alannys came to Castle Glennayre, for the first time?"

The question didn't seem to have any relation to the question he had asked her, but he nodded. "Of course."

"One night while she was here, I went into the study to put out the fire. I found—Lord Malrec had left the art room open." She seemed unable to go on.

Horror bloomed in the pit of his stomach. He had been in that art room himself, once. "You went in?"

She nodded, biting her lip.

"And you saw something."

Kalyn swallowed hard. "I...saw something, yes. I had just gone into the room when I heard Lord Malrec approaching in the corridor. I ran out of there as fast as I could...but when I turned to go...I had a glimpse of something. A painting. One I had never seen before."

"What did you do?" The words rustled like dead leaves in his throat.

She shook her head, like she was trying to shake off the memory. "I kept going. I ran out of the room. I left, and I never tried to go back there. I thought...I thought if I could just put the painting out of my mind, it would go away. I would forget it, it wouldn't bother me anymore. It worked, for a while."

She looked at him then, and her eyes were dark. "But it wouldn't stay gone. I couldn't make it go away completely. I worked harder and harder, trying to leave it behind. But it always found me. I started having dreams about it. So I stayed up later, and got up earlier. Then I started seeing it while I was awake. I knew I had to go back in there. I had to see it again, to find out the truth of the painting I had seen, even if it drove me mad. I was already going mad, do you see?"

Larric nodded.

She turned the knife in her hand, contemplating the flickering light from the lantern reflecting off the blade. "I waited until Lord Malrec retired this evening, and I went into the study and searched for the key to the art room. It wasn't hard to find. The painting was right where I remembered it."

Larric sighed. "Kalyn, I—"

She wasn't listening. "And do you know what was in that painting, Larric? Do you know what I found? The very thing I have seen in my nightmares since I was a child. The smoking remains of Archford. All that's left of my home town."

He couldn't look at her. The painting hung in his memory as well. "I know." He sounded hoarse, even to his own ears.

"Do you? Do you know what that means?" She started pacing the small room, more animated than he had seen her in a long time. "Because in that moment, I knew. I remembered my mother, how she could hardly sit up in bed. How my father clung to her side, how he sent me out to play. The way they both held me close and said goodbye with tears in their eyes...and then coming back to find the ruins, my parents gone...and Lord Malrec surveying the destruction. I used to thank the Muses that he had been there, that he had happened to find me. Because until I saw the painting I didn't know, I didn't understand. Lord Malrec burned Archford. He burned it. He *planned* it. Lord Malrec murdered my parents!"

"I know."

She stared at him, aghast. "What?"

"I know—I know what Lord Malrec did." He sounded hoarse, even to his own ears.

"Larric, what are you saying? You knew—all this time you knew what happened—and you said nothing? You let me live my life serving the man who murdered my parents?"

The hurt and outrage in her voice shamed him. He could not hold her burning, accusing gaze. "Kalyn, wait. That isn't the way of it—you must know that. You loved him—you said it yourself, many times. If I had tried to tell you, would you have listened to me?"

Her face fell. She wanted to argue it, he could see that in her eyes, but she knew the truth. "No." Her voice was faint. "No, I wouldn't have listened to you. I guess I had to find out for myself."

Larric took a hesitant step toward her, holding out a hand. "Kalyn, give me the knife."

She jumped back in surprise, holding the knife out in front of her defensively. "No! I have but one purpose left to me now, and I mean to achieve it!"

His hand dropped to his side. "You have to see you aren't being reasonable—there is no way you can succeed at this."

"I will!" Tears shone in her eyes. "I have to!" Her eyes flitted from him to the door behind him.

"No. No, you don't."

"Larric, you aren't going to stop me." She was right, too; he knew that. How could he, while she carried that knife?

She was gathering herself for a charge to the door. In a moment he would have to make his decision—to stand aside or to fight her and see how far her resolve really extended. He didn't relish the moment—neither choice felt right.

For that matter, nothing about the whole situation felt right.

"You don't have a hope," he said again, vainly. "You can't overpower him. You'll spend the rest of your life in Castle Glennayre's dungeon, as long as he needs the focus-bond."

Kalyn shook her head, and suddenly crumpled to her knees. The knife landed on the dirt floor in front of her, and she caught herself on her hands.

"Kalyn! What's wrong?"

"Malrec," she said faintly. "He paints."

Larric couldn't help but think that Lord Malrec had very good timing. He scooped Kalyn up, ignoring the knife, and put her down on the bed against the wall. "So he isn't asleep after all," he said wryly, looking down at her. "You would not have stood a chance."

She squeezed her eyes shut and looked away. "Yes. It will have to wait."

"Wait? Are you daft? You can't seriously intend to attempt this again?"

"I have to," she said, and though her face was ghostly pale, her eyes still burned with unholy resolve. "I have to, Larric. I can't give up. There isn't anyone else to avenge my parents."

Larric had never seen a person drain of energy as fast as Kalyn did when Malrec used the focus-bond. Every word she spoke sounded like a terrific effort. "You're wrong," he said gently. "There is someone else, someone who has lost just as much as you have. Someone who can help you."

She looked at him like she might not even be seeing him. "Who?"

"The arch-prince." He patted her hand. "He has been where you are now, and believe me, it has never been his plan that Lord Malrec should suffer no consequence."

Kalyn just stared at him. She couldn't seem to form a response to that.

"In fact, it seems to me that the best thing we can do is get you to the Great Palace. The sooner the better."

"What?"

"Think about it, Kalyn. There's nothing you can do here. As soon as Malrec sees you, he's going to know. You can't hide how you feel about this. But at the palace—they are working to stop him. You could help."

She didn't protest, but she didn't look particularly convinced, either.

"Really, Kalyn. Raman has only seen Lord Malrec a handful of times. But you—think of the years you have spent here. Think of the things you know about this castle, about its master, that they could never learn any other way. You could help in the battle against him."

"All right. You win. I'll go to the Great Palace."

Larric sighed in relief he hoped wasn't too apparent, and sat down on the edge of the bed. "There is one thing we need to take care of first. This focus-bond—this has to stop."

She nodded weakly.

"When he finishes painting, Lord Malrec is most likely going to take the canvas down to the art room with the others. While he is gone, I could sneak in and take the statue. All I need is a way to know when he is finished. Can you tell me that?"

Kalyn nodded again. "Aye. I can tell you easily enough when he's done."

Larric braced himself for an ordeal—last time he had seen Kalyn under the effects of the focus-bond, she had been unconscious and suffering the entire time. He really didn't want to witness that again, but what choice did he have?

He needn't have worried, though. Kalyn stayed awake, a grim look on her face and a sheen of sweat on her forehead. He didn't know how she managed it—a sheer effort of will, by the look of it.

It felt like hours passed. Larric was dozing in his chair by the window when her quiet voice broke the heavy silence. "It's time. He is finished."

Larric stood up. "All right. I'll be back soon. You just rest here, will you? I don't want you getting up from there."

She nodded and closed her eyes.

Larric let himself out of the stablehouse and closed the

door quietly behind him. He wasn't looking forward to this, but it had to be done. This was his only chance — if Kalyn and the statue disappeared at the same time, Lord Malrec would naturally assume that she had taken it when she left. So it had to happen now — Larric couldn't take any chance that the theft would be attributed to him.

That didn't mean he had to like it, though. The study door had been open when he passed, but he still stood a moment outside the door to the master's chambers, listening carefully for any movement inside. After a moment, he swallowed hard and pushed the door open.

The sitting room was thankfully empty. Larric released a breath he hadn't been aware of holding, and moved to the big desk in front of the window. He searched quickly, opening and closing drawers, rifling through the contents in too much of a hurry to pay attention to what they were.

At last, in the bottom drawer, he found it. A small stonework statue, chiseled into a rough likeness of a girl with long hair and a long dress rested underneath a stack of drawing paper. Clearly Lord Malrec did not want anyone happening upon this statue.

Larric grabbed it and shoved the drawer closed, pleased with his luck. The whole search had taken under a minute; there was no conceivable way Lord Malrec could be on his way back already. He left the room and hopped down the big stairs two at a time, eager to be clear of the castle and back in the relative safety of the stablehouse.

His night was far from over, he knew that. He would need to pack up some of Kalyn's things, even if she would never need them, to give the impression that she had left on her own. He would need to take her down to Glennayre, and find her a carriage to take her to the Great Palace, from someone he could trust to keep quiet. Her horse would have to be left in town, his own horse brought home and tended to, all before Lord Malrec awoke in the morning.

Fortunately, after such a late night, Malrec was not likely to rise very early. He found he was grateful for the small blessing.

He had a feeling he was going to need all the luck he could get.

♫

Alannys and the Singari spent the entire next day camped out in the same spot, recuperating. The horrors of Eversnow Pass were behind them—coming down the mountain had felt like leaving a nightmare. The forest they camped in seemed more peaceful and beautiful than any they had ever been in, and even Alannys, with her sense of urgency bearing down upon her, could not bring herself to force them to leave just yet. She had to admit that the day of rest did her worlds of good, as well.

The next day, they broke camp and finished their descent. The farther they pushed into Orinthal Holding, the less Alannys could feel that sense of peace she had so enjoyed the day before. It felt more like going back into the nightmare than leaving it behind. Orinthal was full of tall, twisted trees with thorny branches that grasped out in all directions like gnarled, skeletal fingers. They cut a downright creepy silhouette against the gloomy sky, and provided thick mats of tangled shadows where anything could hide. Looking into the darkness of those shadows, Alannys always half expected to see glowing eyes looking back.

Alannys had figured Shadowkeep as an easy day's ride ahead, but it was getting uncomfortably dark and they still weren't there. As the weak sun set, the shadows stretched and grew, and so did Alannys's unease. She wrote it off to paranoia—the darkness, the creepy trees, and the heavy shadows were getting to her. She remembered her trip to Ibira's wagon, and immediately wished she hadn't. She wound Quicksilver's reins around her hands, looking at them instead of her surroundings.

"Expecting someone?" Chen didn't even look at her, riding next to her on Nightfire. His tone was low, but she jumped as though he had shouted.

"No, I—what do you mean?"

"You've been glancing behind us an awful lot. Do you know something I don't?"

She shook her head. "No, I—I just can't shake the feeling we're being followed." She darted a quick look back, and found nothing but the wagon train behind them. "It's crazy, isn't it?"

Chen regarded her thoughtfully. "I don't know, Alannys. I don't think any kind of hunch from someone with the Second Sight should be ignored. But who do you think could be following us?"

Alannys shuddered. "The cloaked swordsman has been following me ever since I left the Great Palace. I don't see why he would stop now."

"Alannys, the cloaked swordsman died in the avalanche."

"No. He escaped." Her voice was low and grim.

Chen looked at her, then looked straight ahead. She'd seen the flicker of worry in his dark eyes, and she didn't like it. "I know how long he's hunted you. I know what it must be like to live with that hanging over you every minute of the day and night. I know that you feel you can never really let your guard down. But Alannys, it took us eighteen hours to dig you out. No man could escape that on his own. The cloaked swordsman is dead."

She shook her head, ignoring the burning in her eyes. Why did it bother her so much that Chen wouldn't believe her? "He is not. I saw him escape. He was gone before the snow hit the ground."

"That's—that's not possible. I don't see how any person could have done that. Did you see how sheer those cliff faces were? I don't want to upset you, but you were injured pretty badly, and in pretty extreme circumstances. Is it possible you only thought you saw him escape?"

Alannys turned her face down to regard her hands on the reins again, twisting them even tighter. She hated to admit it, but what Chen said made sense. It *was* possible that she had imagined what she thought she saw. And if that was true, and she refused to consider it, then what? Did she spend the rest of her life paranoid, anxious, jumping at shadows, always on guard against someone who wasn't there?

"Lady Alannys!"

The shout came from somewhere behind them. Alannys twisted around in the saddle, and saw Drigo riding fast to catch up with them, bent low over his horse's neck. Alarm was plain in his voice and on his face, and her heart leaped into her throat. What new trouble was this?

Chen frowned as Drigo guided his horse up next to Alannys. "Drigo? What news?"

"Chen," Drigo said, "my Lady, we are being followed."

Alannys could feel the color drain from her face. Chen glanced at her, and shook his head.

"Your timing," he told Drigo sourly, "is wonderful."

Drigo looked from Chen to Alannys. "I—I apologize. Did I interrupt something?"

Alannys flushed, and looked away.

"No, of course not," Chen snapped. "What happened? Why do you think we're being followed?"

Drigo looked unconvinced, but nobody spoke so he answered the question. "I saw him. Grald was riding rearmost, and he claimed to see someone following us."

"Grald?" Chen frowned. "I thought you were riding rearmost today, Drigo."

Drigo couldn't quite look at either of them. "I—I was supposed to, yes. Grald was covering for me. Something—

something came up that I had to attend to."

"Ah," Chen said knowingly. "Your mother."

Drigo looked pointedly away.

"Your mother?" Alannys suddenly realized that her long recuperation in her wagon had left her out of a lot. "What's the matter with your mother?"

Chen's short bark of laughter held little humor. "The same thing that's always the matter with Pesia. She can't stand you."

"That's hardly news," Alannys said. "She has always hated me, ever since I came here. But why should that be causing Drigo trouble now?"

"I hope you're not asking for a logical explanation, because there isn't one," Chen said bluntly. "She thinks you've stolen her son."

"What?" Alannys looked at Drigo in surprise. "Is this true?"

"I'm sorry, my Lady." Drigo still didn't look at her. "This was not meant to be your problem."

"Don't be silly," she said. "We're all a team here. I wish I knew what to do to help." The only thing that would make Pesia happy, Alannys knew, would be for Drigo to abandon her completely. And even if Drigo were willing to do that, Alannys wasn't sure she could afford to let it happen. Chen, Drigo, and Grald were her lieutenants—especially here lately while she had been incapacitated by the avalanche and Trago's beating.

Chen held some authority among the Singari for being so close to her—even if their private relationship did not quite fit the bill, the entire tribe considered him *markortha*. But Drigo had status of his own. He had been the younger brother of the previous *kortha*; he already had the respect of his people and they were already accustomed to seeing him in some measure of command. Grald came from a poor family and had no authority of his own, and Chen's status would be reduced when Alannys inevitably left the Singari. If what she had created was to continue, Drigo had to remain in the Three, as they were known in the tribe. "Tell me, Drigo," she finally said, "what do *you* want?"

"Me?" He looked surprised. "You have to ask? I see the changes you are making, my Lady, and they are grand changes. The Singari need to keep moving forward, or we're going to get left behind. Our tradition should be a pedestal to help us reach higher, not an anchor to drag us down and bind us. I want to be part of what you are doing."

"Of course." Chen sounded smug.

"But my mother will never see that. She's too attached to the way things were with Brutagar. A man like that had no business leading anybody, but..." He shook his head. "Of course she'll never see that, either."

"It doesn't sound easy," Alannys said. "Is there anything I can do?"

Drigo sighed, and shot a look at Chen that seemed almost apologetic. "My mother imagines that I am only biding my time until I can supplant you. I am ashamed to say that I let her continue to believe this. It isn't true—you know it isn't—but it seemed the easiest way to get rid of her. This news, it couldn't wait."

"Ah yes, the news," Chen said, as though he hadn't even heard the rest of Drigo's remarks. "Why don't you tell us exactly what happened?"

Drigo cleared his throat uncomfortably. "As I said, Grald told me of the follower. I was skeptical, so after my mother left I rode with him at the rear for some time, keeping watch behind us, and I saw him myself. Swathed completely in black, keeping a constant distance behind us in the cover of the forest."

"Black?" Alannys couldn't quite keep the alarm out of

her tone. "Did you say this stranger is wrapped completely in black?"

Drigo seemed flustered by her intensity. "Indeed. I am quite certain of it—I saw him several times. Either he is not very experienced, or he deliberately chose to let us see him."

Chen and Alannys exchanged a look. If the cloaked swordsman was seen, it was not from a lack of experience. And if he was confident enough to taunt them with his presence, who knew what he had planned?

"We're stopping," Chen said shortly. "Now. I want Alannys's wagon in the center of the camp, with the tents ringed around it, as tightly as we can pack them. The rest of the wagons should form rings around the outside of the tents. Put the horses around the wagons, so they can let us know if anyone is sneaking around the camp. Grab Grald and have him help you get the word out. And do it quickly!"

Drigo nodded sharply and wheeled his horse around to gallop to the back of the wagon train.

Alannys swallowed hard. "Chen, I—"

"Not a word." His face was hard, his eyes cold and steely. "This is not up for discussion. You get yourself into your wagon, and you keep Songstrike in your hand, and you don't come out. I'll come sit with you as soon as we are done setting up camp. I will not have that bastard anywhere near you again."

The look in his eyes convinced her that it was better not to argue.

♫

"This is ridiculous, Chen," Alannys said.

He sat between her and her wagon door, unmoving, implacable. He worked a knife over a whetstone, honing the edge with a concentration that bespoke serious intent.

"You can't do this. You've got hundreds of innocent people and their families between me and a ruthless assassin."

His eyes flicked in her direction, then back down to his work. "Which part of that is ridiculous? The part where we protect our Redeemer, or the part where the assassin doesn't kill you?"

"Both. That's wrong on so many levels I don't even know where to start."

"Pick anywhere," he said quietly. "It doesn't matter. You aren't changing my mind."

She sighed in frustration. "Chen, you say I'm the Redeemer. If that's so, shouldn't I be able to fight my own battles? Isn't it sort of reprehensible to ask innocent families to face this for me?"

"No. You're the Redeemer, you are more important than any of us. Than all of us put together. It would be reprehensible for any of us to stand aside and do nothing while harm came to you."

She shook her head. "Did you miss the 'ruthless' part? This man has no conscience. He won't hesitate to cut you all down if he has to, every man, woman, and child among you."

"And he'll have to, if he wants to get to you. We've waited for you for generations. If you die, none of us have any reason left to live." He stood up and looked her directly in the face. "Do you understand? I will die before I will let that man near you. I will die!"

The room felt suddenly very small. She looked away, stricken, unable to face him. The silence that hung heavy over the entire camp crept into the wagon, and she could hear every ragged breath he drew.

What could she do? She couldn't argue with that kind of blind, zealous devotion. She couldn't acknowledge the deep feelings that drove his outburst, that hung there between them, obvious but unaccepted. In another life, in another existence where she had never met Dorramon, never fallen into a love as fierce as it was doomed, she would have closed the few steps that separated her from Chen and taken him in her arms. He stared at her, eyes aflame, and the urge was almost too much to fight.

She turned away, and reached without meaning to for the Seeing Stone hanging around her neck. Its cool, solid weight was a comfort to her, a tangible reminder of the one whose name she could not speak, of hopes so hopeless she could not admit them, even to herself.

Chen swore from behind her. "Alannys, that thing isn't helping you."

She flinched. "It is. It does help. I think it keeps me sane."

He grabbed her shoulders and turned her back around to face him. "I think it keeps you safe, is what you mean. Safe from us, safe from *me*, because it makes you feel attached to him. It makes it easier for you to bury your feelings for me, to pretend they don't exist. To pretend I don't exist."

She couldn't look at him, but she couldn't look away. Her fingers clenched convulsively around the Stone. "Chen, I—"

"I'm here, damn it! I'm here with you, fighting for you, fighting with you, ready to die for you. He is safe in his palace getting ready to marry somebody else. He'll live out his life with her, and whether you live or die here will not change that."

Tears welled up unbidden in her eyes.

Chen swore again and released her. "Alannys, you can't shut me out forever."

He was right, and she knew it. Everything he had said was right. So why did she still feel like half of her heart was back at the Great Palace? She couldn't have Dorramon. He would marry the Princess of Cadenda; he had no choice about that. There was nothing there for her.

So why couldn't she give Chen what he so desperately needed? Why did she always hold herself at arm's length from him? She could be happy here, with him. She knew that. Why didn't she take it?

Quicksilver snorted and stomped from outside, tied to the wagon. She could hear him whinny, and feel the tiny shakes in the frame of the wagon when he jerked against the rope.

"Trouble," she said.

Chen spun around for the door, and she followed right on his heels. "No way," he said, but he didn't slow down. "We are here to protect you—there is no way you are coming out here."

"There is no way you are stopping me," she said, skipping down the steps after him. "You can stand here and argue with me until the cloaked swordsman comes and runs us both through, or we can go face this together."

He turned and searched her face for a split second, searching for some meaning behind her words that he evidently did not find. Without another word he turned and ran towards the edge of camp, following the sounds of anxious horses.

As creepy as the forest had been during the day, Alannys found it even creepier at night. One of the two moons was full, but its white light couldn't quite seem to penetrate the gloom that seemed to pervade Orinthal Holding. The only light was the flickering, jumping light from the fires that had been set around the camp perimeter. The wavering, unsteady light did not make her feel any better. Anything could be hidden in those dancing shadows, waiting to skewer her and any Singari who stood to defend her.

She swallowed hard, turning away from that line of thought. Drigo and Grald stood near one of the campfires, peering out into the darkness, speaking to one another in tones so low she could not hear them from a few feet away.

Chen jogged over to join them. Alannys could see a few other Singari, scattered around the edges of the camp. She hoped most of them were safe inside their tents and wagons, away from any blood that spilled here. This man's mission was not for them; as long as they stayed out of his way, they would be safe.

She heard a sudden, loud rustling from one of the trees behind her. Before she could even turn completely around toward the sound, a figure swathed completely in black dropped lightly from the tree to the ground, falling into a ready crouch, steadying itself with one gloved hand on the ground.

The figure straightened. Alannys just had time to realize that this figure was too slight and too slender to be the cloaked swordsman, when Chen appeared beside her, grabbed her arm, and pushed her behind him. Before anyone had time to react, he had his knife at the figure's throat.

"Make one move in her direction," he growled, "and you will die."

"Chen?" gasped a voice from inside the cloak, undoubtedly female. "Chen, is that you?"

Chen stepped back, thunderstruck. His eyes bulged, and his sickly pale complexion stood out in the darkness. He couldn't have looked any more shocked if Soth himself had addressed him. "Who are you?"

"Forgotten already. How fickle are Muses and men." The voice had a sarcastic edge. The woman pushed her hood back with gloved hands. She had caramel skin, long black hair, and eyes that looked like they could cut a man down, if she felt like it.

Grald guffawed, a sudden, obtrusive sound that made them jump. "So this was our follower. Don't worry, Chen,

Drigo and I'll go announce the stand-down." He clapped Chen on the back. "Good luck, *markortha*."

Grald and Drigo beat what seemed to Alannys a very hasty retreat.

The woman's eyes narrowed. "*Markortha?* What is this about?"

"That's what I said," Alannys muttered.

"Hush, you." Chen took Alannys by the arm and pulled her next to him. It was a deliberately intimate gesture.

Apparently the cloaked woman did not appreciate it. "Well, Chen?" she demanded.

"This is our new *kortha*," he said, dodging the question entirely.

She made a sound of pure impatience. "I *know* that. But this *markortha* business?"

"It's nothing," Alannys interjected. "Tongues wagging when they would do better to be silent. But it seems to me it upsets you?"

The woman glared at her. "Naturally. Chen and I have been betrothed since we were teenagers!"

For a long, long moment, everything seemed to freeze.

Sandra Miller

Don't miss the exciting continuation of Alannys's story:

Book Three

𝒥rials of the 𝑅edeemer

AS TROUBLE CLOSES IN ON EVERY SIDE, A LEGENDARY HERO ARISES...

𝒥ust when Alannys thought she had earned a little peace at the Great Palace, Lord Malrec and his Dark Alliance stood at Dorramon's coronation and declared war on the new king. She's known for a while that Dorramon has some bad news for her, but she's unprepared for just *how* bad. But it's the midnight attempt on her life that spurs her to action--Ravanmark is imploding around her, and she can't just sit and watch it happen.

𝒮he knows she helped cause it, after all.

𝒜nd what of the prophesied savior, the legendary Redeemer? Time is growing short, and the songs of the Redeemer have yet to be found. Alannys will have to take her fight for Ravanmark's future across the country on her own, while Lord Malrec continues his work on the magical device that will enable him to safely hold her prisoner, and use her as a weapon to destroy the king.

𝒥oin Alannys and her friends again as they continue their epic fight for the kingdom of Ravanmark—because sometimes 'happily ever after' has to wait.